The LAST PHOENIX

ALSO BY RICHARD HERMAN

The Trojan Sea

Edge of Honor

Against All Enemies

Power Curve

Iron Gate

Dark Wing

Call to Duty

Firebreak

Force of Eagles

The Warbirds

The LAST PHOENIX

RICHARD HERMAN

wm
William Morrow
An Imprint of HarperCollins*Publishers*

This is a work of fiction. The characters, incidents, and dialogues are products of the author's imagination and are not to be construed as real. Any resemblance to actual persons, living or dead, is entirely coincidental.

 For information address HarperCollins Publishers Inc., 10 East 53rd Street, New York, NY 10022.

HarperCollins books may be purchased for educational, business, or sales promotional use. For information please write: Special Markets Department, HarperCollins Publishers Inc., 10 East 53rd Street, New York, NY 10022.

FIRST EDITION

Designed by Nicola Ferguson

Printed on acid-free paper

Library of Congress Cataloging-in-Publication Data
Herman, Richard.
The last Phoenix / Richard Herman.
p. cm.
ISBN 0-06-620976-5 (alk. paper)
1. International relations—Fiction. 2. Women presidents—Fiction. 3. Middle East—Fiction. 4. Generals—Fiction. 5. China—Fiction. I. Title.
PS3558.E684 L38 2002
813'.54—dc21 2001044877

02 03 04 05 06 SPS/QBF 10 9 8 7 6 5 4 3 2 1

In memory of my mother,

Mildred Leona Herman

The nation that will insist in drawing a broad line of demarcation between the fighting man and the thinking man is liable to find its fighting done by fools and its thinking done by cowards.

—*Sir William Butler*

ACKNOWLEDGMENTS

I would like to thank those who gave so willingly of their time and shared their insights and knowledge. Master Sergeant Paul Wishart excited my interest and gave me a quick education in military working dogs. But it fell to Major John Probst and his staff—Technical Sergeant Chris Jakubin and Rambo, and Staff Sergeant Uilani Bio and Boyca—at the 341st TRS, Lackland Air Force Base, to fill in the details. They impressed me beyond measure, especially when I donned a bite suit and met Boyca up close and personal.

The role of security police in air base defense was made abundantly clear by Captain Michael Ross, Master Sergeant Grady McGuire, and their staff at Detachment 1, 343rd TRS, Camp Bullis. Technical Sergeant Lisa Johnson was a very knowledgeable and enthusiastic teacher about search-and-clear procedures.

Lieutenant Colonel Herman "Hampster" Brunke gave me a quick refresher course on the A-10 Warthog, proving again that it is an amazing jet that continues to defy age and military planners.

In any story about armed conflict, the issue of morality is always there, often below the surface, but real and demanding. Malham M. Wakin, Brigadier General, United States Air Force (Retired), was kind enough to explain Just War Theory in terms I could understand, and his book, *War, Morality, and the Military Profession,* is a masterful anthology on the ethical dimensions of war.

I owe a special debt of thanks to my editor, Jennifer Sawyer Fisher. Over the course of working on four books with me, she has proven again and again that she is an editor par excellence.

The
LAST
PHOENIX

prologue

South China Sea
Thursday, July 22

Tel heard it first. "Captain," he called in Malay, "something's out there." He stood at the bow of the small fishing boat and looked into the night.

Victor Kamigami strained to hear, but his fifty-eight-year-old ears weren't up to it. Luckily, the boy had excellent hearing. "He's not a boy," Kamigami said to himself in English.

"I'll be twenty in two months," Tel said in Malay.

"And with good hearing," Kamigami replied, still speaking English. He had a voice that was unusually soft and high-pitched for such a big man. "Look away from the sound so your night vision can work better." Automatically, he checked the small handheld GPS that dangled from the throttle lever. On course and four nautical miles to go. At five and a half knots, they'd make landfall in forty-five minutes. He glanced at his Rolex watch—the only clue that he was not a poor fisherman struggling to feed his family on the eastern shore of Malaysia. They would be on the beach and home in time for breakfast.

"I hear two engines now," Tel called. From his rigid stance Kamigami could sense Tel's worry and made a mental promise to install a radar set. It wasn't a question of affording it, but he didn't want to spoil the simple, classic lines of his prahu, a traditional Malay fishing boat. After his family, it was the pride of his life.

Kamigami retarded the throttle to idle, and they coasted to a stop in the calm waters. Now he heard the deep rumble of diesels at high speed. He started to count. "I can hear two, maybe three," he said. "Can you see anything?"

"There!" Tel screamed, his voice tight and filled with fear. He pointed to a spot slightly aft of the starboard beam, as a large shadow emerged out of the darkness and bore down on them.

Kamigami's reflexes were still rattlesnake quick as he shoved the throttle full forward and hit the horn button to blare a warning. A searchlight clicked on and swept over Kamigami's prahu, blinding him with its brightness. The ship's big diesels roared as it turned onto Kamigami's boat. "Jump!" he shouted. He dove over the side and swam down the wake his boat had carved in the water. He was a big man and still physically fit, as befitted a former command sergeant major in the U.S. Army. He took fifteen powerful strokes before the ship smashed into the prahu, crushing it like matchwood. The wake kicked up by the ship's bow engulfed Kamigami and pulled him under.

He came to the surface sputtering and coughing. Another ship cut by him, outlined by the glare of the searchlight. *Son of a bitch,* Kamigami thought, *a fast-attack patrol boat. Who in hell? Singapore?* He didn't know. He watched as the large craft slowed to a crawl. Its searchlight swept the water looking for survivors. The familiar bark of a heavy machine gun echoed over him. "Bastards," he said aloud. The light moved toward him. He simply let his breath out and dropped below the surface. His proportions may have matched those of a sumo wrestler, but he was more muscle and bone than fat. He sank like a rock. It was a long swim back to the surface.

A much bigger ship ghosted by him. *An LST! What the hell is a landing craft doing here?* None of it made sense to him. Now one of the patrol boats circled as its searchlight again swept the water. Then the light was doused and the boat raced after the landing craft. He waited, treading water. He mentally urged Tel to be quiet—if he was still alive. He kept checking his Rolex as the minutes passed. *Seven more minutes,* he calculated. *Is that long enough?* He reasoned that was how long he would have waited.

Six minutes later a diesel roared to life, and a patrol craft cruised by with its two searchlights sweeping the water. Again Kamigami exhaled and sank. But this time he didn't let out as much air and it was a much shorter swim back to the surface.

He patiently treaded water for another five minutes. Finally he judged it was time. He felt for the flat gold whistle on the chain around his neck that May May, his wife, had given him for good luck. It was about the size of his old dog tags and was engraved with a dragon on one side and a tiger on the other. He gave a short toot and waited. Nothing. He blew hard on the whistle—a long blast that carried for a mile.

"Captain!" a faint voice called. "Is that you?"

"You bet your sweet ass!" Kamigami roared, relieved to hear Tel. "Keep talking and I'll come to you." He took three strokes and stopped to listen. Tel's voice was louder. He took an even dozen strokes before stopping to listen. He was getting closer, but there was panic in Tel's voice. "Keep cool," Kamigami urged as he stroked hard, pulling ever closer. His hand touched something in the dark. It was Tel, and the boy jumped on him, holding on for dear life.

Kamigami easily broke his death grip and turned Tel around in the water. His big right hand held him by the back of the head. "Lie on your back," he ordered. "You'll be okay. I won't let you drown." Tel's breathing slowed. "The ocean's our friend. Don't fight it." He could feel the boy's body relax. "Much better."

"Are we going to die?" Tel asked.

"Not tonight. It's only four miles to shore."

"I can't swim"—he gulped for air, the panic back—"that far."

Kamigami snorted. "Who said anything about swimming? Give me your pants." He held Tel's head above water while he struggled out of his light trousers and handed them over. "Okay, you're gonna have to tread water for a few moments." Kamigami let go of him and quickly tied an overhand knot in the end of each leg. He grabbed the waistband of the trousers and found the drawstring. Then he gave a strong kick and rose out of the water. At the same time he waved the pants over his head and filled them with air. He held the waistband underwater as he tied it closed with the drawstring. The pants legs stuck out of the water like two overstuffed sausages. Kamigami handed the pants back. "Here's your life preserver. Lie on it. Keep it wet and it'll stay inflated."

Kamigami did the same with his pants and lay across the crotch with a leg under each arm. "That's not fair," Tel said. "Yours are bigger than mine."

Tel's spirits were definitely improving, and Kamigami played on it. "You want a quick drowning lesson, boy?"

"Not tonight, sir."

Much better, Kamigami thought. "I need to get my bearings," he said. He studied the sky, looking for familiar stars. Finding Polaris was out of the question, as they were too close to the equator. "Okay," he said half aloud, "what's in the west at three in the morning this time of month?"

"Nothing good," Tel answered. "But the Belt of Orion is above the eastern horizon, and you can see Sirius." He pointed to their left.

Kamigami breathed more easily when he found the constellation and the bright star. He was impressed with Tel's knowledge. "Very good," he said, wondering what else was hidden behind that pretty face. "Swim away from it. We'll have the sun later." They started kicking and stroking. There was no doubt in the older man's mind that he could make the long swim, but he hardly knew Tel. The boy might not be up to it. Normally Kamigami was a quiet man and never said much, but an inner sense told him he needed to talk to keep Tel's spirits up. "So you know astronomy?"

"My father left a star chart on the wall when he left. My mother kept it."

Kamigami heard resignation in Tel's voice. He was a very lonely young man, and as long as he lived in a kampong, or village, he would stay that way. That was the main reason May May had asked him to take Tel on as his crew in the fishing boat. "Do you remember your father?" Kamigami asked.

"A little. He's English, very tall and skinny. He had a beard." That was at the root of Tel's problems. He was too different. Not only did he have Eurasian features, with doe-shaped eyes and light skin that made Kamigami think of a teen movie heartthrob, but he was tall and slender, towering above the average Malay. It wasn't a question of virulent racism—the Malays were very tolerant—but rather the pervasive influence of ethnicity in Malay society. Because he was a very visible half-caste, Tel was simply excluded from the mainstream of village life. Kamigami and his family had experienced some of the same rejection when they first moved to the kampong. But thanks to his Japanese-Hawaiian heritage and his wife's beauty—she was a Zhuang from southern China—his children were very Asian in looks and readily accepted by the villagers. It also helped that he was a wealthy man and always ready to help the villagers in time of need.

"Why doesn't your mother move to Kuala Lumpur?" Kamigami asked.

"My father still sends her money. It's not enough for us to live in the city but enough for her to be important to the family." Like most Malays, Tel's family was very aware of economic reality.

Two hours later something rough brushed against Kamigami's leg. "Don't move," he said. "Stay absolutely still."

"What is it?" Tel asked, the panic back in his voice.

Kamigami lied. "Just a big fish." He suspected it was a shark.

"I need to pee."

"Don't," Kamigami ordered. Urine in the water acted like a homing beacon for sharks. The two men waited, but whatever had been there had left. Kamigami could see a faint glow in the east. "Keep paddling."

The sun was just below the horizon when Tel gave up. "How much longer?" Despair etched every word.

"What difference does it make? We keep going until we get there."

"I can't make it," Tel announced.

"At least wait for the sun to come up."

"Why?"

"So you can see the shore and know how close you are." There was no answer. Kamigami took two quick strokes in Tel's general direction and dove. He reached out in the blackness as he swam in a circle. His lungs were bursting for air when he felt skin. He grabbed a handful and kicked for the surface, dragging Tel with him. He broached like a whale, spouting and gasping for breath. He grabbed Tel's face and blew a lungful of air into his mouth. Tel coughed and threw up water. "Damn," Kamigami growled. "We lost our pants. Lie on your back and start kicking."

"No," Tel replied.

"You're stubborn. I like that. Now, start swimming or I'll cut off your balls and feed them to the first passing shark."

"How? You don't have a knife."

"Okay," Kamigami groused, "so no plan is perfect." He thought he heard a laugh as Tel lay on his back and kicked for the shore. Kamigami did the same as they watched the sun break the horizon. He turned to look where they were headed, and saw land. "There," he said, gesturing in the general direction. Tel turned and looked. His spirits soared, and he kicked harder. They were making good time when a series of dull explosions echoed over them.

"What's that?" Tel asked.

Kamigami didn't answer and maintained his even pace. *Mortars,* he thought. The explosions kept up a steady rhythm, growing louder as they swam. Dark smoke rose up and drifted over the shore.

"I can touch bottom," Tel said.

Kamigami looked down and saw a coral formation. He dropped his feet and gingerly felt for the reef. He found a smooth place and let his weight come to rest. "Be careful," he warned. "Don't cut your feet." The explosions abruptly halted, only to be replaced by the sharp report of gunfire. Now he could see flames licking at the bottom of the smoke.

Tel looked at him, his eyes full of concern. "It's our kampong, isn't it?"

Again Kamigami didn't reply. His eyes squinted as he studied the shore, obviously looking for something. The gunfire stopped. "I don't see the ships that ran us down," he said. He set off with a powerful stroke, plowing the water. Tel fell in behind him but was rapidly outdistanced. It was a long swim, and Tel was two hundred meters out when Kamigami waded ashore and disappeared into the foliage behind the high-water mark. Tel struggled ashore and followed Kamigami's footprints into the dense underbrush.

"Over here," Kamigami said quietly. There was something in his voice that cautioned Tel to be silent.

They waited for over an hour.

Kamigami came to a half crouch. "Follow me," he commanded in a low voice. "Do exactly what I do, and don't make a sound." Before Tel could stand, Kamigami drifted silently into the brush. Tel followed, astounded by the speed of the big man. It defied all logic that Kamigami could seemingly disappear at times and then emerge twenty meters farther on. Tel blundered after him, panting hard, following familiar landmarks as they neared the kampong. The stench of burning meat and wood filled his nostrils, and his eyes burned from the smoke. He ran into Kamigami's back.

Tel was barely able to see as Kamigami led him to the upwind side of the village. Kamigami stopped and stared into what was left of their home. "Nothing's alive in there," he said. He sat down to wait for the fires to burn out.

Tel sat on his haunches, overwhelmed with grief, as Kamigami examined the ground around their kampong. He motioned Tel over and pointed out a distinctive footprint. "See the ridges on the sole and heel," he said. "They're everywhere."

"What does that mean?" Tel asked.

Kamigami spat. "Soldiers." He found a stick and poked through the ashes of his home. One by one, the big man carried out the blanket-wrapped remains of two of his children and then his wife. He gently laid her body next to the children's. "Mai Ling isn't here," Kamigami said, his words barely audible. He stood and went in search of his twelve-year-old adopted daughter.

"Isn't she Chinese?" Tel asked.

"Yes" was all Kamigami said as he plodded down a trail to a nearby kampong. They had been there before while waiting for the fires to burn out, but it, too, had been destroyed in the attack and was burning. Kamigami pushed through the still-hot rubble to the house of the old woman who had been the children's amah. The house itself was leveled, but a small shed at the back was still standing. Kamigami pulled open the low door and looked in. For a long moment he didn't move, his face frozen. Then he bent over and disappeared inside. He came out carrying his daughter's body. From the shreds of her clothes and the condition of her body, there was no doubt that she had been tortured and raped. Tel ripped off his shirt and draped it over her body as Kamigami carried it back to his kampong.

Kamigami and Tel placed the nine small tin boxes holding the ashes of their families in the small shrine they had built overlooking the beach. It was a beautiful spot, and willowy casuarina trees and palms curved over them, beckoning at the emerald green sea and the islands that floated on the far horizon. Only the three offshore oil platforms that marched in a straight line spoiled the peace and tranquillity that had originally brought Kamigami to this place.

"We used to come here in the evening," Kamigami said. "May May always said we were looking the wrong way to see the sunset. But it didn't matter." Together they lit joss sticks and placed them on the shrine, one in front of each tin. Kamigami knelt down in the sand, his hands on his knees, and gazed at the shrine. He fingered the flat gold whistle dangling from a chain around his neck. He cocked his head as he studied the dragon engraved on one side. "May May said it made good feng shui at sea." He turned it over to the tiger. "She said the dragon and the tiger are inseparable. Just as the North Pole must have a South Pole, if there is a dragon there must be a tiger." He raised it to his lips and gave a little toot. It was a sad, wistful sound that drove a pang of despair into his heart. "It's all that's left. Everything else was destroyed in . . ." His voice trailed off. Then, more strongly, "I came here to escape all this. But it came after me."

Tel didn't know what he was talking about, but rather than pursuing it, he asked the one question that consumed him. "Why?" He waited for what seemed an eternity.

Kamigami finally came to his feet, looked out to sea, and gestured at the oil platforms. "Maybe something to do with that. I don't know." He picked up a shovel and walked quickly toward the amah's kampong. At a distinctive bend at the halfway point, he stepped off the path. He counted the steps to an open spot and started digging. The shovel clanged off a hard object. Kamigami scooped out more dirt and handed up a metal chest sealed in plastic wrap. He cut away the plastic, knocked off the hasps with the shovel, and threw back the lid. He removed a bundle from the chest and unwrapped it to reveal a submachine gun coated in Cosmoline. "A Heckler and Koch MP5," Kamigami said. "It's time you learned how to clean and assemble one."

For the next hour Kamigami and Tel methodically stripped and cleaned the MP5 and a well-used Beretta nine-millimeter automatic.

When they were finished, Kamigami packed two rucksacks, hiding the two weapons. Then he dressed in dark gray-green pants and a black T-shirt, taking care as he laced his jungle boots. The boots were the only military item he was wearing. He threw Tel a pair of pants and a T-shirt that were much too large for him. "We'll find something that fits later," he told him, shouldering one of the rucksacks and adjusting the straps. Satisfied that it fit properly, he went into a deep crouch as his right hand reached back and snapped open a flap at the bottom corner of the rucksack. The MP5 fell out, into his hand. He slapped in a clip as he brought the weapon to the ready. The sound echoed in the smoky air.

Tel stared at the dark specter towering in front of him. He had never seen such a look on the face of a human being.

Kamigami gestured at the second rucksack. "You coming?"

one

Oakland, California
Saturday, July 24

The formal dedication ceremony of the Matthew Pontowski Presidential Library was over, but Madeline O'Keith Turner did not leave. Instead the president of the United States strolled down the hillside garden chatting with two former presidents and savoring the unusually clear and mild August day. From time to time they would stop and take in the magnificent vista overlooking San Francisco Bay with its view of the Oakland Bay Bridge and the city on the hill. A breeze washed over them, gently ruffling the president's hair, creating a charming effect not lost on the TV cameras that were held at a distance on the veranda of the small library building.

The presidential entourage hovered in the background, nervously checking their watches. Only her personal assistant, Nancy Bender, was unconcerned with what the delay would do to the president's carefully crafted campaign schedule. She alone knew what was on the president's mind.

The deputy chief of staff rushed up to Nancy. "How much longer will the president be?" the young man asked. "I've got a campaign to run . . . can't delay much longer."

Nancy stifled a sigh. Like so many who worked in the White House, he had an overblown opinion of his importance because of the position he occupied. "Yes you can," she replied. But she immediately relented. *He's got a point, Maddy.* Madeline "Maddy" Turner had just emerged from a hard-fought primary campaign and turbulent convention to win her party's nomination for president. It had been a near thing, which was unusual for an incumbent. Now her old rival and nemesis, Senator John Leland, was determined to deny her the election and get his boy elected, the former congressman and now governor David Grau. Leland and Grau's opening salvo was an attack on her legitimacy. They claimed she was a political lightweight and incompetent, not capable of leading the United States, and had come to the presidency only through the vice presidency and the death of President Quentin Roberts. It was turning into a savage personal fight, and the fall campaign and run-up to the November election promised to be a brutal, take-no-prisoners battle.

A woman reporter floating behind Nancy said, "She may be the most beautiful widow in the United States." Nancy agreed, for Maddy was at her best on this particular day. The president's brown eyes sparkled with life, and her makeup was perfect for the sunlight, accentuating her high cheekbones and smooth complexion. "That white linen suit is very elegant," the reporter continued. "She has a fabulous figure."

Indeed she does, Nancy thought. She waited for the inevitable question.

"Off the record," the reporter ventured, "is there anything to the rumor about Matt Pontowski?"

Nancy knew better than to deny it. "Only what the president has said," she answered. "They're good friends and have the same mutual interests as any parents." She didn't have to explain what the "mutual interests" were. The reporter knew that the president's and Pontowski's fifteen-year-old sons were best friends attending New Mexico Military Institute in Roswell. Nancy saw the cause of the delay move down the veranda and walk across the lawn toward the presidential party. She glanced at her watch and went in search of the deputy chief of staff. She found him still fretting over the delay. "Thirty minutes" was all she said. The young man scurried away to set the wheels of the campaign back in motion. "Oh, Maddy," Nancy breathed. "He does light your fire, doesn't he?"

The "he" was Matthew Zachary Pontowski III, the president of the library and grandson of the late President Matthew Zachary Pontowski. Every person, not to mention the TV reporters, at the dedication ceremony of President Pontowski's library was talking endlessly about the physical resemblance of Matt Pontowski to his famous ancestor. Pontowski was exactly six feet tall, lanky, and with the same piercing blue eyes and hawklike nose. His shock of graying brown hair with its barely controlled cowlick was an exact replica of the late president's, and he even walked with the same limp. Like his grandfather and father, he had flown fighter aircraft in combat, but no reporter really understood the significance of that. Still, it was the stuff that made news good entertainment, and they played it to the hilt.

Secretly each reporter hoped there was some truth to the rumor of an affair between Madeline Turner and Pontowski. But a strong sense of self-preservation held them in check—for always lurking in the background was Patrick Flannery Shaw. No one knew exactly what Shaw did as the special assistant to the president; however, he had direct access to Turner at any time and any place. That, plus a well-deserved reputation as the president's pit bull, made it mandatory to stay on his good side. The one White House reporter who had gotten crosswise with Shaw had suddenly found himself reporting local events in Pocatello, Idaho. It was an object lesson that didn't need repeating.

The TV cameras on the veranda zoomed in on Pontowski. "Matt," Maddy called, "what a wonderful ceremony." She extended her hand. "I was quite moved by your words. He was a wonderful man."

"Thank you for coming, Mrs. President," Pontowski said, gently taking her hand. The TV cameras recorded that they touched for a few seconds longer than required by protocol. But that was all. Pontowski shook hands with the two former presidents, and both were eager to recall the last time they had met. The reporters scribbled in their notebooks that the friendly reception was proof that Pontowski had a future beyond that of running the presidential library.

"What a magnificent view," Maddy said, leading the small group to the one secure observation point. Because of two attempted assassinations, the Secret Service made sure that no one was within earshot or, for that matter, any other kind of shot. While security was intense, Maddy still moved without fear among people as the agents standing post worked themselves to a frazzle and into an early retirement. "How's Little Matt?" Maddy asked.

"Growing like a weed," Pontowski replied, "and he's not so 'little' anymore. Maybe that's why everyone is calling him Zack these days."

Maddy laughed. "Brian never told me. It's much better than that horrible name Brian was calling him. I know Sarah will like it." Sarah was Maddy's twelve-year-old daughter, who had a not-so-secret crush on Pontowski's son. Then the tone of Maddy's voice changed as she became all business. "Have you had time to think about it?"

Pontowski nodded. "The ambassadorship to Poland is tempting, but I've got to get the library off the ground. I can't believe the stacks of documents and files we're sorting."

"You're lucky," one of the former presidents said. "No real hard issues like the tapes the Nixon Library has to deal with."

"Anyway, not yet," the other president allowed.

Again Maddy laughed, enchanting Pontowski. "There's always a rat in the woodwork." They all assumed her "rat" was the man ambling toward them. Patrick Flannery Shaw was a shaggy bear of a man given to wearing rumpled plaid suits, scuffed shoes, and outrageous ties. At first glance he seemed totally out of place. But the knowledgeable knew he was a shark swimming in his perfect environment.

"Mizz President," Shaw said, putting on his thickest southern accent, "we got a passel of people who need tendin'."

Maddy pleaded helplessness. "What can I do?"

"Win the election," the older of the two presidents said.

She shook hands all around, coming to Pontowski last. "Matt, please think about it. I don't need an answer until after the election." She turned to go. "Oh, Mazie needs to talk to you. Can you escape from all these dusty archives?" "Mazie" was Mazana Kamigami Hazelton, her national security adviser.

"For Mazie," Pontowski answered, "anytime."

"I believe she's free tonight," Shaw said. "I'll set it up for after the banquet." Then the president was gone, locked in a deep conversation with Shaw.

"Sounds like a command performance," the younger of the two presidents said.

"With the Dragon Lady," the older growled, "damn right."

Pontowski only smiled and shook his head.

San Francisco
Saturday, July 24

"General Pontowski," the Secret Service agent said, "this way please." Pontowski followed the amazingly fit young man into a service corridor on the ground floor of the Fairmont Hotel. They stopped at a guard station, where Pontowski emptied his pockets and was searched. A uniformed guard ran a wand over him, searching for metallic objects. The wand buzzed when it passed over Pontowski's right knee, and three guards immediately surrounded him.

"It's the pins in my knee," Pontowski explained as he pulled up his pant leg to show the long scars on his knee. "Ejected from an F-16," he explained. "Bad landing. Shattered my kneecap."

"Understand, sir," the Secret Service agent said. "But we'll need an X ray to confirm, if you're to see the president."

Pontowski was confused. "I thought—"

"I can vouch for him," a familiar voice said. Pontowski turned to see Chuck Sanford. "Evenin', General. Setting off alarms—again?"

A smile spread across Pontowski's face. "It's been a while, Chuck. I thought you were with Brian." Sanford was normally assigned to guard Brian Turner, the president's son.

"I've been on vacation. I'll pick up the duty when he goes back to the Hill." The Hill was the New Mexico Military Institute, where Sanford headed the detail guarding Brian. Because of the close friendship between Brian and Zack, Sanford and Pontowski had met many times. "I'm lookin' forward to gettin' back to the land of the sane and borin'. How's Zack doin'?" For a moment the two men were silent. It was not a simple question, because Zack had saved Sanford's life in New Mexico. But Zack had had to kill a man to do it.*

Pontowski chose his words with care. "He's doing just fine, and his counselor says he's handled it as well as any adult." The relief on Sanford's face was obvious. "I swear he's grown three inches over the sum-

---

*Editor's note: The story of Zack Pontowski, Brian Turner, and Chuck Sanford is told in *Edge of Honor* by the same author.

mer," Pontowski continued. "He's been working at the library here until school starts."

Sanford signed a clipboard and motioned Pontowski to a service elevator. They rode in silence to the presidential floor. The doors swooshed open, and the security drill repeated itself. "Sorry for the inconvenience," Sanford said.

"I understand," Pontowski replied. "It must be hell during a campaign."

"You wouldn't believe," Sanford allowed. He led the way down the service corridor to a door leading into the Presidential Suite. "I'll wait here for you," the agent said. He held the door open, and Pontowski entered a kitchen.

Pontowski's back stiffened. Mazana Kamigami Hazelton was sitting at a small table with Patrick Flannery Shaw. "Hello, Mazie," he said, ignoring Shaw. "What can I do for you?" Mazie was a petite woman, barely five feet tall, and the best of her Japanese and Hawaiian heritage was captured in her beautiful face and eyes. She came out of her chair and held Pontowski's hand with hers, no longer the cool and aloof national security adviser but an old friend.

"It *is* good to see you," Mazie said. She stood back and studied him. "It's not fair. You just keep getting better and better looking."

"And you're still the charmer."

"Maddy wants to see you," Mazie told him. "But we need to talk first." They sat down at the small table with Shaw. "She really wants you to be her ambassador to Poland." Before Pontowski could reply, she held up her hand. "There's more. Zou Rong is leading the Chinese delegation to the World Trade Organization conference in Chicago next week. He wants to speak to you."

Pontowski frowned as memories washed over him in full flood. He could no more stop them than change the course of the Mississippi River. For a moment he was back in southern China leading the American Volunteer Group—the AVG, a ragtag collection of pilots flying A-10 Warthogs—in support of Zou and his abortive revolution. Zou had saved himself by cutting a deal with Beijing. Pontowski had extracted the American Volunteer Group at the last moment and brought them back to the States. But it had been a near thing. Now Zou was the chairman of the Standing Committee of the National People's Congress—the real power in China—and in line to be the next president. Common wisdom held that Zou was not content to wait until the current president died, and the two were locked in a power struggle.

"Why me?" Pontowski asked.

"That's what we want to find out," Mazie said. Pontowski tightened his lips, not liking what he was hearing.

"We need an inside with the new boys in Beijing," Shaw said.

"Because you're at total odds with the current regime," Pontowski added.

"They are expansionist," Mazie said, "and engaged in an arms race. But we believe that if Zou Rong and his group come to power, all that can change."

"Good luck," Pontowski said under his breath. He had a different take on Zou and what was really going on in Beijing.

"But you will see him?" Mazie asked. Pontowski thought for a moment before making a decision. He nodded once. Mazie pushed back in her chair. "Maddy's waiting."

Shaw humphed for attention, demanding the last word. "The campaign is heatin' up, and the press is sniffin' after her like a pack of Dobermans goin' after a poodle in heat. So far I got their peckers tied to a tree. But if they sense there's anything goin' on between you and her . . . well, let's just say those boys are more than willin' to do themselves an injury if they smell—" Pontowski gave Shaw a cold look, cutting him off in midsentence. But the older man wouldn't let it go. "It doesn't take a rocket scientist to figure out why she lights up like a June bug when you come around. But you're a political liability, son."

"So what are you saying?" Pontowski demanded.

"Cool it until after the election, okay?"

Pontowski stood and followed Mazie into the lounge. Maddy Turner looked up from the briefing book she was reading, and came to her feet as Mazie closed the door behind him, leaving them alone. Maddy rushed into his arms and kissed him lightly on the cheek. Then she led him back to the couch and sat down. For a moment he stood, not knowing what was expected, until she patted the cushion beside her. He sat, and she cuddled against him, caressing his hand. They talked about the boys, their families, and the personalities that walked on their stage. Gently they found what had been lost. Finally she couldn't avoid the one issue they had to lay to rest. "Oh, Matt, I'm so sorry for what happened in Poland. I wanted to do something, but we had to hold it at arm's length for political reasons."

"I thought you had hung us out to dry."

"I'd never do that," she promised.

Terengganu, Malaysia
Monday, July 26

Kamigami and Tel squatted in the brush on the hillside overlooking the small hamlet. Below them, men shouted as they swept through the streets, killing everyone they found. "What can we do?" Tel asked.

"Nothing," Kamigami replied in a low tone. He motioned Tel to silence, and they waited for the attack to end. It didn't take long, and soon the men were looting and torching the wooden structures. Then they climbed into trucks and disappeared down the dirt road to the east. "Let's go," Kamigami said, leading the way into the valley.

"It doesn't make sense," Tel complained. "The other villages were Malay. This one is Chinese."

Kamigami examined a soft spot in the dirt and found a footprint. "Nike or Adidas," he said. "Those were Malay doing the killing."

"So the Chinese are killing Malays, and the Malays are killing Chinese in revenge?"

"Something like that."

"Was our kampong the first?"

Kamigami thought for a moment. "Probably."

The question was back. "Why?" Tel moaned.

"That's what we're going to find out." A shadow moved in the tree line on the hill above them, and Kamigami's right hand flashed, sending Tel a command. Kamigami took refuge behind a burned-out car and dropped his rucksack. He chambered a round in his Beretta and checked the safety while Tel retreated to their original spot on the hillside. Once Tel was safely out of the way, Kamigami slipped into the brush and worked up the hill to circle around to the backside of the area where he had seen the movement. He smelled urine first and shook his head.

Whoever was out there was very deficient in basic tradecraft if they were urinating in the open. He moved at an oblique angle to his target and secured the area. He didn't need any nasty surprises from a lookout or backup that had gone undetected. Satisfied that the area was clear, he closed on the target. He saw two men wearing civilian clothes lying on the ground. They had spread a ground cloth to make themselves comfortable while they scanned the village with a pair of high-power binoculars.

This is too easy, he reasoned. *They had to see us when we were down there.* He listened as they talked loudly in Cantonese—a language he understood. The man with the binoculars pointed to the spot on the far hill where Tel was hiding. *The boy needs more training.* One of them moved, and Kamigami saw the soles of his boots. He froze. The boots had the same ribbed pattern as those in his kampong. His face was impassive as he drew the Beretta and thumbed off the safety. Then he thought better of it.

He holstered the Beretta and moved silently toward them. They never heard him as he stood behind them. He decided he wanted them to see him and reached for the golden whistle hanging on its chain around his neck. He gave a short blast, and as they turned to the sound, he fell on them, banging their heads together. One man groaned, stunned but not unconscious. Kamigami slammed his hands against the man's temples in a clapping motion. He checked the man's breathing and reflexes. He was out cold. Kamigami worked fast, calculating that the man would regain consciousness in a few minutes.

The man's head was racked with pain, and his temples throbbed as he fought his way back to consciousness. He was lying on the ground and, other than this splitting headache, was unharmed. A shadow moved across his face, and he looked up. He forced his eyes to focus on the image swinging in the shadows. His partner was hanging upside down from a tree by his ankles, free from any obvious wounds but totally lifeless. The man staggered to his feet and touched the body. It was still warm but strangely blanched. Confused images flashed through the pain—lying on his stomach and watching the boy on the far hill, reacting to the sound of a whistle, turning in time to see a huge creature descending on them, smothering under its weight. A vague memory of two giant hands crashing against his head kept coming back, demanding his attention. He forced it away as he cut down the body, not sure what to do.

Then he saw the two closely spaced punctures on the neck. He stroked his own neck where the punctures would have been, and felt his carotid artery pulsing with life. His fingers went to his own teeth and touched his canines. The spacing was the same as the holes in his comrade's neck. His eyes searched the ground where the body had been hanging for signs of blood. Nothing. For a moment, he couldn't breathe. The sound of a whistle, far away but clear, echoed over him.

He turned and ran, crashing through the dense foliage.

Kamigami reached the spot where Tel should be. *Okay, where are you?* It puzzled him, for so far Tel had been following his directions to the letter. He felt something poke him in his back and whirled to face the threat, his MP5 coming up to the ready. Tel was standing there with a long stick, a big grin on his face. "Gotcha!"

"Not funny, boy," Kamigami groused. "I could've shot you."

"I don't think so," Tel replied. He felt the need to explain. "I saw the lookouts, and I wanted to draw their attention away from you. I knew you would come back here, so I hid."

"Why did you have to hide from me?"

"Well, I couldn't be sure it would be you, could I?"

"Thanks for the vote of confidence," Kamigami muttered, wondering who really needed more training.

two

Oakland
Monday, July 26

The Annex, the nondescript office building where the real work of the Presidential Library took place, overflowed with files stuffed with documents, photographs, books, reports, letters, diaries, movies, videotapes, newspaper clippings, interviews, memoirs, and magazine articles all devoted to one subject—the life and times of President Matthew Zachary Pontowski.

The librarian, and the real force behind the library, was a little birdlike woman with boundless energy and a no-nonsense disposition. Judy Bloomfield, or Bloomy as everyone called her, was also a dedicated feminist of the very liberal persuasion, and while she liked Matt Pontowski as an individual, she quivered at the notion that she worked for a socially conservative member of the establishment, spoiled by position, wealth, and privilege. When pressed, she would admit that he was a good administrator and served the library well with his astute sense of public relations, his connections, and his good looks. But it upset her when he laughingly described himself as a "retired aerial assassin." It hurt because she knew he wasn't joking.

However, Bloomy had no reservations about Pontowski's son, Zack, who was spending his summer vacation working at the library. She enjoyed his boyish ways and good humor and had put him to work in the foreign collections department, figuring it might give him an incentive to polish up his rudimentary German. She also kept a mental calendar counting down the days to when he went back to school at the New Mexico Military Institute. She was going to miss him.

On the Monday morning following the library's formal dedication ceremony, Bloomy was still basking in the compliments and accolades over the success of the ceremony. But it frustrated her that the staff was more interested in hearing the details of her meeting with Maddy Turner than in the real substance of the day. When she finally broke free for a late lunch, she realized she hadn't seen Zack all morning. She went in search and found him in the special collections department, normally under lock and key. He was reading and didn't see her. She studied him for a moment, seeing a young carbon copy of his father. "Zack!" She feigned indignation. "How did you get in here?"

He gave her the infectious grin that seemed to be in the Pontowski genes, and held up a key ring. He handed her a small diary she had never seen before. "I found this. Grandma Tosh wrote it." Tosh was Lady Wilhelmina Crafton, the elder Pontowski's wife and one of the most elegant first ladies ever to grace the White House. He blushed brightly. "There's some personal stuff in there. Grandma Tosh was jealous because Gramps knew a woman called Chantal Dubois."

Bloomy turned to the marked pages and read. While there were some very racy passages, there was nothing really damaging, as Tosh and the president later married. *It was wartime,* she rationalized. She smiled at the thought of a young couple finding love in the chaos of a war that threatened to destroy them. It only added to the Pontowski legend.

"Then I found this," Zack said. He handed over another small journal. "But it's written in French." Bloomy was fluent in French and scanned the little journal. Now it was her turn to blush. "Oh, my." She read in silence. She would have to verify its provenance, but her instincts shouted, *Authentic!* She looked for the source, but the donor was listed as anonymous. "Is there anything else?"

Zack showed her a formal document written in German. "I think it's a death warrant signed by the German governor of a town called Amiens in northern France. It's for Chantal Dubois and dated February 19, 1944."

Bloomy was fully alert. "Who else has seen all this?"

"Only me that I know of."

She made a decision. "Come with me." She carried the death warrant and two small books to her office, where she locked them in her personal safe. "Are you hungry?" From the look on Zack's face, she knew she had gotten that one right. "Let's go for a pizza. We need to talk."

Zack had found the Pontowski rat.

"General Pontowski," Bloomy said, "do you have a moment?"

Pontowski looked up from his desk. "For you, always." He motioned her to the most comfortable seat in his spartan office on the sixth floor of the Annex. It surprised him that she closed the door without asking. *Why is she so nervous?* Pontowski thought.

"Zack unearthed these." Bloomy handed him the death warrant, Tosh's diary, and Chantal's journal.

Pontowski glanced at the warrant and thumbed through the little books. "My French is very rusty, and I don't read German. What am I looking at?"

"The document is a death warrant for the execution of one Chantal Dubois, incarcerated in Amiens prison in France. According to Zack, it says she had committed crimes against the Third Reich and is dated February nineteenth, 1944."

Pontowski pulled into himself. "If I remember right," he said slowly, "Gramps bombed that prison." He brightened as it came back. "Operation Jericho. Gramps was flying Mosquitos for the RAF, and they bombed the prison the day before a group of French resistance workers were scheduled for execution. The idea was to blow the place up so they could escape. He was shot up something fierce and wounded but managed to land the Mossie in England. His navigator was killed."

"Unfortunately," Bloomy said, "we know very little about his wartime record after that. He was grounded and couldn't fly. The president never talked much about the last year of the war. I call it 'the missing year.'"

Pontowski gave her a little smile. "He could be the great stone-mouth at times." He glanced at the pages Zack had marked in Tosh's diary. Pontowski chuckled as he read. "It looks like they went at it like bunnies."

Bloomy ignored the remark and was all business. "Near the end there's a reference to Chantal Dubois. Apparently the first lady was quite jealous." Pontowski read the marked passages and again chuckled. "I assure you," Bloomy said, "it is not funny." She picked up Chantal's journal and translated. Pontowski's eyes opened wide. "To paraphrase your words, General, it looks as if the president and the Dubois woman went at it like bunnies."

"Oh, boy," Pontowski murmured. Then his basic good humor reasserted itself. "Well, Gramps always said the Pontowskis were a tight-lipped and lusty bunch. Just good peasant stock from Poland."

"The dates on the Dubois journal are after February the nineteenth," Bloomy continued. "Apparently the Dubois woman did escape. But I keep asking myself, why were the death certificate and Dubois's journal given to us? Memorabilia like these are worth a great deal of money at auction."

"Maybe they're not authentic," Pontowski replied. But even as he said it, he knew they were.

Taman Negara, Malaysia
Wednesday, July 28

They hadn't come that far from the destroyed Chinese hamlet, perhaps forty miles. But the trek through the jungle-covered hills was an excursion into hell, and Kamigami wanted the fleeing man to get the full experience. Unfortunately, in his panic the man had bolted, leaving all his gear behind, and Kamigami couldn't push him too hard. He had to have time to find water. But Kamigami made sure he didn't get any rest, especially at night, and a little toot on the whistle would get him moving.

At the end of the second day the man was on the verge of collapse, and he needed help. Kamigami left Tel behind to keep an eye on things while he ranged ahead. He found a well-used path, almost wide enough for a small truck. A squeaking noise caught his attention, and he barely had time to hide before a line of men came lumbering down the path from the east, pushing bicycles heavily laden with supplies. Kamigami waited until they had passed, and then set out after them, stalking the last man. As expected, Tail End Charlie was last for a good reason—he couldn't keep up with the others, and the gap was widening. The man leaned his bicycle against a tree and took a short smoke break.

Kamigami didn't even bother to drop his rucksack. He unsheathed his knife and slipped up behind the man. Kamigami had no compulsions about killing him—he had killed many others before—but it bothered him that it was so easy. Fish in a barrel were better fighters. In one smooth motion he grabbed the man's hair, which was too long for the jungle or combat, jerked his head back, and drew the knife across his neck. It looked easy, but Kamigami had put all his strength into the attack and almost decapitated the man. He threw the body over the bicycle and retreated down the path until he reached the place where he had come out of the bush. He pushed the overloaded bike into the dense foliage and retraced his steps.

It was hard going, and Kamigami had to lighten the load. He tossed the body into a ravine and pressed on. When his small GPS placed him near the location where he had left Tel, he dropped the bike on its side, certain that it was too heavy for one man to lift. He rifled through the bags strapped to the bike and pocketed a few items. He dumped the rest on the ground so his quarry could easily find it. Then he sat down to rest, and within seconds dozed off.

"You do sleep a lot," Tel said from a deep shadow.

"That's the idea," Kamigami said, instantly awake. "Where is he?"

"About two hundred meters behind me. Coming this way."

"Good. Let's vamoose."

"What's vamoose?" Tel asked. "Something to eat, like a McDonald's?"

"You don't *eat* a McDonald's, you eat *at* a McDonald's."

"I could eat a McDonald's right now," Tel told him. But all he could see was Kamigami's back as he headed for the path.

Tel sat on his haunches and munched the soy cake Kamigami had taken from one of the bags on the bicycle. He was puzzled, since they had been watching the path for over a day and nothing had happened. "This tastes terrible," Tel said.

Kamigami handed him a granola bar. "Drink lots of water." Tel savored the bar as Kamigami turned on his GPS and unfolded a map. It was time for a navigation lesson. "We're here," he said, pointing to a spot near the Tembeling River in Malaysia's Taman Negara, or National Park. Suddenly Kamigami's right hand flashed, palm down, close to the ground. Tel lay on the ground, certain he could not be seen. Again Kamigami signaled by pointing a finger to his eyes and then pointing into the jungle. He held up a finger indicating that one person was coming their way. The man they had been stalking pushed through the brush and stepped onto the path, a relieved look on his face. He had a bag strapped to his back and was in much better shape. He looked both ways and set off toward the east. Kamigami didn't move.

"Aren't we going after him?" Tel asked softly.

"He'll come back," Kamigami replied.

"How can you be so sure?"

"The stupid ass is going the wrong way." He pointed to the west. "That's the way the pack train was going. I think he wants to go the same way."

Twenty minutes later the man came back, making good time. He trudged by, less than three feet from Tel's hiding place. Again Kamigami didn't move. After what seemed an eternity to Tel, Kamigami stood and shouldered his rucksack. "He's going in the right direction," he announced.

"What now?" Tel asked.

"We follow. Stay alert for lookouts or guards." Kamigami set off, moving silently along the path. His forward motion was a series of short moves from shadow to shadow, which Tel tried to copy, but it was hard going. He was just hoping that Kamigami would take a break when the big man stopped and motioned him to join up. Tel heard voices, and Kamigami pushed a leafy fern aside. Tel looked where he was pointing and, far down the path, saw their man talking to a guard. After a few words the guard motioned the man on and stepped off the path to light a cigarette. "Stupid," Kamigami said under his breath, the professional in him disgusted with the lax security.

He carefully slipped out of his rucksack and signaled Tel to cover him. He stepped onto the path in full view of the guard. But the guard just kept puffing on his cigarette and was oblivious to the danger coming his way. Kamigami shrugged in resignation and walked toward him. Kamigami spoke a few words of Cantonese in greeting as he approached, finally capturing the man's attention.

The guard bent over to stub out his cigarette butt. Kamigami, still speaking in Cantonese, called him a fool. The guard looked up to see

Kamigami's hands flashing down on him in a clapping motion. Kamigami's palms slapped the man's temples—hard—stunning him. He easily shouldered the unconscious body.

Tel followed and watched in fascination as Kamigami carried the guard into the jungle, hung him by the heels from a tree, tied his hands, and stuffed part of his shirt into his mouth. Satisfied that the guard was immobilized if he regained consciousness, Kamigami searched the foliage until he found a certain thornbush. He cut off a slender shoot and carefully extracted the core, leaving a hollow tube. He cut the tube in half to make two before retracing his steps to the tree where the guard was hanging.

The man was now fully awake, his eyes wide with fear as Kamigami scooped out a hole in the ground directly underneath him. Kamigami sharpened an end of each of the tubes and jammed them into the guard's neck, side by side, about an inch apart. Blood spurted from the tubes and dribbled into the hole as the man twisted and turned, trying to shake the tubes out. He slowly weakened as his life drained away. "Why are you doing this?" Tel asked.

Kamigami gave him a cold look. "These are the men who butchered our families." He paused to let the lesson sink in. "Follow me," he said.

They had barely regained the path when a smoky smell drifted over them. "I can't believe it," Kamigami said. "Cooking fires. They're not really serious about this." Tel didn't know what "this" was, but he was afraid to ask, especially after witnessing the guard's execution. They moved off the path and came to a ridge overlooking a shallow valley. The smoke of numerous cooking fires floated over the treetops, and off to the far side, men were exercising in an open area. Beyond the open area, and dug into the high limestone ridge at the northern end of the valley, were three tunnels.

"What is it?" Tel whispered.

"Don't whisper like that," Kamigami said. "It travels too far. Just speak in a low voice." He paused to let that lesson register. "It's a military base camp. A big one." He sat down and made himself comfortable. "We'll move out when it's dark. Now we get some rest. Wake me in an hour, and don't let me snore."

Tel came awake with a jolt. Kamigami's hand was over his mouth. "It's time," Kamigami said. He handed Tel a pair of night-vision goggles and helped him adjust the straps. "You lose a lot of depth perception, so go slowly at first or you'll get a stick in your face." Kamigami moved slowly until Tel was comfortable with the goggles. Then he moved quickly, heading down the path and away from the base camp. He relied on his GPS to guide them to the body that was still swinging from the tree.

Kamigami covered the hole where the blood had pooled and cut the body down. He carried it back to the path and again strung it up by its ankles. "It's blocking the path," Tel said.

"That's the idea," Kamigami murmured. He took a few sips of water and told Tel to do the same. "Rest. We're going to be moving very fast the next few hours. You up to it?"

"Do I have a choice?"

Kamigami shook his head as they sat down. When he judged that Tel was ready, he stood up and tightened the straps on his rucksack. Then he unsnapped the side pocket, and the MP5 fell into his hand. He slipped in a clip and charged a round. "Make sure your shoelaces are tight," he said. He carefully inspected the boy. "Ready?" Tel nodded, and Kamigami put the gold whistle to his lips.

"What are you doing?" Tel asked.

"Sending a message," Kamigami replied.

"Which is?"

"Vampire." Kamigami gave a long blast on the whistle and moved out, setting a blistering pace.

Washington, D.C.
Friday, July 30

The spook sitting in the national security adviser's office was a nondescript man, five feet ten inches tall, in his late forties, hunch-shouldered, and slightly balding. He was a man people passed every day and never saw. Franklin Bernard Butler was also a lieutenant general in the Air Force, the chief of a shadowy organization quartered on the mezzanine of the Pentagon's basement, and an operational genius in the netherworld of covert intelligence. Mazie looked up from the thin folder she was reading, a very worried expression on her face. "Bernie, how in the world did you get this?"

"The old-fashioned way."

Mazie arched an eyebrow. "Which is?"

"Spying."

"I was afraid you were going to say 'work,' which is something the Boys never do." The "Boys" was shorthand for Butler's group, known only as the Boys in the Basement. She gave a very audible sigh. Levity was not going to lessen the reality of what she was looking at. "How good is this?"

"It doesn't get any better," Butler told her. Although he trusted the national security adviser, he wasn't about to reveal how the Boys had recruited three moles in Iraq during the Persian Gulf War in 1991. The moles had been left behind to burrow into Saddam Hussein's infrastructure, and now all three were talking. "The president needs to know," Butler said, telling her the obvious.

Mazie looked at the elegant carriage clock on her desk. Again she sighed, giving in to the inevitable. "Why does it always hit the fan on a Friday afternoon?"

"It's an immutable law of nature," Butler replied.

The chairman of the Joint Chiefs of Staff, General Mike Wilding, United States Army, was the last to enter the White House Situation Room. Wilding nodded at the three people sitting at the table—Mazie, Vice President Sam Kennett, and the director of Central Intelligence, or DCI. The four of them were the heart of the National Security Council and among the president's most trusted advisers. As expected, Wilding's boss, the secretary of defense, was not there, as he was reluctant to attend any meeting that included the vice president. Wilding stared at the outsider who was sitting against the back wall. "Bernie Butler," he muttered. "I should have guessed."

The door opened, and Patrick Shaw came into the room. "Mizz Hazelton, gentlemen, the President." Madeline Turner entered the room and sat down.

"Patrick," Mazie said, "I'm afraid this one is above your pay grade." Shaw was dumfounded. It was the first time Mazie had ever asked Shaw to leave a meeting. Normally Shaw would have treated it as a power play and responded accordingly. But Mazie never played silly Washington games. He nodded and closed the door as he left.

"This must be serious," Turner said.

"I believe it is," Mazie replied. She looked at Butler, her eyes full of concern.

Butler stood and keyed his remote control. The large computer monitor mounted in the wall opposite the president came to life, and a map of the Middle East flashed on the screen. "My sources claim that the radical Islamic states"—the map flashed, and Iraq, Iran, and Syria were highlighted in red—"have joined in a secret alliance. They're calling themselves the United Islamic Front—the UIF for short."

The DCI raised his hand slightly to interrupt, a condescending look on his face. "Syria has been on board in the war against terrorism, Iran is cooperating under the table, and we've effectively isolated Iraq. So, why in the name of Allah would they form such an alliance at this time?"

"Oil," Butler said. "They are going to attack Kuwait, Saudi Arabia, and the United Arab Emirates." Again the map changed, and the target states changed to blue.

The DCI shook his head. "Not hardly," he announced.

Vice President Kennett scratched his empty left coat sleeve. His missing arm always itched when he was worried. "How good is your source?" he asked.

"Extremely reliable," Butler answered.

"Confirmation?" General Wilding asked.

"We have two other independent sources saying the same thing," Butler told him.

"And why haven't I heard about this?" the DCI barked, his anger showing.

"We forwarded it to Langley yesterday," Butler explained, his voice a monotone. "When it didn't show up in the PDB this morning, I took it to Mrs. Hazelton." The PDB was the President's Daily Brief, a slick summary of the best intelligence the United States had. It was compiled by a committee at the CIA and seen by only twelve people.

The DCI was outraged. "You're not on distribution! How did you see it?"

Mazie caught the crinkle in Butler's lips, the closest he could come to a smile. "Don't ask the question," she said, "if you can't stand the answer."

"It's my business to know," Butler replied. In five simple words he had summed up what intelligence was all about.

The hard professional in Wilding came out. "When? Do you have an order of battle?"

"Not order of battle, sir," Butler answered. "We're working on it." He paused. "But my sense of the matter tells me before the first of the year."

"What's the NRO and NSA saying?" This from Vice President Kennett. Like the others, he was at home dealing with the alphabet soup that made up the intelligence community. The NRO was the National Reconnaissance Office, which controlled the Keyhole series of spy satellites, and NSA was the National Security Agency, which monitored communications.

"I'll have to check," the DCI said. He hit a button on the small control panel in front of him and spoke into the microphone. "We need the latest satellite imagery for the Persian Gulf and the latest CIS for the same area." A CIS was a communications intelligence summary produced by the NSA. The DCI looked at Turner. "We should have something in a few minutes."

"I hate surprises," Turner told the DCI.

A woman's voice from the control room said, "NRO coming on the number-two screen now. And a courier has a message for General Butler."

Butler walked to the door as the second screen came to life. He stepped outside. His second in command was waiting in the hall and handed him a sealed envelope. "The shit is hittin' the fan over there," he told Butler.

Butler carried the envelope back into the Situation Room and glanced at the monitor displaying the latest satellite coverage from the Persian Gulf. The DCI was talking. "We're seeing nothing unusual." The screen scrolled, and the NSA summary appeared. Listening posts had detected no change in the normal traffic for the region. Butler glanced at the screen and shook his head as he opened the envelope. He read the message twice and cleared his throat. Everyone turned toward him. "Iraq,

Syria, and Iran are planning a joint training exercise. No announced time frame."

General Wilding snorted. "Joint exercise, my—" He caught himself, remembering whom he was talking to.

Turner came to her feet. "The word you're looking for, General, is 'ass.' Which is what they're making of us and which I'm ending right now. No more surprises. We will stay ahead of this."

"Level of response?" Mazie asked.

"I want everyone awake and looking at this, but I don't see any reason for moving up the DEFCON in the Middle East—not yet." They all agreed with her, fully aware of the political ramifications of such an action during an election year. "Mazie, start talking to your counterparts in NATO." She pointed a finger at the DCI. "And find out why the CIA missed this. It won't happen again. Okay, that's it for now. We'll reconvene tomorrow morning and see where we are."

three

The White House
Saturday, July 31

Butler leaned against the wall in the corridor outside the Situation Room in the White House basement and yawned. It was early Saturday morning, and he needed a cup of coffee to jump-start his heart. Patrick Shaw emerged from the kitchen across the hall with two cups of steaming coffee and handed one to Butler. "I hear you're a patient man," Shaw said.

Butler took a sip before answering. *What does he want?* He allowed a cautious "It goes with the territory."

"What do you think they're talking about in there?" Shaw asked.

He doesn't know? Butler thought. *Fat chance. Shaw knows everything that goes on around here.* Before he could answer, the door to the control room opened, and one of the duty controllers told Butler he was wanted inside. Butler gave Shaw a shrug as if to say he was sorry as the Marine guard opened the door to the Situation Room. One glance around the room as he entered told Butler all he needed to know. Every major policy player in the Turner administration was there, including the irascible secretary of state, Stephan Serick, and Robert Merritt, the secretary of defense.

"Well, Bernie," the president said, "you certainly stirred up a hornet's nest on this one."

"I take it you have verification," Butler said.

Serick coughed for attention. "My people tell me it's all a false alarm. There is no secret alliance between Iraq, Iran, and Syria. There is no joint exercise. We've all lost too much sleep over this."

"I'm not ready to totally discount it," the DCI said, surprising Butler. The DCI had just admitted to a major intelligence failure.

Serick turned on him. "So what do you know now that you didn't know twelve hours ago?" His voice filled with sarcasm. "No doubt you've unearthed the real expert on the Middle East—the little old lady who wears purple dresses and sleeps under her desk in the CIA's basement?"

Secretary of Defense Merritt chuckled at the DCI's embarrassment. "Not exactly," the DCI replied, glaring at Merritt. "What I did discover was a power struggle going on between my China and Middle Eastern division chiefs." He spoke without emotion. "Both those gentlemen were fired, and their replacements are taking a fresh look at the situation. So far the assessment isn't good." Madeline Turner's warning about its not happening again had not gone unheeded.

Serick snorted. "Are you saying the Boys in the Basement made you look like fools?"

The DCI took a deep breath to control his anger. "What I'm saying is that we have a new development in the Middle East that needs close monitoring."

Serick was shouting. "My people would know if—"

The DCI interrupted him. "Your people don't know diddly—"

"Gentlemen," the president said, her voice full of authority. "Enough." A heavy silence ruled the room. Then, "Bernie, what is your sense of the situation?"

Butler thought for a moment. "The Islamic radicals have sensed a weakness and are moving in a new direction. It has the potential for serious trouble."

"Don't you think," Serick said, "that our allies in the Gulf would be shouting for help if what you say is true? Besides, who exactly are these sources that are revealing all of this? Some janitor in an embassy? Pickpocket? Pimp? A whore?"

Butler almost laughed, but it wasn't in his nature. Serick would never know how close he came to the truth. "Some things in my business," Butler murmured, "never change." He let that sink in. "Unfortunately, our erstwhile allies in the Gulf tend to rely on us for their intelligence. They know what we tell them."

"If I may," the DCI said, trying to speak with authority in his domain, "let me summarize. One: Iran, Iraq, and Syria have joined together in an alliance, calling themselves the United Islamic Front, or UIF. Two: We have an unconfirmed report from General Butler that the UIF intends to attack and capture the Kuwaiti and Saudi oil fields."

Merritt finally spoke. "Which will never happen."

"So you keep reassuring us," Vice President Kennett said. There was no reply as Merritt slipped into one of his characteristic funks. He hated the vice president.

The DCI took the silence as consent to continue. "Three: The UIF has announced a joint training exercise to be held sometime in the future. We've seen this before. They flex their muscles, we cry wolf and react, they do nothing, and we end up with egg on our face. For now it's fair to ask how much coincidence or speculation are we dealing with?"

The president sank back into her chair. "Patrick is fond of saying that 'once is chance, twice is coincidence, three times is enemy action.'" She leaned forward, her face frozen. "Every instinct tells me this is enemy action." Again a silence came down in the small room.

"Madam President," the DCI finally said, "we must not overreact. No one starts a war with the United States in an election year. Even the Arabs know that."

"Assuming they're rational actors," Butler said quietly. The number of heads nodding around the room was ample indication that he was not alone in his doubt.

The president thought for a moment. "No more surprises. So what can we expect, and what options are available to us? I want to stay ahead of this, and *they* do not drive events in my country. Further, I will not be held hostage in the White House monitoring the Middle East. Mazie, I want you and Sam"—she nodded at her vice president—"along with the secretary of defense and the DCI to form a working group to spearhead our response. Call it the Executive Committee. ExCom for short. Mazie, you have direct access to me, anytime, anyplace. Anyone you need, you have. All doors are opened to the ExCom." She looked around the room. "I hope everyone understands what I'm saying." She rose to leave.

"Stephan, please join me." Everyone stood as the president left the room with the secretary of state in tow.

Butler allowed an inward smile. By taking the cranky Serick with her, the president had removed a major obstacle to progress.

"Well," Mazie said, "I think the president was quite clear in what she wants. Sam, who do we need working with us?"

The vice president didn't hesitate. "Bernie Butler."

Mazie glanced at the DCI. "Anyone else?" He shook his head.

She turned to the secretary of defense. "I'd prefer General Wilding to stand in for me," Merritt answered, refusing to work with the vice president.

Maddy walked into her private study next to the Oval Office and nodded at her assistant, Nancy Bender, to close the door. She motioned Serick to a comfortable seat. "Well, Stephan, what's your take on all this?"

All the posturing, the grumpiness, the irritability that made him a legend, was gone. No longer was he the devil's advocate keeping everyone honest. Now he was a trusted adviser giving his president the best advice he could. "There still exists a deep hatred of our country in the Arab world, and Butler certainly understands the Middle Eastern mind-set. We may have convinced them to forgo terrorism as a national policy, but if they sense a weakness they may well be striking out in a new direction. Timely action now might convince them otherwise."

"We're going to need allies."

"I'll do what I can, but France is going to be a major problem."

"Why am I not surprised. Talk to them. The Russians?"

"I can neutralize them."

"And the Chinese?"

Serick shook his head. "Still to be heard from."

Taman Negara
Sunday, August 1

The soldiers trudging down the path in a line were nervous as they looked right and left, afraid of what might be lurking in the jungle around them. Less than five meters away, Kamigami and Tel lay under a low bush counting them as they filed past. But there was more. Kamigami was taking their measure as soldiers, judging the way they moved and carried their weapons after being in hot pursuit for three days. He was not impressed. The signs of exhaustion were evident, the result of poor conditioning. But even more telling was the way they bunched in a tight group and clung to one another like ducks in a row. It had been easy leading them in a series of circles, always coming back to the path that led to the east. He seriously doubted they even knew where they were. It would be simple to render them. When the last man had passed, Tel started to speak. Kamigami waved him to silence. On cue, four stragglers stumbled past. Kamigami held up his hand and waited. A lone man came into view, driven by the fear of being left behind. He struggled to keep from collapsing as he disappeared down the path.

"I count twenty-seven," Kamigami said.

"My feet hurt," Tel said in a low voice.

"It's only pain," Kamigami told him.

Tel pulled off his boots and rubbed his aching feet. In all his nineteen years he had never been so bruised and abused. Yet for some strange reason he felt good. "Will they come back this way?" he asked.

"Eventually," Kamigami replied. "When they realize they're out of the park, they won't go much farther. Might run into civilization. They'll rest, maybe ten, twelve, hours before returning to base." He pulled out his chart and GPS. "Go back to where I left the bicycle." He pointed to the spot on the chart where he had dumped the bicycle laden with supplies. "There's claymores in one of the bags. Bring back as many as you can carry. Meet me here." Again he pointed to the chart. "Memorize the coordinates and never mark them on a map."

"What's a claymore?" Tel asked.

Kamigami stifled a sigh. *Don't kids know anything these days?* he lamented to himself. He described what the olive drab, three-and-a-half-pound antipersonnel mine looked like and how it was carried in a canvas bandolier. Tel listened attentively as he pulled on his boots. "Off you go," Kamigami said. "Heads up. Hurry." He watched approvingly as Tel moved out, staying low and in the shadows. "The boy is a quick learner," Kamigami mumbled to himself. He leaned against a tree to rest. He calculated he could make the journey in three hours, so Tel should do it in four or five—if he didn't get lost. Then he fell asleep.

The inner alarm was there, cutting through the fog of sleep. Kamigami came alert, pleased that the sixth sense that had saved him so many times in combat was still there, undiminished by time. There was movement in the brush off to his right. He cracked an eyelid as he freed the Beretta in his holster. It was Tel. He faked sleep to see what the boy would do. Tel emerged from the brush weighed down with bandoliers, paused, and gazed at Kamigami. Certain that the big man was asleep, Tel retreated back into the bush and made a loud noise.

"Bull elephants in mating season make less racket," Kamigami said half aloud.

"I didn't want you to shoot me by mistake," Tel replied.

Kamigami knew that Tel was only being polite and didn't want to embarrass him by catching him asleep. "I saw you the first time."

Tel grinned, not believing him. "Yes, sir."

"Cheeky bugger," Kamigami grumbled as Tel shed his cargo. "How many did you bring?"

"All of them. Twelve."

"Six is the normal load," Kamigami explained. He checked his watch. Tel had made it back in less than three hours. "Well done," he conceded.

"What now," Tel asked, eager to get on with it.

"Impatient bugger," Kamigami groused. He set to work and showed Tel how to rig one of the small mines. He unfolded the short scissor legs and sat the mine on the ground. He read the words on the face of the claymore: "'Front Toward Enemy.' Pretty simple." He attached the firing wire and rigged the firing device.

"Why are the words printed in English?" Tel asked.

"Because these particular puppies were made in the good old US of A and probably sold to some government in the name of military aid."

"Then they were resold into the black market."

"Something like that," Kamigami allowed. "Okay, ambush time." Tel watched as Kamigami found a relatively open area and set three mines twenty-five meters apart. Then he strung the firing wires to a concealed position fifteen meters back from the trail and connected the claymores to a common firing device. "Normally this is all I would set along a trail like this. But since you were such an industrious little pack mule, we're going for overkill." He moved up the trail and planted another set of three. After rigging and camouflaging the mines, he moved farther along the trail and set up another three. Kamigami showed Tel how to activate the firing device and gave him his orders.

"Your job is to fire this last set of claymores when the Gomers are in range."

"Gomers?" Tel asked. "My uncle said that was a bad name Anglos used for us." Kamigami stared at him, not understanding. "I mean . . . ah . . . Gomers are Asian. Aren't we Gomers, too?"

Kamigami laughed. "Naw. Gomers are the bad guys. Never identify with the enemy you're about to render. Give 'em all a name, something derogatory." He turned very serious. "Never forget what those bastards did to your family." He studied Tel for a moment, wishing he could read the look on his face. "Here's the drill: I detonate the middle set of claymores when the main body of Gomers is in range. It won't get 'em all, and I expect a few to head your way. Your part of the contract is to nail them. But only detonate your claymores if you've heard mine go off first. Otherwise you'll be taking them all on. After firing your claymores, fall back into the jungle and rendezvous at the bicycle. If I let the Gomers go past, wait for me here. If something goes wrong and you don't know what to do, hide for twelve hours, then rendezvous at the bicycle."

"What will you do?"

"Good question," Kamigami said. "If the conditions are right, I'll initiate the ambush. Then I'll fall back on the first set of mines and render any Gomers coming my way. I'll clean up and meet you at the rendezvous."

"Why can't I clean up?"

"No weapon," Kamigami replied. "Just do what I tell you this time. You'll have plenty of chances later. Let's do it." Tel followed him as they walked the trail, checking the camouflaged mines.

"Why did you pick such an open area for the ambush?"

"They won't suspect it here. I'm betting the survivors will be afraid to run into the bush and will stay on the trail."

"And right into a second ambush."

"That's the idea," Kamigami replied. He walked Tel through the initial part of his escape route three times. Satisfied that it was burned into Tel's memory and he could do it in the dark, he then helped Tel camouflage his observation post. "Whatever you do," Kamigami cautioned, "keep your head and butt down when the claymores go off." He returned to the middle set of claymores and scooped out a depression in the soft earth before covering it with foliage. He crawled inside, rigged the firing device, and made himself comfortable.

Once more he fell asleep.

It was almost dark when it all went wrong. The man serving as point for the main column of soldiers was not concentrating as he came down the path. Instead he was daydreaming about his girlfriend and the reception he knew was waiting for him at the base camp. That, plus the fact that they were no longer chasing a shadow and hadn't heard the so-called vampire's whistle once, made him indifferent to the task at hand. As a result he trudged past the first string of claymores without seeing a thing. That's when luck took over. He was lost in an erotic vision when he stumbled off the path—right into the first claymore of Kamigami's string. For once his training held, and he simply cut the firing wire with his knife. But a little success went to his head, and he then forgot his training.

Rather than warn his comrades coming up behind him, the man bent over and pulled at the wire as he followed it to a thick clump of foliage twenty-five meters from the trail. He got down on all fours and pushed a leafy branch aside to look directly into Kamigami's big brown eyes. Before the man could shout a warning, Kamigami's left hand flashed out as he jammed the point of his knife into the man's Adam's apple. He thrust hard, twisting at the same time, and cut the man's vocal cords. The man instinctively jerked backward as Kamigami reached for his shirt to drag him under the bush. He missed. "Damn," Kamigami mumbled. He scrambled backward out of his hiding place while the wounded soldier crawled toward the path, all the time making a gurgling sound like a perking coffeepot.

The man had almost reached the trail when Kamigami got to him. Kamigami bent over, placed one hand on the back of the man's head, grabbed his chin with the other, and made a hard pull-push jerking motion. The soldier heard the sharp crack of his own neck snapping. The gurgling sound stopped.

Kamigami grabbed the man's shirt and pulled him away from the trail, reaching the low foliage just as the main column came into view. The first two men missed it, but the third man in line saw a pair of feet disappearing under a bush and shouted a warning. Two things happened; most of the column retreated back down the trail, while the first five men took cover and unleashed a hail of fire. The distinctive chattering bark of their Type 56 submachine guns echoed over the clearing. The Type 56 was a knockoff of the Kalashnikov AK-47 assault rifle and put out the same heavy rate of fire. The soldiers, all believers in the tactical principle of concentration of fire, sprayed the vegetation above Kamigami, burying him in debris.

That's when he detonated the two remaining claymores in his string.

Officially the claymore is described as an antipersonnel mine with 700 steel spheres embedded in a plastic matrix. That's the part of the mine that says "Front Toward Enemy." Behind that is a layer of C-4 explosive that sends the steel balls and fragments into a killing zone that is 2 meters high and spread over a 60-degree arc out to 50 meters. Beyond that is a danger area that spreads over a 180-degree fan and out to 250 meters. Even the area directly behind the claymore is highly dangerous, and a secondary missile area extends to 100 meters behind the mine.

The five men hosing down the area with their Type 56 submachine guns were simply outvoted by the claymores and shredded. Kamigami was well inside the secondary missile area behind the mine and pressed his body into the shallow depression he had scooped out underneath the foliage. He felt a hot, searing pain across his left buttock as a ricocheting steel fragment cut into his flesh. A cloud of debris and dust rained down on him. The silence was deafening. "I'm getting too old for this," Kamigami groused aloud as he dug himself out. He came to his feet and quickly donned the web harness with his fighting load, shouldered two bandoliers with extra magazines and grenades, and checked his

MP5. In less than twenty seconds he was moving through the jungle and headed for the first string of mines a kilometer down the trail.

Although Kamigami knew the numbers, he never hesitated. For him it was a matter of tradecraft and experience against twenty-two half-trained and poorly led young men. He blew a long blast on his whistle to give them a motivational boost. Then he really put on some speed, figuring that at least two or three of the men would react correctly and home in on the sound. Six minutes later he found the location he was looking for.

He paused at the edge of the small jungle clearing. The grass was thick and even, almost chest high. *Perfect,* he thought. He listened. Nothing. He sensed a gentle breeze blowing in his face and sniffed the area. Still nothing. Then he heard movement deep in the jungle behind him. *Do I have enough time?* He didn't know, but it was worth a chance. He ran across the clearing in a zigzag pattern, getting to the far side in seconds. He quickly cut a long, thin tree branch and sectioned it into fourths, each two feet long. He retraced his steps across the clearing. He planted two sticks in the grass as far back as he could reach without leaving the trail he had made. The sticks were about eight feet apart and parallel to the path. Then he stretched a trip wire between them and tied a grenade to the base of one of the sticks. He carefully extracted the safety pin and used one end of the trip wire to hold the safety lever in place. It was a delicate operation, and even a strong gust of wind could move the grass enough to set off the grenade. He moved another ten meters and rigged a similar trap on the other side of the trail. Now he could hear definite movement in the jungle. He quickly moved to the near side of the clearing where the sound was coming from, and took cover.

He didn't have to wait long before a shadow in the trees materialized into a single soldier. The soldier glanced directly at the spot where Kamigami was hiding, but didn't see him. *Take the bait,* Kamigami mentally urged. The man moved cautiously onto the path Kamigami had cut through the grass. The soldier paused, surveyed the clearing, and motioned his comrades to follow. Two men followed him into the clearing. Kamigami's eyes drew into narrow slits as he watched their backs. When they reached the booby traps, he raised his MP5 and squeezed off a short burst. The bullets struck the last soldier in the back and blew out large chunks of his chest. The two men in front of him dove off the trail.

A few seconds later Kamigami was rewarded with the sound of two grenades going off. A high-pitched scream cut the air.

Kamigami worked his way around the clearing as the screams tapered off to a loud moan. He heard the man pleading for help. *You got to be smart in this business, and you weren't smart,* Kamigami rationalized. Then he relented and walked back into the clearing. He found the man still alive, curled up on the ground and holding his intestines in. The wounded man looked up, pleading for help.

Kamigami's face softened. He hesitated, drew his Beretta, and shot him in the head. It was the best he could do for him. *Eight down, nineteen to go,* he thought.

The sharp echo of three claymores washed over him. *Tel!* Nothing made sense. He had driven the men back down the trail, away from Tel's ambush. Now Tel's claymores had detonated. Had the soldiers reversed course and stumbled into Tel's killing zone? Or had they captured Tel and set off the claymores? A vision of Tel staked out in front of his own claymores as they exploded flashed in Kamigami's mind. He headed for the sound of the explosion. But this time he moved slowly and with caution.

He heard it first—the sound of swarming insects. Then he caught the faint scent of blood that cut through the smell of decay and rotting vegetation that marked the Malay jungle. As quickly as it came, the scent was gone. But Kamigami knew he was in the presence of death. He moved through the underbrush without a sound until he could see the area where he had left Tel. The vegetation was chopped and torn, spattered with human remains—the work of claymores properly sited and detonated. He moved through the death and destruction, getting a body count and looking for Tel. *Eighteen.*

"Here, sir," Tel said. Kamigami whirled around to see Tel emerging from behind a tree. His lips were trembling and his body shaking as he stood there, unable to go on. Kamigami recognized the symptoms—he had seen them many times before. Tel was lost in an emotional wasteland, trying to reconcile his basic humanity with the carnage he had caused.

Kamigami knew what to do. "Report." No answer from Tel. "I need to know exactly what happened," Kamigami explained.

Tel hesitated, his lips working. Then, slowly and with increasing confidence, "I'm not sure. I heard your ambush go off, but then nothing happened. Then I heard your whistle and waited. Then they came running toward me. I got all but one. He got away." Tel motioned in the direction of the base camp. "I'm sorry."

"Don't be," Kamigami told him. "I wanted one to escape."

Tel's voice was stronger. "Why?"

"To get their attention," Kamigami replied. "Come on. We need to identify the bastards. Look for ID tags, papers, personal effects." Again Tel hesitated, still shaking. "Look, kiddo, do you have any idea what they'd have done if they'd caught you?" A slow shake of Tel's head. "They'd have tied you to a tree and peeled away strips of skin until you told them everything you knew. After cutting off your balls and stuffing them in your mouth, they'd have used a claymore to make whatever was left of you insect-friendly." He paused for effect. "Got the picture?" Tel nodded, his shaking gone. "Okay, get to work."

They worked through the bodies until Kamigami was satisfied they had found all that was useful. Tel was fascinated by the amount of photos, letters, and pornography they found stuffed into the soldiers' pockets and packs. "What are you going to do with this, sir?"

"Take it to Kuala Lumpur."

"Why?"

"To get *their* attention," Kamigami answered.

four

Oakland
Monday, August 2

Zack hunched over the chart spread out on the worktable. He was alone in the basement of the Annex and surrounded by silence as he worked. He had never seen a map like this one, a survival chart used by downed airmen in World War II, but thanks to his orienteering class at New Mexico Military Institute, he knew what it was. He reread the memo establishing the map's provenance. The source was good: the archives of the British Imperial War Museum. He turned the map over and read the notes penciled on the back. There was no name or signature, but he recognized his great-grandfather's cramped handwriting. He methodically listed the dates written by each note. All were in what Bloomy called "the missing year."

Something deep in his fifteen-year-old psyche told him his great-grandfather was sending him a message. But what was it? Frustration gnawed at him like a Rottweiler worrying a juicy bone. "Fido," he muttered to himself. His best friend, Brian Turner, had adopted "fido" as his favorite expression: fuck it—drive on. But the gnawing wouldn't go away. Zack carefully folded the map along its original creases, gathered up his notes, and headed for Bloomy's office. Another emotion puzzled him. Why did holding the map make him feel so good?

He found the chief librarian in the small workroom next to her office. "Miss Bloomfield," he said from the doorway, catching her attention.

She gave him a smile. "I thought you were going back to school?"

"I am. But I'm waiting for Dad to finish up some business, so I had some time to kill, and I found this." He came in and handed her the map and his notes.

He enters a room just like his father, Bloomy thought. *Was the president the same?* She made a mental note to follow up for the biography she was planning to write. It was the stuff that made the subject come alive. She studied Zack's latest discovery for a few moments before carefully folding it and replacing it in its envelope. "The dates check," she told him. "I've been doing some research on my own. It appears your great-grandfather never talked about this period in his life because he was absent without leave from the Royal Air Force and at one time had been classified as a deserter."

A look of pure shock crossed Zack's face. "That's serious! Why would he do that?"

"I have no idea," Bloomy replied. She paused for a moment. "There's so much I don't understand about him, but he was very strong-willed."

"I want to know," Zack announced. He had never felt so sure of anything in his life.

"Know what?" Pontowski said from the doorway.

Automatically, Bloomy glanced at him. He was wearing his summer working uniform: khaki pants, a light blue chambray dress shirt without a tie, and a blue blazer. A battered briefcase was resting against his shoes, an old but well-cared-for pair of English jodhpurs, a low dress boot with a strap that buckled on the side. *He is good-looking,* she conceded. "Well," she said, "Zack has made another interesting discovery about the 'missing year.'"

"I found a map, Dad. Gramps made notes on the back." He stopped. "Anyway, it looks like his writing."

Bloomy became all business. "It corresponds with the time he was reported absent without leave . . ."

Pontowski's head came up. His eyes were wide and alert. "Where did that come from?" His words were measured and calm.

"Nothing conclusive in the research," she murmured. *He knew!* she thought.

Pontowski bent over the map. "This could be significant," he said in a low voice.

"Maybe," Bloomy allowed, now convinced it was a family secret that had finally surfaced.

"We'll have to look into it," Pontowski said.

Bloomy gave a little nod. "I'll treat it as confidential," she promised. She changed the subject. "So you're off to New Mexico."

Zack came alive. "Yeah! We're flying the Mentor, and Dad's gonna let me fly in the front seat." He felt the need to explain. "I've already soloed and passed the written test for my pilot's license."

Pontowski laughed. "And he won't let me rest until he gets his hands on it." He shook his head. "That's what I get for letting him help me restore it." The aircraft in question was a T-34A, a two-place, tandem-seat trainer built by Beech Aircraft for the Air Force in 1958. It had been a family project restoring it to pristine condition, and now it was better than new.

"After I drop Zack off at NMMI," Pontowski said, "I'll fly to the World Trade Organization meeting in Chicago. Should be back by Friday." He didn't mention that he was going to the WTO to see Zou Rong at the national security adviser's request.

"Fly safe," Bloomy said.

Pontowski laughed. "Always do."

She knew it was a lie, and that bothered her as well. How could any sane human be so cavalier about life and death?

Over New Mexico
Monday, August 2

Never teach your own kid to fly, Pontowski told himself. He bit his tongue, waiting for Zack to make the decision. He ran the numbers for the third time. They had refueled at Las Vegas and had taken off with fifty gallons of fuel. He glanced at his watch, the best fuel gauge on the aircraft. They had been airborne for two hours and thirty minutes, with another hour to go to Roswell. They were consuming gas at fifteen gallons per hour, and that meant they needed to land and refuel. *Come on, Zack,* he urged. *Think!*

He did. "Dad," Zack said from the front seat, "we need to land to refuel. Socorro's on the nose at thirty miles."

Pontowski breathed easier and keyed the intercom. "Sounds like a plan." Then the father in him took over. "The outside air temperature is pushing a hundred, so carry a little extra airspeed coming down final. Full flaps."

"Got it, Pop."

Pop! Pontowski thought. Was there condescension in his son's voice? He didn't know. Then he laughed out loud.

"We might have to stay overnight to take off in the morning," Zack said.

"Why?" Pontowski asked, knowing the answer.

"Well, the field elevation is almost five thousand feet, and the temperature has got to be over a hundred on the ground. I haven't calculated the density altitude, but it's gonna be high. It's safer to take off in the morning."

"Make a decision," Pontowski said.

"How do you like Mexican food?" Zack replied.

"Love it," Pontowski said, meaning that he really loved the chance to spend some time with his son. The World Trade Conference and Zou Rong could wait another day. Zack flew a standard pattern into the airfield and came down final at eighty knots. He flared and made a sweet touchdown. "Beginner's luck," Pontowski grouched.

The amount of food Zack consumed amazed Pontowski, and the dark-haired teenage girl serving them was more than happy to keep his son's plate full. "I think you've got an admirer," Pontowski conceded. "She's pretty enough."

Zack's reply surprised him. "Dad, do you really think Gramps went AWOL?"

Pontowski thought for a moment. "I can see him doing it."

"Why?"

"We'll probably never know for sure, but that's the way your great-grandfather was. Once he decided to do something, he did it. But knowing him, you can bet it was for a damn good reason. He put principle above everything else." Zack shoveled more food into his mouth. "If you eat like this at NMMI, I'm getting one hell of a bargain on room and board."

Zack nodded as the girl brought out another plate of tamales. "Bloomy said Gramps was a very strong-willed man."

"When he believed in something," Pontowski said, "the strongest. It was his best trait. I wouldn't want to get in his way when he set out to do something."

"I hope I can be like that," Zack said quietly.

I hope so, too, Pontowski thought, hearing the resolve in his son's voice.

Kuala Lumpur, Malaysia
Wednesday, August 4

The cabdriver turned onto Tun Razak and pulled over to the curb. He pointed across the busy boulevard. "That's the American embassy," he said in Malay. "The police won't allow me to stop in front." Kamigami got out and stretched while the driver opened the trunk. "Bags extra," the driver said to Tel. "Twenty dollars U.S."

Tel protested. "You said twenty ringgit." He looked at Kamigami. "That's what he said at the hotel."

"Twenty dollars U.S. or no bags," the driver barked. Kamigami shrugged and shouldered the driver aside. He lifted two of the duffel bags out of the trunk. "I call police!" the driver shouted. He reached to close the trunk lid on the two remaining bags.

Kamigami brushed the driver back like a fly and dropped one of the heavy bags on his foot. The driver bent over in pain. "Twenty ringgit or I drop the other one on your head," Kamigami said in Malay. The driver looked up into Kamigami's face and, before Tel could hand over the money, hobbled down the sidewalk as fast as he could, abandoning his cab and forgetting about collecting the fare. Kamigami picked up the two heaviest bags and motioned for Tel to get the two others, which were still in the trunk. "I expect the guard will stop us at the entrance. Just do what they say until I can get it sorted out."

"I thought you said they know you," Tel said.

"They may not remember me," Kamigami said. They dodged a few cars crossing the street, and Kamigami led the way to the Marine guard. They deposited the four bags at the corporal's feet, and Kamigami gave him a friendly smile. "My name is Victor Kamigami. I'm an American. These are for Mr. William Mears. I believe he's still here, an administrative officer, if I remember correctly."

Kamigami's soft, high-pitched voice surprised the guard. "Please wait over there," he said, pointing to a spot closer to the street. "And please take your bags with you." He keyed his radio while Kamigami and Tel moved back. "Two individuals, one who claims to be an American citizen, are here with four duffel bags for Mr. Mears." It was common knowledge inside the embassy that William Mears was the CIA chief of station. The guard gave Kamigami a questioning look as he listened to the reply. "He said his name is Victor Kamigami."

"You might not want to stand too close to me," Kamigami said in a low voice. Tel obediently moved a few feet away, not understanding why. He discovered the wisdom of the request a few seconds later when a large unmarked van drove up, slammed to a stop, and a tactical squad of Malay police in full battle gear burst out the side and rear doors.

"Down!" the Marine guard shouted. "On the ground! Spread-eagle!" His automatic was out and leveled directly at Kamigami. Tel fell to the ground. He was amazed that Kamigami was already down and spread-eagle. He looked at Kamigami in confusion.

"I guess they remember me," Kamigami allowed.

"Gentlemen," the Marine guard said, "the Ambassador." He stepped aside as Winslow James minced into the basement room of the embassy. He nodded at the two CIA agents, William Mears and Charles Robertson, and surveyed the weapons and other items spread around the room. "Well, well, what do we have here?"

"Sir," Mears said, "this is Victor Kamigami." He read from his clipboard. "Twenty-four years in the U.S. Army, all of it in the Rangers and special operations. Reached the rank of command sergeant major before deserting and fighting as a mercenary for Zou Rong in southern China in . . . ah, 1996. After that he went into hiding on the east coast near . . ."

"Near Kemasik," Kamigami said. "Terengganu Province. Mr. Ambassador, may I present Tel Zaidan? He and I were the only survivors when our kampong was destroyed."

Winslow James nodded in gracious acceptance, always the polished diplomat. "I am pleased to meet you, Mr. Zaidan." A concerned look spread across his face. "I must apologize, for I haven't heard of the tragedy that befell your village." Mears and Robertson exchanged glances. It had been included in the daily intelligence summary that was placed on the ambassador's desk every morning. The ambassador looked at the two CIA agents, effectively dismissing Kamigami and Tel. "I take it that you know Mr. Kamigami?"

"We've met," Robertson, the junior CIA agent, said. Robertson instinctively felt the scar on his neck, the result of their first meeting when Kamigami had jabbed his fingers into Robertson's neck and crushed his larynx. Only the quick action of May May, Kamigami's wife, had saved him from suffocating.

Kamigami couldn't help himself. "The last time we saw each other, Chuck and Bill were hanging around in Singapore." The two CIA agents had been transporting Kamigami to Singapore for extradition to the States when he escaped. In the process Kamigami had handcuffed them together and left them dangling from a bridge railing.

"I see," James said, not understanding at all. "And what do we have here?"

"We took these off soldiers in the National Park," Kamigami said. "They were operating out of a large base camp and were from the same group that destroyed our kampong."

"Do we know anything about this so-called base camp?" James asked. No answer from the CIA agents. James rummaged through the uniforms, ID tags, and papers on the table. He glanced at the weapons stacked against the wall. "It appears they were well armed." He picked up a pair of boots and examined them.

"They were Chinese regulars," Kamigami said.

James's reaction was immediate. "Because they were wearing these? Nonsense." He turned for the door. "Please dispose of this," he told Mears. Then he was gone.

Mears and Robertson stared at each other. They would never admit to an outsider that the ambassador refused to believe anything that ran counter to current State Department policy with regard to Malaysia. "The official position is that we're seeing an indigenous political faction of farmers dissatisfied with the current regime," Mears said.

"If that's dissatisfaction," Kamigami said, "you don't want to be around when they get angry."

Mears took a deep breath. "You better tell us everything you know." He listened while Kamigami detailed all he had learned. A heavy silence came down in the room. "This is not a disgruntled bunch of farmers," Mears finally said. He made a decision. "You need to talk to Gus."

Robertson moaned. "Ah, no. Give me a break, Bill."

Singapore
Thursday, August 5

The white Bronco with Malay license plates drove down Admiralty Road and turned into the walled compound. Its wheels crunched on the raked gravel that led to the main house. "You're meeting Deng Shikai," Mears explained from the front passenger seat. "He looks like some old grandfather, and you'll swear he's one of the nicest guys you ever met. Don't be taken in. He's the head of Singapore's Security and Intelligence Division and will cut your throat in a heartbeat."

Robertson pulled to a stop under the canvas awning and spoke to the young man waiting for them. The visitors' bona fides established, two more servants rushed up and opened the doors to the Bronco. The very visible bulges under their white jackets left little doubt they were armed. Tel followed Kamigami out of the backseat and stood in awe of his surroundings. "I've never been in a house like this," he said.

"Keep your mouth closed and you'll be fine," Kamigami told him. But even he was impressed as they walked through the main atrium of the mansion and into the garden. Their host was waiting for them under a flower-covered lanai by the pool. Two beautiful girls—one Eurasian, the other Caucasian—were swimming in the pool. The old man stood as the men approached. He was tall for a Chinese, almost six feet, very thin, and slightly stooped.

Mears made the introductions. "Sir, may I introduce Victor Kamigami and Tel Zaidan?"

The man extended his hand. "I am pleased to meet you." He spoke with a crisp English accent. “Call me Gus.” They shook hands all around, and Gus motioned them to seats. “LeeAnn, Cari,” he called. The two girls smiled at him and climbed out of the pool. They were both nude and wrapped themselves in big towels as they scurried across the grass and into the main house. Tel couldn’t take his eyes off them.

“Close your mouth,” Kamigami muttered.

Gus waited until the girls were out of earshot. “Your reputation precedes you, General Kamigami. I can’t help but wonder what brings you out of retirement.” He laughed at the look on Tel’s face. “Your big friend here was a general, I believe. That was in China, was it not?”

Kamigami nodded. “I was with Zou Rong.”

Gus’s face went blank. “Ah, yes, Mr. Zou. A most interesting creature, don’t you think?”

“He’s a survivor,” Kamigami replied.

“Indeed,” Gus said. “But Mr. Zou is not why you’re here, is it?” He thought for a moment. “Tel, I’m afraid this conversation will bore you. Perhaps you’d like to meet LeeAnn and Cari?”

“I wouldn’t know what to say to them,” Tel replied.

“I’m quite sure they’ll think of something,” Gus said. He motioned to one of the servants in the cabana on the far side of the pool. The man hurried over, and Gus told him to escort Tel into the house. “I imagine they will find your young friend a pleasant distraction,” he said to Kamigami.

When they were gone, Mears extracted a map from his briefcase and spread it on the low table in front of Gus. Kamigami pointed to a spot on the eastern coast of Malaysia. “This was my home,” he began. He spoke in a low voice, without emotion, as he detailed everything that had happened from the time the patrol boat sank his prahu.

When he finished, Gus tapped the map with his right index finger. “Why your kampong?” he asked.

“Mr. Deng doesn’t believe in coincidence,” Mears added.

“I have no way of knowing for sure,” Kamigami said. “But considering what happened afterward, I suspect it was the opening move of a plan to stir up ethnic conflict in eastern Malaysia.”

Gus was aware of Kamigami’s reputation, and there was no doubt that he could be useful. But recruiting him was another matter. Gus turned it over in his mind and then did the one thing that was totally contrary to his nature: he told the truth. "Your village was destroyed for a number of reasons. I believe it was the first step in a plan to set the Malays and indigenous Chinese at each other's throats. I also believe that this problem will soon be ours. Further, I have reason to believe that Zou Rong is involved and that he wanted you eliminated." He paused, waiting for Kamigami's reaction. He found it in the set of the big man's jaw. "Interesting, yes?"

"Very," Kamigami said.

"We've created a special operations unit to deal with this type of problem," Gus said. "But as this type of organization is new to us, we've encountered many . . . ah, difficulties." Again he waited for Kamigami's reaction.

"Special operations are always tricky," Kamigami allowed, speaking with authority. He was a legend in the field of special operations, and only a very few men, none living, had a combat résumé that matched his.

"I am told you're fluent in Malay and Cantonese," Gus said. He paused for a moment. "I can offer you the command of our little task force."

"I'd like to think about it," Kamigami said. "Would tomorrow morning be okay?"

"You and Tel are more than welcome to stay here tonight," Gus said. "Your young friend will not be bored."

Kamigami was still awake after midnight and sitting on the veranda leading into his suite when Tel came in. He sat down beside Kamigami in a wicker chair, propped his feet up on the railing, and savored the night air. Kamigami glanced at him. There was no doubt Tel had crossed one of the divides that mark a boy's transition into manhood. "Had a nice time?" he asked. A slight nod answered him. *Good,* Kamigami thought. *He knows when to keep his mouth shut.* A warm breeze brushed against them. "What did you talk about?" he asked, his curiosity up.

"My name. They said it was very unusual. LeeAnn really liked it."

"LeeAnn was the dark-haired girl?"

"No. That was Cari. LeeAnn was the blonde."

"They're right, it is an unusual name. Where did it come from?"

"My father was English, and he named me. He used the initials for Thomas Edward Lawrence."

"Lawrence of Arabia?"

"My father was a great admirer and said Lawrence was one of the greatest amateur soldiers who ever lived."

"He wasn't an amateur," Kamigami replied. "He spent most of his adult life in the service."

"Wasn't he a lieutenant colonel?"

"At one time. Later he was a private in the Tank Corps and then an aircraftsman in the Royal Air Force."

"That's sort of like you in reverse. You were a sergeant and then a general."

Kamigami chuckled. "That was different."

"Which did you like best?"

"Sergeant." He was silent for a moment. "Gus has offered me a job. It involves special operations, and I'm thinking of taking it. You're welcome to come along, but if not, I'll help you find your relatives."

"I'll stay with you," Tel said.

"Before you make a decision, there's two things you've got to know. First, you'll have to go through training on your own." He described the various forms of torture Tel would have to endure to qualify for special operations. "Most who try, fail."

Tel listened impassively. "What's the second thing?"

"This is what I am."

five

San Antonio, Texas
Thursday, August 5

The shiny black 1956 Ford pickup eased into a parking space in front of the 341st Training Squadron at Lackland Air Force Base. For a moment the driver didn't move as he gripped the steering wheel. His mind made up, Chief Master Sergeant Leroy Rockne climbed out of the cab. He was a big man, well over six feet tall, given to hard workouts and seven-mile morning runs. The Air Force was his only family, he wore his uniform with pride, and on first impression many thought of him as a five-hundred-pound gorilla with muscles. But those who served with him in the security police knew better. Professionally, he was a walking, talking advertisement for a security cop: dedicated, smart, and by the book.

Rockne reached behind the seat and pulled out a leather leash with a silver-plated chain dog collar. He slipped the collar into a pocket and deliberately folded the leash into fourths. He slapped it against his pant leg like a riding crop. He closed the door and checked his image in the window. His black beret was set at the correct angle on his closely cropped Marine-style haircut, and his square jaw was cleanly shaven. He wasn't a vain man, but he knew the value of appearances.

Technical Sergeant Paul Travis saw him first. He came to attention as he greeted him. "Good morning, Chief. What brings you down here? Headquarters getting too much for you?" There was respect in his voice.

"Personal business," Rockne replied.

No reply was called for, and the sergeant hurried past a training flight of students marching to the line of aircraft fuselages used for antihijacking training. He skidded to a stop and spoke to the training NCO, Staff Sergeant Jake Osburn. "Over there," Travis said, pointing to Rockne.

"Ah, shit," Jake muttered. He halted his training flight. "Listen up. That's Chief Master Sergeant Leroy Rockne over there. He's called 'the Rock' for a damn good reason."

"What makes him so special?" an airman asked.

"He just happens to be the best security cop who ever wore the beret."

Rockne walked into the building and turned into the operations section. The clerk, Airman First Class Cindy Cloggins, came to her feet. Rockne's reputation had preceded him, and she was nervous at meeting him face-to-face. "Good morning, sir."

Rockne fixed her with a hard look, taking her measure. She was a big girl, young and immature. He made a decision and eased off a notch. "It's 'Chief.' I'm not an officer."

"Yes"—she caught herself in time—"Chief." She buzzed the captain and sent Rockne right in. She waited until the door was closed, and called the squadron commander, a newly minted major. "The Rock's in the building," she told him. The major said he'd be right over.

The captain in charge of operations stood and smiled. "It's been a while, Chief. What can I do for you?"

"I heard Boyca was scheduled for disposal tomorrow. I want to adopt her."

"The veterinarian and kennel master say she's not adoptable," the captain replied.

Rationally, Rockne knew that euthanasia for an old dog like Boyca, who had exceeded her working life and could never adjust to family life, was the humane thing to do. She was a working dog, and, like he was a security cop, that's all she was. "Screw the vets. We got a history."

"She's too old, Chief," the captain said, telling him the obvious.

"She's got another year or two left in her," Rockne replied.

The captain was about to say that he couldn't approve of the adoption, but one look at Rockne's face convinced him otherwise. "I'll take care of the paperwork."

"Thank you, sir. I owe you." Rockne snapped a sharp salute and left, heading for the kennels out back. The captain punched at his intercom to tell his secretary to start the paperwork rolling, his day now pure gold.

Rockne walked along the double row of kennels as he searched the cages. A dog started to bark, setting the others off. On the backside a dog smashed into the cage's wire fence in a frenzy. "How ya doin', Boyca?" he said. The dog barked at him. "You remember me, don'tcha?" Rockne's lips compressed into a tight line when he saw the red *X* in grease pencil on the gate's metal note plate. Tomorrow's date was written below the *X*. "I almost missed it."

He opened the gate, but Boyca retreated to a far corner and growled at him. "Come," he ordered. No response. "Feelin' bitchy today?" He slapped the leash he was holding against his thigh. Boyca's head came up as a vague memory stirred. He slapped his thigh again. "Come," he repeated. The dog immediately came to his side and stood quietly, eager for whatever came next. Rockne bent over and ran his hands over Boyca's coat, careful not to touch the open wound where she had rubbed herself raw against the wire. He felt her conformation, surprised that she was still in good shape at fourteen years of age. But the deterioration in her muscles was obvious, and he knew she tired easily. He dropped the collar over her head. "You're a good old girl, aren'tcha?" Boyca was a Belgian Malinois with a reddish-brown, short-haired coat. Size-wise, she was smaller than a German shepherd with much the same conformation. But Malinoises didn't suffer from the same hip-degeneration problems.

Rockne stood and clipped the lead onto the collar and headed for the parking lot as the major in command of the squadron walked up. He glanced down at Boyca. "She's done good, Chief. Take care of her."

"I will, sir." Rockne led Boyca to his pickup and pointed to the back. "In," he ordered. The dog looked at him and didn't move. He relented. "Okay, so you're too old for jumpin' in and out the back." He opened the passenger door, and Boyca crawled onto the new leather seat. Rockne settled into the driver's seat and started the engine. The big, highly tuned V-8 came to life with the distinctive lope of a high-lift cam. Boyca leaned her head over the edge of the seat and vomited on the carpet. "Didn't like the food?" He bent over to clean it up. "Do you have any idea what this carpet costs?"

Boyca licked his cheek.

Chicago
Thursday, August 5

Pontowski worked his way through the small group of protesters crowding the sidewalk outside the Chinese consulate. For the most part they were young, scruffily dressed, and carrying placards denouncing the WTO. A young girl stepped in front of him and waved one in his face. "Where you going, bud?" she demanded.

"In there," Pontowski said.

"No way."

"It has nothing to do with the WTO," he said.

Three rough-looking young men joined her. "Get lost," the biggest one said.

Pontowski shook his head and pushed past them. The man grabbed his arm, stopping him. Pontowski looked at the man's hand and then at the other protesters. Without exception, they were thin, in poor shape, and showed signs of drug use. He looked for indications of a concealed weapon. Nothing. He had seen it before. They were there for show and not really serious about getting physical and going one-on-one. He tried to be reasonable. "You have no argument with me. Please, I urge you to reconsider if—"

"If what, fuckface?"

Pontowski's voice hardened. "If you want your hand back." The man released him, and Pontowski was all reason again. "I'm being polite and don't want trouble. But I'm perfectly willing to oblige you, if that's your choice." He leaned into the man and lowered his voice. "Didn't your daddy teach you to be very careful when you pick a fight? You gotta know who you're taking on." He paused. "You've already made two mistakes."

"I ain't made no fuckin' mistakes."

"Make that three," Pontowski replied. He looked in the direction of the four policemen heading toward them. The protesters turned, and Pontowski slipped past, into the consulate.

A dark-suited young Chinese woman was waiting for him. "Good afternoon, General Pontowski. This way, please. Mr. Zou will be a few minutes late, please forgive. But there is someone who wishes to speak to you." She smiled at him. "I saw the way you handled the protesters. Most impressive." He followed her up to the second floor and into a small reception room.

He froze when he saw the woman sitting there. He was vaguely aware of the door closing behind him, leaving them alone. The woman stood, her hands clasped demurely in front of her. She was five feet six inches tall, possessed beautiful dark almond-shaped eyes, lustrous black hair, and a delicate facial structure with high cheekbones. She was not Han Chinese but Zhuang from southern China. She was perhaps the most famous fortune-teller in China, and Zou's mistress. "Jin Chu," Pontowski said, "you're as beautiful as ever." The memories were all there—the time in China, the American Volunteer Group, and Zou's abortive revolution.

"And you are charming above all men." She beckoned for him to sit beside her on the couch. It was a royal command he hurried to obey. She folded her hands in her lap and gazed at him, looking deep into a world he could not see. "How is Victor?" she asked.

There was no emotion in her voice, but Pontowski knew it was there. Before Zou, Jin Chu had been Kamigami's mistress. "I haven't seen him since 1996," he said. "I understand he's living in Malaysia."

"How is your son?"

"Zack is growing like a weed. He's turning into a fine young man." They talked, and the time flew by. A clock chimed four, and Zou Rong entered the room. His ever-present entourage of bodyguards and advisers trooped in behind him. Pontowski stood, and the two men shook hands. He was surprised at how Zou had aged. He had grown fat, and his hair was thinning. The boyish countenance that had charmed people was forever gone, replaced by a shrewd cunning.

"Mr. Zou has only a few moments," an aide said.

"What brings you to Chicago?" Zou asked, knowing full well that Pontowski was there at his request.

"Politics," Pontowski answered. "What else?"

"I was hoping for friendship," Zou answered smoothly. He had just delivered the first part of his message to the Americans.

"There is always friendship. But that is a constant in my life, and I could never intrude for that alone."

Zou laughed, and they sat down. "You were always the smooth devil. It is good to see you again." He continued to dissemble, playing the surprised host glad to see an old friend. "How may I help you?"

"My president is worried about the trends in China. To be honest, her advisers are not sure how to read your government's intentions."

"Our admiration and friendship for the United States remain unchanged. But we are engaged in the new world order, which is economic. We must not lose sight of our friendship even though we are competing economically." That was the second part of his message.

The aide interrupted. "Mr. Zou, your schedule, please."

Zou frowned. "Please forgive me, there is so much to do." He stood and spoke in Cantonese to Jin Chu. "See what you can learn."

Pontowski stood with him. "Thank you for your time." The two men shook hands again, and Zou was gone. "That was quick," Pontowski said.

Jin Chu took him by the hand and led him to a window overlooking the interior courtyard. She held him in the light and placed her hands on his cheeks. "I have never told your fortune," she said. Again he had the impression she was looking into another world. She took his right hand and held it against her cheek without speaking. Then she opened his hand and studied his palm. Slowly she moved a finger over his life line. "I see a mountain pass in a land I do not recognize. There is a man. It is you, but it is not you. There is a beautiful dark-haired woman." She started to tremble. "I also see a great struggle and many deaths. But I cannot see further. There is so much confusion." She looked at him, her eyes filling with tears, and whispered, "Victor." She ran from the room.

Pontowski walked to the open door. The dark-suited aide was waiting for him. "You are the most privileged of men," she said. "Jin Chu has not told a fortune in eight years."

The White House
Friday, August 6

Patrick Flannery Shaw exploded in a loud guffaw as he read the *New York Times*. The sound carried out of his corner office and into the quiet halls of the West Wing. It was the modern equivalent of a bull elephant trumpeting victory or a lion roaring over the dead carcass of his latest kill. The president's staff knew the sound: Maddy's special assistant had barbecued some feckless politician. They didn't know who was on the receiving end of Shaw's attention or why, but they would figure it out in time. They always did.

Shaw's intercom buzzed. He pulled himself off the couch and lumbered over to his desk. A short, thick finger jabbed at the buttons. "Hello, darlin'."

The caller came right to the point. "Leland's at the west gate with eight of his staff."

Shaw checked the president's daily calendar: Senator John Leland was scheduled for a personal conference with her in fifteen minutes. Shaw snorted. "Thanks for the heads up," he said, breaking the connection. He pulled on his coat and ambled down the hall. "Lordy Lord," he mumbled. "Eight sounds like an attack." He plugged that number into his unique algebra of Washington politics. On one side of the equal sign, Leland thought eight was a show of strength. On the other side of the equation, Shaw saw political weakness. And he knew how to cancel Leland's side. Shaw paused at the door leading into Maddy's private study next to the Oval Office. He knocked twice, counted to three, and walked in.

Maddy looked up from her rocking chair and dropped the thick report she was reading. "Good morning, Patrick. I take it you've seen today's *New York Times.*"

"Yes, ma'am. I did."

"Enjoy it?"

Shaw nodded. It was all that would ever pass between them about the congressman who had made the mistake of spreading a malicious lie about the president and Matt Pontowski sharing the same bed.

"Leland brought eight of his advisers."

Maddy arched an eyebrow. "I was expecting him, not his staff." She paused. "Do I want to see all of them?"

He thought for a moment. "Why not? They're totally outmatched." Maddy nodded in agreement. "Let me set it up," Shaw said.

"Make your entrance at the right time," she told him. They were on the same wavelength.

The man entering the West Wing looked and sounded like a senator. John Leland was an accomplished orator with a deep, rolling southern accent, a full head of gray hair, and the jowly cheeks his constituency expected of the most influential and powerful senator in the Imperial City. His career in Congress stretched over forty years, and he was the chairman of the powerful Foreign Relations Committee. With a few well-chosen phone calls he could change the political weather of the capital and move whatever legislation he wanted through Congress. Shaw thought of Leland as the South's permanent revenge on the United States for losing the Civil War. It was a quip he was saving for the right moment, preferably on a Sunday-morning political talk show.

Leland led the way into the room and sat down in one of the two easy chairs placed near a window. His staff found seats in the chairs grouped to his side, out of Leland's line of sight. They were facing a single straight-back chair placed next to the door. Turner swept into the room, alone, and closed the door behind her. "John," she chimed as the senator stood. "It's good to see you."

They exchanged the customary courtesies and sat down. The battle was joined. She let Leland take the conversation where he wanted. "Madam President, my committee is fully aware of developments in the Gulf and your creation of the ExCom to monitor the situation and advise you. What concerns me is the role of the secretary of defense in that process. Mr. Merritt appears to be marginalized and left out of the decision-making process, which is contrary to the intent of the Goldwater-Nichols Act."

Turner grew very solemn, for Merritt was Leland's man, a holdover from the Roberts administration whom she kept on board to appease the senator. "I asked him to serve on the ExCom, but he asked for General Wilding to serve in his place. I, of course, honored his request. I'm not sure why, but it's his choice."

Her answer seemed to satisfy Leland, and they moved on to her foreign policy agenda. At a critical point one of Leland's aides jumped in. "Madam President, we are concerned about the deterioration of Franco-American relations. France is one of our oldest allies, and—"

Turner interrupted him. "John, exactly who am I talking to here?" Before Leland could reply, Shaw entered the room and sat in the single chair near the door. The entire constellation of the room changed as Leland's eight advisers were looking directly at Shaw and Shaw was looking straight back at them. Shaw was carrying a yellow legal pad and made a big show of writing down everyone's name. He smiled at them. Suddenly the five men and three women wanted out—the quicker the better. It was Washington game playing—trivial, childish, but of consequence. And Shaw was the master.

Leland stammered a reply. "I . . . we . . . that is to say . . ."

Turner reached out and touched his hand. "I, too, am concerned about our relations with France. In fact, the secretary of state is in France speaking to their prime minister with the express goal of improving relations."

"Madam President," Leland replied, finally recovering, "I am also totally aware of your concern with the Middle East. But I do believe that our French allies have the matter in the proper perspective and that we should follow their lead in this matter."

"Really?" Turner said as a secretary entered. The meeting was over.

Shaw chuckled as he followed Maddy into the Oval Office. "Those folks couldn't get out of there fast enough."

"Patrick, is there something going on between Leland and the French? He's never been overly concerned with them before."

"I'll check it out."

Richard Parrish, Maddy's chief of staff, joined them. "The embassy in Paris is on the phone. It seems the secretary of state is cooling his heels at the Quai d'Orsay waiting to see the prime minister."

Shaw chuckled at the thought of the cranky Stephan Serick being put on hold by the French. "What's keeping the chief Frog busy? A late lunch?"

Parrish checked his notes. "It seems Monsieur Cherveaux is meeting with a delegation from Iraq tomorrow, and the French don't want to send them the wrong message by Monsieur Cherveaux's being too friendly with us."

Maddy let her anger show. To treat the president's official representative in such a cavalier manner was a diplomatic slap in the face. "I thought this was all arranged?"

"Indeed it was," Parrish replied.

Shaw grunted his disapproval. "Sounds like the Froggies are sending the Iraqis—and us—a message about their priorities."

Maddy thought for a moment. "I need to send *them* a message. Tell

Stephan to leave immediately and return home. Recall our ambassador for consultations. Also, am I scheduled for anything with the French?"

Parrish checked his calendar. "A dedication ceremony at the French Cultural Center next week."

"Send my regrets that I cannot attend and have the secretary of state send one of his assistants. The lower the better."

"Are we overreacting, Madam President?" Parrish asked.

Shaw answered, "Nope, just choosing up sides."

six

Camp David, Maryland
Sunday, September 5

It only hurts a little, Pontowski thought as he pushed up the low hill. He was careful to favor his right knee and jogged slowly. Even though it was late morning and the heat hadn't started to build, sweat poured down his face. *Give it a rest,* he cautioned. He slowed to a walk, and the pain went away. *Maybe your running days are over.* He hated the thought. He paused at the crest of the hill and took in the view. Low rolling hills stretched out in front of him, and he could see the presidential lodge. Movement in the trees off to his side caught his attention.

A soldier dressed in camouflage fatigues and carrying an M-16 stepped onto the trail. "General Pontowski, the national security adviser is at the lodge. She requests your immediate person."

What an odd way to say it, Pontowski thought. "Thanks," he said. He turned and headed for the lodge. His knee felt better after the short rest. Maybe his running days weren't over.

Mazie was waiting for him on the deck of the big cabin. "Thanks for coming so quickly," she said. They stretched out in deck chairs, and a steward materialized to ask if he could be of service. Pontowski noticed he also was wired with a whisper mike and a radio. They ordered, and the steward retreated.

"Security seems tighter than usual," Pontowski ventured.

"Maddy's arriving later this afternoon," Mazie said. "She's taking one day off the campaign trail. By the way, Maura and Sarah are here." Maura O'Keith was Maddy's mother and Sarah her precocious fourteen-year-old daughter. "I imagine Sarah will want to know all about Zack."

Pontowski grinned and shook his head. "Kids."

Mazie turned to business. "I read your memo on the meeting with Zou."

"Sorry, but there wasn't much there. We met for less than five minutes."

"What was your sense of the man?"

"He's changed, put on a lot of weight, balding. He keeps a big entourage around him."

"Do you trust him?"

"I never trusted him."

"My people tell me he's leading the moderates in Beijing," Mazie said. "Zou could be a friend."

Pontowski shook his head. "It doesn't matter if he's a moderate or a hard-liner. They all dislike and distrust the United States. It's a natural reflex with the Chinese."

"But Zou's not a problem right now?"

Pontowski caught the tension in her voice. *Something's going down,* he thought. "I can't say. My sense of the situation says there's something cooking, but what, I don't know. Maybe a change in leadership." Mazie leaned back in her chair as the steward returned with a pitcher of water and one of lemonade. When he was gone, Pontowski took a sip of the lemonade. "I take it there are problems. The Gulf again?"

"What do you know?"

"What everyone can see on TV or read in the newspapers. Iran, Iraq, and Syria making common cause isn't good, no matter which way you cut it."

"They've joined in a secret alliance called the United Islamic Front," Mazie said.

"They do hate us." He thought for a moment. "We've underestimated them before. I hope we're not making that mistake again."

"This morning Baghdad officially announced a joint training exercise starting next Saturday, called Shield of Islam. It's been scheduled for some time."

"Not good," Pontowski said. "Who are they in bed with?"

"Their allies? The usual suspects."

Pontowski started to make connections. "No country in its right mind is going to take us on militarily unless they're suicidal." Then he saw it. "Or they have one hell of a friend backing them up."

"Like Russia," Mazie added.

"I'm thinking China."

"In either case," Mazie assured him, "we can handle it. The president is telling the voters we have the best and most powerful military in the world."

"That's a true statement. But we've been focused on the war against terrorism and we're out of balance. In the more conventional forces, our levels of readiness are down to fifty, sixty percent. Also, we have severe airlift and sealift problems. What happens if we have to respond quickly, say, in a matter of days and not months, on a massive scale to a conventional MTW?" An MTW was a major-theater war, much like the Gulf War of 1991. "Even worse, what if we have to fight two MTWs at once? We're going to be hard-pressed to fight one, much less two."

"We don't have to worry about that," Mazie told him. "Maybe an MTW in the Middle East with the UIF, but with China? Where? The Chinese can make life difficult for us, but they don't have the capability to project their power much beyond their borders. Besides, they would pay a heavy economic price. North Korea? Not as long as South Korea is itching for a fight."

"I hope you're right. But I can see us getting kicked around a bit if we're not careful."

Mazie changed the subject. "Here comes your future daughter-in-law."

Pontowski followed her gaze and saw the president's mother and daughter walking toward them. He grinned. "I wonder how Zack feels about that?"

"I don't think he's going to have a choice in the matter," Mazie replied.

Pontowski stood and gave the seventy-one-year-old Maura a hug. "Me next," Sarah demanded. Pontowski gave her a hug, surprised at how she was filling out. "Tell Zack to answer my e-mail," she said.

"Well," Maura said to Pontowski, "Maddy will be delighted to see you here."

"Don't you think it's time you started sleeping together?" Sarah asked.

"Sarah!" Maura scolded.

Pontowski rubbed his chin. "Not tonight. I haven't shaved and need a shower."

"I'm being serious," Sarah said.

By the time Marine One landed on the helipad with the president aboard late Sunday afternoon, all the signs of a building crisis were in place. Chief of Staff Parrish was huddled with Mazie and a Navy vice admiral in the Camp David communications center while two brigadier generals—one from the Army, the other from the Air Force—waited in the hall. Pontowski was sure of it when a second helicopter arrived and perched on the helipad, its crew also standing by for a quick launch. To his way of thinking, what else would cause her to return unannounced to the capital during the height of a campaign? And her arrival at Camp David would set off no alarms.

Later that same evening they found some time to be alone. Maddy cuddled against his shoulder as she gazed wistfully into the fire crackling in the stone fireplace. "I do love this place," she murmured.

"It is beautiful," Pontowski allowed. He waited, sensing she wanted to have a serious talk.

"Mazie talked to you," she said. It wasn't a question. Pontowski gave a little nod. "Do you know a General Bernie Butler?"

"I've heard of him. The Boys in the Basement. He's got a good track record, lots of credibility."

"He's saying the UIF is going to attack Kuwait and Saudi Arabia. The CIA gives it a lower probability. Mazie's on the fence." A discreet knock at the door caught their attention, and Maddy moved away. "Come," she said.

The Air Force brigadier entered the room. "I'm sorry to disturb you, Madam President. The UIF military command in Baghdad has implemented a communications blackout in conjunction with their joint exercise."

"Effective when?" Pontowski asked.

"As of twenty minutes ago," the brigadier said.

Pontowski shook his head. "A communications blackout before the start of a major exercise is not business as usual." He checked his watch and ran the numbers. "It's four o'clock Monday morning over there. Sunrise is when?"

"In an hour and forty minutes," the brigadier replied.

"Madam President," Pontowski said, "I believe you need to return to the White House."

Maddy stood and walked to the fireplace. A log flared, and sparks rose up the chimney. "I didn't want this," she said.

"No sane person does," Pontowski told her.

Maddy gave a little nod, her lips compressed tightly. She picked up the phone. "Please tell Mr. Parrish that I'm returning to the White House." She turned to Pontowski. "Would you mind staying here with Maura and Sarah?"

"Not at all," he answered, wondering why.

The White House
Monday, September 6

Secretary of State Serick joined the Executive Committee gathered in the Situation Room. He took his seat and did a head count: Mazie, Sam Kennett, the DCI, General Wilding, and Bernie Butler were all there. The door opened, and Secretary of Defense Robert Merritt entered. "Well?" Merritt demanded.

Serick shot him a contemptuous look. The secretary of defense was Leland's boy, appointed only to appease the senator, who demanded a presence in the administration in return for political peace. "The National Intelligence Officer for Warning has declared a WATCHCON I for the Persian Gulf," Serick said. "The president is on her way and should be here any moment." They waited in silence, each drawn into his or her own personal world of doubts, fears, and concerns about what the next few days would bring.

The president entered. "Thank you for all responding so quickly," she said. She took her seat opposite the big computer monitor. The DCI stood as the screen scrolled to a map of the Arabian Peninsula. He pointed to the Iraqi-Saudi border 135 miles west of Kuwait. "The combined UIF ground-force strength has reached corps levels in this area. The necessary logistics infrastructure is in place and fully functional. These forces could move in a southerly direction at any time with no warning."

"It looks like a good place to hold an exercise," Vice President Kennett said. "And it is a fair distance from the oil fields."

Merritt coughed. "There's nothing between them and Riyadh except some sand dunes." Silence.

General Wilding finally spoke. "King Khalid Military City is in their way, which we have been quietly reinforcing."

"What's the latest satellite coverage?" the president asked.

The DCI spoke into his intercom, and a heavy cloud cover appeared on the screen. He listened for a moment before speaking. "We are experiencing a most unusual weather pattern for this time of year."

"Coincidence?" Butler said in a low voice.

"And what happened with that new Keyhole satellite with the wide-aperture synthetic radar?" Serick asked. "Can't it penetrate the cloud deck?"

"Indeed it can," the DCI replied. "But it's currently positioned to monitor China's nuclear tests. Unfortunately, it's low on fuel, which the National Reconnaissance Office is reluctant to use until the shuttle resupplies it later this month."

"Coincidence?" Butler repeated, a shade louder.

"It would be nice to know what is going on under those clouds," Turner said.

"Madam President," General Wilding said, "we'll know more in a few hours without repositioning the satellite." Every head turned toward the four-star general. "The Air Force has been developing an F-117 Stealth fighter as a reconnaissance platform. It carries a very sensitive high-resolution infrared imaging suite and is on its way to Saudi Arabia as we speak. It has the sensing capability to get up close and very personal. But we'll have to wait for darkness." He checked his watch. "It's 0830 hours in Saudi. We should know something in another eighteen hours."

"Why haven't we deployed it sooner?" Kennett asked.

"Because," Wilding said, "the Saudis have not given us permission to ramp up our capability until now."

"It does make you wonder whose side they're on," Kennett muttered.

"The Saudis," Butler said, "have been walking a political tightrope for years, buying off and appeasing their fundamentalists. But even they know when they're about to get their ass kicked by their brother Muslims."

"And they know who can help them," Kennett added.

The door to the control room burst open, and the duty officer rushed in. "Madam President . . ." He pointed at the screen.

**TANKS SUPPORTED BY APCS
MOVING IN FORCE ACROSS
IRAQI/SAUDI BORDER.
FORWARD OBSERVATION POSTS OVERRUN.**

Serick came to his feet and leaned across the table. "The bastards!" Butler only stared at the screen, his worst fears confirmed. Kennett and Wilding looked at each other. The DCI contemplated mayhem. It was the worst intelligence failure since the CIA had missed the attack on the World Trade Center, and heads were going to roll. Mazie concentrated on Turner, who was staring at the screen, her face a frozen mask.

The secretary of defense seemed relieved at the news and gave a little grunt. "A bad mistake. A very bad mistake." He wondered if Leland was aware of the invasion. It didn't matter, for he would soon tell him.

Madeline O'Keith Turner, the forty-fourth president of the United States, looked at the master clock on the wall opposite her, the date and time seared into her memory.

It was Labor Day.

seven

Camp David
Monday, September 6

Maddy's mother, Maura O'Keith, was fixated on the TV as she watched the coverage leading up to the White House press conference. "Don't you know Liz Gordon?" she asked Pontowski, referring to CNC-TV's White House correspondent.

"In the biblical sense?" Sarah Turner asked.

"Sarah," Maura scolded, "you have an obsession with sex. Stop it this minute. Hear?" Sarah knew when not to cross her grandmother and flounced out of the room, her fourteen-year-old worldliness insulted. Pontowski was surprised to see Patrick Shaw come through the open door.

"Mind some company?" Shaw asked.

"Please join us," Maura said, being very civil. She detested Shaw and wondered why he hadn't returned to Washington with Maddy. He settled onto the couch next to Pontowski and turned his attention to the TV.

"Many insiders," Gordon said, standing on the White House lawn with the West Wing in the background, "are asking if this crisis is being exploited by the administration to prove to the voters that Madeline Turner can lead the military as commander in chief."

"That lady," Shaw grumbled, "is out to do some crucifying."

The scene on the TV switched to the press conference room as the press secretary took the podium. His words were solemn and matter-of-fact as he detailed the situation. "We can confirm that the combined military forces of Iran, Iraq, and Syria have crossed the Iraq–Saudi Arabian border and are driving southward into the heart of Saudi Arabia. The situation is very fluid, and we are not certain of the scale and intensity of this incursion. But we are responding accordingly and treating it as a full-scale invasion. The president has returned to Washington and is with her advisers. We are confident that we can contain this aggression with the forces currently in place."

Shaw caught the frown on Pontowski's face but said nothing. "I have one announcement," the secretary said. "Starting in one hour, DOD will be holding regular press conferences in the Pentagon's Briefing Room. We should have a better understanding of the situation on the ground by then, and you can talk to the experts who have the latest information." He paused, the signal for the questions to start.

Liz Gordon was first. "Will the president be holding a press conference?"

"The president will be making a statement as soon as the situation stabilizes. I expect that should happen at some point later this afternoon. We'll notify you well in advance."

"Is there any truth to the rumor," Gordon shouted, "that the president was at Camp David with Matt Pontowski when the crisis broke?"

"The president did stop by Camp David for a few hours yesterday on her return to the White House to see her family. General Pontowski was there, but so was the national security adviser and key members of her staff."

"Did she know about the invasion?" another reporter asked.

"This was before the invasion," the secretary replied. "Of course, we were monitoring the buildup, which was taking place under the guise of a joint exercise, and the president was concerned."

"What did she and Matt Pontowski talk about?" a woman shouted from the back of the room.

The secretary ignored her. "Next question, please. I would ask that you stay focused on the crisis at hand."

Shaw let his contempt show. "Them id-jits only think about one thing."

Another reporter asked, "What about casualties?"

The press secretary glanced at his notes, carefully selecting his words.

The number of soldiers killed was going to be a critical issue. "The initial reports are still coming in. We do know that at least four observation posts and nine defensive fighting positions were overrun. Again, we should have better information for you at the Pentagon briefing in one hour."

The UPI reporter gained the microphone. "In the past, deep background briefings indicated Syria and Iran were cooperating with us in the war on terrorism and trying to reenter the world community of nations. Why should they choose this course of action now?"

Silence claimed the room. "Anything I say at this time would only be speculation," the press secretary replied.

"Is it safe to say," the reporter answered, "that we were so preoccupied with the war on terrorism that we were ambushed?"

The press secretary repeated himself. "Anything I say at this time would only be speculation."

It was exactly the wrong thing to say, and the reporters jumped on that subject. Shaw heaved his bulk to a standing position. "General, can we talk?" Pontowski stood and followed him out onto the deck. Shaw leaned over the rail and gazed into the trees. "It hurts when them id-jits get it right. We were looking the wrong way and got ambushed. How bad is this?"

Pontowski trusted rattlesnakes more than he trusted Shaw, and went into a deep defensive crouch. "I imagine the CIA has a better grasp of this than I do."

"Then how come they missed it comin'?" Shaw paused to let that sink in. "I'm askin' for Maddy."

"Officially?"

Shaw shook his head. "Gimme a break. You know how the system works, and you know the Pentagon. So what's your take?" No answer. "For Christ's sake," Shaw grumbled. "We're on the same side." He pulled out all the stops. "Maddy needs to know the worst, and she trusts you."

Can I trust this guy? Pontowski thought. "Give me a moment," he said. He made a decision. "I don't know the numbers."

"Which means?" Shaw retorted.

"I don't know what they're throwing at us and exactly what we have in place. But if this is a major offensive, my guess is that we're in a world of hurt."

"Would it help if you knew that the Seventh Marine Expeditionary Brigade from Camp Pendleton is arriving at Dhahran International and a squadron of Maritime Prepositioning Ships is waiting for them at Ad Dammām?" He almost laughed at Pontowski's reaction. "Them MPSs are handy things to have around, and the Air Force has one AEF in place at Prince Sultan Air Base." An AEF was an Aerospace Expeditionary Force, a response force made up of different aircraft for rapid reaction to trouble spots around the world. "Seven more are on the way."

The fact that the Air Force had committed eight of its ten AEFs was very troubling. Pontowski's face hardened as a cold feeling swept through him. "So Maddy knew it was coming," he said in a low voice.

"She had strong suspicions and was quietly movin' things and people around. She didn't want to set off any false alarms, not during an election."

Well done, Maddy, Pontowski thought. His president did need his best advice, even though it would have to go through Shaw. This was why she had asked him to stay. "I'm guessing that the UIF is going for broke. This is going to be a real slugfest. With a little luck we should be able to halt their advance somewhere in the desert. But it's going to take major reinforcements to stabilize the situation and a hell of a lot more to go on the offensive. Given our state of readiness, it's not going to happen fast. The system is going to be strained to the limit."

"Will it break?" Shaw asked.

"I don't think so. But it will take time, which is exactly what the UIF is trying to deny us."

"So the bottom line is that we can do this," Shaw said.

"At a price."

"Which is?"

Pontowski pulled into himself, not liking what he had to say. "We're going to take some heavy casualties."

"Sweet Jesus," Shaw muttered. He ran his mental abacus, calculating the political cost of the war. "I don't know if Maddy can take that. Not in an election year. She's got to keep the body count down."

"There's no such thing as a bloodless war," Pontowski told him. He doubted that Shaw understood the grim cost accounting of warfare, where the very effort to avoid bloodshed only prolonged it.

Shaw pounded his fist on the wooden railing. "God damn it all!"

Washington, D.C.
Monday, September 6

The Marine colonel giving the briefing was short, stocky, and bullet-headed. From all appearances he was all muscle, hard lines, and not much else. But that was wrong. Colonel Robert Scovill had authored the textbook on the formation, training, and deployment of Marine Expeditionary Battalions and was one of the best briefers in the Pentagon. Everything Scovill said was tailored to the president's level of understanding, and his voice was cool and modulated as he described the situation on the ground in Saudi Arabia.

"Our border defenses gave a good account of themselves but were overwhelmed. Minefields have slowed the advance, but apparently the enemy has reached its first objective, the Tapline Road that parallels the border twenty to thirty miles inside Saudi Arabia, and has laagered for the night. We expect them to resume their advance at first light. If they continue in the same direction, our main force should come in contact here." He pointed to a line fifteen miles north of King Khalid Military City. "In conjunction with the Saudis, we have deployed six infantry battalions of approximately three thousand men and four tank battalions with a hundred thirty-seven tanks."

"I was under the impression a tank battalion had fifty-eight tanks," Turner said. "Can't four battalions put more tanks in the field than that?"

"Fifty-eight is the number for a standard army tank battalion," Scovill replied. "But we are at approximately sixty percent readiness in the forward area due to the lack of spare parts and fully trained crews."

"Do we have enough to stop them?" the president asked.

"Probably not," he answered.

"I'm not going to sacrifice our troops."

Scovill shook his head. "They are not going to be sacrificed. We're going to engage the enemy, inflict as much damage as we can, and fight a retrograde action, making him pay for every meter of ground as he advances."

"So what exactly are you telling me?" the president demanded.

The colonel never hesitated. "We've got some tough fighting ahead of us before we can stabilize the situation."

Silence. Madeline Turner pulled inside herself as the one thing she feared most loomed in front of her. She was going to be a wartime president and send men and women to their deaths. Every instinct she possessed rebelled at the thought. *So this is the price of power,* she thought. *So be it. I didn't start this war.* But even as her resolve turned to steel, the pain remained. She would have to live with it. "Any word on casualties?"

"No hard numbers yet."

"Then give me some soft numbers."

Scovill thought for a moment. "Four observation posts overrun, nine defensive fighting positions wiped out, hard fighting as we retrograde—I'd guess at least fifty KIA, an equal number WIA and MIA."

Madeline O'Keith Turner fought the pain, not letting them see what was tearing at her. "Thank you, Colonel." She waited for him to leave before she turned to General Wilding. "Why weren't we better prepared?"

Wilding looked at her, never flinching. "Madam President, we've been telling Congress this for years. But no one was listening. We have repeatedly identified our shortfalls to the secretary of defense, and, in all fairness, we are in a better position now than two years ago."

The president felt sick. She knew how it had happened. "Every intelligence estimate I've seen has stressed that there was no credible threat on this scale in the near future." She paused for a moment. "I need to speak to the ExCom." Everyone but the five members of the Executive Committee rose to leave. "Robert," she said to the secretary of defense, "please stay." The room rapidly emptied as Merritt sat back down.

"I have two questions," the president said. "First, how did intelligence miss this so badly?" No one answered. "So what happened?" she demanded. The room was silent.

"Our estimates," Mazie said, "were based on the assumption that no two Arab countries, much less three, would form an effective alliance to attack another Arab state." The silence grew heavier. "Madam President," Mazie finally asked, "what was your second question?"

"How many casualties can we expect? Leland will make it a major campaign issue, and we need to get a handle on it—now."

Again no one answered as Merritt stared at his hands. It was a subject he had to discuss with one Senator John Leland—the sooner the better.

Over the Strait of Singapore
Tuesday, September 7

The helicopter flew high over the water as it headed for the small island that marked Singapore's southern boundary with Indonesia. Kamigami tried to count the number of cargo ships and tankers transiting the Strait of Singapore, but the number escaped him. "It looks like a freeway down there," he told Gus.

"Approximately forty thousand ships transit every year," the old man said. "Singapore handles over four hundred million tons of cargo a year, which puts us ahead of Rotterdam."

Kamigami counted three supertankers, deep in draft, lumbering toward Japan, China, and Korea. "Does that tonnage include oil?" Gus shook his head. Kamigami was not a geopolitician, but he understood what he was seeing. Geography had made Singapore the major transshipment hub of Asia, as it was on the shortest sea route between Europe and Asia. But more important, the island nation was at the narrowest point in the Strait of Malacca and had strategic control of the Middle Eastern oil that fed Asia's economy. "No wonder England didn't want to give it up," Kamigami said.

"It is a prize," Gus replied. Even over the noise of the helicopter, Kamigami heard the worry in his voice. The scene rapidly changed as they crossed the main channel and headed for an island. "Palau Tenang," Gus said.

Kamigami had the pilot circle the island. It was big for a Malay Archipelago island—five miles long and over two miles wide. A low hill, almost two hundred feet high and covered with dense foliage, dominated the center. Deep ravines radiated out from the dome and ran down to the shore. A dirt road ran along the shore, and Kamigami estimated he could jog around the island in full battle gear in under three hours. *Not enough,* he thought. "Fly over the center of the island and hover," he told the pilot. The pilot did as ordered to give Kamigami a bird's-eye view of his new domain. Because of the hill and thick jungle scrub, most of the island was uninhabitable. The ridges were very steep and reminded him of the spokes of a wheel. From his vantage point he could see the main camp on the south side of the island on a small alluvial plain. With his binoculars he picked out a route that led directly from the camp, along a ridge, over the island's center, and then down to the road on the north shore. He estimated the direct-line distance at under two miles. A distinctive pair of boulders dangled over the north road, and the name "Devil's Gonads" flashed in his mind.

"Take it down. I want to see the camp," he told the pilot.

"The First Special Operations Service," Gus explained, "takes the best from the British and the United States. Our staff structure parallels your army, but much of our equipment is British. All of our officers and senior NCOs train in England or the United States at one point in their career. Colonel Sun Dan, the commander of the First, was an honor graduate at Sandhurst."

"Did he train with the SAS?" Kamigami asked. The SAS was Great Britain's Special Air Service regiment, arguably the best special operations unit in the world.

"No. I believe he trained with the British Parachute Regiment and your Rangers."

"I never met him when I was with the Rangers," Kamigami said as the helicopter descended. He grimaced when he saw a hardened command bunker flying the flag of the First SOS. He had his work cut out for him.

As Kamigami had requested, only Tel was waiting for them at the helipad. He had changed in the month since Kamigami had last seen him. He had put on weight and was standing tall in freshly washed jungle fatigues. His hair was cut short, his boots were polished, and a big smile was spread across his face. He snapped a sharp salute when Kamigami emerged from the helicopter. "Good morning, sir," he said.

"I'm not a 'sir,'" Kamigami grumbled, "and you don't salute retired sergeants."

Tel refused to drop his salute. "They teach about you here," he replied.

Kamigami gave in and returned the salute. "I was hoping you'd learn something useful."

"I guess not," Tel said. "I washed out."

Gus came up behind them. "Actually, I recommended he be removed from training." From the look on Kamigami's face, an explanation was in order. "It's a language problem," Gus said. "His Chinese isn't good enough to understand the instruction."

"It's good enough," Tel said, a newfound confidence in his voice. "But

I got into some arguments with my instructors. They didn't like the way I set up an ambush. I did it just like we did on the trail."

Kamigami instinctively understood what had happened. It was the ethnic problem that cursed Tel's life. The First SOS was made up of Singapore Chinese, and while they may have been Singaporean, they were still Chinese. And Tel was anything but. "Every ambush is different," Kamigami said. "You got to learn the basics."

"He can fly back with me," Gus said.

"I want him as my butt man," Kamigami said.

Gus looked amused. "Butt man?"

"A gofer and bodyguard," Kamigami explained.

"You won't need a bodyguard here," Gus said.

Kamigami changed the subject. "Time to meet the troops."

"Your staff is waiting in the command post," Gus said. He led the way into the nearby bunker. It was an impressive structure with blast doors, an air lock, a decontamination chamber, and highly polished floors. It was a perfect setup for a regular-army unit and the last thing Kamigami needed. Colonel Sun Dan was waiting for him with five lieutenant colonels and seven majors. To the man, they were a perfect match for the building: neat, trim, and wearing highly polished boots. For Kamigami the next two hours were an exercise in frustration, as he went through the motions of assuming command and meeting his staff. But he endured, taking the measure of each man. Colonel Sun impressed him, but he made a mental note to transfer out four of the lieutenant colonels and three of the majors at the first opportunity. Finally it was time to meet the men of the First Special Operations Service.

"We're organized in four squadrons of eighty men each," Colonel Sun explained as they approached the parade ground.

"They look very . . . ah, military," Kamigami wryly observed.

"As you can see," Sun replied, missing the cynicism in Kamigami's voice, "we select only the elite."

We'll see how elite, Kamigami thought. He had learned the hard way that the truly elite special operations units had little time, or respect, for the conventions of the normal military. They had to be totally committed to battle discipline, and everything else was garbage. He stepped up onto the low platform as every face turned toward him. "My name is Victor

Kamigami," he began. "I'm your new commander, and while I hold the rank of brigadier, you will not salute me, or any other officer, at any time. To help you remember, remove your berets." As one, they snatched off the black berets they were wearing, and shoved them under an epaulet. "Very good," Kamigami said. "Now fall out and return here with full battle gear in thirty minutes." He stepped off the podium and turned to Colonel Sun. "I'll need to borrow a rucksack," he said.

"We use bergens here," Tel said.

"Ah, the English influence," Kamigami said. He preferred the British backpack, as it could carry more.

"You can use mine," Tel offered.

"You'll be needing it," Kamigami replied.

Exactly thirty minutes later Kamigami stepped back onto the platform. Only this time he was shouldering a sixty-five-pound bergen, wearing a belt kit, and carrying his personal MP5. For a moment he stared at the men. "Follow me," he commanded. He stepped off the podium and set a quick pace to the road that led around the island.

Two hours later he reached the two boulders he called the Devil's Gonads, and called a halt. "How are the men doing?" he asked Colonel Sun.

"Four men have dropped out, and Three Squadron is falling behind," came the answer.

"Four in only two hours?" Kamigami replied. Both he and the colonel knew that it was an unacceptable number. "Tell Three Squadron to keep up," he ordered. He drank from his first canteen, emptied it, and set off again. But this time he increased the pace, and they made it back to camp in ninety minutes. He let the men rest for fifteen minutes, refill their canteens, and then he headed out again, this time running the road counterclockwise. He maintained a killing pace but stopped every fifty minutes. This time they made the circuit in three hours, and again Three Squadron tailed in, strung out over a quarter of a mile. Kamigami shook his head. "How many men have dropped out?" he asked Sun.

"Seven," Sun replied.

Kamigami snorted, showing his displeasure. "Send them home," he ordered. He walked through the squadrons, again taking their measure. He was not impressed. He called the squadron COs together and asked for a chart of the island. The four majors looked at one another. "We all know the island and don't need a chart," one finally answered.

"I'm glad to hear that," Kamigami replied. "So you all know where the Devil's Gonads are?" He waited in silence, and when he didn't get an answer, he described the two boulders on the north shore. "I'm sending a squadron over the center of the island to set up an ambush at the Devil's Gonads."

A major protested. "That's very rough terrain. No one would do that."

"That's what special operations is all about," Kamigami replied. "Doing what nobody else would do. While the squadron mounting the ambush is crossing the island, the rest of us will do one and a half circuits on the road to end up at the Gonads. Gentlemen, it's a race to see who gets there first. Any volunteers?" The four majors were silent. "Okay," Kamigami said, "Three Squadron has it."

"Brigadier," the major commanding Three Squadron said, "I must protest. You don't know the island. I do. No one can cross the center of the island that quickly."

"Tell your men," Kamigami said in his quiet voice, "that if we get there before they do, they're gone, eliminated."

"But some of my men have blisters," the major said.

"It's only pain," Kamigami replied. "Split your squadron into fast and slow movers." He stood back and watched as the majors returned to their squadrons in a state of shock. Within minutes Three Squadron filed past as they headed into the brush. Kamigami's eyes drew into narrow squints as he studied each man. He estimated about half would make it, not including the major.

"Colonel Sun," he called. "Follow me." To Kamigami's way of thinking, the leader of a combat unit had better be able to do what he demanded of his men and demonstrate it from time to time in a way they understood.

Exactly three hours later Kamigami led the main force back into camp after the first circuit. He didn't stop to refill canteens and kept right on going. Tel came up behind him. "Some of the men are making threats against you," he said.

"Anyone collapse yet?" Kamigami asked. No answer. "Then keep on pushing," Kamigami said. Ninety minutes later he reached the Devil's Gonads.

A lieutenant emerged out of the brush and reported in. He was close to exhaustion and, in his confusion, almost saluted. “Three Squadron in place, as ordered.”

“Well done. How many made it?”

“Thirty-two, sir. Counting me.”

“Your name?”

“Lieutenant Lee Go Sung.”

Kamigami nodded. “Lieutenant Lee, as of now you’re the CO of Three Squadron. Move your men to the end of the line.” He turned to Colonel Sun. “Select twenty men from One Squadron and have them report to me in fifteen minutes. I’ll be leading them back over the island.” Sun turned to give the order. “Colonel, you’ll be leading the main body on the road. One and a half circuits back to the main camp. Tell the men that if they all make it before I do, they’ll never see me again.”

A wicked smile crossed Sun’s face. “My pleasure, Brigadier.”

“Split your men into fast and slow movers.”

“That won’t be necessary,” Sun replied.

Fifteen minutes later Kamigami led his men into the brush as the major and the last of Three Squadron arrived. “Take them to the barracks,” Kamigami told the major. “I want you all off the island by sundown.”

A corporal stepped forward. “Brigadier, I want another chance.”

Kamigami studied the corporal for a moment. He was small and too thin for special operations. But there was a driven look in his eyes that Kamigami recognized. “Fall in behind me.”

The corporal hesitated. “I know a way along a ridge. But the major wouldn’t take it.”

“Really?” Kamigami replied. “Take the lead.” The corporal jerked his head and trotted to the head of the column.

Tel came up and spoke quietly. “He’ll never make it.”

“He will,” Kamigami replied.

“I’m almost out of water,” Tel said.

“Go thirsty,” Kamigami muttered.

Sweat poured off Kamigami as he followed the corporal up the ridge that led to the center of the island. It was hard going, and many of the men slipped and fell. Twice they had to stop and pull a man out of a ravine. A sergeant fell into a thornbush and was a bloody mess by the time they got him out. But he refused to quit and slogged on, determined to keep up. A heavy rain started to fall, and Kamigami called a halt to let the men fill their canteens. Then they were moving again as the rain poured in sheets. Visibility was down to fifty feet when they crested the hill in the center of the island, but Kamigami never stopped. Tel seriously wondered if the big man was human.

The corporal stopped. "There, sir." He pointed to a break in the brush that opened into a ravine. He swayed on his feet, his face gaunt. He was on the edge of total exhaustion. "The brush thins out about one-third of the way down. It will be easy going into camp."

"Lead the way," Kamigami said. The corporal turned like an automaton, took a few steps, and collapsed. Kamigami was beside him in a flash and stripped off his bergen and helmet. He felt for the artery on the side of his neck. There was no pulse. "Medic!" he shouted. A corporal rushed up and went to work on the prostrate body. But it was too late.

"He's dead," the medic announced.

Kamigami stood over the body, holding the man's helmet. He bowed his head. Then he knelt and picked up the body, surprised at how light it was. "Bring his weapon and gear," he ordered. He led the way down the ridge and into camp, not stopping once. He marched up to the flagpole in front of the command post and gently laid the body on the ground. "Have the First fall in here," he ordered. "When they arrive." He squatted on his haunches, and his right hand reached for the gold whistle around his neck. He absently stroked it as he gazed at the body.

Tel stood behind him, not sure what to say. He had seen the same look at the village when they built the shrine to hold the ashes of their families. "Can I get you anything?" he finally asked.

"Get his poncho and weapon," Kamigami said. "I wish I had known him." Tel rummaged in the dead corporal's bergen and handed Kamigami the poncho. Kamigami tenderly wrapped it around the body. Then he fixed a bayonet to the corporal's M-16 and drove it into the earth, making a temporary head marker as Colonel Sun and the road team straggled into camp. They formed up while Kamigami reached into his own bergen and pulled out the red beret he had worn in China. He jammed it on his head and stood.

Colonel Sun marched up and stopped. He almost saluted before remembering. "First Special Operations Service reporting as ordered," he barked.

Kamigami jerked his head in acknowledgment and turned to face his command. "We lost one of our comrades today," he began. "I didn't know his name."

"We called him Tiger," Lieutenant Lee said.

"I wish I had known Tiger. But I do know this. He wouldn't quit." Kamigami paused, carefully selecting his next words so there would be no confusion. "Earlier today I had you remove your black berets. It was my intention to replace them with a red beret like the one I'm wearing. But you had to earn it." He removed his beret and placed it on the butt of the corporal's M-16. "Tiger earned his today." Again he paused. "As of now, Three Squadron no longer exists. It is now Tiger Red."

Something in the thirty-two men of Tiger Red caught Tel's attention as Kamigami spoke. He wasn't sure what he was seeing, but they were standing straighter, and there was a look of determination on their faces he had never seen before. It was as if they had been reborn out of the ashes of Three Squadron.

eight

Palau Tenang, Singapore
Tuesday, September 7

Kamigami dropped his bergen by the door of his quarters as a blast of cool, air-conditioned air washed over him. He walked around the modern and well-appointed three-room suite before turning off the air conditioner. "Open the windows," he told Tel. He walked into the bathroom and peeled off his clothes. "I'll need a mosquito net over the bed," he called. He stepped into the shower, savoring the hot water. Every muscle in his body was protesting the abuse he had given it. *Can I still do this?* he wondered, feeling his age.

"Am I your personal servant?" Tel called from the kitchen.

"Not exactly," Kamigami replied. He thought for a moment. *How to explain it?* "The idea is to take care of small details for me so I can devote my time to other things."

"So I polish your boots?"

"Clean them. No polish. Pass the word that I don't ever want to see a polished pair of boots here again." He paused. "Turn off every air conditioner on the island. Now."

"They won't like that," Tel said.

Kamigami came out of the bathroom and fell into bed. "We're ninety miles north of the equator, a long way from Mother Nature's air conditioner. The tropics are our area of operations, and they've got to be a part of it."

"Sir, what was going on out there today?"

Kamigami yawned. "A new day. Reveille at four-thirty tomorrow morning." He was asleep.

Tel adjusted the mosquito net over the bed and turned out the light. He closed the door and checked his watch. Six-thirty in the evening. *A new day?* he thought. *What does that mean?*

The White House
Tuesday, September 7

At the same time Tel was turning off the lights in Kamigami's bedroom, Maddy was sipping her first cup of morning coffee in the residence. She was still wearing slippers and a white fuzzy bathrobe that enveloped her. She curled up in the corner of the couch and cupped the mug in her hands. An image of Matt slipped through the door of her carefully guarded emotions, and for a moment she was in New Mexico when they first met. She held on to the image for a few moments and wished she could return to that magical time and place. But reality intruded, and she willed the image back into its hiding place. Matt was flying back to Oakland and she didn't know when she would see him again.

She steeled herself for what was to come, and set the mug down. "Day two of the war," she said half aloud. It was a new day.

At exactly 7:30 A.M. President Turner stepped into the hall outside her bedroom. Her personal assistant, Nancy Bender, was waiting for her. "Good morning, Madam President," she said, taking Turner's briefcase. They walked to the elevator.

The dark-suited Secret Service agent standing at the end of the hall lifted his left wrist to his mouth and spoke into the whisper mike. "Magic's moving," he said. "Descending in the elevator." In the basement office directly below the Oval Office, the lighted board that monitored the president's movements flashed. The agent on duty sent out the word that the day had started.

The ExCom was waiting for her in the Oval Office, and they stood as one when she entered. "Thank you for coming so early," Turner said as she sat down. She picked up the President's Daily Brief and read as her five advisers refilled their coffee cups. It didn't take long for her to finish. As expected, the PDB was devoted entirely to the conflict in the Persian Gulf. But it didn't tell her what she most wanted to know. She looked at General Wilding. "Do we have a casualty list?"

"Yes, ma'am, we do." Wilding's face was grim as he handed her a single sheet of paper.

Her face paled as she read the numbers. "Two hundred and three killed in action. Sixty-four wounded in action. Over four hundred missing. Am I to assume they're all KIA?" She hated the term "KIA." It was a shorthand that allowed her to sidestep the reality of people's dying because of her policies and decisions.

"No, ma'am," Wilding said. "Most likely a large percentage are in POW status. What you're seeing is the result of the UIF's initial attack."

"The current situation?" she asked.

"The bombing campaign is under way. The Air Force and Navy have flown a combined total of a hundred and ninety-three sorties, and the tempo will increase as more aircraft arrive in the area. For now the main objective is to interdict their forces in the field."

"Which means?" Turner asked.

"We're going to cut them off and isolate them," Wilding replied. "Then we're going to kill them. We do have a few surprises in store for the UIF tonight. The Forty-ninth Fighter Wing is launching twelve F-117 Stealth fighters out of Khamis Mushayt in southern Saudi Arabia, and the Five Hundred Ninth Bomb Wing at Whiteman Air Force Base is launching ten B-2s. Target Baghdad. They plan on taking out every bridge, turning the lights off, and hammering their main command-and-control centers."

"We're doing all this with just twenty-two aircraft?" Turner asked.

Wilding allowed a tight smile. "An F-117 carries only two bombs, but each of those ten B-2s has a mix of sixteen smart bombs, mostly GBU-31s, for a total of a hundred and eighty-four weapons." She gave him a quizzical look, not understanding what a GBU-31 was. "The GBU-31," Wilding explained, "is a two-thousand-pound bomb with an inertial guidance system updated by GPS. Given the accuracy of that weapons mix, we expect ninety-two percent—that's a hundred and sixty-nine bombs—to impact within the target structure."

"And the other fifteen bombs?" the president asked.

"We're trying to keep collateral damage to a minimum," Wilding answered.

"You mean killing civilians." It wasn't a question.

"Yes, ma'am."

Turner stared at her hands, not saying a word. The DCI spoke up. "Madam President, please remember the Iraqis deliberately shield targets with civilians to discourage us from bombing them." He let that sink in.

Wilding continued with his update. "On the ground our forces engaged at first light and are falling back on King Khalid Military City. K squared . . ." He paused, embarrassed that he had used the nickname the military had given to the desert outpost. "Excuse me, I meant to say King Khalid City. The city is under artillery attack, and all noncombatants have been evacuated. Demolition teams are at work in King Khalid destroying everything of value before we withdraw."

The president came to her feet and leaned across the desk, resting on her hands, her face flushed with anger. "You mean we're abandoning our major base to the enemy and retreating? Why wasn't I advised of this, and who made the decision?"

"It was a tactical decision made in the field by General Riddenblack, the commander of Central Command. I concurred with the decision at one-thirty this morning, Eastern daylight time. We are not going to defend King Khalid but continue a tactical withdrawal to a more defensible line."

"That was a decision I do not approve of," Turner said.

Again General Wilding paused. They had come to a crossroads. He firmly believed in civilian control of the military. Not only did he support his commander in chief's policies, he fully accepted one of the basic premises of civilian control—that civilian leaders have the right to be wrong. He was also a professional in every sense of the word, proven in combat, and true to his oath—but he would resign rather than serve under a civilian official with a Napoleon complex who insisted on seizing operational control of the actual fighting. That job belonged to him and his subordinate commanders, and if he made a mistake, she could fire him. "In my judgment the withdrawal from King Khalid was the only sound decision if we were to preserve our forces and keep fighting." He waited for her reply.

Turner sat down and stared at him. *He's been up all night,* she thought. "My primary concern," she said, "is to stop this aggression and defend our allies."

"Madam President, just tell me what you want to do. Set the general guidelines, but, please, let your commanders in the field handle operations." He bowed his head, fully ready to resign if she didn't understand.

Her reply surprised everyone in the room. "How do I know if you're doing it right?"

Wilding's face turned to granite. "When they're bleeding so hard they have to stop advancing and we can stabilize the situation and go on the offensive."

"What will that take?"

"A lot of hard fighting and sacrifice."

"Is that a euphemism for heavy casualties?" she asked.

"We are going to take casualties," Wilding said. "But so will they. If we do it right, it will be forty to one in our favor."

"I hope I've made this clear: I am not going to sacrifice our men and women. Nor, for that matter, am I going to kill innocent civilians."

"Neither am I." How could he make her understand? "Madam President, my oldest son is at King Khalid leading a tank battalion."

His son is in harm's way, she thought. The reality of modern warfare beat at her, threatening her humanity and all that she believed in. She looked at her advisers, carefully shielding her own doubts and fears.

"Madam President," the DCI said, "a more complete brief is ready in the Situation Room."

Turner nodded. "I'll meet you there in fifteen minutes." The meeting was over, and all but the vice president filed out of the Oval Office.

"General Wilding's a good man," Kennett said.

"Is he going to resign?" Turner asked.

"Only if you don't let him do his job," he replied.

Chief of Staff Parrish and the president's personal assistant were standing in the door waiting to escort her to the Situation Room. "Nancy," Maddy said, "please call Brian."

Nancy understood. "He should be up by now." She hurried out to make the call.

Warrensburg, Missouri
Tuesday, September 7

Maggot was waiting when Pontowski taxied his T-34 Mentor up to the fuel pumps at Skyhaven Airport. As usual, he was wearing a flight suit, but this time brand-new eagles were sewn on its shoulders. He waved a salute at Pontowski, not expecting one in return, and set the wheel chocks. Physically, it was impossible to distinguish Dwight "Maggot" Stuart from the average middle-aged male citizen of Missouri. He stood five feet ten inches tall and had close-set gray-green eyes and graying red hair. He was on the lanky side and hadn't put on a pound of weight in ten years. There was nothing in his friendly manner or easy way of speaking to indicate that he was, without doubt, the best A-10 Warthog pilot in the United States Air Force.

The Mentor's canopy slid back, and Pontowski stood up. "Maggot, good to see you. Congrats on the eagles. Much deserved." He climbed onto the wing and stretched before removing his earplugs. He loved the old Mentor, but it was a noisy bird. "Thanks for coming."

"Nothing else to do," Maggot groused. He studied the pristine aircraft for a moment, appreciating what he was seeing. "She is a pretty thing," he said. Pontowski climbed down, and they shook hands.

"What are you up to these days?" Pontowski asked.

"Nothing since I pinned on eagles," Maggot answered. He had been the commander of an Air Force Reserve squadron of A-10 Warthogs at the nearby Air Force base but had been promoted out of a job when he assumed his new rank. "I've been cooling my heels waiting for an assignment to come down. I was hoping to get the Wing, but everything is on hold now."

"Shooting matches do that," Pontowski said. He told the ramp rat to top up the Mentor's fuel tanks and check the oil as they walked into the fixed base operations building. "What's happening at the squadron?" he asked.

"We're getting ready to deploy," Maggot replied. He shook his head. "Problems."

"Such as?"

Maggot frowned. "We're undermanned, especially in maintenance, and half the women are bailing out. Also very short on spare parts. Forty percent of our aircraft are down."

"Ouch," Pontowski said. "Pilots?"

"Young. All the old heads have left for the airlines. We're basically okay but low on experience."

"The first ten days are going to be hell," Pontowski said ruefully. Combat had taught both men a hard lesson: the highest attrition rates occurred in the first ten days, and the lower the experience levels, the higher the attrition. "I remember when I had the squadron," Pontowski said. "Just hint at a shooting match and the old heads couldn't get here fast enough."

"Things change," Maggot said. "The damnedest thing, Waldo showed up."

Pontowski laughed. "George Walderman? The last I heard he was flying C-130s for the CIA out of South Africa."

"He was, but he quit. Claims it was too boring. For a while I thought he wanted back in. But he took a look around, talked to the training folks, and voted with his feet. We could use a stick like him." Maggot thought for a moment. "I've got the feeling we're going to need every pilot we can get."

"Is the squadron in bad shape?" Pontowski asked.

Maggot thought for a moment. "Just low on experience. Compared to the rest of the Reserves, the squadron's in great shape. But the tactical air force is living with the sins of the past ten years and rebuilding. We needed another two or three years to rebuild. Given enough flying time . . ." He shook his head in resignation. "This hit us too damn soon."

"I take it you're not deploying to the Middle East."

A pained look crossed Maggot's face. "I'm not on the roster." Pontowski felt sorry for Maggot, but there wasn't a place for an extra full colonel when a squadron went to war. That was when lieutenants and captains counted. Inside the building they walked up to the counter. Maggot glanced at the TV mounted in the corner. "There's your old friend." Elizabeth Gordon, CNC-TV's star reporter, was on the screen, her mouth moving in silence. "Nice teeth," Maggot said. "I bet she gives one hell of a blow job with that overbite."

"I wouldn't know," Pontowski replied. Maggot gave him a look that said "Really." A map of the Middle East flashed on the screen with the words SPECIAL REPORT FROM BAGHDAD in prominent letters. Pontowski turned up the volume.

"The following scenes," Gordon was saying, "document graphic brutality and definitely should not be seen by children or those upset by violence."

"Which guarantees everyone will watch," Pontowski muttered.

Maggot couldn't resist the chance to rag his old commander. "But I thought you really liked her."

"Yeah, right," Pontowski said.

Gordon's voice was louder. "Again, I must warn you not to watch if children are present or if you are upset by violence. The videotape you are about to see was recorded from Baghdad TV earlier this morning. We have superimposed an English translation over the narrator's voice."

The scene in the news studio dissolved to one of tanks driving across an open desert, their cannons firing on the move. The excited narrator's voice speaking in Arabic faded out and was replaced by a matter-of-fact voice speaking English. "This is not the mother of all battles but the mother of all victories. Our forces are sweeping with deadly force through the ranks of the demoralized and worthless American soldiers."

"Now, that's impressive," Maggot said. "T-72s shooting on the move. Never saw that before." He had killed fourteen tanks in the 1991 Persian Gulf War, and it was common knowledge that the Russian-built T-72 had to stop in order to fire its cannon with any degree of accuracy.

"Publicity," Pontowski replied. "Stock footage."

The scene changed to one of soldiers charging fearlessly across the desert and jumping into trenches. "Our brave soldiers quickly overran the cowardly Americans, who could not surrender fast enough."

"Looks like training trenches to me," Maggot said.

The scene changed to real footage from the field, and Maggot fell silent. An armored personnel carrier was churning across the desert floor dragging a long rope with a bundle at the far end kicking up a cloud of dust. The APC slammed to a stop, and the camera zoomed in on the bundle as the dust settled. It was an American soldier. An Iraqi soldier ran up, cut the rope, and kicked the lifeless body. But the American was not dead and raised a hand in supplication. The soldier kicked him in the head and motioned at the APC. The driver gunned the engine and spun the APC around, pivoting the vehicle over the American and grinding him into the gravel before stopping. The camera panned to laughing soldiers dragging two more American soldiers out of the APC. They held one upright and propped him against the side of the APC. A man ran at the prisoner with a fixed bayonet. The American grabbed the bayonet with his bare hands but couldn't stop the soldier from driving it into his abdomen. The soldier twisted the rifle until the man fell to the ground. The Iraqi leaned on the rifle butt, driving the bayonet completely through the American's body.

The camera focused on the last soldier, a woman. Rough hands tore away the top of her fatigues, exposing her bra. A knife flashed, and her bra was cut away. Two soldiers grabbed her arms and twisted them out, behind her back, as they forced her to a kneeling position. Another soldier grabbed her hair and pulled her head straight forward as a man advanced holding a ceremonial sword. The scene suddenly went blank as he raised the sword above her neck. The waving flag of the UIF filled the screen. "Thus Americans receive justice," the translator said, his voice flat and unemotional.

Pontowski's hand was a blur as he hit the power button to the TV. "Son of a bitch," he growled.

"Why did they show that?" Maggot asked, his voice shaking.

"In a word," Pontowski said, "ratings."

"I mean the Iraqis," Maggot said.

Pontowski shook his head and reached for the direct line to the Flight Service Center. "Cancel the flight plan for Mentor 4315. I'm refiling for Washington, D.C."

He was airborne and over St. Louis when the call from Patrick Flannery Shaw was patched through.

Palau Tenang
Wednesday, September 8

Sweat streaked the faces and fatigues of the officers waiting in the hardened bunker that served as the 1st SOS's command post. A lone fan in the doorway stirred the air and moved it toward the opened emergency escape hatch in the rear wall. Kamigami entered and spoke in Chinese: "Please be seated." Although it was early in the morning, he estimated the temperature at ninety degrees and rising. "I know this is uncomfortable. Bunkers in the field are. They also make good targets. From now on, everything we do, all our training, is based on the assumption we are in the field on operations. We will train as we plan to fight. Our motto is 'Mobility is life.' For you who don't understand that, remember three words"—he switched to English—"shoot and scoot."

Kamigami waited while his staff talked among themselves, deciding what "shoot and scoot" meant. He knew how the Chinese mind worked, and it would take some reinforcing on his part. But he accepted that. "Our first exercise is to create a mobile command post in the field and establish contact with Headquarters Central in Singapore. You have four hours, gentlemen. At that time I expect the new command post to be up and operating." He spun around and walked out. "I'll be with Tiger Red," he called over his shoulder.

Tel followed him outside. "What now?"

"We're leading Tiger Red on the morning run," Kamigami said.

"Oh, no," Tel said, mostly to himself.

"Is that a problem?"

"Those guys are charged up after yesterday."

"That's the idea."

Two hours later Kamigami led Tiger Red back into the camp. The men were all bunched together and jogging in lockstep, more than willing to run over Kamigami should he stumble and fall. First, Second, and Fourth Squadrons were right behind them, threatening to do the same. "How many have dropped out?" Kamigami asked Tel.

"Three," came the answer. "I think."

"Find out," Kamigami ordered. "I want them all off the island by sundown." He turned to the four squadron commanders. "Dismiss your men for breakfast."

Colonel Sun Dan was waiting and escorted him into the brush, leading him to their new command post. They trudged along the base of one of the low ridges that radiated out from the center of the island. Sun pushed aside some heavy foliage and motioned Kamigami toward a group of canvas-covered shelters hidden below the crest of the ridge. "We established contact with Headquarters Central an hour ago," Sun announced, "and received our first message." Sun checked his watch. "Mr. Deng Shikai is arriving by helicopter in twenty-four minutes."

"Gus coming back so soon?" Kamigami mused. "I must have pissed someone off."

"Two of the men who fell out yesterday and who you ordered to leave are from very prominent families. Very well connected politically."

Kamigami shrugged. "Too bad they couldn't hack it. Well, let's go meet the gentleman." They walked in silence back to the helipad. Kamigami understood too well how the Chinese did business and fully expected to be on the helicopter when it left. He waited patiently until he heard the familiar beat of rotors. Then he snapped to attention as the aircraft came into view and landed.

Gus was off the helicopter before the blades had stopped turning. "We need to talk," he said.

"Alone?" Kamigami asked.

"It would be better if Colonel Sun and your staff were there."

So it's going to be a public humiliation, Kamigami thought. He led the way into the brush and to the new command post. It started to rain, and they took shelter under the canvas of the largest shelter. Colonel Sun called for the staff to squeeze in around them.

Gus came right to the point. "I have just received word of unusual activity around the Chinese base camp in Malaysia's National Park."

Kamigami caught the surprised look on Sun's face. The colonel obviously had not been told about the Chinese presence in the Taman Negara. Kamigami fingered the gold whistle hanging from his neck as he related what he and Tel had discovered after their kampong was destroyed. His soft voice hardened into granite as he spoke, and Tel recoiled at the rage he sensed was lurking below the surface. He gave a silent prayer of thanks that he would never have to face Kamigami in combat.

Sun didn't hear the fury in Kamigami's voice, but he understood the implications for Singapore. "So we have a real threat on our doorstep," he said when Kamigami finished. "We could have been training for this." Gus didn't answer. "I assume you are here for a reason," Sun said.

"I want you to find out what they're doing," Gus said.

Sun stared at him in disbelief. "We'll need time to prepare." Like most commanders, Sun was hesitant to commit his men to a new operation on short notice. "Don't the Americans have satellite coverage?"

"I have asked the Americans, but all their so-called resources are committed to the Middle East. They aren't willing to reposition a satellite at this time. Time is the one thing we don't have right now." His voice was as cold and flat as the look in his eyes. "I take it your men are not ready?"

Before Sun could answer, Kamigami coughed for their attention. "If this is reconnaissance only, I'll take four teams in. Colonel Sun, you know the men better than I do, so please select the teams, eight men each." He couldn't read Sun's reaction.

The officers and senior NCOs were busily making notes as Kamigami stood over a chart table and recapped what he wanted done in his absence. "Drive everyone hard." He placed his hands flat on the table and leaned on his arms, his head bowed. "The First is too large. We need to weed out the weak links. You must be merciless. Better now, in training, than in the real event. In your training stress small-unit mobility with mutual support. When I return, I want to see a live-fire exercise attacking and destroying a hardened target."

"We'll need to build the target first," Sun said.

"I was thinking of your old command bunker," Kamigami said. He rolled up his chart. "I should be back in two weeks. I want to see progress."

Sun's wicked grin was back. "Indeed you will, sir."

nine

Washington, D.C.
Wednesday, September 8

It was after midnight when the taxi stopped at the intersection of Connecticut Avenue and K Street, two blocks short of the Old Executive Office Building. "Sorry, General," the driver told Pontowski. "This is as close as I can get." Like many denizens of the Imperial City, he recognized Pontowski. He flicked on the dome light to calculate the fare. "I voted for your grandfather," he said. "Best president we ever had. He'd know what to do with those fuckin' Aye-rabs messin' with us."

"I imagine President Turner has a good idea what to do," Pontowski replied. He handed over the fare and included a two-dollar tip. "We've got a lot of friends and allies in the Middle East who are depending on us," he added.

The driver relented a little. "Yeah, I know. But we only hear from them when they raise oil prices or someone is kickin' their asses."

Pontowski got out of the cab and headed for the first security checkpoint, located a good block from Pennsylvania Avenue. Ahead of him, and despite the late hour, the old office building was lit up like a gingerbread monstrosity. Across the street he could see the White House, also fully lit. He stopped at the checkpoint to identify himself. The police officer recognized him but still checked his ID before calling for an escort. "Be careful, General," the officer warned. "We stopped a car bomber just after dark near the airport . . . an illegal immigrant who's lived here since 1980."

A uniformed Secret Service agent arrived and escorted Pontowski inside. *It still looks the same,* he thought, remembering the last time he had been in the building, eight years before. *We were putting the AVG together then.* The elevator stopped at the third floor, and the doors swooshed open. The highly polished black-and-white marble floor stretched out in front of him. "Just like old times," he told his escort. They walked down the hall to the national security adviser's corner office overlooking the White House.

Mazie was waiting for him. "Thanks for coming so quickly."

"Why all the secrecy?" he asked.

She glanced at his escort and didn't answer. He got the message—the reason for his summons from Patrick Flannery Shaw would have to wait. Mazie gathered up her briefcase and headed out the door with a brisk "Come." They took another elevator to the basement and went through a series of checkpoints as they walked the tunnel leading to the White House.

"Okay, what's going down?" he asked.

Mazie glanced at the people around them. "Personal problems," she said in a low voice. When they reached the basement of the West Wing, she turned into the Situation Room.

Shaw was waiting for them. A relieved look spread across his face. "You need an update before we see the president." He motioned at the duty officer sitting at a workstation against the sidewall. His fingers flew over the keyboard as he called up a situation map on thc big monitor. "King Khalid Military City fell three hours ago," Shaw said, "and we're falling back toward Riyadh."

Pontowski studied the map for a moment. "It's bad," he said. "But it could be worse."

"How?" Mazie asked.

"They haven't broken out or flanked us. Our line is intact, and given the slowness of their advance, I suspect they're paying a heavy price."

Shaw made a decision. "You need to talk to the president. Now." Pontowski blinked at the worried tone in his voice. Was Shaw, Washington's political wizard, losing it under the pressure of war? Shaw turned to the duty officer. "Call for an escort." Pontowski arched an eyebrow at the tight security. "You haven't heard," Shaw said. "The FBI rolled up four terrorist groups in D.C. yesterday. Deep sleepers."

"The way a poor man fights a war," Pontowski said.

Shaw snorted. "One group had five canisters of sarin nerve gas and detailed maps of the subway system." He paused. "And of the White House." Their escort led them to the elevator, and it was obvious neither Shaw nor Mazie was going to talk about the reason for his summons within earshot of another person. They rode the elevator in silence to the second floor. A Secret Service agent checked Mazie's briefcase and ran a wand over all of them before allowing them to proceed. Pontowski counted five Secret Service agents along with two armed Marines and a Navy lieutenant commander who was sitting in the hall. As expected, the Navy officer had the football, the soft leather briefcase containing the nuclear launch codes, chained to his wrist. There was no doubt that the White House was an armed camp. "Are you ready?" Mazie asked. Pontowski steeled himself, fully expecting to find a devastated president, perhaps on the edge of collapse.

He couldn't have been more wrong.

Madeline Turner was pacing the floor in front of the fireplace like a caged tiger. Her chief of staff, Richard Parrish, Vice President Sam Kennett, and the secretary of defense, Robert Merritt, had all taken defensive positions well away from her line of fire. She moved with a quick, feline grace as she turned to Pontowski. Her brown eyes were clear and flashed with determination. "Matt, what brings you here?"

Before he could answer, Shaw said, "I asked him."

She whirled on Shaw, and they stared at each other, some form of unspoken communication between them. A little of the fire seemed to drain from her. She crossed her arms and hugged herself as she turned, focusing on the fireplace. "Did you see how they executed those three prisoners?" She didn't wait for an answer. "And they had the audacity to show it on TV! Not to mention a car bomber headed directly for Reagan International. And sarin! Right here! They were going to use it on innocent people! I won't have it! I simply won't have it!"

"Madam President," Kennett said, "a nuclear response is not appropriate at this time."

Pontowski was stunned, and he stood there, not sure what to think, much less say. Silence held the room as the president resumed her pacing. Then he saw it. She was venting her anger and frustration—but she was in total control. "Madam President," Pontowski ventured, testing the waters, "if we start creating parking lots in the Middle East, who knows what the terrorists here will do."

"And just what can they do?"

"Detonate a nuke." He paused to let it sink in. "The FBI needs time to roll them up. Give it to them."

Mazie sensed rather than saw a slight change in the president's mood and shot Shaw a look. "Mrs. President," Shaw said, "we all need a short break." On cue, her advisers stood and filed out, leaving Pontowski and the president alone. Mazie was the last out and closed the door behind her.

Maddy turned to face him. "Oh, Matt, it was terrible. Thank God our media edited the tape. But I saw it all. The Iraqis actually showed the beheading on TV."

Now Pontowski understood. "It was meant to be horrible," he told her.

"But why? They were prisoners."

"From their point of view it made sense. Remember all the coverage of Iraqi soldiers surrendering in the Gulf War? This was payback and geared to inspire their soldiers."

She was incredulous. "Inspire?"

"That's the way they think. Also, they wanted to intimidate us."

Her back grew rigid. "Well, they thought wrong!"

"By our standards they're not rational."

"Rational or not, if—"

He interrupted her. "We hit them with our strength and they hit us where we're vulnerable. It's called asymmetrical warfare."

She glared at him. "I will respond with force. They must know that."

"They fully expect you will. But they're betting you won't go nuclear."

"Why?"

"We'd pay too high a price with our allies and world opinion." He paused. "Are you willing to create a nuclear Armageddon, level three nations, maybe destroy Israel in the process, in retaliation for a few thousand American deaths?"

She looked at him, and every bit of her humanity was on full display. Of all things, Madeline O'Keith Turner was not prepared to be a wartime president and had never steeled herself for the reality of what it entailed. Despite that, she stood in front of him alone and defiant, not about to collapse, not needing comfort or a refuge.

Pontowski gave a little humph. "I could use a drink." She stared at him, not believing he'd said that. "Coffee." She shook her head, her mood broken, and buzzed the steward. The steward carried in a tray and quickly retreated. Pontowski poured a cup of coffee and handed it to her. She took a sip and sat down while he poured one for himself. "After you've heard all the options, set clear objectives for the military, but don't—"

She interrupted. "But don't micromanage operations. I've been through that with General Wilding."

"You can trust Wilding. Merritt I don't know about. But you've also got to give Wilding the means to win the war. Big emphasis on 'win' here. That's where Congress comes in. I assume you're talking to them."

Her head came up. "Congress starts consideration on a bill funding the war tomorrow."

"With Senator Leland leading the opposition," Pontowski added.

"He's so damn partisan," she said. "Patrick says he'd do anything to see his boy Grau win in November." She gave a little shudder. "I need to put him in a box."

"Show Congress the unedited TV tape of the execution. Take the high ground and turn it into a Pearl Harbor or World Trade Center."

"But what if the parents or spouses see it? You know there is at least one bastard who will leak it. I don't know if I can do that."

"You've got to beat the average congressmen over the head to get them focused," he told her. "How often do they quit playing politics and do the right thing?"

"Not often," she said. "You mentioned options and objcctives. Mazie and the ExCom are doing a good job with that."

Pontowski gave a little shake of his head. "Mazie will do whatever you ask and is totally reliable. But she's so rational and loyal that she may not be able to consider the unthinkable, which is exactly what you need to know. You've got this big bureaucracy at your beck and call, which has a lot of talent and brains. Make it work for you. Call your advisers in and tell them you want six options, with consequences, about how to conduct the war. Two that are the easiest; two that make the most sense, given the players and means available; and two that are totally out of the box."

"What do I do if they detonate a nuclear weapon?"

"You want six more options. Now. Before it happens."

She set down her coffee cup and stood. "Where did you learn all this?"

"I had a good teacher."

"Your grandfather."

"Well, he did have a clue."

Maddy walked to the door to call in her advisers. "Matt, thank you for coming, but . . ."

He gave a little smile. "I know. You've got a war to run, and you don't need me around to complicate things with the media."

"It won't always be this way," she promised. She reached out and touched his cheek.

He touched her hand. "Better not." Then he was gone. The president stared at the open door as her advisers filed in again.

Outside, Bernie Butler escorted Pontowski back to the Situation Room. "Matt, you were in Israel the last time the Israelis and Arabs went at each other. I'm worried the Israelis might get involved. If you've got some time, would you mind taking a more detailed look at the situation?"

"Can do," Pontowski said, a little too eagerly. It had been a long time since he'd had access to current intelligence. He gave Butler a sideways look. "What are the Boys telling you?"

"They don't like all the signals they're seeing. But nothing concrete."

"I'll take a look," Pontowski told him. Butler cleared him into the Situation Room, and the duty officer called up the current intelligence summary for the Middle East. While Pontowski read, Butler waited patiently and soon dozed off. He hadn't slept in over thirty hours. When Pontowski finished with the Middle East, he glanced at Butler, saw that he was asleep, and decided to go fishing. *What the hell? They can only say no.* He asked to see the summary for Russia. Since Pontowski had been in before with Shaw and the national security adviser, the duty officer simply gave it to him. There was nothing of interest, although the Russian economy was showing signs of growing stability. "Latin America." Again the screen scrolled with the latest intelligence summaries. The drug lords were effectively consolidating their political power. "China," he said. The duty officer pulled up the most current summary for him to read. Something started to scratch at the back of his mind, but nothing came into focus. He rapidly scanned India and Pakistan. But the itch refused to go away. "Southeast Asia," he said, about ready to give it up.

The screen scrolled, and again he read. "What the hell is this?" he said, reading a report about recent disturbances in eastern Malaysia.

Butler came awake, and Pontowski pointed to the report. Butler's eyebrows furled into a worry line as he read. "We're seeing conflicts like this everywhere. At last count forty-four this year alone have reached the level of what we class as ethnic war." He changed the subject. "So what's your take on the Middle East? Do you think Israel is coming in?"

"Not at this time," Pontowski replied. "But I keep wondering why the UIF aired that tape on TV. It's almost like they wanted us to see it and overreact."

Butler shook his head. "They don't think like we do."

New Mexico Military Institute
Wednesday, September 8

Brian Turner rolled over in his bunk, which was built into the overhead above his desk, and looked directly into his best friend's face. "Sumbitch," he muttered, turning back over, not wanting any trouble from one of New Mexico Military Institute's TLAs, or training and leadership advisers.

"Get your lazy ass moving," Zack Pontowski said in a low voice.

"Don't need ten more D's for missing a bed check," Brian mumbled. A D was a demerit, and each one meant he was restricted to post until he walked off a fifty-minute punishment tour. "Go back to bed. Wait for reveille."

Zack ripped the blankets away. "It's on TV," he said. "Live coverage." Zack had no trouble dragging him out and depositing him on his feet. "You don't want to miss this," he promised.

"Sumbitch," Brian growled. "I can remember when you needed a ladder to reach the freakin' washbasin and couldn't lift anything heavier than your pecker."

"Things change," Zack said. It was true. He was taller than Brian and outweighed him by ten pounds.

"Knock it off," Brian's roommate said, now also fully awake. "What's up?"

"They got live coverage from the Gulf on the TV in JRT," Zack said. JRT was John Ross Thomas Hall, where the cadet lounge was located. "Let's go."

"Shee-it," Brian's roommate said. "I just got off restriction. No way I'm missin' a bed check." He rolled over and went back to sleep as Brian hurriedly dressed in the dark.

The two cadets slipped out of the room and hurried down the stoop to the stairs. Without a word a Secret Service agent trailed after them. They heard him report in with a curt "Merlin's moving." "Merlin" was the code word a Department of Defense computer had cranked out for Brian when his mother assumed the presidency of the United States. They slipped through the deep shadows as they made their way to JRT, which was lit up like a Christmas tree. The TLA who had the night duty saw them immediately and waved them inside, where forty or so upperclassmen were clustered around the big TV set.

A scene straight out of hell was on the screen. Men were running as explosions ripped the ground. A Humvee disappeared in a fireball as the camera captured a T-72 main battle tank firing at point-blank range. A wire-guided antitank missile streaked overhead, missing the tank and slamming into an eight-wheeled armored personnel carrier. "Christ," the TLA said. "That's a BTR-60. Those fuckers are mobile."

On the TV the voice of a woman reporter could be heard shouting above noise. "A tank has broken through—" The clatter of heavy machine-gun fire cut her off as the camera swung around. The woman was lying in a crumpled heap in a shallow depression behind a burned-out Land Rover. The words PRESS CORPS could still be seen on the scorched paint. The tank fired again, and the Land Rover disintegrated. Now the cameraman was running, his camera still on. Men were streaming out the back of the disabled BTR-60 as the cannon on the tank lowered, then lifted.

"The T-72," the TLA explained, trying to be the cool professional, "lowers the cannon muzzle to eject the spent shell casing, then raises the muzzle to autoload a fresh round." The cadets watched in horror as the barrel started to come down, directly toward the running cameraman. Another Humvee raced into view, crossing in front of the cameraman. The soldier manning the TOW wire-guided antitank missile mounted on top of the Humvee swung it around and fired. The missile leaped out of the tube and headed for the tank as the cannon's muzzle dropped. The cadets held their breath as the duel played out. The missile hit the turret just as the cannon fired. The sound of the cannon round passing inches above the cameraman's head filled the room as the tank exploded.

"That is one lucky dude," the TLA said. Again the camera swung, and the woman reporter was up and running, her Kevlar vest in tatters, her helmet gone. She jumped into a ditch as another much heavier, and slower-sounding, machine gun swept the field, ripping apart the soldiers from the BTR-60. The TLA breathed easier. "That's an MK-19 grenade machine gun doing the damage," he explained. "It fires a forty-millimeter, high-explosive, dual-purpose round. We're talking industrial-strength deterrence here." Suddenly the scene was silent as the cadets erupted in cheers. The TLA took a deep breath. "I got to tell you, I was in the Gulf in '91 and never saw action like that."

Zack looked at Brian. "We're gonna miss it," he said in a low voice.

The TLA worked his way through the cadets to the TV. "Gentlemen, you are indeed fortunate that I suffer from poor night vision. I'm gonna turn off the TV, and when I'm finished with this laborious and time-consuming task, I hope to hell this room is vacant and that I find you all safe as bugs in a rug in your bunks."

It was, and he did.

Lackland Air Force Base
Wednesday, September 8

The two sergeants waiting inside the 341st Training Squadron's orderly room jumped to their feet when Rockne walked in. "Thanks for coming down, Chief," Tech Sergeant Paul Travis said. "I believe you know Staff Sergeant Jake Osburn." The men shook hands all around. "The squadron deployed this morning to backfill for units headed for the Gulf," Paul told Rockne. "There's only four of us left, and we can sure use some help around here."

"Who are the other two?" Rockne asked.

"Staff Sergeant Jessica Maul," Paul replied. "She was a no-show for the deployment. The other is Airman First Class Cindy Cloggins. She's your admin clerk."

"A real bimbo," Jake muttered.

Paul gave him a long look. "She's just young. She's doing okay and will make a good cop."

"Let's get to work," Rockne said. Travis nodded and escorted him into the administration section.

Cindy Cloggins jumped to her feet, not quite as frightened as the last time she had met Rockne. "Good afternoon, Chief."

"You remembered," Rockne said. Cindy Cloggins gave a little nod and relaxed. "I need to speak to Sergeant Maul," he told her.

"I haven't seen her today, Chief," Cindy replied.

Rockne stared at her. "The squadron deploys, and she's still not here?" he said. It wasn't meant to be a question. "Find her." He turned and walked into his new office.

Rockne was on the phone when a young woman knocked on his door. "Chief Rockne," she said, out of breath. "No excuse, but I'm ready to go now."

He read her nametag. "Staff Sergeant Maul—as in shopping mall?"

Jessica grimaced at the play on her name. "That's correct, Chief."

"Why did you miss the deployment?" he asked.

"My asshole husband changed his mind and said he wasn't gonna baby-sit while I was gone. It took me some time to sort it out."

"And?"

"He changed his mind. Which he won't do again."

Rockne liked the determined look on her face. "I imagine he won't."

"Are we going to the Gulf?" she asked.

"Nope."

A frown crossed Jessica's pretty face. "Damn."

"As of now," Rockne told her, "you're the acting kennel master."

Jessica brightened. "I can do that."

"My dog's in my pickup out front. Please put her in the kennel."

She smiled broadly. "I know Boyca."

Washington, D.C.
Wednesday, September 8

President Turner escorted Senator Leland into the Situation Room. "We try to keep these briefings short," she explained as she sat down. She had invited Leland to the White House to meet with the ExCom in the hope of moderating his opposition before the politics of waging a war divided Congress into the hawks and the doves.

Patrick Shaw stood and offered his seat to the senator. "Glad you could make it, Senator." He stood against the wall, thankful that Leland was not at his back. *Can't trust that bastard at all,* he thought.

Turner nodded at Colonel Scovill, the Marine briefer who was standing in front of the computer-driven monitors. His voice was under strict control as he started the briefing. "Madam President, we have the results of last night's missions over Baghdad. As of now every bridge over the Tigris River in the city is down and all electrical power is off. Only the water system remains untouched." He allowed a tight smile. "I can reconfirm that all aircraft returned undamaged."

"The French," Leland said, "claim we bombed Saddam Hussein's palace. Is that true, and if it is, isn't that a violation of the Geneva Convention?"

"Yes to the first question and no to the second," the colonel answered. From the frown on Leland's face, it wasn't the answer he wanted.

"Do you have the details?" Turner asked.

Scovill managed to keep a straight face as he spoke. "Yes, ma'am, we do. But the language is a bit—" He paused, searching for the right words. "—shall we say risqué."

"I'm quite sure we're all adult," Turner replied.

A little grin played on the Marine's lips. "Yes, ma'am." He keyed the remote control in his right hand, and the monitor on the left came to life. "This is the unedited target video from the F-117 Stealth fighter that bombed Saddam's main palace."

A greenish image filled the screen, and the pilot's voice could be heard as he described the bomb run. "There's the Tigris," the pilot said. He laid the crosshairs on a bridge spanning the river. "The Jumhuiya Bridge. Follow the main boulevard to the southwest . . . there's the government conference center . . . which points to the palace. All checks with the GPS." The image was unbelievably sharp as he positioned the crosshairs over the huge doors that led into the main entrance hall. A light flashed at the bottom of the screen. "Bomb gone," the pilot said in a conversational tone. Nothing betrayed the fact that he was deep over hostile territory.

"Please note the time-to-go timer in the lower right-hand corner of the screen," Scovill said. "When it reaches zero, the bomb will impact on the crosshairs." Silence held the room in thrall as the seconds counted down. The crosshairs on the screen never moved from the big doors as the pilot flew an arc around the palace. When the timer touched four, the pilot said, "Knock-knock, muthafucker." The bomb flew through the door and into the main hall. The screen mushroomed as the bomb detonated, and then it went blank.

Shaw let out a loud guffaw as Leland came to his feet. "That's not funny!" Leland roared. "How can we protect innocent civilians when our pilots have that kind of attitude? I want that pilot court-martialed and made an example of." He stood there, his jowls quivering as the room echoed with his fury. "Do not misjudge me on this," he warned. He spun around and stormed out of the room.

"Must've been something the good senator et," Shaw muttered in his best Texas accent as he sat down in the empty chair.

Turner shook her head. "Well, I tried. Do we have a problem here?"

"Only if you court-martial the pilot," General Wilding replied.

"How so?" Turner asked.

"We'll have sent the wrong message about mission accomplishment," Wilding said.

"Court-martial any pilot for hitting his assigned target," Butler added, "and half the pilots will abort for mechanical problems before they even take off. The other half will be hard-pressed to find their targets, and we'll be lucky to see ten percent of our bombs on target. Even then not one will press the envelope."

"What does that mean?" Turner asked.

"They won't take any unnecessary risks."

"Isn't that a form of mutiny?"

"Call it what you will," Butler answered, a rare emotion in his voice. "But it is human nature. If we order them into combat, we had damn well better back them up."

"Are you suggesting I give him a medal?"

"It's worth thinking about," Butler replied.

Turner nodded. Then, "I do worry about civilian casualties. Do we have any idea? Leland will make it an issue."

The Marine thought for a moment before answering. "The Iraqis claim we've killed over five thousand civilians and wounded thousands more. We're monitoring their hospitals and have noticed a nominal increase in activity, but nothing that supports the casualties they claim. The hospitals are certainly not swamped, and for the most part it's business as usual. We do expect to see more activity when casualties are brought in from the fighting in Saudi Arabia."

"If they can get across the river," Turner added.

"Yes, ma'am. That's correct."

The president arched an eyebrow in Shaw's direction—his cue to leave. "Ah," he groused, "the dreaded executive session." He ambled back to his corner office in the West Wing and sifted through the stack of notes and telephone memos on his desk. One note caught his attention, and an hour later he told his secretary that he was going to his favorite restaurant, four blocks away, before it closed for the evening.

As expected, the young lady was waiting for him in the bar. They chatted for a few moments before the maître d' escorted them to a table in a far corner of the dining room. "Well, love, anything exciting going on in the wonderful world where you seem to spend most of your days?"

"You know I can't talk about that," she murmured. He nodded, accepting the truth of it. She worked in the bowels of the National Security Agency and specialized in monitoring electronic communications—of which sort, Shaw had no idea. He felt her hand on his knee and reached for it, covering it with his own. Then he withdrew his hand and dropped the cassette tape into his pocket.

They spent the next hour in idle chatter as they savored the exquisite meal. "Well, love, I've got to return to the dungeon. War to win and all that good stuff."

"Patrick," she asked, "what exactly do you do?"

He smiled at her. "Whatever needs doin'." He called for the bill and headed back to the White House. Once in his office, he fished the cassette out of his pocket and examined it. The slickly printed label announced EXECUTIVE ESCORTS FOR YOUR LISTENING PLEASURE. He dropped the cassette into a player and leaned back to listen as a woman's sexy voice announced the discreet pleasures offered by some of Washington's most beautiful and captivating ladies. His dinner companion's voice cut in and said, "Recorded today at five twenty-two P.M."

A man's voice with a heavy French accent said, "What exactly do you have in mind?"

Leland's voice replied, "You brokering a cease-fire."

The French voice answered, "We can do that."

His dinner companion's voice was back. "If you would like to learn more, please give me a call." The tape ended. Shaw gave a loud sigh and dialed a number. His dinner companion answered on the first ring. "I thought you'd be interested."

"How much?" Shaw asked.

"Five thousand."

Now who's the hooker? Shaw thought. He knew the risks she was taking using the National Security Agency's superclassified equipment to monitor phone calls in the United States. It was worth twenty years in Leavenworth. But, more important, did he want to take the risk? He decided he didn't. "Later, doll."

"I'll be here," she cooed, "if you change your mind."

ten

The Plains of Pahang, Malaysia
Thursday, September 9

The tour bus was within walking distance of Mentakab, a small town on the Jungle Railway, when the engine coughed and sputtered. The driver nursed the bus over to the side of the road and radioed the lead bus, which quickly turned around. After talking to the two drivers, the tour leader called for a replacement bus and tried to make the best of it by reorganizing the sixty-seven people under her care.

While most of the young couples from Singapore explored what few attractions Mentakab had to offer, she discussed the problem with the older man who seemed to be the nominal leader of the group. She beamed and tossed her hair as they talked, all for the benefit of the man's son, a very attractive and physically fit young man about her age. She was glad she had brought her thong bikini to wear on the beach. After discussing the situation and delays involved—the replacement bus wouldn't arrive until midnight—it was decided to split the group. The wives would go on ahead to Kuantan on the eastern coast and check into the luxury hotel they had booked for the weekend.

The tour guide was surprised at how easily the men reloaded the baggage, throwing heavy suitcases and bags of sports equipment around with ease. She smiled as the young wives said good-bye and boarded the first bus. "Are they honeymooners?" she asked.

"I wouldn't call them that," the older man said. "But they haven't been married long." The tour guide was the last to board and waved as the bus pulled onto the highway. An odd thought struck her as she looked at the men waving back. They all seemed relieved that their wives had gone on ahead.

The relief bus arrived after midnight, pulled up behind the disabled bus, and turned off all its lights. Eight men slipped off the disabled bus in total darkness and fanned out to ensure that the area was clear. One by one they checked in on their pocket-size, short-range radios. Their voices were low and barely audible as they reported the area clear. The rest of the men then streamed off the bus, and the baggage doors of both buses were quickly opened. A service light came on. It was quickly extinguished, but not before it illuminated a strange scene. All the men were dressed in dark green jungle fatigues and wearing combat boots. Their faces were streaked with camouflage paint, and they moved with a ghostly silence.

Heavily laden bergens were passed out and bags ripped open to reveal a variety of small arms and assorted ammunition pouches and bandoliers. Within minutes the men had their night-vision goggles on as they loaded up.

Kamigami handed Tel a Minimi light machine gun along with three ammo boxes of two hundred rounds and six thirty-round magazines. It was an awesome amount of firepower, and the light weapon could be used as a rifle in an attack. "You know how to use this?" Tel nodded in answer. "Good. I want the radio operator right behind me and you right behind him." While Tel shouldered his load, Kamigami spoke to the man carrying the patrol radio, a PRC319 set capable of sending and receiving short-burst encrypted messages. Satisfied that he was in contact with his four eight-man teams and that they had all adapted to night vision, he ordered them to move out. Tel fell in behind the radio operator, bent forward under his 180-pound load.

Two hours later Kamigami called for a quick-reaction drill, and the four teams went into defensive fire positions. Satisfied with their response, he transitioned into an ambush scenario. While less than happy with the way Team Alpha sited its fields of fire, he thought the covering and fallback teams were well situated. Rather than break radio silence, he passed the word to bivouac in place for the night. They would move out at first light. "Too difficult to move in the jungle at night," he told Tel. "We can make better time in the morning." He went to sleep.

The White House
Thursday, September 9

Shortly after Kamigami had drifted off to sleep, the ExCom gathered outside the Oval Office for their second meeting with the president that Thursday. Nancy Bender checked her watch. It was exactly 2:00 P.M. "She's with her campaign advisers, and—" Before she could finish, the door opened and four people trooped out of the Oval Office. There may have been a building crisis, but Madeline Turner was still driving her schedule. Mazie led the four men inside. Turner rested her elbows on her chair, folded her fingers together under her chin, and watched them as they sat down.

Mazie looked at the men and told the president the bad news. "Seven hundred and seventy-three as of midnight."

Turner's head came up. "Less than seventy-two hours into this and almost eight hundred casualties."

General Wilding made it worse. "That's KIA only."

The president did the math. "Ten an hour." She thought for a moment, trying to balance the personal with the political cost of the war. She wasn't sure if she could do it. "How much longer will it go on?"

Wilding didn't hesitate. "Another seventy-two hours at the earliest before we can stabilize."

"Does that mean another eight hundred killed?" she asked.

"Probably more," Wilding replied.

"We have the largest and best military in the world," Turner said. "Surely there's something we can do . . . tactically or strategically."

"Not unless we go nuclear," Wilding replied.

"Out of the question," Turner said.

Now it fell to Wilding to give his president a quick lesson in the realities of warfare. "Amateurs think of war in terms of strategy and tactics," he told her. "A professional thinks in terms of logistics. It takes a mountain of equipment to support even a small unit in the field." His voice was a monotone. "When a land power invades a neighboring country, the forces taking the brunt of the attack will experience heavy casualties until they are reinforced and their logistical base is in place."

Nothing betrayed the emotion Turner felt, and for all appearances she was the cool politician working toward a decision. "I was under the impression that the modern nature of war had changed all that."

Wilding's voice changed, now more that of the professor lecturing a student. "Ah, yes, future war based on high-tech, precision-guided weapons and information. All politically correct and trendy. But reality is different when you're facing a determined enemy who is fighting on his terms. For now all we can do is fight a holding action until we build up. Thanks to the Civil Air Reserve Fleet, the necessary troops are arriving in country, but until their equipment arrives, think of them as heavily armed tourists."

Kennett looked sick. "And we lost most of our predeployed equipment when King Khalid City fell."

"Which is why it was the UIF's first objective," the DCI added.

Wilding continued. "Fast Sealift Squadron One will sail from Savannah within twenty-four hours. That's eight ships with enough equipment to field a heavy division."

"How long before it arrives?" Turner asked.

Wilding ran the numbers. "It's eighty-seven hundred nautical miles and, averaging twenty-five knots, fifteen days. That assumes no breakdowns. Then the units still have to marry up with their equipment and check it out. Figure at least another four or five days before they deploy. So until those ships arrive, it's all airlift, and we simply don't have it. The Air Force is at max effort. Air Mobility Command has every airlifter they own in the system. Tactically, every available A-10 is in theater, and they are starting to make a difference. More F-16s and F-15 Strike Eagles are on the way."

She held up a hand and stopped him. "Do I need a full situation brief?"

"I could certainly use it, Mrs. President," Kennett replied.

Turner stood and led the way to the Situation Room, where the Marine colonel was waiting. "It's not a good afternoon, Madam President," Scovill said. He launched into his briefing, and, as warned, it was not good. "The center of the UIF's drive across the desert has slowed as it expands its flanks. They're trying for an end run, and so far we've blocked their eastern flank. But they're expanding to the west, into the desert."

A glimmer of hope crossed the president's face. "Does that mean the fighting has slowed as they maneuver?"

"No, ma'am, it doesn't. We're throwing everything we've got at them."

Again she had to ask the one question that couldn't be avoided. "Casualties?"

The colonel's reply was merciless. "As of an hour ago, eight hundred and sixty-five KIA, three hundred and ten missing in action. Of the three thousand wounded, slightly over two thousand have been evacuated."

"Why only two thousand?" she asked. "Surely those aircraft flying troops in can take them all out?"

"Many of the less seriously wounded have returned to their units," Scovill explained.

"Why?" Turner asked.

"They do it voluntarily. But we're replacing them as fast as we can."

"But why do they do it? I don't understand at all."

For a brief moment silence held them all. Finally Mazie started to talk. "One time in China, I asked Matt Pontowski the same question. He couldn't answer. But he did tell me the story of an Air Force colonel named Muddy Waters. Waters commanded the Forty-fifth Tactical Fighter Wing during the fiasco before the Gulf War."

"I remember that," Turner said. "That was before the Soviet Union collapsed, and everyone was worried it would turn into World War Three. As I recall, we withdrew the Forty-fifth at the last minute."

True to his nature, Bernie Butler had been hovering in the background and mostly listening. Now he had to talk. "Not exactly," he said. "The base was under heavy attack, and they had to fight their way out. Waters fought like a demon while he evacuated his people. But many of them wouldn't go at first. They wanted to stay with him and fight. He held on long enough to get most of them out, along with his last five aircraft. Waters gave the pilot who led those five aircraft, a Captain Jack Locke, his personal call sign before they took off. But Waters was killed before he could surrender the base."

"According to Matt," Mazie added, "Jack Locke was the finest leader he ever knew."

"Knew?" Turner asked.

"Locke was later killed in a training accident," Mazie said. "Matt said Locke set the standard, and he only hopes he can measure up." She searched for the right words. "It's like a torch they pass on, and for some reason it reminds me of the legend of the Phoenix—the giant bird of mythology that is consumed in the fire of its own nest and then arises reborn out of the ashes."

The Marine colonel shook his head. "It's not that complicated, Mrs. Hazelton. It's a combination of leadership and unit identification. They go back because that's where their buddies are."

Turner came to her feet, a decision made. "As of now I'm ordering an all-out effort. Pull out all the stops short of going nuclear." Anger filled her voice. "And let them know that option is *not* off the table."

Maddy retreated into her private study next to the Oval Office. "Nancy, please close the door. I don't want to be disturbed for a few moments."

"Yes, Madam President." Nancy closed the door and leaned against it, her eyes closed. *I wish I could help,* she thought. But no one could.

Maddy stared out the window as tears streaked her face.

The Plains of Pahang
Friday, September 10

Kamigami's internal alarm clock sounded, waking him up. Automatically, he checked his watch. He had been asleep three hours, and it was the beginning of morning twilight. He carefully shifted his weight and blinked twice. Tel was sitting against a tree devouring a cold meal pack. His Minimi and bergen were beside him, ready to go. "The rest of the men are ready," he told Kamigami.

"I must be getting old," Kamigami said. He called the team leaders together for a final briefing. "Nothing's changed," he told the four men. "This is a reconnaissance mission. Get your team into your assigned area as quickly as possible and find the bastards. I can't stress it enough—silence is golden. Transmission protocols are standard, and maintain radio silence to the maximum extent possible. Do not engage unless attacked. Shoot only if shot at, and then scoot for all you're worth. If you find anything that resembles a main camp, they'll be using motion detectors and urine sniffers to monitor the perimeter." He pointed at his map. "Our current location. Memorize the coordinates and rendezvous here in six days. Any questions?" There were none. "Okay, good hunting."

He listened as the four teams moved out. Satisfied that all was well, he hoisted his bergen. "Let me guess," Tel said, his voice barely audible. "We're going to the base camp."

Kamigami gave a little grunt as he settled the bergen on its shoulder straps. "Wouldn't hurt to pay them a visit." He set a fast pace, moving silently as they headed into the heart of the Taman Negara.

eleven

Oakland
Friday, September 10

D*on't jump to conclusions,* Bloomy cautioned herself for perhaps the hundredth time. She slowly rearranged the note cards on the table, searching for another pattern. But nothing else made sense. Feeling the need for a caffeine jolt, she checked the clock on the wall. It was exactly 9:00 A.M. She grabbed her empty coffee mug and walked briskly to the break room. The entire staff was there, oblivious to the television and transfixed by Matt Pontowski. He was leaning against a wall, his hands wrapped around a coffee mug. Bloomy filled her mug as she listened.

"General," one of the volunteer graduate students from UC Berkeley said, "eleven hundred have been killed so far. How much longer will this go on?"

"The number is one thousand ninety-five," Pontowski replied.

"What's five, more or less?" the grad student replied.

"A great deal, if you're one of the five. But you're right to be worried about the high casualties—as are the commanders."

"I seriously doubt that," the grad student said. He stood and walked out of the room, leaving a stunned silence behind him.

"General," Bloomy said, "I apologize for—"

Pontowski shook his head. "No apology is needed." He motioned at the screen, where an attractive young couple was dancing around a bed in an underwear commercial. "It's the fifth day of the war, and you're seeing raw, unedited coverage directly from the battlefield. What you're not getting is the big picture." He walked over to the map of Saudi Arabia tacked on the wall. He drew a broad, slashing arrow from Iraq through King Khalid Military City, with the arrowhead fifty miles to the south. "The UIF's goal is the capital, Riyadh, approximately a hundred and seventy miles away." He drew a flat, oblong circle under the arrowhead. "This is where the fighting is." Next he drew what looked like a set of horns on each side of the oblong circle, curving back toward Iraq. "As the UIF advances into Saudi Arabia, it must extend its flanks to the east and west, making the front much wider. This also reduces their mass in the center." He made the horn on the right, or eastern side, much longer than the horn on the west. "Slowly their eastern flank is extending, inviting a counterattack." He drew a perpendicular arrow from the right that pierced into the side of the arrow representing the UIF's advance.

"They must know that," a voice said.

"Indeed they do," Pontowski said. "That's why speed is critical. I figure they've got three weeks max to capture Riyadh before we have the forces in place to mount a major counterattack." He pointed to the TV, which now showed a dirty and tired reporter standing in front of a first-aid station.

"Peter," the reporter said, "I recorded the following scene thirty minutes ago, less than a mile from where I'm now standing." He turned and pointed to the north as the screen flickered, showing a squad of American soldiers hunkered down behind a low ridge as they moved a TOW antitank missile into position.

"Incoming!" a voice shouted. The scene twisted and turned as the cameraman jumped into a shallow depression. An explosion blasted smoke and debris over the camera lens, but the audio was still good.

"Oh, God!"

"Medic!"

"Shit! Sarge got it!"

A fourth voice took command. "Forget Sarge! Get that weapon in action!"

Before the screen could clear, Pontowski's calm voice was there. "The fact that the reporter had time to set up and broadcast so soon, and so close to the action, tells me the UIF is slowing down. The next two or three days are going to be critical, and I'm afraid we're going to lose a lot of good men before we can stop them."

Bloomy studied Pontowski's face as he spoke. *Had the president been like that?* she wondered. Suddenly she had to know.

Before he left his office that evening, Pontowski telephoned his son at NMMI. He listened to Zack's excitement over the TV coverage coming from the war and let him unwind. A knock at the door demanded his attention, and he turned around. Bloomy was standing in the doorway, nervously fingering a letter. "Zack," Pontowski said into the phone, "can I call you back in a few minutes?" He listened to the reply before he broke the connection. "What's up?"

"My resignation," Bloomy said. She handed him the letter.

The announcement stunned Pontowski. "Why? Is it something I've done?"

She shook her head. "The letter explains it."

He carefully read the letter while Bloomy waited nervously. "I think it's great you want to write Gramps's definitive biography. But why do you have to resign from the library to do it?"

"Because of what I might find," she answered.

He shook his head. "I don't think there's any big surprises lurking in the woodwork."

"There's the missing year," she said quietly.

His brows knitted in worry. "Have you found something?"

Again she was certain that he knew. "There is a most unusual pattern that I can't explain."

Pontowski kicked back in his chair. "The only thing that matters is the truth. So find it."

Bloomy couldn't believe what she was hearing. "No other conditions?"

"None."

"Why?"

"Because I trust you to do the right thing." He handed back the letter. She gave a little nod and quickly left. Pontowski stared at the vacant doorway for a moment and gave a little shake of his head. *You're in for some real shockers. But better you than someone else.* He hit the speed dial to telephone his son.

"Zack," he said, "you calmed down yet?" He listened for a moment. "Hey, you're not even sixteen yet. This ain't your war to miss."

The White House
Friday, September 10

"It's a good one," Shaw said as the crew filming the TV clip quickly cleared the Oval Office. More and more, Shaw was managing Turner's election campaign and portraying the president as a resolute but embattled leader in the mode of Winston Churchill. She leaned back in her chair, taking a few moments to relax. "I've got Sam slated to cover the talking heads Sunday," Shaw told her. The talking heads were the Sunday-morning political talk show pundits. "Unfortunately, he's on with Leland."

"I think the vice president is more than capable of handling the good senator," she said. A vision of Sam Kennett strangling Leland with his one hand on national TV played in her mind.

Nancy Bender appeared in the doorway as an assistant straightened the office. "The deputy chairman of the Joint Chiefs is on six," Nancy said. Button six on the intercom was the hot line to the National Military Command Center in the Pentagon. Nancy closed the door to give her privacy.

Turner picked up the phone. "Good morning, General." She listened for a few moments and closed her eyes. "No, he hasn't arrived yet. I'll tell him." She dropped the phone in its cradle and looked at Shaw. "General Wilding is on his way from the Pentagon for a meeting with the ExCom. Please show him in the moment he arrives. I need to speak to him in private."

Her look told Shaw everything. "Yes, Madam President." He quickly walked to the entrance to the West Wing to wait for the chairman of the Joint Chiefs. The Army staff car arrived exactly four minutes later. "The president would like to speak to you," Shaw told Wilding. "Alone," he added. *Please read me right on this and get your act together,* he mentally begged. The general jerked his head yes and handed his aide his briefcase.

Maddy came to her feet the moment Shaw ushered Wilding into the Oval Office. She took a little swallow as the door closed behind him, leaving them alone. "I'm afraid there's bad news, General. We just received news that your son was . . ." She swallowed harder, hating what she had to say. "Killed in action." She reached out to touch him but thought better of it. For a brief moment she was back in time, telling another general that his only child, his daughter, had been killed in an aircraft accident. "Is there anything I can do?"

Wilding's eyes turned misty. "Thank you, Madam President, but no." Unbidden, he sat down on a couch. She joined him and waited. The general looked at her. "It was what he wanted, to lead men in combat. He knew the risks. He once told me that he would rather be killed than taken prisoner."

"Because of who you are?" she asked.

Wilding shook his head. "No. Because of who he was." A long pause. "I think he knew he didn't have much time. He did everything at full speed. He turned down an appointment to West Point so he could finish college early. Did it in two and a half years and earned a commission through ROTC. But you have to be twenty-one to be an officer, so he enlisted and went armor. He loved those machines. The day he turned twenty-one, I administered his commissioning oath. By then he had two children." He stared at his hands. "He saw this coming and moved heaven and earth to get to Saudi Arabia."

Maddy had to ask the question. "Did he use your influence?"

Wilding gave a little snort. "Out of the question. For a moment I almost did intervene and cancel his assignment. But he would've disowned me and transferred to the Marines. He told me so."

"I have considered keeping the children of flag officers from combat, at least when their parent is on active duty."

"Save that for the politicians." The general stood up. "Madam President, please excuse me. I need to tell my wife."

"Certainly."

Now he was the military professional again, rigid and unbending, determined to answer the call to duty. He hesitated for a moment.

"Madam President, I must warn you. The next thirty-six to forty-eight hours are going to be horrendous. But it's either fight or surrender." She stared at him in shock. She had never thought of it in those terms.

Maddy nodded. "Thank you, General, but surrendering is not an option. Take care of your wife and family."

You're part of my family, too, Wilding thought. "I'll be back in an hour."

Taman Negara
Sunday, September 12

A small bean pod bounced off Kamigami, and he looked up. An unbroken jungle canopy stretched over him, effectively hiding the sun. High above his head, Tel's hand emerged from foliage. Two fingers made a V sign, followed by a finger pointing at the base camp. Tel made a fist, and then fingers extended as he counted. The hand disappeared back into the foliage. *Nine enemy in camp,* Kamigami thought. They had been watching the old base camp for two days, and this was the first sign of activity.

A few minutes later the radio operator motioned to Kamigami when the LED display on the PRC319 radio flashed. A message was coming in. He entered the decryption code on the keypad, the screen blinked, and the message started to scroll. Delta Team under Lieutenant Lee operating in the north sector had finally reached their objective, some fifty miles north of Kamigami's position. *They made good time,* Kamigami conceded. *But not worth breaking radio silence.* He made a mental note to knock some heads when they got back to the island. The radio operator scrolled the message. Delta team had discovered a wide and well-constructed dirt road hidden underneath the tree canopy. A diesel-powered, eight-wheeled vehicle carrying a forty-foot missile had passed their position and was heading south. Two support trucks accompanied it. Again the message scrolled. Unless otherwise directed, Lee was going to recce the road to the north.

Kamigami nodded. He had been premature in deciding to knock heads. *Good thinking. Silence implies consent.* Another bean pod bounced off his head, and he looked up again. Tel's hand was sticking out of his perch high in the tree and moving furiously. A large number of men were returning to the base camp. Kamigami checked his watch. Forty minutes to sunset. He looked up and flashed a hand signal for Tel to climb down when it was dark. Now he had to wait, something he was very used to. He went to sleep.

Tel nudged him awake forty-five minutes later. "Over two hundred men and women returned to camp," he said in a low voice. "They came down the road from the north and were carrying shovels, picks, buckets, things like that."

"Sounds like a work detail building the road," Kamigami said. He showed Tel the message that had come in earlier. "We need to find out if that missile is headed for one of those tunnels dug in the ridge." He thought for a moment. "Too many people around now. We need to pull back." Within minutes the three men were up and moving, with Tel in the lead. They had gone less than fifty meters when Tel made a waving motion by his ear and pointed straight ahead. He had heard something. Kamigami quieted his breathing and closed his eyes. He was not straining to hear but in a receptive mode. Finally, over the slight ringing in his ears that plagued him, he also heard it. A man and a woman were talking softly. Kamigami flashed a hand signal, and the three of them melted into the brush.

After a few moments the voices changed into moans and breathless pants. The couple was making love. It didn't last long, less than a minute, and the man started talking much more loudly. He spoke in Chinese and was anxious to get back to the camp. The girl protested in the same language, demanding that he treat her with respect. They walked by, less than six feet from Kamigami, easy targets. *How old are they?* he thought. *Eighteen? Nineteen? How do you tell turbocharged teenagers that sex in a combat zone can kill you? Where the hell are their commanders?*

They waited to ensure that no one else was wandering around in the dark in search of more nocturnal pastimes. Kamigami didn't stir for over an hour and was ready to move out when the distinctive sound of a diesel engine drifted up the path. He came to his feet, but Tel was already moving, ghosting down the path leading to the Tembeling River. Kamigami followed and immediately lost contact.

"Here," Tel said in a low voice. Kamigami followed the sound and almost stepped on him in the dark. The big man dropped to the ground, and Tel pushed a low branch aside. The big open area was directly below them, and they could see lights in the three tunnels. The sound of the diesel engine grew louder, and finally an eight-wheeled, camouflaged vehicle carrying a missile emerged from the jungle. "Scud," he said to Tel.

"The Chinese don't have Scuds," Tel replied.

"They do now."

Tel pulled out his camera to photograph it as Kamigami pointed to his radio operator and signaled for the detachable keypad. He punched at the keys with his blunt fingers. Frustrated with the small keys, he handed the keypad to Tel. "Retransmit Delta Team's message to GHQ. Also tell them we found a Scud at these coordinates." Tel drafted the message to General Headquarters in Singapore and handed the keypad back to the radio operator. Kamigami motioned for the other keyboard to send a second message. He used a pencil to punch in a simple RETURN TO RENDEZVOUS ASAP and keyed the code that sent it to his four teams. He stood and motioned at Tel and the radio operator. "Time to get the hell out of Dodge."

twelve

Washington, D.C.
Sunday, September 12

The guard at the security checkpoint on the Pentagon's main concourse recognized Pontowski and quickly came to his feet. "Good morning, sir." He stood at half attention as Pontowski signed in.

"Busy for a Sunday morning," Pontowski said.

"Hasn't been like this since the Gulf War in '91," the guard replied. "The place is going crazy." He glanced at his clipboard and noted the office Pontowski was visiting, then handed him a visitor's badge. "Take the first set of stairs to the basement," he said as Pontowski passed through the turnstile.

Pontowski followed the basement corridor to the purple water fountain everyone used as a reference point. "Almost there," he said to himself. He stopped in front of a heavy steel door and waited. The lock clicked, and he pushed the door open. Bernie Butler was waiting inside. "Thanks for coming," Butler said as they walked down a narrow hall.

"How bad is it?" Pontowski asked.

"In the Gulf? I think we're over the hump. We should stabilize in the next few hours."

"How's Maddy doing?"

"She's a rock," Butler replied. "But the casualties are causing her a problem. Over four hundred KIA in the last twenty-four hours. The media are starting to make it a major issue. But she's handling it."

"I was thinking of the personal cost," Pontowski said.

"It's high," Butler replied. "I saw it when she told General Wilding that his son was killed fighting a rear-guard action. He held the center for ten hours with eight tanks. Completely stopped the UIF advance while a Marine battalion retrograded in force. He was twenty-three years old." Butler pushed open the door to his cramped office, where a tall, elderly man was waiting. "Matt, I'd like you to meet Mr. Deng Shikai from Singapore."

The man extended his hand. "Please, call me Gus."

"I know who you are, sir," Pontowski said, shaking his hand. Pontowski looked at the two men. "I'm not here because of the Gulf, am I?"

Butler shook his head and motioned them to seats. "We have a problem on the Malay Peninsula." He handed Pontowski a folder holding two messages Kamigami's team had sent to Central Headquarters in Singapore.

Pontowski quickly read the messages. "Your people send these?" he asked Gus. A nod answered him. "I'm not impressed."

Gus said, "Victor Kamigami identified the Scud." Pontowski arched an eyebrow but didn't respond. "Also," Gus continued, "there's a large contingent of regular PLA operating in the area."

Pontowski's head came up at the mention of China's People's Liberation Army. Gus had his undivided attention. "How large and what are they doing?"

Gus's voice was matter-of-fact. "Their exact size is unknown, but special units destroyed several Malaysian villages. That set off a series of reprisals between Malay and Chinese villagers, which has turned into a full-blown civil war between the Malays and local Chinese. As a result, Chinese villagers are turning to the PLA for protection. In fact, Kamigami's kampong was the first target, and his family was slaughtered."

"That was a very bad mistake," Pontowski said.

Gus nodded. "That's why I was able to recruit him for our Special Operations Service." Butler handed Pontowski a map, and Gus pointed to the Taman Negara. "The Chinese have built underground bunkers at this location. Which is where Kamigami found the Scud."

"The Chinese don't have Scuds," Pontowski said. "So where did it come from? Why not a CSS-7? That's a much better missile."

"North Korea supplied the Scuds," Gus said. "We believe that the Chinese want to appear as indigenous rebels supported by radical Islamic factions."

"And the Scud is part of their cover," Pontowski said.

Gus agreed. "It appears so. We also have reports of numerous small Chinese ships operating off the northeastern coast of Malaysia."

"Why Malaysia?" Pontowski asked.

"We have reason to believe," Butler said, "that their objective is Singapore and the Strait of Malacca." He was treading a thin line with Pontowski and was over the line with Gus. He could not tell either of them what he knew, and had to protect his sources at all costs. That was part of his business. It was only when Gus had contacted one of the Boys asking for help that Butler had gotten involved and asked Gus to come to Washington for "discussions."

Pontowski frowned. "From one of your unimpeachable sources?" Butler ignored the sarcasm. "I can see the Chinese stirring up a civil war," Pontowski continued, "but chancing a major war to gain control of the Strait? No way. The Chinese coerce and punish, they don't invade and occupy."

Butler thought for a moment. He wanted to involve Pontowski, but what would it take to convince him? He could never reveal that his source was Jin Chu, Zou Rong's consort. "Let's just say we believe there's a substantial threat there."

Pontowski studied the map in his hands. "And you've got to honor the threat. Why are you telling me all this?"

"Because," Butler said, "we want you to spearhead the U.S. response."

Pontowski was incredulous. "What U.S. response?" The pieces fell into place even as he said it. "I see."

"Do you?" Butler asked.

"Yeah, I do. If China's objective is to capture Singapore and control the Strait, we've got to get involved. Which right now we can't do because we're up to our ass in alligators in the Middle East. That means we have to adapt a win-hold-win strategy. Win in the Middle East while we hold in Malaysia—then redeploy to Malaysia in time to win there. I think that strategy, for lack of a better word, sucks. You say 'response' and I hear 'hostage force.' No, thank you very much. I'm not your boy." He paused to let it register. "I've bounced between here and the West Coast so much

I feel like a Ping-Pong ball that qualifies for frequent-flier miles." He headed for the door. "I've got a library to run."

"Since you're here," Butler asked, "can you wait at least twenty-four hours?" Pontowski skidded to a stop and hesitated. "I'll owe you," Butler added, upping the ante.

"Twenty-four hours," Pontowski muttered. He disappeared out the door.

The two men looked at each other. "What now?" Gus asked.

Butler reached for the telephone and dialed a number. "How would you like to meet the secretary of state?"

For one of the rare times in his life, Gus showed surprise. "What are you up to?"

"Taking it one bite at a time."

Gus tried hard to be inscrutable, but he knew that Butler could read him like an open book. Both men believed that the United States would have to be dragged kicking and screaming into the coming conflict on the Malay Peninsula. The best way to make that happen was to have a U.S. presence in place that could be quickly overrun, thereby forcing the politicians to do something. But it was a sword that cut two ways. By having a so-called hostage, or trip-wire, force in place, a potential enemy might be discouraged from attacking because it would guarantee a U.S. response. It had worked with the Berlin garrison during the Cold War. "You want Pontowski for the . . . ah, trip wire?"

Butler gave him a hard look. "He's no bleating sheep being led to the slaughter. He fights back."

Butler was waiting when Mazie arrived for the ExCom's Sunday meeting in the Situation Room. Without a word he handed her a thin folder containing a threat estimate for the Malay Peninsula and the same two messages Pontowski had seen. She read through it and shrugged. "Worrisome but not critical."

"And if I said we had a very reliable source confirming the threat?"

"It depends on your source," Mazie replied.

Butler knew what he had to do, and it grated on every instinct, every bit of tradecraft he believed in. He had to compromise his source to gain the support he needed. "Jin Chu. She contacted us."

"The ExCom needs to see this," she told him. He didn't reply. "You don't want to reveal your source, right?"

"You know how the CIA works."

"Unfortunately," Mazie murmured. The CIA would "validate" Jin Chu and, in the process, reveal their interest in her. That, in turn, could be a death sentence. "I doubt if the DCI would buy it even if he knew." They waited in silence. Wilding soon entered, and Mazie passed him the folder. "You need to read this."

The DCI slipped into the room. But before he could sit down, Secretary of State Serick burst through the door. "We have problems in Malaysia." He stamped his cane for emphasis and then sat. "I've been in conversation with a Mr. Deng Shikai . . . very well connected in the Singapore government. He claims the Chinese are set to mount a major offensive on the Malay Peninsula to capture Singapore and the Strait of Malacca."

"Nonsense," the DCI said. Wilding shoved the folder across the table for him to read. He did and then closed the folder with a firm finality. "Someone's obsessing."

"We can't ignore it," Mazie told him.

Wilding punched at a hand controller, and one of the computer monitors came to life with a listing of the United States' order of battle that enumerated all the forces available for deployment. "We don't have the capability to respond. We're fully committed to the Gulf. At best we could mount a win-hold-win strategy."

"That would be political suicide," Serick said. "Leland would see to that."

"So what do we tell the president?" Mazie asked.

At that very moment Maddy was in the residence enjoying herself. It was a rare moment as she watched the vice president spar with Leland on *Meet the Press.* Kennett had effectively boxed the wily senator into a corner, making him choose between selling out America's troops in combat, as well as its allies, and continuing to fight. "The choice is yours to make, Senator."

The camera zoomed in on Leland's face. "That choice will be forced on the president," Leland shot back. "Look at the casualties. She alone is responsible for this slaughter. And it is not a matter of selling out our allies. France has been against this from the very first and can still broker a cease-fire. We need to listen to our allies, not act unilaterally when it is against our best interests. The UIF will need a market for its oil. The industrialized West is that market. There are workable options here."

"Defeat is a workable option?" Kennett asked.

The moderator interrupted them. "Gentlemen, we've just received a report from Malaysia that I believe you'll be interested in." He turned to the screen behind him.

They watched as a reporter stood on the rooftop of a hotel and described the chaos below him. "Widespread rioting erupted today in Kuala Lumpur following nerve-gas attacks on three bus stations. Mobs of angry Malays blame the Chinese and are looting and burning Chinese homes and businesses. Farther south, Singapore police arrested eight terrorists at Changi Airport. All eight were from Malaysia and suspected of being involved with the attacks here."

Maddy gave a little grimace and clicked off the TV when her personal assistant entered the room. "Madam President," Nancy said, "the ExCom is waiting in the Situation Room. Secretary Serick is with them."

The president read Butler's threat estimate in less than thirty seconds and looked around the table. "How serious is this?"

"Given the recent news from Kuala Lumpur," Serick said, taking the lead, "I don't think we can ignore it."

Turner came to her feet and paced the length of the room. "Why is it that we live in a world where we have to use force to make people live peacefully together?" There was no reasonable answer to her question, and she knew it.

"This is a local problem," the DCI said. "What we're seeing is a combination of economics and ethnic hatreds. Rather than addressing the basic economic problem, the government is making a scapegoat of the Chinese minority. The Chinese are fighting back. It's a situation that we do not—I repeat, *do not*—have to address at this time."

"Madam President," Serick said, his voice calm and reasoned, "in conversations with a representative from the Singapore government, a Mr. Deng, I have learned that Singapore, Malaysia, Thailand, and Indonesia are very concerned. In fact, they are forming a military alliance—

Southeast Asia Command, SEAC—under the provisions of the Southeast Treaty Organization."

"I thought SEATO was alive in name only," she said.

"Indeed it was," the secretary of state replied. "But this threat has breathed new life into it. Singapore is taking the lead."

"Chinese fighting Chinese?" the DCI scoffed. "I find that hard to believe."

"The Singaporeans know what's at stake here," Serick replied.

Vice President Kennett entered and sat down. Mazie handed him Butler's threat estimate to read. "We don't need this," he said, thinking about his recent argument with Leland.

The DCI decided it was time to set it all in perspective and establish his authority. "Madam President, I have analysts spending twenty-four hours a day, seven days a week, monitoring every area of the world. They are area specialists and intimately familiar with local conditions. Neither they, the NRO, the NSA, nor the State Department has turned up any evidence to even suggest that this is more than an indigenous group of angry farmers and dissatisfied ethnic groups."

"Who have Scuds and nerve gas," Butler said in a stage whisper.

The DCI ignored him. "We have more important things to consider and are wasting too much time on this."

Mazie sensed it was the right moment to intervene. She glanced at Butler, and he gave a little nod. "Can SEATO handle this alone?"

"Absolutely," the DCI said.

"They're going to need help," Butler said.

"After talking with Mr. Deng," Serick said, "I agree."

Wilding thought for a moment. "We have a Military Advisory and Assistance Group attached to the Singapore diplomatic mission. We can funnel aid to SEATO through it."

Butler felt like cheering. But, true to his nature, he said nothing.

"Sam," Mazie said, "what's the political downside with Leland?"

The vice president considered it. "He'll howl a bit. But we can handle him."

Mazie turned to the secretary of state. "How do we signal to both sides that we're serious?"

"It's quite simple," Serick answered. "We send a high-ranking and prominent officer to head the MAAG."

"Who do you suggest?" Turner asked.

Mazie glanced at the president and took her cue. "Matt Pontowski."

Butler gave a little cough, gaining their attention. "Matt's not really an administrator. He's more operationally oriented and at his best in command of a combat unit. I doubt if he'll be interested in a MAAG."

"So what do you suggest?" Mazie replied.

"Sweeten the offer. Say, reactivate the AVG?"

The DCI was shouting. "The American Volunteer Group? Not necessary!"

As one, six heads turned to the president. "I'll ask him," she said.

A uniformed Secret Service agent escorted Pontowski down the long corridor to the national security adviser's office in the Old Executive Office Building. The number of guards was mute testimony to the increase in security. The agent held the door and stepped back, allowing Pontowski to enter. Butler was waiting inside. "I should have known," Pontowski said.

"My apologies," Butler said. "I handled it wrong. Mazie will fill you in." He led the way into Mazie's office. "I don't believe you've met General Wilding," Butler said, making the introductions. "And this is Colonel Prouder." An Air Force colonel stood. "Colonel Prouder is from Checkmate." Checkmate was a shadowy organization in the Pentagon that hovered in the background, always present when trouble reared its ugly head. Originally Checkmate was formed to integrate intelligence, threat assessments, targeting, and weapons capabilities into effective air campaigns. But in the international chaos following the demise of the Soviet Union, it had grown into much more.

"I didn't know you were involved with Checkmate," Pontowski said.

"Since its inception," Butler replied.

"When you wake up in the morning," Pontowski asked, "do you know who you work for?"

"He knows," Mazie said. "Matt, the situation in Malaysia has the potential to escalate into a full-fledged civil war that could threaten the stability of the entire region. Fortunately, our allies in the region are aware of the danger and responding. SEATO has activated SEAC, South East Asia Command, and formed a unified command. But they need help."

"So why am I here?" Pontowski muttered.

"We want you to head up the MAAG in Singapore," Mazie explained.

Wilding handed Pontowski the folder he was carrying. "Here's what we can offer SEAC." He sat back and folded his hands, waiting for the inevitable reaction. It wasn't long in coming.

Pontowski scanned the document and shook his head. "They can do better at a war-surplus store."

"Between the war on terrorism and the Gulf," Wilding explained, "we're maxed out."

"Obviously," Pontowski shot back. "So where am I to get the means to make a difference?" There was no answer. "This," Pontowski grumbled, "is turning into the proverbial goat rope. Get honest with me, folks. Earlier you tell me that the Chinese are lusting after Singapore and the Strait. Now you tell me that SEAC can handle it but they just need a little help, which we can't really provide but are going to do anyway. So what's it really going to take to do the job?"

Butler said, "That's why Colonel Prouder is here."

"We've run it through Checkmate's computers," Prouder began.

Pontowski interrupted him. "The dreaded threat-and-capability analysis?"

Butler heard the sarcasm in his voice. "It does work," he said.

"Like in the Gulf?" Pontowski asked.

Prouder folded his hands and looked at General Wilding—an obvious challenge. Wilding did the mental equivalent of biting the bullet and said, "One of the Middle East threat scenarios Checkmate produced bordered on the prophetic."

"Then why were we blindsided?" Pontowski demanded.

"Because Secretary of Defense Merritt," Wilding said, "refused to forward it. It stayed in-house."

Pontowski shook his head in disgust. "Politics."

"You will notice," Mazie said, "that Merritt is not here."

"So what does your threat-and-capability analysis tell you about Malaysia?" Pontowski asked.

"SEAC needs tactical air support," Prouder replied.

"Why do I feel like a virgin being led down the primrose path?" Pontowski asked.

"This is not a hostage force," Mazie assured him. "In addition to serving as the head of the MAAG, we want you to reactivate the American Volunteer Group. If you can find the pilots, we can provide twenty A-10s."

Suddenly Pontowski was more alive than he'd been in over a year. "Where are the Hogs coming from?"

"Don't ask," Wilding replied.

thirteen

Palau Tenang
Monday, September 13

It was the little things that impressed Kamigami as he walked through the compound with Colonel Sun—the way the men talked quietly among themselves, the slight changes in equipment that stressed function over spit and polish, a lean and hungry look, and even the occasional can of Skoal chewing tobacco. "A big change in six days," he said.

"It was always there," Colonel Sun replied. "We only had to let it come out." Sun pulled into himself for a moment, trying to give meaning to what had happened. "It seemed the more we cut our size, the more we . . ." He paused, searching for the right words.

"The more you became focused," Kamigami said. "It's all about battle discipline. What made the difference?"

"The swim," Sun replied. "When Tel was in training, he told about the time you and he had to swim ashore. Did you know he was afraid of the water and could hardly swim before then?" Kamigami looked at the colonel in surprise. "So," Sun continued, "I decided it was time we went for a swim. All of us. Four kilometers. Two men drowned, and we think a shark got another. The next day forty-two men resigned. But not the men I expected to quit. In fact, many were the ones I was counting on. I was worried what it would do to morale, but didn't have a choice. The change was almost immediate, as if some major obstacle had been removed."

"It's often like that," Kamigami said quietly.

Sun nodded. "After that it was easy. I reorganized into two squadrons—Tiger Red and Dragon Gold. Sixty men each."

"So that explains the gold berets," Kamigami murmured. "But are they good?"

Sun nodded. "The best."

"You sound convinced."

"I trained them. I'd bet my life on it."

"You may have to," Kamigami said. He gave Sun a sideways look. The short, wiry colonel seemed taller than before. "What about the command post?"

"We're not going to blow it up," Sun answered. He waited for Kamigami's reaction as they stood in the morning sun. But Kamigami said nothing. "We're using it for training."

Tel emerged from the brush where the temporary command post was located, and joined them. "From Gus," he said. He handed over a message and waited while Kamigami read it. Acting on a tip, the police had arrested eight Chinese men at Changi Airport before they could board a Air China flight to Hong Kong. All were members of the PLA and suspected of being involved with the nerve-gas attacks in Kuala Lumpur.

"No doubt," Kamigami said, handing the message back, "the tip was from Gus."

He turned to Sun. "I'd like to see a training exercise."

Sun's wicked grin was back. "My pleasure." He spun around and walked away without saluting. He beckoned for the two remaining squadron commanders to join him and issued quiet orders. He was back in less than two minutes. "This will be a live-fire hostage exercise." Kamigami arched an eyebrow in surprise. Live-fire exercises were iffy at best, and to use live ammunition in a confined space was asking for trouble. "Our best team will do the demonstration," Sun explained. "They've done this many times before." The four men detailed for the exercise joined them. Each was equipped differently, but all carried a Heckler & Koch MP5 with a silencer and thirty-round clip. Sun knelt and drew a sketch of the command post in the hard dirt as he reviewed the rules of engagement. "This will be a live-fire exercise with dummies. Reliable sources report there may be two terrorists, maybe more, holding a single hostage inside. Your assignment is to extract the hostage unharmed and kill the terrorists. I'll place the dummies, and you go in five minutes. Any questions?" There were none. Sun nodded and disappeared inside as the men took their places outside the main entrance.

Exactly five minutes later the four men slipped through the main entrance in order: low man, high man, cover, and backup. Kamigami and the two squadron commanders followed at a safe distance. The men moved without making a sound, and the fourth man moved backward, covering their rear, relying on the third man to warn him of any obstacles. At the first door they stacked against the wall, boot touching boot. The leader sent a signal down the line by reaching back and touching the arm of the man behind him. When the backup man was in place and the rear clear, he sent a signal up the line by touching the thigh of the man in front of him. The leader knelt and held a listening probe against the door, listening for the sounds of breathing. Satisfied that the room was empty, he gave a signal and they moved quickly, keying off boot movement. The low man threw open the door and buttonhooked around to the left, while the high man went through at an oblique angle, clearing the room.

Within seconds they were out, and the team flowed down the half-lit corridor, repeating the drill at the second room. At the third door the leader listened and held up a finger, then two, finally three. Three people were in the room. He pointed to the left, the middle, then the right side of the room, signaling where he thought the sounds were coming from. He stowed the listening probe and removed his headset. Again his hands flashed, signing his intentions. He crossed to the other side of the inward-opening door, next to the latch, and readied a concussion grenade commonly called a flash-bang. The second man reached for the door latch and, on signal, tested it. In one quick, smooth motion he cracked the door open. The leader threw in the flash-bang, and the second man slammed the door shut. A bright light flashed through the cracks around the door, and a loud bang echoed from inside.

The leader threw the door open, and the second man burst through at an angle. The leader followed him at a cross angle. Both fired in short bursts as they entered. There was no deafening clatter of submachine-gun fire but only a popping sound mixed with the clatter of bolt actions and spent cartridges hitting the floor. The stun grenade had blown out the lightbulbs, and they were firing in almost total darkness. Then it was silent, and the third man, who was now crouched beside the door, directed the beam of his flashlight into the room, making sure he was shielded from any return fire a terrorist might send his way. "All clear," Colonel Sun said from inside.

"What the—" Kamigami muttered. He pushed into the room with two majors close behind. Three dummies were lying on the floor, their upper torsos shattered by gunfire. It was a mute tribute to the accuracy of the two shooters and the horrible efficiency of the MP5 at close range. But instead of a dummy in the chair, Sun was sitting there, a rope looped around his body to make him look like a hostage.

"Good shooting," Sun said.

Kamigami allowed a rare excursion into profanity. "Damn, Colonel. You could've been killed."

"I told you they were the best," Sun replied, "and I am willing to bet my life on them."

The first shooter sank to the floor on one knee, shaking slightly. "I didn't expect to find a live person in here." His voice cracked with emotion.

"What did you expect to find?" Sun demanded.

The second shooter blurted an answer. "We expected to find terrorists who we were to service."

Kamigami's words were barely audible. "Does that mean kill them?"

The first shooter stood up, still struggling to control his emotions. "Yes, sir. Two bullets in each head."

"And are there?" Sun shot back.

Kamigami examined the three mannequins. "There are," he said. "Very good." It was a rarc compliment, and the men knew it. Kamigami paused for a moment. "Outside." He led the way out of the building, to where Tel was waiting. "Please show Colonel Sun the message," he said. Tel extracted the message from a shirt pocket and handed it over.

A slight flexing of Sun's fingers betrayed what he was thinking as he read the message. Then he read it a second time. "Eight 'terrorists' in custody. Most interesting."

"What do you think we should do about it?" Kamigami asked.

"Interview them," Sun said.

"My thoughts exactly." Kamigami suppressed a smile. Without doubt, Sun was the commander he needed.

The White House
Monday, September 13

Shaw stood in the doorway of the Green Room as the reporters took their seats for the Monday-morning press conference in the East Room. Normally they reminded him of a flock of magpies, talking and jabbering among themselves. But this time they sat quietly and studied their notes. "They're loaded for bear," he told Pontowski. "You just tag along behind the others and stand against the wall. I imagine them id-jits will figure you're here for a reason, and that may distract them. The president wants you to say a few words when she announces your appointment. Keep it brief. The fewer words the better." A voice spoke in his earphone telling him the president was ready. "Okay, you're on," he told the small group standing bchind him.

Vice President Kennett led Serick and Merritt, along with General Wilding, out the door. Pontowski fell in behind and, as Shaw had directed, stood against the wall. In unison, the three TV cameras panned around to him but immediately swung back to focus on Madeline Turner as she walked down the main hall toward the East Room. As always, she entered alone, holding a slim leather folder in the crook of her left arm. "Ladies and gentlemen," the press secretary intoned, "the President of the United States." Everyone stood, and an eerie silence descended over the room.

Turner stepped up to the podium and opened the folder as the reporters shuffled back into their seats. "I want to thank you all for being so patient. I hope we can meet more frequently after this. Before I answer your questions, I do have an announcement. Central Command reports they have halted the enemy's advance on a line approximately one hundred miles north of the Saudi capital of Riyadh. For now the fighting has all but stopped, and we have suffered only three wounded in the last twenty-four hours. How long this will last, I can't say. But if I may quote a former president, 'This aggression will not stand.'"

She lifted her head and looked directly into the cameras. "We have paid a horrendous price, and eighteen hundred and two of our valiant soldiers have given their lives in the cause of peace. We will not forget their sacrifice." She nodded in the direction of the dean of the press corps.

"Madam President," he asked, "it appears we are stalemated. Is this turning into a 'phony war,' and what happened to our European allies?"

"There is nothing 'phony' about this war, and we will go on the offensive. But it's not going to happen in the next few days. When it does, the issue will not be in doubt. As to our allies, you are all aware that the debate in the United Nations has stagnated. But England is sending three squadrons of fighters and two regiments. They should be in place within a few days."

Shaw retreated into the Green Room and stood in front of a bank of TVs watching the coverage. He listened carefully as Turner answered question after question, never once losing her way. When one reporter asked if it wasn't all about oil, she fixed him with a steely look and cut him dead. "Only from their perspective."

"Well done, Madam President," Shaw said. He licked his lips in anticipation of what was coming. He didn't have to wait long.

"Madam President," the reporter from *Japan News* asked, "how serious are the riots and killings sweeping through Kuala Lumpur?"

"We view it as a very serious problem, but from all reports the authorities are gaining control. SEATO has asked for our help, and we are responding accordingly. To that end I am strengthening the presence of our Military Assistance Advisory Group in the area. Brigadier General Matthew Pontowski has agreed to head the mission." She turned to Pontowski and gestured for him to come forward. The TV cameras zoomed in as he stepped to the podium. "General Pontowski," Turner said, "has commanded advisory groups in the past in Asia and South Africa." She stepped aside for him to speak.

"Thank you, Madam President. I do appreciate your trust in me and hope we can achieve what has been done in the past, namely, to help our allies so they can help themselves." He stepped back.

In the Green Room, Shaw shook his head in admiration. "And I thought I knew how to spin it."

"Madam President," Liz Gordon from CNC-TV called. "Earlier today Senator Leland said our allies are not supporting the war in Saudi Arabia because of your leadership."

Turner never missed a beat. "I hadn't heard that. I have talked to Senator Leland, and we have disagreed on the conduct of the war. I can tell you this: I have set the broad objectives and trust our men and women in uniform to achieve them. Our military goal is simple—we will stop this aggression and drive the invaders back. We will hold them accountable in a way that is fair to those they have hurt and, yes, even to their own people. Of course, the good senator is entitled to his opinion, but I do hope he will work with us in a constructive way."

In the Green Room, Shaw's eyes narrowed into tight slits. "Leland, you make a damn good case for retroactive abortion." He exhaled deeply. "Learn from the past or get bit in the ass."

Jurong Camp, Singapore
Tuesday, September 14

"This way, please," the colonel said as he escorted Kamigami and Gus across the immaculate grounds of the Armed Forces Training Institute. Colonel Sun and Tel followed at a respectful distance. "We conduct most of our advanced professional military education here," the colonel explained. He led the way into what looked like an armory. "We're holding them in isolation."

"Have they been interrogated?" Gus asked.

"Yes," came the answer, "but we learned very little."

"Do you know which one is the leader?" This from Kamigami. The colonel shook his head. "I need to see them together," Kamigami said. "But bring them in one at a time. The order makes no difference. Keep them bagged."

The colonel issued the necessary orders. "At this point," he explained, "we're not sure if they had anything to do with the riots in Kuala Lumpur."

"We'll soon know," Kamigami said. His voice was so soft and low that it was barely audible. Guards brought in the eight suspected terrorists one at a time. Each one was handcuffed, with a canvas bag over his head. The moment one cleared the door, Kamigami grabbed him by the shirt and slammed him into a chair. "Don't move," he ordered in Cantonese. When all eight had been brought in and seated, he walked up to one and grabbed the canvas bag. He gave it a good shake and ripped it off. The man blinked in the bright light as Kamigami loomed over him. "Who is your leader?"

The man stared at Kamigami in defiance and said nothing. Kamigami hooked his rigid fingers under the man's jaw and lifted him out of his seat. He banged the man's head against the low ceiling before dropping him to the floor. He placed his right foot over the supine man's Adam's apple and started to bear down.

The man's eyes darted to a man sitting across the circle, and Kamigami lifted his foot. The man nodded in the same direction, as if to confirm that that individual was their leader. Kamigami lifted the man off the floor and dumped him in his chair before walking over to Tel. He spoke in English, a mere whisper. "Watch his face." He then circled behind the men, not making a sound as he fingered the gold whistle dangling around his neck. He stopped behind the supposed leader and placed his hands on his shoulders. At the same time he gave a blast on the whistle. All the prisoners jumped with surprise, and Kamigami could feel the man shaking in fear. Still bearing down, Kamigami spoke in Cantonese. "Do you know who I am?" The canvas-covered head bobbed in answer. "I'm more than you think," Kamigami said. "You must make a choice. Answer my questions truthfully and live. Or you can spend the next three days dying. It will be a most miserable, painful death. When you pass out, you will dream of pain and wake up screaming, only to learn the pain is real. You will curse your mother for giving you birth. Your comrades will tell me all they know, and beg me to end it. When I finally slit your stomach and let you hold your own intestines, you will thank me and kiss my feet in gratitude as you bleed to death. Choose now."

A torrent of words erupted from the man, and the others quickly joined in. They were members of the Ninety-second People's Liberation Regiment. It was an independent and elite unit of the People's Liberation Army, whose mission was terrorism and insurgency. None knew how big the Ninety-second was or who commanded it, only that their unit specialized in urban terrorism. Their first and only assignment had been to start a riot in Kuala Lumpur. They all had entered Malaysia from Thailand, but when Kamigami asked a second time, one revealed that the first man he had interrogated had entered by another route. "Who burned the Malay fishing village the last week of July?" Kamigami asked. The man sitting in front of him shook his head in confused silence. They had nothing left to give. Kamigami walked over to Tel and motioned at the man who was looking directly at them. Kamigami spoke in a low voice. "What did he do?"

"He never said a word," Tel replied. "He only listened."

Kamigami grunted and turned to the man, who lost control of his bladder when he saw the look on Kamigami's face. Tel also saw it and took a step backward. He bumped into Sun. "What's going on?" Sun asked. Tel motioned him to silence, afraid to speak. The prisoner's eyes were wide with fear as Kamigami loomed over him. He babbled in Cantonese, pleading for his life. Kamigami's hands were a blur, grabbing the man's chin and the back of his head. He gave a sharp jerk, and a loud snap echoed over the room. He dropped his hands, his face now impassive and calm, as the lifeless body slumped to the floor.

"Free them," Kamigami said. "In the Taman Negara." The colonel rushed to the door and shouted for the guards. The prisoners were dragged out as Kamigami nudged the lifeless body with his toe.

"Why him?" Tel asked.

"He was the leader."

"When did you know?"

"When I sat them down," Kamigami answered.

Tel was confused. "But how?"

"He was the only one who resisted. The others did as they were told. I knew for sure when they talked and he said nothing."

"Your threat," Gus said, "about taking three days to die. Would you have done that?"

"It wasn't a threat."

Tel alone understood. "It was a promise," he explained. "Why did you kill him?"

Kamigami headed for the door. "He was there."

"At the village," Tel said. It wasn't a question. Then, "Why did you release the others?"

Kamigami stopped at the door and stood in the sunlight. "So they can tell their comrades they met the vampire." He walked outside.

fourteen

The White House
Wednesday, September 15

The woman noted the time the lights came on in the president's bedroom. Her mouth pulled into a little grimace as she shuffled toward Lafayette Park across the street from the White House. "Forty minutes early," she murmured in Arabic, maintaining her image as a mumbling old woman who liked to feed pigeons in the early morning. Normally Madeline Turner's morning routine was set in concrete, and the change had to be reported. The woman walked slowly across the park toward the statue of Baron von Steuben and Connecticut Avenue.

Once across the street and clear of the park, she pulled out a cell phone and hit the speed dial. The number connected, but all she heard was a loud screeching sound. She panicked and looked around to find the source of the jamming. But her training held, and she forced herself to be calm. She punched the number off and dropped the phone down a drain as she hurried north. She stepped into a doorway, shrugged off her overcoat and shook out her hair, shedding thirty years of age. Feeling more confident, she crossed the street and headed west on L Street. A nondescript SUV coasted to a stop beside her, but before the doors opened, two men were beside her. They easily picked her up by her arms and carried her to the truck. "You can't do this!" she screamed. "I'm an American citizen!"

A man jabbed a needle into her arm. "Of course you are," he agreed.

The Secret Service agent standing in Maddy's bedroom spoke into her whisper mike. "Copy all. Tell the guys good work." She smiled. "Thank you, Madam President. We caught a watcher and made a connection. This looks like a good one."

"Was it the old woman?" Maddy asked.

"Yes, ma'am," came the answer. "But she wasn't old. Probably in her mid-thirties. We'll know more in a few hours."

"Please keep me informed."

"Yes, ma'am." The agent made a mental note to relay the president's request, which wasn't really a request. The woman would be interrogated and rendered in short order as the FBI, the Secret Service, and a few other nameless agencies closed in on the terrorists stalking the White House. It was a race against time as they went head-on-head with no holds barred. "Shall I turn out the light?"

"No. I'm awake now." Maddy sat on the edge of the bed as the agent left. Then the door opened again, and Maura came in. A woman followed with a coffee tray. "You're up early, Mother."

"Well, it is all exciting, isn't it? I mean, helping catch a spy."

"I suppose it is." She stepped into her dressing room, where her maid was waiting.

"The news is good from Saudi Arabia," Maura called.

"For now," Maddy replied. Maura poured a cup of coffee and waited. A few minutes later Maddy stepped out, ready to start a new day. She snatched a tissue from a holder and dabbed at the corners of her eyes. Then she was back in control.

But Maura saw the tears. "Oh, dear." Maddy sat down as Maura pulled a comb and brush out of her ever-present handbag. She stood behind her daughter. "Well? Are you going to talk about it?"

"It's Matt," Maddy said. Her mother was silent as she did her magic, combing Maddy's hair into a very simple but stylish arrangement. "I'm worried."

"About helping SEATO?" Maura replied. "Malaysia's a lot better than the Gulf."

"I'm not so sure." Silence. Then, "I'm using him."

"A man like Matt," Maura said as she finished, "is used only if he wants to be used." She tapped Maddy's shoulder with her comb. "Have you told him you love him?"

"He knows."

"Have you told him?" There was no answer. "I think," Maura fumed, "that you should do it before it's too late."

The Pentagon
Wednesday, September 15

Butler introduced the men and women gathered in the basement workroom. "This motley crew," he told Pontowski, "has forgotten more about putting together expeditionary forces and creating forward operating bases than I ever wanted to know."

The working group's leader, a trim and elegant lieutenant colonel who took pride in her ability to get things done quickly and efficiently, stood up. "Good morning, General. I'm Lieutenant Colonel Janice Clark from Installation Plans and Requirements." She cut to the heart of the matter. "Think of your MAAG as the logistics pipeline and the AVG as your operational arm. The MAAG is already in place and functioning, so it's not a problem. However, we have two immediate problems with the AVG. One, you need a place to form up in the States, and two, you need a base to deploy to. As for the first, we have identified Kelly Field in San Antonio, Texas. The old Air Material Command hangars and offices have been vacant since the logistics center was closed, and are available." She waited for Pontowski's reply. Was he going to staff a decision to death, or was he capable of making a decision? The answer was critical, for it determined how they would proceed.

Pontowski didn't disappoint her. "Kelly Field sounds good."

She jotted down a note and said, "As for the second problem, there is no suitable base in Singapore."

"We need to get as close to the action as possible," he told her.

Janice Clark allowed a tight smile. This was a man she could work with. "We may have something. Major."

A major standing by a worktable spread out a series of photos. "This is satellite imagery of Camp Alpha," he began. "It's a full-up base hidden in the Malaysian jungle approximately sixty miles north of Singapore and meets all the requirements for A-10 operations." He gave a very audible sigh. "I wished it belonged to us."

"Will the Malays let us use it?" Pontowski asked.

"Who knows?" the major replied. "It was built under the SEATO treaty, and supposedly we don't even know about it."

"I don't think," Butler said, "that access will be a problem." He added mentally, *Not if they want us to get involved.*

Pontowski studied the high-resolution photos. "Okay," he muttered, "you've stumped the student. Where the hell is it?"

The major handed him a magnifying glass and pointed to what looked like a straight stretch of highway carved out of the jungle. "Here's the runway. You've got ten thousand feet of reinforced concrete and enough room to land a C-17. The parking ramp at the south end is a bit small and can accommodate only one cargo plane at a time. If you look closely, you can see the taxiways leading to the runway here, here, and here. This is the control tower." His pencil circled what looked like the top of a tall tree.

"Clever," Pontowski said. "You called it a 'full-up base.' What exactly does that mean?"

The major unrolled a large-scale map of the base. "This is compiled from synthetic aperture radar imagery, which can penetrate the foliage. You've got twenty-four hardened aircraft shelters, each capable of housing maintenance and munitions." His pencil flicked from shelter to shelter. "Here's a hardened command post, and we think these structures are barracks and a mess hall." He pointed to a series of igloolike structures on the far side of the runway. "Munitions storage."

"Water and fuel?" Hard experience had taught him that the four essential prerequisites for a forward operating location were a runway, a weapons-storage area, a fuel dump, and a secure water supply. Everything else they could bring with them.

"Civil engineers," the major replied, "claim that the base is built over a limestone aquifer. So there's your water. I suspect they've already sunk wells. If they haven't, our civil engineers can correct that in a heartbeat. Unfortunately, we haven't identified a fuel dump."

Pontowski bent over the map and cross-checked it with the photos. He gave a little humph. "The Israelis built this, didn't they?"

The major agreed. "It certainly looks like their work."

"They like to refuel in bunkers," Pontowski said.

Now it was the major's turn to humph. "Which sounds like a recipe for disaster."

"Not the way the Israelis do it," Pontowski explained. "There's a main dump somewhere that feeds small underground holding tanks, which in turn feed the shelters through a network of pipes, sort of like a spiderweb. The fuel lines are automatically purged after each refueling with a fire retardant, which also serves for firefighting. When they want to use a line for fuel, the jet fuel pushes the retardant back into the web.

A skinny captain hovering behind them coughed for attention. "Excuse me," he mumbled. He paused, embarrassed by his rashness. Pontowski's reputation was well known, and the captain, like many junior officers, stood in awe of him. "There may be a problem with fuel. The base is only serviced by a laterite road that may be impassable during heavy rains, and there is no pipeline."

"So check it out," Pontowski said.

The more Pontowski paced the office, the more Butler envisioned a tiger stalking its prey. But this tiger had a slight limp as he circled the computer bench. Finally the captain looked up from his computer and said, "I wish we had a pipeline, but we can work around it."

Pontowski bent over a worktable and studied the map of the air base. "What else is out there that can come back and bite us?"

Janice Clark ticked off all the variables. "Runway: good. Aircraft shelters: state of the art. Water: may have to drill wells, not a problem. Fuel: we can do it with work-arounds. Weapons storage: I can vouch for that." She continued to run the long list.

Pontowski made a mental note to ask her if she would be the base commander. It was a critical decision, for whoever ran the base had to be a hard taskmaster, perfectly capable of driving people until they dropped but able to work for a wing commander whose primary orientation was flying operations. He split his attention as she talked, thinking about what he needed in a wing commander. There was only one real choice: Colonel Dwight "Maggot" Stuart. That decision made, he focused on Clark. She finished, and he asked the key question: "Is Alpha doable?"

"It's doable," she said.

Pontowski looked around the room. "Anything else I need to know?"

"There is one thing," Butler said. He walked to the big chart of Malaysia hanging on the wall. He used a wide-tip felt pen to trace two sweeping arrows down the peninsula, one on the west coast, one on the east coast. Then he tapped the chart. "These are the two invasion routes the Japanese used when they invaded the Malay Peninsula in World War Two." He extended the arrows and brought them together over Camp Alpha, where he formed one big arrow pointed directly at Singapore. "They merged forces here for the final push on Singapore in 1942. My guess is that SEATO took a lesson from history in building the base where they did."

"Well," Pontowski said, "I did ask to get close to the action, didn't I?" He thought for a moment. "Camp Alpha it is," he said, bending back over the map on the worktable.

Butler's image of a tiger changed to one of an eagle swooping down on its prey.

"We're transferring to a permanent office in my directorate," Janice Clark told Pontowski. "Butler will be glad to see the last of us." She signed for a box of classified material and sent the sergeant on his way. "We should be up and operating by the time you get to Kelly Field in San Antonio."

Pontowski looked around the now-vacant office. It had been a long day, and he desperately needed some exercise to brush away the mental cobwebs. "I'll walk with you, if you don't mind." He loaded a cart with boxes and pushed it out the door. It amazed him how quickly the paperwork had piled up once the decision was made to activate the AVG at Kelly Field and deploy to Camp Alpha. He checked his watch. "Butler wants me at the NMCC." The NMCC was the National Military Command Center and the closest thing the United States had to the command centers Hollywood and TV fantasized about.

"The dreaded marching orders?" Clark asked.

"I suppose," he said, pushing the loaded cart into the hall. "Where's the elevator?"

"You better let me push that," Clark said. "It might upset the sergeants if they saw a general doing something physical."

Pontowski laughed. "Ouch." They headed for an elevator. "What do you think they'll be?"

"Your marching orders?" she asked. He gave a little nod. "Formally and in writing, pretty standard. Diplomatic boilerplate, nothing surprising. Informally, I'd guess you'll be given a great deal of latitude. Just don't screw up."

"Or they'll disavow all knowledge of my mission and claim I was a cowboy out playing shoot-'em-up at the OK Corral."

She grew very serious. "That's the way it works."

He pushed a button to call the elevator, then looked around. They were all alone. "Colonel Clark, I'd like you to be the base commander at Alpha."

"And the wing commander is?"

"I've got a body in mind. He's all fighter jock, hair on fire. A certified aerial assassin. I haven't asked him yet."

"He'll say yes," she predicted. "If he can make a decision, I can work for him." She looked at him, thinking. "How long do I have to decide?"

"How about the same length of time you gave me?"

She laughed. "Ouch." Then, "You've got yourself a base commander, General." The elevator doors opened, and she pushed the cart inside. "You'll want the second floor to get to the NMCC," she told him. The doors swooshed closed.

Pontowski stood next to the glass in the commander's cab high above the main floor of the NMCC and watched the president as she moved over the main floor. A two-star general, puffed with pride, escorted her, explaining the function of each position. Even from this distance Pontowski could sense Turner's impatience.

"He's running out of time," Mazie said from behind him. Pontowski turned to see the national security adviser standing less than two feet away. She gestured at the president to indicate whom she was talking about.

"It's the general's chance to shine," Pontowski said.

"Not for long," Mazie replied. She pointed to a briefing room off to the left. "The ExCom is meeting inside."

Pontowski followed her into the small room. He stiffened when he saw the secretary of defense, Robert Merritt, sitting in the chair next to the president's position. *Why do I distrust that man?* he wondered. Butler motioned him to stand immediately behind him and against the sidewall.

"Shall we get started?" Mazie asked.

The big TV screen built into the wall came to life, and Colonel Scovill updated the ground situation in Saudi Arabia as a series of maps and graphs scrolled on the screen. The room was absolutely silent. Finally a simple chart flashed on the screen, tabulating casualties. Four soldiers had been wounded in action in the last twenty-four hours but not one killed in the last forty-eight. "Thank God," Merritt said sotto voce.

"Are there any questions?" Scovill asked. There were none, and he made his escape.

"Stephan," Mazie said to the secretary of state, "you wanted to discuss the political situation before the president arrived."

"Indeed," Serick said. "This is a replay from twenty minutes ago." He fiddled with his hand controller and cycled to the channel covering the Senate.

Leland was on the floor speaking. "Two thousand of our valiant soldiers have given their all in the first ten days of this bloodbath."

"Eighteen hundred and two," Wilding muttered, correcting the misstatement. "And none in the last two days."

On the screen Leland was looking directly at the camera. "We, as a God-fearing, peaceful nation, cannot, will not, tolerate such a wholesale destruction of the flower of our youth." A slight movement at the door drew Pontowski's attention away from the screen. Turner was standing there, her head slightly cocked as she listened to Leland. "We are at a crossroads," Leland intoned, "and can stop this senseless killing if we listen to our allies and reassess our current policies and strategy accordingly."

Butler snorted and shook his head. "The man's an asshole."

Merritt glared at the intelligence officer as Turner entered the room. "Turn him off," the president said.

Patrick Shaw was right behind her. "Bad timing, General," he whispered to Butler as he passed.

"My apologies, Madam President," Butler said.

"We've all been under a strain," Turner said as she sat down. "While I disagree with the good senator's implication that we're responsible, I do agree with his concern over casualties, as do most Americans. Now that we've stabilized the situation, we must keep it that way."

Wilding stood by the screen. "Madam President, we're entering the second phase of the war—stabilization and buildup. What we do now will determine how and when we go on the offensive. With your permission, we'd like to summarize how we're creating the logistical base to defeat the UIF. After that we'd like to discuss the emerging threat on the Malay Peninsula." Turner nodded, and Wilding turned the briefing over to a young Army lieutenant colonel.

Pontowski listened as the lieutenant colonel ran through the logistical details. *The guy's good,* Pontowski thought. *But Clark is better.*

Twelve minutes into the briefing, a military aide entered the room and handed Wilding a note. He glanced at it and stopped the briefing. "I think you need to see this, Madam President." He called up the Senate channel on the TV. But this time it was a replay of Leland's closing remarks.

"By all reports," Leland said, "our government made no attempt to defend King Khalid Military City, and as a consequence we suffered a disaster that can only be compared to Pearl Harbor. This august body must discover what went wrong. Therefore, I'm recommending we approve and appoint a special committee to commence an immediate investigation into this disaster." He turned and looked into the camera. "I don't know where this investigation will take us, but I can promise the families who lost their loved ones that their sacrifice will not have been in vain. We will hold those responsible accountable."

Turner stood. "For some reason it totally escapes the good senator that those responsible happen to command the UIF. Please excuse me while I stomp out this brushfire." Everyone stood as she left with the vice president. Shaw ambled out after them.

"I believe we're finished here," Mazie said.

Pontowski stayed behind as the room emptied. Finally he was alone with Butler. "I still haven't got a clue as to what I can and cannot do with the AVG."

"We'll get something to you," Butler said. "Please be patient. We're playing this by ear."

Pontowski arched an eyebrow. "That's becoming more obvious by the moment." He changed the subject, afraid he would say what he really felt. "I need to make a phone call."

"You can use a phone outside." Butler led him to a phone in the now-deserted battle cab and punched in his personal access code. He handed Pontowski the phone and turned away, surprised to see Patrick Shaw sitting in one of the commander's chairs overlooking the main floor.

Pontowski waited while his call was put through. Then, "Maggot, Pontowski here. You got a job yet?" He listened to the reply. "I don't think headquarters Air Force Reserve Command is ready for you. We're reactivating the AVG. How'd you like to be the wing commander?" He held the phone away from his ear.

A loud "Shit hot!" echoed from the earpiece.

Pontowski grinned at Butler. "I think he wants it." He spoke into the phone. "Get your body to Kelly Field ASAP, like Friday. Meet you there." He broke the connection and dropped the phone into its cradle. "I'm going be at Kelly Field if you need me." He headed for the door.

Butler started to follow, but Shaw waved him to a stop. "We need to talk." He heaved his bulk to an upright position. "Can you find out what the hell Leland is up to?"

"I thought you'd never ask," Butler said in a low voice so Pontowski wouldn't hear.

fifteen

New Mexico Military Institute
Wednesday, September 22

Brian Turner stuck his head into Zack's room. "Going to the briefing?"

Zack looked up from his computer and glanced at the clock. It was 3:51 in the afternoon. "Yeah. Let's go." He grabbed his hat and joined his friend. They walked quickly down the stoop to the stairs, hit the box running, and hurried out the Sally Port. "According to the news, not much is happening," Zack said. They skirted around the drill team that was practicing close-order drill, and headed for Dow Hall for the daily update on the war. The briefing, given by an active-duty Army captain in the senior ROTC unit, lasted about twenty minutes and was held in a classroom. As they were late, they had to squeeze into the rear and stand against the back wall. The captain was standing at the podium next to the big-screen TV.

"In Saudi Arabia it's 0200 hours Thursday morning," the captain said, "and day eighteen of the war. The opening stage, attack and stabilization, has ended. As we've discussed before, we're now in interdiction and buildup, and, as you know, this phase of the war lays the foundation for what comes next—attack!" A loud cheer erupted from the cadets. The captain grinned and calmed them down. "You've all seen the videos from the air war, smart bombs, things going boom in the night. What you haven't seen is the logistical buildup, which is about as exciting as counting trucks driving by. So today I want to look at political considerations the military has to deal with—specifically, the growing protest movement in the States." He hit the play button on the videocassette player, and the TV came on. The scene was a big student demonstration at the University of California–Berkeley campus. The camera panned over the crowd and then zoomed in on a girl. On cue, she stripped off her clothes as friends wrapped an antiwar banner around her.

"Hey, nice tits!" an upper classman shouted as the camera zoomed out. The scene changed to one of a cameraman running through the crowd following two nude girls who were carrying a banner. The cameraman stumbled and fell. Three sets of bare legs ran over him.

"Raise the camera!" a cadet shouted from the back.

An excited reporter in the crowd described the scene as a modern bacchanalia. "It's make love, not war all over again!" the reporter shouted. "At my last count at least twenty young women have shed their clothes in the quest for peace."

"Do it here! Do it here!" four cadets chanted in the back of the room.

Brian laughed. "Skip and go naked for peace! What a great idea."

"Let's hear it for the demonstrators!" another voice called, obviously pleased with the coverage.

The four cadets picked up the chant. "Here, here, do it here!"

The TV screen went dark. "Knock it off!" the captain shouted, quieting the cadets. "The goal of the protesters is not to end the war but to gain political power. It's a sophisticated process, and the first step is to gain the attention of the media. Once that is accomplished, they'll make common cause with the doves in Washington, D.C. Then they'll attack the military, blaming us for the war. The big lesson here is that democracies cannot fight long wars."

The briefing was over, and Zack and Brian made their way back to Hagerman Barracks entering through the sally port. As they turned left and climbed the steps to their rooms, they stopped and leaned over the rail, watching the cadets below march back and forth, walking off the demerits they had accumulated. "Okay," Brian said, "what's bugging you?"

"I'm worried about my dad going to Malaysia."

"Ain't no war there," Brian said. "He'll be bored to death."

Washington, D.C.
Thursday, September 23

The five trays were ready when the ExCom gathered at 5:30 A.M. in the national security adviser's office in the Old Executive Office Building across from the White House. Each tray was a special creation, tailored to the needs of each member of the committee, and while it was a small touch, it got things off to a smooth start. The DCI let the heavy Colombian blend he preferred, with its massive caffeine jolt, work its magic. "How's the election campaign going?" he asked conversationally.

Kennett savored his milder brew before answering. "Going as well as can be expected. Good TV coverage and enthusiastic crowds. The 'Support Our Troops' theme has worked well in spite of the antiwar protesters. She'll wind up at Sacramento tonight and return to Andrews tomorrow."

"Is there anything we need to alert the president to?" Mazie asked. She sipped at her Lady Grey tea.

"I don't think so," Wilding replied. He had been up two hours, and his coffee was untouched. "Other than an occasional exchange of artillery fire, it's quiet at the front. The air-interdiction campaign is going well, and nothing is moving during the day." He allowed a little grunt of satisfaction. "And they're not getting any sleep at night. Over two hundred sorties last night, four aircraft reported battle damage, nothing serious, but the British lost a Tornado on landing. The crew was unhurt. The first two fast sealift ships are scheduled to arrive tomorrow." He looked satisfied. "The pipeline is open." He paused for a moment. "Two more died from wounds received in combat and three more from motor-vehicle accidents. All at night, driving under blackout conditions. That brings noncombat deaths to nine."

"Can we do anything about that?" Mazie asked.

"We're working on it," Wilding replied.

"NSA intercepted an interesting message between Baghdad and Damascus," the DCI said. "It was a summary of the total casualties the UIF has experienced so far. Much higher than we calculated. We might want to get it to the president."

Mazie agreed. "Anything else?"

Butler swallowed the last of the doughnut he was munching, and washed it down with a gulp of hot chocolate. "A problem with the AVG. Pontowski tells me it's coming together much faster than expected. He needs guidance on what weapons they can employ so they can build a training program and set up the ROE." The ROE were the rules of engagement, normally a collection of very good ideas designed to keep fighter jocks alive. That is, until politicians got involved. Then they became a political statement that had nothing to do with engagement. Pontowski wanted to short-circuit that process by creating his own.

"That's a problem," Kennett said. "We've got to hold the AVG at arm's length, or Leland will crucify us in the press. The president needs distance on this one, like our involvement in Afghanistan in the 1980s. We were there, but we weren't there."

"So exactly what is Pontowski doing there with the AVG?" the DCI asked.

"Meeting the functions of a Military Assistance Advisory Group," Kennett replied. "In other words, he's there to help SEATO help itself."

"Leland's going to love that one," Mazie said.

Kelly Field, San Antonio
Thursday, September 23

"Okay, how does this work?" Pontowski muttered to himself. He stared at the computer screen for a few moments. "Hey," he called. "Does someone have a clue how to access an encrypted e-mail?"

One of the young pilots walking by his open office door nodded and ambled in. "Treat it as a secure phone call," he said.

Pontowski grumbled as he unlocked the safe where he stored classified documents. He found the key and inserted it in the base of the STU-V, the secure phone sitting on his desk. He turned the key, and the LED screen blinked a message at him to press the aux message button. He did, and the scrambled e-mail message on the computer screen metamorphosed into plain text. But now the normal text was scrambled, and he grumped in frustration. He wasn't going to have it both ways. The message was from Lieutenant Colonel Janice Clark.

1. ADVON TEAM ARRIVED CAMP ALPHA THIS MORNING. INFRASTRUCTURE BETTER THAN EXPECTED.
2. SEAC POSITIONING WEAPONS AND FUEL FOR YOUR ARRIVAL.
3. AIR BASE DEFENSE INADEQUATE, BRING OWN SECURITY TEAM WHEN DEPLOY. CONTACT CMSGT LEROY ROCKNE AT HDQTRS 37 TRW AT LACKLAND AFB FOR SUPPORT.
4. LIST OF REMAINING SHORTFALLS TO COME.

"Very good," he said to himself. Not only had Clark quickly identified what she considered the major problem, she had proposed a solution and a person to contact for help. "Maggot's going to like working with her," he said. "And I've got to stop talking to myself." Pontowski hit the print key to print the message. The printer whirred, but the message it spit out was gibberish. "Technology is a wonderful thing," he groused. He rooted around in his desk drawer and found the telephone directory for Lackland Air Force Base, which was next door to Kelly Field. He called the Thirty-seventh and left a message for Chief Master Sergeant Rockne to call him.

Then he kicked back in his chair and thought for a moment. Two questions loomed large in his mind. First, what were his marching orders? Lacking an answer, he couldn't set up a coherent training program for his pilots, much less create the ROE he wanted. Second, when could they deploy? His gut instincts told him the sooner the better, but how close were they? The answer would come in two parts: one from Maintenance, the other from Operations. It was the excuse he needed to escape the confines of his office, with its never-ending flow of paperwork. He grabbed his flight cap and headed for the hangar next to his building. Outside, ten A-10 Warthogs were lined up on the ramp, ready for the morning's training missions. If the schedule held, eight would be turned for the afternoon's flights and two would join the other nine in the hangar being prepared for the long flight across the Pacific to Malaysia.

Pontowski ran the numbers through his head: 19 aircraft, 29 pilots, and 310 maintenance troops. It still amazed him how quickly it had all come together. That was the wonder of modern communications and

Air Force organization. The downside was that the aircraft had been scrounged from around the system, and most needed major maintenance. On the plus side they were swamped with pilots who wanted to sign on. Maggot had posted a message on the Air Force's personnel Web page advertising for pilots with A-10 experience who wanted to travel to foreign lands, meet strange and exotic people, and drop bombs on them. The ad was deemed politically incorrect by the powers that be and pulled within three hours. But the damage had been done, and the word had gone out that the American Volunteer Group was back in business and under the command of one Brigadier General Matt Pontowski. The phone had started ringing immediately, and the pilots couldn't get to Kelly Field fast enough. But it had been a balancing act, blending experience with youth. Fortunately, Maggot knew most of the pilots personally or by reputation, and he culled the wheat from the chaff. But he still wanted a few more.

Pontowski jammed his flight cap on his head, careful to dent it in the back in the approved fighter-pilot style. He watched as four pilots walked out to the aircraft, carrying their helmet bags and gear. He wished he were going with them, and for a moment he was back in the cockpit. Over the course of his career he had flown numerous aircraft and seen combat in two, the F-15E Strike Eagle and the A-10 Warthog. The Strike Eagle had been a beauty, sleek and graceful, and performed like a demon straight from the environs of hell as he visited death and destruction on those who would do harm to innocent people.

But the A-10 was still his favorite, slow and ungainly-looking with its blunt nose and big thirty-millimeter cannon that could destroy tanks with deadly efficiency. How many times had he challenged death in that bird? Suddenly, standing there in the bright Texas sun on a lovely September day, it didn't matter. He had done it.

Pontowski was not an introspective man, given to self-examination or doubts. His wife, Shoshana, had told him it was the major flaw in his personality. But she forgave him for it and had given him a wonderful son before she had been killed. Was that the price extracted for his survival? He hoped it didn't work that way. For some reason he had never remarried. But he didn't think about it. Later on, other women had moved through his life, challenging and changing him, sometimes loving him. Some had used him and, in the case of Liz Gordon of CNC-TV, hated him with a pure and unrefined passion. And then there was Maddy Turner. He forced her image away, not knowing what the future held for them.

He watched as the pilots finished their walk-around and climbed up the boarding ladders. How many times had he done that? A sharp dagger of regret cut through him. He would never do it again—not with his bad leg and at his age. *Be honest,* he told himself, *flying a jet is a young man's game.* Now it was his job to lead them, not from the cockpit like Maggot Stuart but from a different place in time and space. His decisions would determine who would live and who would die. *What gives me the right?* Shoshana's voice was there. *Because you did it and risked all, because you care and know the price.*

He watched the four A-10s taxi out. Another thought came to him. It was also the challenge, the testing, the adrenaline flows. For reasons he would never understand, he was most alive, most sure of himself, when he was flying and fighting. *And ego,* he thought. *What part does that play in this strange brew?* He forced that thought away, too, not ready to deal with it. He waited until the four jets took off at twenty-second intervals. His eyes followed the lead aircraft as it turned out of the pattern, giving the following jets cut off in order to join up. "Please, Lord," he prayed, "forgive me, for this is what I am."

He turned and walked into the maintenance hangar. Inside, the cavernous bay was alive with activity as men swarmed around the nine Warthogs being prepped for deployment. Like any military facility, the hangar was spotless, but any similarities ended there. The men were all middle-aged or older, and dressed in civilian clothes. A few had been with the original AVG in China and later with him in South Africa on a peacekeeping mission that had been anything but peaceful. Some had come out of retirement, and more than half were Air Reserve technicians on a leave of absence from their regular jobs. He was thankful for the wealth of experience they brought with them.

Maggot stepped out of the office where Maintenance Control worked, and walked toward him. Much to Pontowski's envy, he was wearing a flight suit and his face was still etched with the lines from his oxygen mask. He had been up on a test flight earlier. "Our last jet is inbound," Maggot told him. "It should be on the ground in a few minutes."

"What sort of shape is it in?" Pontowski asked.

"According to Maintenance, it's right out of the depot. Total rebuild."

"So we finally lucked out and got a good one," Pontowski said. "Let's go howdy the pilot." They walked outside to wait. In the distance they saw a follow-me truck leading an A-10 into the parking area. The engines had a different sound, and the plane's fresh jungle green paint job glistened in the bright sun.

"It's one of the reengined birds," Maggot told him. The Warthog came to a stop, and the ground crew quickly installed wheel chocks and safety pins as the engines spun down. The canopy lifted, and the pilot removed his flight helmet, revealing a full head of dark hair streaked with gray. His potato-shaped face broke into a smile as he scampered down the boarding ladder. The crew chief was surprised that a pudgy, middle-aged man with a body that matched his face could move so quickly. "Son of a bitch," Maggot said, smiling broadly.

On the ground, George "Waldo" Walderman spread his arms wide and announced to the world, "I have arrived. You may start the war."

Pontowski gave a very audible sigh. "Misfits. We're nothing but a collection of misfits."

"Ain't it wonderful," Maggot said.

Mather Field, Sacramento, California
Thursday, September 23

The half-light of sunset played with the rain that danced across the area where nuclear-armed B-52s had once sat cocked and ready for takeoff. But that was over twenty years ago, and the bombers were gone. Now only a blue-and-white Boeing 747 sat behind the fence, its reflection casting long shadows in the standing water. The plane stood there in quiet majesty, the words UNITED STATES OF AMERICA emblazoned on its side proclaiming it was the president's aircraft, Air Force One.

Because it was a secure area, the small army of agents detailed to guard the president breathed easier while she was in Sacramento. At first Turner had objected to parking in the area because she hated any appearance of being walled off from the people. But there wasn't a choice. The high number of casualties suffered during the first nine days of the war had triggered numerous death threats against her life, three from the Sacramento area alone.

Consequently, security was tighter than ever, surrounding Air Force One like an invisible wall. It wasn't there until you tried to breach it, and then, as one reporter from the local newspaper found out, it was solid as the Rock of Gibraltar.

As were so many, the newspaper's editorial staff was genuinely appalled by the heavy casualties coming out of the Gulf and, not understanding the nature of modern warfare, had severely criticized the president's conduct of the war. In an editorial that received national attention, they charged she had deliberately started the war for political gain. Then the same editors were furious when Turner declined to be personally interviewed by their star political reporter, Lacy Bangor. They would have attained heights of unknown apoplexy had they known that Shaw also wanted to pull their Washington bureau's credentials and cast their reporters into an informational limbo. But the president had vetoed that. In retaliation for the interview snub, and not aware of the bullet they had dodged, the editors decided on the lead headline for their Sunday op-ed section: PRESIDENTIAL STRATEGY AND SECURITY—MASSIVE FAILURES. But the editors needed a story to go with it, and over Lacy Bangor's loud protests they told her to test the security around Air Force One before she was apprehended and arrested. The follow-up story would document how freedom of the press and her civil rights were violated. Needless to say, that was a mistake.

The president was sitting in the aft lounge aboard Air Force One with her campaign staff when a Secret Service agent told her that the reporter had tried to penetrate the security cordon by driving her car through a checkpoint. Guards had stopped the car before it went thirty feet, and Bangor was spread-eagle on the asphalt. "Is she still there?" Turner asked.

"In a mud puddle," the agent replied.

"Release her," Turner said. "Have someone from Justice give her paper a call and explain a few facts of life to them."

"They'll probably withdraw their endorsement," an adviser said.

"They already have," another adviser replied. "It's the numbers." For a moment no one said a word. Turner's opponent had made the high casualty rate the number one issue of the campaign and was using it to drive the polls.

"Her editors," the first adviser said, "are going to make this an issue no matter what we do."

"Then make it a nonissue," Turner ordered.

"Maybe they need a distraction," a third adviser suggested. "Perhaps a visit from the IRS?"

Turner gave the speaker a steely look. "We don't play that way. They may, but I don't." Then she relented. "You're right. They do need a distraction. Have Patrick call them instead." A chuckle worked its way around the lounge as her advisers speculated about what Patrick Shaw would say. Most were willing to bet he'd say something about the president listening the next time he wanted to pull the newspaper's White House press credentials. They went back to work, firming up her next day's campaign schedule before they returned to Washington.

Richard Parrish, her chief of staff, interrupted them. "Madam President, we have a message from the NMCC. Perhaps in your private office?" He followed her forward, through the passenger compartment, where a group of reporters were working.

"Madam President," one of them called, "what are you going to do about that reporter?"

"Lacy Bangor?" Turner replied. "Dry her off and send her home." She stopped. "I like Lacy. She's a good reporter, but . . ." She hesitated and smiled. "You all know the 'buts' as well as I do. I'll talk to her after we find out what happened."

"Thank you, Mrs. President," a reporter said. They all had a new story and considered that a dunk in a mud puddle was worth a private interview.

The president's personal assistant held the door to her private office. "Thank you, Nancy. Anything from the family?"

"I talked to Maura a few minutes ago. All's quiet on the home front. Sarah's doing her homework."

"I'll call later this evening," Maddy said, looking directly at Scovill. "It's bad, isn't it?" Parrish followed her in and closed the door.

"Yes, ma'am," the colonel answered, "it is. The first two fast sealift ships transiting the Straits of Hormuz struck mines. Both sank. One of the two escort frigates also struck a mine but didn't sink. The other six sealift ships are still in transit and being diverted to safe waters until we decide how to proceed."

The agony was back, unrelenting and constant. "How many?" the president asked. Nothing in her voice betrayed her feelings.

"So far," Scovill replied, "fourteen known dead. The undamaged frigate and three minesweepers are recovering survivors. More help is on the way. Apparently most of the crew members on the cargo ships are okay."

Turner paced her small office. "What happened? I was told the Navy was going to sweep the straits before the ships arrived."

"They did, ma'am. In fact the minesweepers were in sight when they hit the mines."

A red light flashed on the intercom panel on Turner's desk. Parrish picked up the phone and hit the button connecting him to the aircraft's communications deck. He listened and handed the phone to the Marine. "Another message from the NMCC," he said.

Scovill listened, his face impassive as he jotted down notes. He almost asked his president to sit down but thought better of it. Madeline Turner could take bad news. "Three Libyan ships were blown up by their crews in the Suez Canal. It's closed. For how long, we don't know." He glanced at his notes. "One of the minesweepers picking up survivors in the Straits of Hormuz retrieved what looked like a life-raft canister. Luckily, they recognized it as a mine and knew what to do. It's a new type of mine we've never seen before. Made of ceramic and self-propelled."

"So it escapes magnetic detection and moves," Turner added.

"Apparently so," the colonel said.

"Richard," Turner said, "we're returning to Andrews immediately. I know what it will do to the campaign." She looked at him as he made the phone call. "It may cost me the election."

"Not necessarily," Parrish replied. "We change our strategy to 'Embattled president wages war on ruthless enemy.' Or something like that." He warmed to it, proving why he was a consummate politician. "I'll get Shaw on the line, and we'll work it with the committee on the flight back. Should have something by the time we land."

"We need to defuse the casualty issue. Perhaps it's time for a few reporters to receive a deep-background briefing from a highly placed, unidentified source in the administration."

"How high?" Parrish asked.

"The highest," she answered. She looked at Scovill. "I'd like for you to be there."

"My pleasure, Madam President. Anyone in particular you want me to strangle?"

"Not today," she answered.

"I have a few candidates," Parrish said.

Over Missouri
Thursday, September 23

By definition, reporters are cynics. They are also firm believers in the axiom that everyone is entitled to his or her own opinion. But in their special case they are also permitted their own special truth, and any fact that runs counter to their view of reality is wrong by definition. But what they were hearing now was beyond their special truth and could not be discounted, denied, or damned. It was a view of reality, straight from the top and devoid of the special interpretations they labeled "spin." All tape recorders were off, no notebooks were out, their pens were still as they listened to the Marine colonel simply repeat all he had told the president during the day. He finished by telling them about the sinking of the two ships and the closing of the Suez Canal. "I'll tell you this," Scovill said. "This is the worst job in the Pentagon. I'd much rather be with my unit facing the enemy. The decisions there are simple."

The president sat down beside Scovill and touched his hand. "This is the first time I've seen you display any emotion. I know it's been hard for you, and I appreciate it." She turned to her chief of staff. "Richard."

"Most everything you've heard so far," Parrish began, "will be released within twenty-four hours. Of course, certain items will not, like the mine we recovered. We need to keep that a secret so we can exploit it." Parrish paused and looked at Turner. She nodded, giving him the go-ahead. "We want to show you a report that is very close-hold for reasons that will become obvious. But before we do, I must have your promise that what you see stays here."

"Is this more important than the mine?" a reporter asked.

"In a way, yes," Parrish replied.

The reporter stood. "I'm not going to sell my integrity for a peek at some intelligence report. No thank you very much." He walked out.

"Anyone else?" Parrish asked. The remaining nine reporters didn't budge. He passed out a sheet of paper.

"Oh, my God," one of the reporters whispered. "Are these our real casualties?"

"No," Parrish answered. "Theirs. This came from a UIF message the National Security Agency intercepted less than twenty-four hours ago. The information it contains is not classified, but the fact that we caught it and were able to decode it is highly classified. We want them to keep using this channel, as it's one of our best sources of intelligence."

Now it was Scovill's turn. "The standard planning factor for the opening phase of a war like this calls for an exchange rate of approximately forty to one in our favor. It doesn't take fuzzy math to figure out that with a hundred thirty-eight thousand killed alone, the exchange rate is seventy-six to one."

"Seventy-six and a half to one," a reporter who was good with numbers said. "I don't believe it."

"Believe," the Marine answered. "The UIF planned and trained for a conventional attack, not appreciating the lethal nature of modern warfare or not giving a damn about their soldiers. They bogged down in the desert because we bled them dry and they outran their supply lines. We plan to keep it that way with the air-interdiction campaign. We're going to cut them off and bomb them until they have two options: surrender or die."

"Why is this close-hold?" another reporter said. "You should be shouting it from the tallest buildings."

"Because of the source," Scovill told him.

Turner stood up. "There's another reason." She started to pace. How could she make them understand? "Those are real people, not just numbers on a sheet of paper. For the most part they want the same thing everyone wants—a home, a safe place to raise their children. They hurt and cry like we do, and they only want to get on with their lives. I doubt that many really wanted to fight this war, but they had no choice. We have no quarrel with them, and we're not fighting for revenge."

"Madam President," a reporter said, "how can you say that? I saw the unedited tape of our three soldiers being executed."

"I saw it, too. I don't know what motivated them. Considering the way we've slaughtered them—and it has been a slaughter, there's no other word for it—they may still feel the same and will do it again. But we have to look beyond that." She paused to make her point. "They are not our teachers!" She stood before them, all that she was out there to be seen. "My generals tell me that these numbers are nothing compared to what will happen when we go on the offensive. But this time our casualties will be minimal. Make no mistake, I will give that order if they do not surrender and withdraw."

Her voice was firm. "We didn't want a war, and we didn't provoke it. But even so, no person should be asked to kill others on such a scale. Yet that is exactly what I've ordered our men and women to do. But how can I reconcile such killing with everything we stand for without appealing to hate and prejudice? Hate . . . the most accessible of all human emotions. Is this what we're all about? Must we sacrifice our humanity to the gods of war?"

She turned and looked out a window. "I think that's Missouri below us. The heartland of America. B-2 bombers from Whiteman Air Force Base are recovering from missions over Iraq. They'll be rearmed and launched on more missions. I would much rather be sending the world grain grown in Missouri. This is not what I wanted." She turned and walked from the cabin.

Without a word, the reporters stood. One by one they handed the sheet of paper they were each holding to Parrish as they filed out. The lone reporter who had walked out of the meeting was waiting for them. "Did I miss much?" he asked, his voice heavy with sarcasm.

"Only the best speech Maddy Turner will ever give" came the answer.

sixteen

Palau Tenang
Friday, September 24

The rain slugged down, working its way through Tel's poncho and sending a rivulet of water down his back. He hoped it was the last rainstorm of the southwest monsoon and that they would have a break until December, with the onset of the northeast monsoon. He joined the officers and senior NCOs gathered under the tightly stretched tarp and shrugged off his poncho, glad to be out of the rain.

"The brigadier and colonel will be here in a few moments," he announced. He stifled a grin as he listened to the Chinese equivalent of bitching and moaning. If Kamigami was correct, he was hearing exactly what they needed to hear. The First SOS had changed from a highly disciplined, regimented, spit-and-polished outfit to a totally focused collection of aggressive shooters totally committed to battle discipline. But there had been a price—the First was half its former size. Tel made a mental note to ask Kamigami what had happened.

Kamigami and Colonel Sun emerged out of the rain. They were a strange combination, Kamigami's seemingly placid bulk dominating the diminutive but very active colonel, whose face was still pale from the helicopter flight from Central Headquarters on the main island. They shucked off their ponchos, and Sun tacked up a chart of Malaysia on the easel. As they had agreed on the flight in, the colonel would do the talking to avoid any confusion. "CHQ offered us an assignment," Sun explained in Chinese.

"Offered?" one of the majors asked.

"That is unusual," Sun replied. "But it's an unusual situation." He pointed to an outlined area in the center of the chart. "Units of the PLA effectively control this region of Malaysia and are holding the local population hostage, forcing them to supply food and shelter for their soldiers. There are also reports of forced prostitution of younger girls. If a kampong resists, they loot and burn it, killing every able-bodied man and boy. CHQ has asked us to insert rescue teams and move the villagers to safe areas."

"You mean we have a choice?" a captain asked.

"Yes, we do," Kamigami said, his voice barely audible over the rain drumming on the tarp inches above his head. The men fell silent, for it was a choice that went to the heart of who and what they were. With the exception of Kamigami and Tel, the First was composed of Straits Chinese. The assignment meant they would be fighting Mainland Chinese—a break with their ethnic identity. "Think about it," Kamigami said.

The men talked among themselves, and to the uninitiated it was a wild conversation. But it had purpose and direction. Finally they quieted, and the senior major spoke. "We do not think of this as a choice but as a challenge," he said. "When do we leave?"

Sun was ready and passed out a schedule. "We will move in stages, starting tomorrow. Each squadron will send an advance team to be followed by the rest two days later. We will move in force and take all our equipment with us to set up a permanent base camp."

"Have they identified the location?" a senior NCO asked.

Kamigami tapped the map with a finger. "Here. Sixty miles north of Singapore." His finger was pointing directly at Camp Alpha.

The Pentagon
Friday, September 24

The sergeant handed Butler the message that had come in earlier that morning. "We've got a valid decode, sir."

Butler leaned back in his chair and adjusted his glasses as he read. It was from the agent he had sent to New Delhi to monitor Zou Rong's secret talks with the new Indian prime minister. Somehow the agent had contacted Piepmatz, which, all things considered, was a major feat in itself. Details of exactly how the agent had accomplished that would come later during an extensive debrief. But for now it was the message that had Butler's undivided attention. Piepmatz had said only "When the rains end."

The general shot to his feet, knocking his glasses askew. "Oh, shit," he moaned. "How could I have been so fucking stupid?"

Piepmatz was German for "dickey bird" and the code name assigned to Jin Chu. Butler dropped the message and reached for the phone.

The small conference room at the back of the battle cab had turned into a war room for the ExCom, partly because it was central to the NMCC and partly because the members of the ExCom, with one exception, were spending most of their time in the Pentagon. Only the DCI had not fully made the transition to the war room and spent half his time at CIA headquarters in Langley, Virginia. But there was a dedicated helicopter at his disposal to whisk him back and forth.

However, the heart of this war room was not the classic wall charts with pins and magnetic icons but a bank of TV screens and computer monitors. The big table and chairs had been replaced with six small tables with comfortable chairs clustered in front of the TV bank. As a consequence the five members of the ExCom were able to quickly access the information flows flooding into the NMCC. Mazie and Sam Kennett were cycling through the most recent logistic status reports when Butler joined them. "General Wilding," Mazie said, "is in the Tank with the Joint Chiefs and the SecDef." The Tank was the conference room on the second floor above the River Entrance where the JCS met. "He'll be here as soon as we get an ETA on the DCI."

Butler sat down next to the vice president. "When you see Shaw, tell him I've got what he asked for."

"So soon?" Kennett asked. "About Leland, right?" He gave Butler his most serious look. "Shaw told us."

Butler's worst fears about politicians were reconfirmed. They simply couldn't keep their mouths shut. Butler shrugged and decided to save himself the trouble of trying to be discreet. He reasoned that whatever he said would within minutes be on the jungle telegraph that linked the masters of the Imperial City. "Leland's cut a deal with the French. The Froggies keep NATO out of the Gulf War, the war stalemates, and he delivers the election for his boy."

"So what's the quid pro quo?" Kennett wondered.

Butler was disgusted, and it showed. "The Frogs get to negotiate a Middle East cease-fire and in the process become the daddy rabbit of oil for Europe."

"Son of a bitch," Kennett muttered.

Mazie continued to stare at the screens as if she hadn't heard. She had to talk to the secretary of state. Wilding and the DCI walked in, cutting off any further conversation about Leland. "I take it," the DCI said, "that it's hit the fan. Again." His tone was a mixture of sarcasm and heavy doubt.

Butler rose. "Not quite." He called up a map of Southeast Asia on the center screen. It was time for a geography lesson. "It rains all the time in Malaysia, and there's no distinct dry season. But there are two monsoon periods when rainfall is much heavier. The southwest monsoon runs from June to September and is coming to an end. There will be a relative dry period until December, when the more robust northeast monsoon kicks in." He took a deep breath and plunged ahead. "We have reliable information that the Chinese are going to exploit that dry period."

"For what?" the DCI asked.

Wilding saw it immediately. "So obvious." He stood, almost at attention. "We can expect the PLA to open up an offensive."

The DCI shook his head. "I've said it before—you've got to stop obsessing. I assure you my analysts are on top of this. The intentions may be there, but the means are not."

"Remember Korea?" Butler asked. "The PLA intervened when they could cross the frozen Yalu River." He paced the floor. "Tell me this isn't timed to the situation in the Gulf. Our supply lines are now stretched around the tip of Africa, taxing our logistics buildup to the limit. It has effectively delayed offensive operations by two months and taking everything we got."

Wilding gulped. "That's exactly what we were discussing in the Tank."

Butler continued. "Meanwhile, with the exception of the British, our allies are dragging their heels, refusing to get involved, while the French maneuver for a negotiated cease-fire before we go on the offensive."

"Thank you very much, Senator Leland," Kennett muttered.

"So while we're fully occupied in the Gulf," Butler said, "the PLA intends to capture as much territory as possible in Malaysia before the northeast monsoon sets."

"Which will cut off military operations," Wilding added. "That will give them three months to consolidate their gains." He paused. "Brilliant, absolutely brilliant. And we missed it."

"All while the president," Kennett said, "is focused entirely on the Middle East, being blamed for the heavy casualties, and fighting for her political life."

"There's one problem," the DCI said. He pulled himself to his feet. "The Chinese simply can't do it. They don't have enough men or supplies available for the job, not with an alert and ready SEAC."

"I hope you're right," Mazic said.

"If the AVG were in place," Kennett asked, "would that discourage them?"

The DCI scoffed, dodging a direct answer. "The dreaded trip-wire force? Or should I say hostage force?"

"But it wouldn't hurt," Butler said. "Just to be on the safe side."

The DCI conceded the point. "No, it wouldn't. But do we have the airlift?"

"We can divert it," Wilding said.

Kelly Field
Friday, September 24

The chief master sergeant waiting in his office was without doubt the biggest man Pontowski had ever seen wearing an Air Force uniform. The uniform was obviously tailored to his bulk, and his highly polished boots were at least size fourteens. There wasn't an ounce of fat on his body, and the way his neck muscles strained at his collar was ample proof he spent time in a weight room. An inner alarm went off in Pontowski's subconscious, warning him not to underestimate this man.

"Lieutenant Colonel Clark gave me your name," Pontowski said.

"She was the commander of a weapons-storage site in the Netherlands," Rockne replied. "I was the NCOIC for her security flight."

Pontowski was impressed. The NCOIC, or noncommissioned officer in charge, at a weapons storage site held an awesome responsibility. "Did you like working for her?"

"Yes, sir. She was an excellent commander. No nonsense. She gets the job done."

Everything about the man told Pontowski to be direct. "She's the base commander at our forward operating location. She said air base defense was inadequate and to bring our own security team when we deploy. She said to contact you for support."

"Was that her word?" Rockne asked. "Inadequate?" Pontowski answered in the affirmative. "Then you've got problems. Was 'support' her word?"

"That's her exact word," Pontowski told him.

"She wants me for her NCOIC of security."

Pontowski was perplexed. "Is this some kind of special code you two use?"

Rockne shook his head. "No, sir. That's the way she works. When she asks someone for support, she means support. Like personal and committed."

Pontowski made a decision. "Do you want the job?"

"Where is it?"

The same warning bell went off in Pontowski's mind. You didn't hold back with this cop. "Malaysia, sixty miles north of Singapore. In the jungle."

"Shit."

"I take it that means you don't want the job?" Before Rockne could answer, a real alarm went off down the hall. Pontowski came to his feet. "Crash alarm. I've got aircraft airborne." He grabbed his handheld radio and ran out the door.

Rockne was in hot pursuit. "I'll drive, sir. The security pickup outside." Pontowski was fast, but nothing compared to Rockne. By the time he reached the truck, Rockne was behind the wheel, the engine started, the light bar flashing, and the passenger door open and waiting for him. "The approach end of the runway?" Rockne asked.

"Right. Follow the crash trucks."

"I know where it is, sir." He gunned the engine and raced for the end of the runway. "There," he said, pointing to the southwest.

Pontowski could barely see the two small dots. He keyed his radio and called the SOF, supervisor of flying, who was in the tower. "SOF, this is Bossman. Say emergency."

A voice he didn't recognize answered. "Miser One experienced catastrophic gun failure on a strafing pass. Lost all hydraulics plus wrapped the gun-access door around the nose and jammed the nose-gear door. He's in manual reversion, but since he's got two good engines, he's gonna land it."

"Say pilot," Pontowski radioed.

The SOF answered immediately. "Lieutenant Colonel Walderman."

"Waldo," Pontowski said, half aloud.

"Is that good or bad?" Rockne asked. He coasted the pickup to a stop halfway down the runway and well back from the taxiway. They were merely spectators.

"Both," Pontowski replied. "Manual reversion is an emergency procedure when you've lost hydraulics to get you to a safe area to eject. That's good. The book says you can attempt a landing if you've got two good engines, which he does. He'll try to land. Not good. He can't get the wheels down, but the Hog's main gear sticks out enough to land with it up." Again he keyed the radio. "SOF, tell Waldo to jettison that Hog. I've got lots of aircraft but only one him."

"I've advised him of same," the SOF said. "It's his option."

Another voice came over the radio. "No sweat, Bossman." It was Waldo. "And you speak with crooked tongue, white man. We no have lots of aircraft."

"White man?" Rockne asked Pontowski.

"A play on words. We were in the Three Oh Third at Whiteman in Missouri."

"I was stationed at Whiteman," Rockne told him. "During the Jefferson court-martial."*

Pontowski looked at him in surprise. "You were mixed up with that?"

"The whole damn Wing was mixed up." His eyes narrowed as the two aircraft approached. "I see smoke." A thin trail of smoke was trailing from Waldo's aircraft.

"I got it now," Pontowski said. "You got good eyeballs."

They watched as the two aircraft came down final. Waldo's wingman moved away for a go-around as Waldo crossed the approach lights. Waldo set the disabled aircraft down on the centerline just beyond the runway numbers, leaving plenty of room to drag the jet to a stop. "Pretty as a picture," Pontowski said. And it was. The Warthog touched down on its partially exposed main landing gear, and Waldo held the nose up as long as he could. Finally the nose came down and sent out a shower of smoke and sparks.

"Why isn't the crash wagon following him?" Rockne asked.

Pontowski took his eyes off the jet and looked back up the runway. The crash wagon was not moving. Two firefighters were off the truck and ripping open a side panel. "Hell of a time to stall," Pontowski growled. A loud screeching sound jerked his attention back to Waldo's Hog. Without hydraulics Waldo had five applications of the emergency brakes. When he tapped the brakes, the big jet started to slide off to the left. He tapped harder to straighten it out, but that only made matters worse. The Warthog jerked around and skidded sidewise down the runway. The right wingtip dug in, and the left wing lifted high into the air. For a brief moment Pontowski was certain it was going to do a cartwheel. Then the wing lowered back down as the big jet came to a halt on the runway. Waldo's head was slumped forward.

---

*Editor's note: The saga of the 303rd Fighter Squadron and the Jefferson court-martial is told in *Dark Wing, Iron Gate,* and *Against All Enemies* by the same author.

Rockne gunned the engine and raced for the Warthog. "When we get there," he said, "you drive. Give me enough time to get the fire extinguisher out of the back and then go tow the crash wagon here. A tow strap is behind my seat."

"Got it," Pontowski said as the pickup slammed to a stop. Rockne was out in a blur of motion, and before Pontowski could slip behind the steering wheel, he had jerked the fire extinguisher from the back and was running for the Warthog. Waldo's head was still down and not moving. Pontowski spun the wheel and headed for the crash truck. He glanced in the rearview mirror in time to see Rockne hit the button to open the canopy.

Pontowski pulled up in front of the crash truck and jumped out. He threw the tow strap at a fireman. "Hook it up," he called. He jumped back in and waited. Within seconds the driver gave him a thumbs-up, and he gunned the engine. The transmission whined in protest. "Go!" he yelled. Slowly, they started to move. Then they were picking up speed, reaching fifteen miles an hour. Ahead of him he could see Rockne pulling Waldo out of the cockpit as the back of the aircraft was enveloped in smoke. An ambulance drove up, and two med techs headed for the aircraft, but the heavy smoke drove them back. "Oh, no," Pontowski moaned as he stopped on the upwind side of the Warthog. The crash truck slammed into the rear of the pickup, its brakes not working. A silver-suited fireman jumped out of the crash truck and headed into the smoke as three others unlimbered a hose. Rockne and the rescue man stumbled out of the smoke, half carrying, half dragging Waldo.

The med techs were on Waldo and Rockne in a flash and loaded them both into the ambulance. It sped away as the fireman hosed down the back of the Warthog with fire retardant. It was over.

Pontowski walked around the aircraft with one of the firemen. "That was quick thinking, sir," the fireman said. "Towing us like that."

"I've never seen one of those stall before," Pontowski said.

"Budget cuts," the fireman said. "Maintenance sucks." He examined the pickup. "Well, that's one way to stop. But I don't think you'll be driving this anywhere soon."

Pontowski agreed. "No kidding." He looked around for a ride and saw Maggot with the chief of Maintenance, a Reserve colonel, examining the A-10. "How bad is it?" he called.

"I've seen worse," the colonel replied. "We'll know better when we get it in a hangar."

"So we deploy without it," Maggot said. "While you were out having fun and games on the runway here, we got orders to deploy." He automatically answered the next questions. "Advance team tomorrow, the Hogs on Sunday. Personnel to follow on Monday."

"So we go to war with nineteen jets," Pontowski grumbled.

"Maybe not," the colonel said.

Pontowski and Maggot walked through the main hangar where one group of technicians tore into the damaged Warthog while others swarmed over four other A-10s being prepped for the long flight to Malaysia. "This is organized chaos," Pontowski said.

"We've seen it before," Maggot replied. "These guys are all professionals and know what to do." They went into the Maintenance offices, but it was just as hectic. "Let's check the ramp," Maggot suggested. They walked outside and stood by the cargo pallets and mobility bins that were rapidly accumulating. "The support we've been getting is fantastic," Maggot said.

"That's an understatement if I ever heard one," Pontowski allowed. The buildup for their deployment wasn't pretty or by the book, but it was effective. He made a mental note to make sure the generals in the Pentagon knew what the men and women of Lackland had done. They stood there, comparing notes as the sun set. "It always hits the fan on Fridays," Pontowski observed.

"An immutable law of nature," Maggot replied. A minivan drew up by the operations building, and three men got out. "I think that's Waldo." He snorted. "I'll be damned, that's the Rock."

"You know Rockne?"

"From Whiteman. A great cop."

"He's the guy who pulled Waldo out," Pontowski said. "Let's go talk to them. Who's the other guy?" Maggot didn't answer and only shook his head. They followed the three men into the building.

Inside, Maggot stared at Waldo. "Cheated death again, Walderman?"

Waldo grinned. "Hey, you got your jet back." He turned serious. "I want to go."

"Are you okay?" Pontowski asked. He knew how physically and mentally punishing even a minor crash could be.

"Other than a stiff neck, I'm fine. The doc here can verify."

The major introduced himself. "Bob Ryan. I'm a flight surgeon. Lieutenant Colonel Walderman is fine."

"It's up to Colonel Stuart," Pontowski said, deferring the decision to Maggot.

It was an easy decision. "We got work to do," Maggot said. "Can't stand around here all day and yak." He gave Walderman a little shove and followed him out the door.

Pontowski turned to Rockne. "Chief, I can't thank you enough. I'll make sure your boss hears about it. But like the colonel said, we've got work to do."

Rockne didn't hesitate. "I want to go."

Pontowski was confused and it showed. "But you said—"

"I said 'shit,' sir, because I wanted to go to the Gulf. But what the hell, if this is the only action available, I'll take it."

"Can you get clear by Monday?"

"If I can't, then it's time to retire."

"I don't suppose," Pontowski said, going for broke, "that you could also get a security team together?"

Rockne's face was impassive. "I'll shake the tree until someone falls out. Excuse me, sir. But I've got some heads to crack, arms to twist." He spun around and was gone. Only the flight surgeon remained.

"Doctor," Pontowski said, "thanks for the help, but you didn't need to make a special trip."

"You need a flight surgeon," Ryan said. "I want to go."

Pontowski thought for a moment. His eyes narrowed into a squint. "Weren't you at Okinawa during the blockade?"*

Ryan never hesitated. "Yes, sir, I was. I'm that Ryan." The look on Pontowski's face told him he wasn't going. But he had to try. "I was an asshole and screwed up big-time. After it was over, General Martini told me everyone benefits this earth; some do it by living, others only by dying and freeing up space. I still had time to make a choice."

---

*Editor's note: The blockade of Okinawa and the near mutiny of Robert Ryan is told in *Power Curve* by the same author.

"I can hear Mafia saying that," Pontowski murmured. "Sorry, I'm not convinced."

Ryan knew he was begging, but he didn't care. "Martini told me something else. He said the Air Force is not about making money or getting your name in lights. It's about accomplishment, and we do it by placing service, sacrifice, and obligation over the individual. I didn't understand that then. I do now." He pulled himself to attention. "Sir, I'm asking for another chance."

Pontowski sat down behind his desk. "You said the right words. You've got your chance."

Ryan snapped a sharp salute. "You won't regret it," he promised.

I hope not, Pontowski thought. *But beggars can't be choosers.*

seventeen

Camp Alpha, Malaysia
Saturday, September 25

The dark green minivan pulled to a halt on the taxiway, still under the jungle canopy and well short of the wide highway that also functioned as a runway. The driver parked under the camouflage netting that covered an entrance to a hardened aircraft shelter, and Lieutenant Colonel Janice Clark got out. She motioned for the driver, who also served as her interpreter, to join her. "Let's talk to the guard," she told him. Together they approached the guard post, a sandbagged observation bunker at the edge of the tree line. The guard, a very nervous teenage Malay, fingered his M-16 as they approached. "Do you need food or water?" Clark called. The driver translated.

The boy held up his canteen, top down, cap off. "Damn," Clark growled. "Why don't they take better care of their people?" She sent the interpreter back to the minivan for water and a meal packet. She chafed at the delay, but there was little she could do about it—yet. The guard grinned at her. "Just a kid," she said to herself. "Ask him if there's been any activity," she told her driver. Again she waited as the two carried on an interminable discussion in Malay.

"He say nothing happening here, Missy Colonel," her driver said. She suppressed the urge to strangle him. For some reason he couldn't get her name and rank right. But rather than fight it, she went with the flow. "He's been here two days and wants to go back to barracks."

"Soon," she called. "Also tell him four helicopters are arriving in a few minutes and don't shoot at them." Clark keyed her handheld radio and radioed her command post. She quickly explained the situation to the duty officer and told him to check all the guards. She ended, "We've got to get the Malaysian Army organized." She signed off when she heard the helicopters. "I hope *they've* got a clue," she said in a loud voice, her frustration showing.

"Singapore Army much better, Missy Colonel," her driver replied.

The urge to strangle him grew stronger. She walked to the edge of the trees but didn't step into the open. A French-built AeroSpatiale 332 Super Puma with its twin Turbomeca engines crossed overhead and landed in the high grass next to the runway-cum-highway. The subdued Singapore roundel on the side of the fuselage was barely visible against a fresh jungle green camouflage paint job. The four-blade rotor spun down as twenty men jumped out the side doors and moved quickly into the tree line. The last man off was huge and moved with an agility and speed that belied his bulk. He headed straight for her. "Colonel Clark?" he asked. She nodded. "Victor Kamigami, First Special Operations Service." A second helicopter landed, and more men streamed off as a third came into view.

Just then a shot rang out, and Clark jumped back into the trees. When she looked back, all the men had disappeared and the helicopters taken off. "Get down," Kamigami ordered.

"It's okay," Clark told him. "He hasn't hit anyone—yet." An explanation was in order. "We've got a sniper who takes an occasional potshot. The MA can't seem to find him."

"MA?" Kamigami asked.

"Malaysian Army. They gave up, and we worked a deal with him: he misses us and we leave him alone."

Kamigami gave her a look she couldn't read. He spoke into the whisper mike pinned to his shoulder and issued orders. It was a strange mixture of Chinese and English that made absolutely no sense to her. "We'll take care of it," he said. "Tell your people we're here and to stand down while we . . . uh, renegotiate with your sniper."

Clark relayed his message to her command post. "Tell the MA we've got friendlies on base and to hold their fire."

"Hell," the duty officer replied, "they don't shoot at anything unless they think they can eat it."

"Problems?" Kamigami asked.

"You wouldn't believe," Clark said. "Is it okay for us to move around?" He nodded, and they walked toward the minivan. "Are you familiar with Alpha?" she asked.

"Only what I've seen on paper." Kamigami sat in the backseat as they drove down a taxiway and onto the base proper. He studied the camouflage netting overhead, the reinforced-concrete aircraft bunkers, and the way the buildings were sited to blend in with the terrain and trees. His initial impression after flying over was confirmed—the base was next to impossible to see from the air and impervious to satellite reconnaissance. Only the straight stretch of highway that served as its runway provided any clue as to its location. The more he saw as they toured the base, the more he was impressed. Alpha was a masterpiece. "Very nice," he allowed. "Israelis?"

"They built it two years ago," she explained. "Under contract to SEATO. Unfortunately, it's been neglected since then. We had to chase squatters and pig farmers out of the shelters. Luckily, the MA has managed to keep the locals from stealing—" A burst of submachine-gun fire cut her off. "What the . . . ?"

"Ours," Kamigami assured her. "Pull up over there." He pointed to a revetted entrance to a low concrete building.

"That's the base medical station," she told him. "It's locked up—I hope." Another burst of submachine-gun fire echoed over them. This time much farther away.

Kamigami got out of the minivan as Sun and Tel emerged from the shadows of the entrance. Kamigami introduced them to Clark, and without being asked, Sun briefed them on the situation. More gunfire. Sun stopped and pressed a hand to his ear, covering the earpiece linking him to his radio. "We're bringing them in now," he said.

"Them?" Clark asked. Sun nodded as a team of four shooters emerged from the nearby trees. They were carrying a body. Another team was right behind them, but this time they had two very live, and very frightened, prisoners. She listened as Tel interrogated the prisoners in Malay while Kamigami and Sun held back in the revetted entrance. Tel waved an arm in the direction of Kamigami's dark shadow, and the two men fell to the ground, wailing loudly. Two more teams of shooters drove up in a truck they had commandeered. They unloaded three more bodies and piled their equipment on the ground. Clark circled the four bodies, struck by how young they were. "They're just boys," she said.

Sun spoke into his radio as Tel joined her. Tel pointed at one of the men kneeling on the ground. "He says there were six."

"Then all are accounted for," Sun said.

"Ma'am," Tel said, "may we speak in private for a moment?" He played the gentleman and motioned her around the corner of the building.

Clark glanced back over her shoulder as Kamigami stepped out of the shadows. A lightning bolt shot out of her subconscious and jolted every fiber of her being. "You're going to kill them!"

Tel gently touched her elbow, urging her around the corner and out of sight. "Only one," he told her, refusing to lie. "The other one will be released."

"Why?" she asked.

"So he can tell his comrades he met the vampire. They won't be back." He tried to make her understand. "It's much better this way. We won't have to kill so many."

"I will *not* be a part of this," Clark told him, her anger in full play. She spun around and marched back to Kamigami, determined to do something. But the two prisoners were gone, and only the four bodies remained. "What exactly do you think you're doing here?" she demanded.

"Doing here?" Kamigami asked. "I thought you'd been briefed." It was obvious she hadn't. "We're here to relocate as many villagers as we can. Before they get butchered."

Clark stormed back to her van.

The White House
Saturday, September 25

"I hope this won't take too long," Richard Parrish said as he escorted them into the study. "The president will be here shortly. It may be Saturday, but she has a full schedule. I don't know how she does it, balancing an election campaign with running a war. It would drive a normal person over the edge."

"President Turner is far from being a normal person," Secretary of State Serick conceded.

"We only need fifteen minutes," Mazie told him as they sat down.

Parrish held the door when the president entered. Mazie and Serick stood. "It looks like a quiet day in the Gulf," Turner said. "Nothing is moving." She sat down in her rocker and motioned for them to sit. "But you're not here to tell me what I already know."

"No, ma'am," Serick began. He shot Mazie a cautious glance. He cleared his throat. "Mrs. Hazelton has a most intriguing idea that we might want to pursue."

The president's lips crinkled, the beginnings of a smile, at his formality. Then it was gone. "Not the unthinkable I hope?"

Serick breathed deeply. "Not unthinkable, but a new vector, one that we haven't considered."

"But one sensitive enough that no one else should know?" Turner asked.

"At this point," Serick said, "that might be the wisest course."

"Stephan," Turner said, now smiling at her two most trusted advisers, "would you please be more direct and less diplomatic?"

Mazie decided to do just that. "Madam President, we want to open a second front in the Gulf."

"I'm quite sure General Wilding can give me a dozen reasons why that's impossible," Turner said. "And they all start with the word 'logistics.' With the Suez Canal closed, our supply lines are simply too long."

"But the Mediterranean is still open to us," Mazie said.

Turner saw it immediately. "Are you suggesting perhaps Israel?"

"Not Israel," Serick replied. "Turkey." The president sat upright.

"All our intelligence," Mazie said, "indicates that the UIF is strained to the limit as it regroups in Saudi Arabia—in the south. If we were to open a second front through Turkey, in the north, we could catch Iraq in a giant pincer. Baghdad is approximately three hundred miles south of the Turkish border, and we could split Iraq right down the middle."

"It has the added advantage," Serick said, "of driving a wedge between Syria and Iran, placing each in a much more isolated position."

"I need to see a map," Turner said. Serick opened his briefcase and unfolded one. He spread it across her desk, and the three gathered around it. Turner's eyes narrowed as Mazie measured the distances.

"The Iraqis," Mazie explained, "believe that the mountains are a natural barrier between them and Turkey. But the mountains didn't stop Alexander in 331 B.C. when he came down the eastern bank of the Tigris. He fought and defeated the Persians here, near Mosul." Mazie tapped the city in the northwest corner of Iraq. "After that it was open country to Babylon."

"Which was not far from modern Baghdad," Serick added. "Approximately two hundred miles of wide-open country. Good terrain for armor."

Turner considered it. She shook her head. "The Iraqis would see our buildup in Turkey and be ready. They'd stop us in the mountain passes, before we broke out into open country."

"So what if it wasn't us?" Mazie said. "But one of our allies who trains in Turkey."

"And that ally is?" Turner asked.

"Germany," Mazie replied. "They do extensive tank training near Urfa in southern Turkey. They have a training program modeled after our National Training Center in the Mojave Desert."

"The Turks would never allow it," Turner said.

"Unless they thought they were next," Mazie replied.

"But they're not," Turner objected. "We know that."

"But do the Turks?" Mazie asked. "What if they were convinced otherwise?"

Turner thought for a moment. She reached for the phone and hit a button. "Patrick, would you step in here for a moment?" She didn't wait for an answer and buzzed her chief of staff's office. "Richard, please clear my schedule for the next hour." Again she didn't wait for an answer. "Convince Patrick," she told them.

Patrick Shaw's sarcasm was in full flow as he poked at the map on Turner's desk. "What do you people use for brains around here? Alexander the Great, my ass. The next person who wants to play strategy around here is gonna get a lobotomy. Sans anesthetic." He shambled to the door, a shaggy bear at bay. "Totally unthinkable. If you wanna split the UIF, make Syria or Iran an offer they can't refuse." He paused. "Anything else, Mizz President?" She told him no and he was gone, closing the door behind him.

Turner carefully folded the map and handed it to Serick. "Thank you for listening, Madam President," Serick said. Mazie stood to leave.

The president turned sideways in her chair as her fingers beat a little tattoo on her desk. They both recognized the signs. "He may be right, Stephan. Approach Syria and Iran with a deal. Make it a good one."

"We can use Jordan as an intermediary," Serick told her.

A long pause. Then, "Can you bring Germany and Turkey in?"

Mazie stared at her, and Serick sucked in his breath, both totally surprised. The president had never disregarded Shaw's advice before. "Patrick," Turner said, "has a crude saying: 'Learn from the past or get bit in the ass.' I don't think the Iraqis have learned a damn thing." She stood. "And we're going to teach them."

"I have a contact in Bonn," Mazie said. "Herbert von Lubeck."

Serick was impressed. "You'll have to go to him."

"I can go today," Mazie told them. "That leaves the Turks." She thought for a moment. "I believe Bernie can help. At one time, the Boys were very active in Turkey."

"Get him moving," Turner ordered. "We need to make something happen. The sooner the better."

Shaw stood at the window in his corner office, looking at the bright day outside. But he didn't see a thing. His fingers played with the laboratory report he was holding. "Do it, Maddy," he said under his breath. "You know how." He paced the floor, talking to himself. "Leland, you miserable bastard." More mumbling. "Fuckin' investigation . . . makin' common cause with the Frogs . . . I'm gonna shred your ass." He wadded the report he was holding, and threw it into the wastebasket to be shredded.

eighteen

Over the Philippine Sea,
Wednesday, September 29

This isn't as easy as it used to be, Pontowski thought as he crawled into the seat next to the boomer in the refueling capsule of the KC-10. Jet lag was taking a fearsome toll, and he wasn't sleeping well. He slipped on the headset and settled into the comfortable seat next to the boom operator. The three seats were a far cry from the narrow pit where the boom operator lay in the older KC-135 for refueling. The protective shield over the view port was open, and he could see eight Warthogs, four on each side, flying in a loose formation. Far below him puffy clouds dotted the blue Pacific. "How's it going?" he asked.

"Not bad," the boomer replied. "The KC-135 from Okinawa was on station as planned. Mindanao coming under the nose in a few minutes." Pontowski felt the tension ease a bit. The one KC-10 and three KC-135s escorting his twenty A-10s did not carry quite enough fuel to refuel the Hogs for the entire leg, and they had to make a midocean rendezvous with an additional tanker. While it sounded simple, it was anything but. Pontowski dozed.

On the face of it the deployment from Kelly Field in Texas had gone smoothly enough. Pontowski and eighty others had boarded the KC-10 the Air Force had laid on to serve as a mother ship for the deployment and launched with the Hogs on Sunday morning. They rendezvoused with four more tankers and flew to Hickam Air Force Base in Hawaii, a flight of eight and a half hours.

On Monday morning the twenty Hogs and the KC-10 had taken off from Hickam, again rendezvoused with four KC-135s, and flown nine and a half hours to Guam. But thanks to crossing the International Dateline, they had landed on Tuesday. Now they were on the last leg, an eight-hour hop to Malaysia. On its own, the KC-10 could have made it in much less time, but the Warthogs did nothing fast.

The boomer's voice brought him back to life. "Steamer One, you're cleared to precontact." Steamer One was the call sign for Bag, the flight lead for Steamer flight, the formation on the right. Bag slid into close trail. The boomer cleared Bag into position, and he moved smoothly under the KC-10's tail. The boomer guided the flying boom and hooked up on the first try. Bag's Hog never moved as he took on five thousand pounds of fuel. "Very nice," the boomer said over the intercom.

Indeed it is, Pontowski thought. *How old is Bag now? Forty?* He couldn't remember. *He's changed since Africa.* The pilot had been a captain on the peacekeeping mission to Africa, full of life and dedicated to the pursuit of women and the search for the perfect beer. During a stopover on that deployment, he and six other Hog pilots had set a new record on the island of Saint Helena for beer consumption and had been arrested by the local constabulary. The governor of the island had ordered the police to make sure they departed the next day, never to return. But four lovely young ladies had come to see them off with flowers and tears.

Pontowski hit the transmit button. "Bag, how did it go last night?" He expected to hear a tale of debauchery and consumption to rival the Saint Helena episode. Whether it was true or not didn't matter—it was the image that counted.

"Hit the sack early," Bag replied.

"Hair not on fire?" Pontowski asked.

Another voice answered. "Naw. He burnt it off years ago."

"Flying for the airlines does that to you," a second voice said.

The years tame us all, Pontowski thought. Maturity had its own demands, and the airlines paid much better. Like most of the pilots, Bag hadn't flown an A-10 in over two years. But no fighter jock really wanted to be an airline pilot, and after four flights and hitting the books for a few days, he was back in the groove, more than ready to ferry a Hog across the Pacific. Steamer flight cycled smoothly on and off the boom, proof positive that they hadn't lost the old skills.

Maggot's four aircraft, Bruiser flight, were next. "Clear Waldo on first," Maggot radioed. "Higher fuel consumption."

Pontowski watched as Waldo moved into the precontact position. "He's not trimmed up," the boomer said.

It was true; the A-10 appeared to be in a skid. "Waldo," Pontowski said over the radio, "say problem."

"This Hog's a real pig. It's out of rig."

A voice that sounded suspiciously like Bag said, "You pranged it, you fly it."

Waldo was flying the jet he had dumped on the runway, and the other pilots were not about to let him forget it. "Hey, meathead," Waldo shot back, "I got it down."

"One of your better landings," another pilot observed.

"Landing, hell," another voice said. "That was supposed to be a touch-and-go."

Pontowski grinned. *Some things never change.* There was no doubt in his mind that the AVG was going to do just fine. *Thanks for making it happen, Maggot. I can't do this without you. But who would have ever thought it would be you?* How many times had he seen it happen when a young and superb pilot—but all stick and balls, no forehead—matured into a leader men would follow into combat? Was this the same Maggot who bet that he could eat an oyster without its touching his lips or tongue and then won the wager by sniffing the oyster up his nose? Or during a flyby at a football game really took it low, thrilling the crowd? *You drove me crazy! How ironic. I did the same to Jack Locke.* But when the battle was joined and the odds overwhelming, Maggot was always there, ready to do what he did best—fly and fight. *You saved my ass in China, and now I'm going to risk yours. What gives me the right?* He would never find a satisfactory answer to that question.

"General Pontowski," the KC-10 pilot called over the intercom, "we've got an incoming for you." The KC-10 had recently been upgraded with a sophisticated communications suite that not only handled routine radio traffic over a broad bandwidth but also allowed encrypted message traffic, weather reports, and maps to be sent and received through an onboard computer and then printed out.

Pontowski heaved himself from his seat and worked his way forward, past the pallets of cargo and sleeping men. It hadn't been the pilots who were partying on Guam. He stopped at the galley in the area aft of the flight deck. Rockne was standing by a window deep in thought. "How's it going, Chief?"

"Problems. I talked to Colonel Clark on the phone while we were at Guam. She's worried about security when the A-10s land. I've only got thirty cops with us. I've been promised a mobility team of four flights plus a headquarters element—max of a hundred eighty-nine people—with an officer in charge. But I haven't got a clue when they'll arrive."

Pontowski thought for a moment. "We'll have to use maintenance troops until they get here."

Rockne was appalled. "Give a wrench bender a weapon and he'll shoot his foot off."

"You've got fifty or so bodies on board you can use," Pontowski told him. "We land in four hours. Make something happen." Rockne jerked his head yes. It was exactly the type of challenge he loved.

Pontowski went forward to the flight deck, and the copilot handed him the hard copy of the message addressed to him. It was from the NMCC and very short. When the American Volunteer Group crossed 125 degrees east longitude, they were chopped (change in command) to South East Asia Treaty Organization. However, as the commander of the MAAG, Pontowski was to maintain operational control of the aircraft at all times.

He scratched his head. *How in the hell am I supposed to make that happen?*

Camp Alpha
Wednesday, September 29

Janice Clark was waiting on the parking ramp when Pontowski climbed down from the KC-10. She made a mental note to get boarding stairs; one more item in the long list of what they needed to make the base more efficient. "Missy Colonel," her driver said, "he is a general." The man had simply confirmed what she already knew—Pontowski looked like a general. His jungle fatigues fitted his lanky frame perfectly. He jammed a dark green beret with SEAC's badge over his close-cropped hair as he walked toward her. His slight limp added to the image.

It's a good thing I'm happily married, Clark thought. She walked out to meet him. Much to her surprise, her driver trailed along. She snapped a salute. "Welcome to Alpha," she said. Her driver was also trying to salute, his hand against his forehead in the British way, his mouth open.

Pontowski waved a salute back. "Glad to be here." He checked his watch. "The jets are right behind us. We came on ahead after the last refueling to get the crew chiefs on the ground and let a KC-135 bring them in." He pointed to the west. "There they are." A KC-135 flew by at twenty-five hundred feet and turned away, its mission complete. Two miles behind, the first flight of four A-10s flew down final, level at fifteen hundred feet. They smoothly echeloned to the left, each slightly behind the other. Farther to the south, four more A-10s came into view. "Got all twenty," Pontowski told her.

The three stood there as the flight crossed the approach end of the runway. "In the break . . ." Pontowski murmured. "Now." On cue the flight lead pitched out to the right and circled to land. At exactly five-second intervals his flight pitched out in order. Clark glanced at Pontowski and caught the satisfied look on his face as the fighters lowered their gear and flaps to land at three-thousand-foot intervals. It was a classic overhead recovery, the way fighters recovered from combat. She smiled at her driver, who was transfixed by the sight. All around them the ramp was alive with activity, crew chiefs hurrying to marshal their charges in and a crew offloading the KC-10. The first four jets cleared the runway as the second flight of four approached for an overhead recovery.

"What a sight," Clark said. The third flight came into view. "They do look good."

"Good enough," Pontowski allowed. His eyes narrowed in recognition of the first aircraft as it taxied in. *That's Bag. Maggot should have landed first.* He shrugged it off. One of Bag's flights was probably low on fuel, and Maggot had changed the landing order. No big deal.

"It's too bad no one's here to see this," Clark told him. Now the fourth flight was in sight.

It doesn't matter, Pontowski thought. *The jocks know.* Suddenly the tension was back as the fifth flight came into view. There were only two aircraft. "I need to talk to the tower," Pontowski said, his voice calm.

Clark turned to her driver to tell him to get the minivan with its radio. But he was already running for the van. She shook her head. "He's never moved that fast before." In less than a minute he drove up and handed Pontowski the mike, its cord stretched out the window.

"Tower," Pontowski radioed, "this is Bossman. Say status of last flight." His eyes were fixed on the horizon, looking for the two missing aircraft.

"Bossman," the tower answered, "Bruiser Three and Four are in the pattern now. One and Two are five minutes out." Bruiser Three and Four were the second element in Maggot's flight. Maggot was Bruiser One, and Waldo was Bruiser Two. "Bruiser Two reports partial hydraulic failure," the tower reported.

"It figures," Pontowski said to himself. He keyed the radio. "Have they declared an emergency?"

"Negative," the tower replied. "Precautionary landing only."

Now they had to wait. Clark saw the two aircraft first. "There," she said. One of the aircraft was trailing smoke.

"That's Waldo," Pontowski muttered.

Clark took the mike. "Tower, scramble the crash trucks. I want to use this as practice." She handed the mike to the driver. "We've got a new crash-response team from Singapore. I hope they're better."

"Better than what?" Pontowski asked. He walked toward the runway.

"What was here before," she answered. Two crash trucks and an ambulance roared out of the trees, lights flashing, and stopped short of the runway. "Much better," she announced.

Pontowski walked with measured steps back to Clark's minivan, his eyes locked on the landing aircraft. As expected, Waldo landed first as Maggot flew a loose formation, escorting him down. Pontowski opened the van door, ready to jump in. The driver, sensing the emergency, was already behind the wheel and starting the engine. Waldo made a smooth touchdown and rolled out. He turned off at midfield and taxied into the trees. "Let's go howdy the man," Pontowski said, meaning he wanted to find out what had happened. Clark jumped in, and they raced down the access road.

They reached the taxiway where Waldo was stopped and got out of the van. Waldo was still sitting in the cockpit, the canopy raised, talking to a crew chief who had climbed up the boarding steps. When Waldo saw Pontowski and Clark, he climbed down. When he reached the pavement, he dropped his helmet and spread his arms. "I have arrived. You may start the war."

Pontowski shook his head. "You need a new line, Waldo," he called.

Bonn, Germany
Wednesday, September 29

The dark gray Mercedes sedan drove through the Wednesday-evening traffic. In the backseat Mazie sat with her hands folded while Butler read a highly confidential dossier that should never have left the confines of the State Department. He was still getting up to speed on the situation. "Have you met von Lubeck before?" he asked.

"A few times," she murmured, not willing to say more. She had dealt with Herbert von Lubeck numerous times and was apprehensive. Von Lubeck was a tall, handsome man in his early fifties with salt-and-pepper hair and penetrating blue eyes. On the face of it he was a minor functionary in the German government, the first secretary to the deputy minister for economic research and trapped in the old Cold War capital while the political action swirled in Berlin. But in reality he was a plenipotentiary with wide-ranging powers and influence in the German government. Von Lubeck preferred to remain in the shadows, but the knowledgeable knew that he was the man to see on truly important issues involving the German government. Supposedly only four people in the U.S. government knew who he really was, and Mazie was one of them. However, a fifth person now knew—Bernie Butler. But he would deny it with his last breath.

"So he's quite the . . . uh, ladies' man," Butler said. He was careful in his choice of words, for one couldn't ask the national security adviser if von Lubeck had hit on her. But according to the dossier, Mazie Kamigami Hazelton was exactly the type of woman who appealed to von Lubeck.

"He was"—Mazie paused, searching for the right words—"always the gentleman."

Butler worked to keep his face expressionless. The answer to his unasked question was obviously yes, and she was obviously attracted to von Lubeck. But he had seen it all before; for the rich and influential of the world, power was the ultimate aphrodisiac, and they sought each other out. Butler closed the dossier as the car drove into the basement garage of a nondescript government office building. The driver knew where he was going and pulled into a guarded back bay where two dark-suited young men were waiting. They were most polite in escorting the two Americans to the top floor in a private elevator.

The man waiting for them in the ornate study was a throwback to a previous age—aristocratic, gracious, and gallant. He could have been a cavalry officer mounting a charge during the Franco-Prussian War or a courtier at the court of Frederick the Great. "Mrs. Hazelton," he said, taking her hand and almost kissing it, but not quite. Butler was certain Mazie wanted her hand kissed. "It is always a pleasure to see you." He spoke with an English accent. Then he turned to Butler and extended his hand. "And General Butler, I presume." The two men shook hands. Even von Lubeck's handshake was perfect for the occasion, just the right strength and duration. He motioned them to comfortable overstuffed chairs in front of the fireplace. "Our first fire of the season," he said.

He settled into a chair and turned directly to business. "No doubt you're here because your government wants mine to become involved in the Gulf."

Mazie allowed a little smile. "No doubt." Butler listened as they played cat and mouse, circling in on the purpose of the visit. He was surprised how quickly Mazie dropped the first bombshell. "I assume you're aware of the arrangement our Senator Leland has worked out with Monsieur Cherveaux and his cohorts at the Quai d'Orsay?" Von Lubeck gave a little nod, which meant he wasn't. "Of course," Mazie added, setting the hook, "the quid pro quo is based on Leland's candidate winning the election."

Von Lubeck smiled. "As your Mr. Shaw is fond of saying, 'the dreaded quid pro quo.'"

"That always bites someone in the ass," Mazie replied, startling von Lubeck. She returned his smile. "Which Patrick is also fond of saying." Now she dropped the second bombshell. "In this case a European backside."

It was Butler's turn. "We have reason to believe that if the French can keep NATO out of the war, that will force a stalemate in the Gulf. Which, in turn, will stir up a political firestorm in the States and give the election to the senator's boy."

"Your election is five weeks away," von Lubeck replied. "I seriously doubt if NATO's intervention would make a difference by then."

"But it might force the UIF to withdraw or negotiate," Mazie said.

"Perhaps," von Lubeck allowed.

"If NATO stays out," Butler said, "and his boy wins, Leland will allow the French to broker a cease-fire and in the process become the middle man for marketing the UIF's oil to Europe."

Again von Lubeck nodded. A noncommittal look played across his face that hid his shock and anger. But, true to the game, he said nothing and waited for the Americans to put something on the table.

"We were hoping," Mazie said, "that your government would be willing to act in the best interests of the European community." She was asking the Germans to "do the right thing," a very weak offer in von Lubeck's world.

Butler pulled off the diplomatic gloves. He clasped his hands and leaned forward in his chair. "Sir, we know that your government is as concerned as ours and is thinking along the same lines."

"And how do you know that?" von Lubeck asked, showing a little surprise.

"Because," Butler replied, "you are building up your forces in Turkey. At last count you have over a hundred Leopard tanks in place at your training camp outside Urfa. They're fully operational, along with two army regiments and the required logistical infrastructure to keep them in the field for six weeks. That, sir, is a formidable presence—all within two hundred miles of Iraq's border." Mazie shot Butler a startled look. She knew of the training area used by the Germans but hadn't heard of their buildup. Butler realized he had made an assumption that wasn't true. That was a very bad mistake in his business. "My apologies, Mrs. Hazelton. I thought the DCI had briefed you and Secretary Serick."

"And you are suggesting?" von Lubeck asked.

Mazie recovered and said, "We are suggesting that you open a second front in the north to advance on Baghdad and drive a wedge between Syria and Iran."

"The UIF," Butler said, "is fully committed to the buildup in the south. Iraq has bled its northern forces dry, and what's left in place is a shadow force meant to intimidate the Kurds."

"The Kurds have always been a thorn in the side of the Iraqis," von Lubeck said, dissembling as he reviewed his bargaining strategy. German intelligence had accurately predicted the war, and his government had secretly increased its military presence at Urfa in anticipation of a two-front war. But timing was everything in his world, and everything had a price. How much more could he get from the Americans—or was it time to commit?

Mazie decided to lay her cards on the table. "We need your help. I shudder to think what would happen under an administration controlled by Leland." She stood and walked to the fireplace. "We also believe that it's time Germany takes its proper place on the world stage."

Von Lubeck stood beside her. "What is our place in the new world order—or should I say the new world disorder? My country is searching for an answer to that question, but we seem to have lost our identity in a sea of modernity."

"Perhaps," Mazie said, "you need to return to the old virtues, but without the madness of the last century."

Von Lubeck gazed into the fire and committed. "It will take some convincing on my part." He paused, marshaling his thoughts. "There also remains the problem of Turkey. We cannot act without their agreement, which I don't believe they'll give."

"I can solve that problem," Butler promised.

The meeting was over, and von Lubeck was the gracious host as he escorted them to their car. They were silent until they were clear of the garage and in traffic. Mazie reached out and touched Butler's hand. The warmth of her hand surprised him. "I was blindsided in there," she said. "Secretary Serick and I fully discussed this with the DCI after speaking to the president. Why didn't he tell us about the German buildup in Turkey?"

"Maybe he didn't know," Butler replied. "It won't happen again." It was a promise he meant to keep.

Mazie thought for a moment. "Von Lubeck wants something. What is it?"

"Who knows?" Butler replied. "He's probably thinking he can play Bismarck."

Camp Alpha
Thursday, September 30

Clark's office was austere in the extreme. A gray metal desk occupied one end, and plastic file boxes lined two walls. Three folding chairs completed the furniture. The only spot of color was a small vase on her desk holding a beautiful orchid. "Very pretty," Pontowski said, sniffing at the orchid.

"My driver," Clark said. "He says they grow wild and brings me one every day." She closed the door and sat down behind her desk. The gentle whir of the air conditioner seemed to fill the room. "I've a problem we need to discuss," she announced. "I believe you know Victor Kamigami."

Pontowski sat in one of the folding chairs and tried to get comfortable. "We have a history," he admitted. "In China."

She took a deep breath and plunged ahead. "He may have committed a crime on my base. Specifically, he murdered a prisoner in his custody."

"I didn't know he was here," Pontowski said, hedging an answer. He had been busy the last eighteen hours bedding down the AVG and needed sleep.

"SEAC deployed the First SOS to Alpha as its base camp," she explained. "Their mission is to extract villagers out of areas controlled by the PLA. I assigned them an empty barracks on the perimeter and a bunker for their helicopters. We haven't seen much of them since. I assume he's still on base." She folded her hands and related the incident with the snipers. "They hadn't been here two hours when it happened." Her voice hardened. "No one—I don't care who it is—commits murder on my base."

"You didn't actually see it?" Pontowski asked.

She shook her head. "I only know what one of his men told me. But I was there, just around the corner. In fact, I was escorted there so I wouldn't see it."

Pontowski tried to adjust his body to the chair but failed. In exasperation he turned it around and straddled it, his arms resting on the back. "Let's ask him. He won't lie. Unfortunately, under the right circumstances, I can see him doing it."

"And what exactly are the right circumstances?" she asked, her words laced with sarcasm. "What kind of man would do that?"

Pontowski searched for the words to explain. "First, Victor is the national security adviser's father—"

"So he has political protection?" Clark snapped.

"No. Not at all. But he operates from a different set of rules. It's hard to explain. It's like he's the ancient warrior."

"Which means what?" Clark shot at him.

"That's all he is—a warrior. It's almost like war seeks him out and draws him in to correct some horrible wrong. Do you know what happened to his family?" She shook her head. As best he could, Pontowski filled in the details. When he was finished, he said, "I would not want to be one of the soldiers who murdered his family."

Clark mulled it over. "Let's ask him." Then, "Breakfast?" Pontowski readily agreed. They walked outside and headed for the mess hall. But before they were halfway there, her handheld radio beeped at her. A C-17 was inbound with eighty passengers and cargo. She gave Pontowski a sideways glance and said, "Shall we go 'howdy' the folks?" She turned and motioned at her driver, who was following them in the minivan. "My shadow," she said. They drove to the parking ramp and arrived in time to see the big C-17 land. Rockne joined them as the high-winged cargo plane taxied slowly off the runway and onto the confined parking ramp. "It might be your cops," Clark told him.

Together they watched the cargo ramp come down and people stream off the back. A loadmaster handed Clark a passenger list and cargo manifest. "A flight surgeon with eight medics," she announced. "And seventy-two cops." She handed Rockne the manifest. "And one K9."

Rockne came alert, and his eyes narrowed as he searched the people milling around in confusion. The flight surgeon and eight medics gathered around three pallets with their baggage and equipment. Then someone issued an order, and a young airman, who looked suspiciously like Cindy Cloggins, lifted a fanion, a small unit flag on a six-foot staff. What had been a shapeless amoeba flowing around the plane formed on the fanion in ranks of eight, nine deep. Jessica Maul marched to the front with a dog at her side. But the dog's leash was not attached, and she held it in her left hand, folded in fourths. She came to attention and slapped the leash sharply against her thigh. "Squadron," she called, her voice full of command. "A-ten-hut!" As one, the formation responded. Her commands were crisp as she formed them up. Then, "Squadron! For-ward harch!" They marched across the ramp directly toward Pontowski, Clark, and Rockne. Twenty feet short, Jessica halted the squadron and saluted. "Sir, ma'am, Three Forty-third Training Squadron reporting for duty."

Pontowski returned her salute. "Welcome to the American Volunteer Group," he said.

Clark was shocked. Without exception, they were all young—too young. "A training squadron?" she said in a low voice.

Jessica heard it and dropped her salute. "Actually, ma'am, this is last Friday's graduating class from basic security police training." She looked at Rockne. "Your dog, Chief." She whispered a command and sent Boyca on her way.

Rockne stroked Boyca as he looked them over. He had a new challenge. "Glad to see you could make this deployment," he told her.

"Wouldn't have missed it for the world," she told him.

nineteen

The White House
Thursday, September 30

The silver-haired senator followed the president through the door of the Situation Room and sat down next to her. *I'll be damned,* Shaw thought. *Savane's one of the good guys.* In Shaw's political order of battle, Senator Philip Savane was truly a member of the loyal opposition and not to be confused with the likes of his fellow party member John Leland. *She's reaching out,* Shaw decided. To his way of thinking, she couldn't find a better ally in the Senate.

"I wish Mazie and Bernie were here to see this," Vice President Kennett said, also impressed with the turn of events.

"Mazie's due back this afternoon," Shaw said.

"And Butler?"

"No idea," Shaw replied. He fell silent as Colonel Scovill took the podium and waited for the signal from Wilding to start the morning's briefing for the ExCom.

"President Turner, Senator Savane, gentlemen," Scovill said, "I'd like to begin with a recap of last night's B-2 missions." He allowed a tight smile. "I can reconfirm that all ten aircraft returned undamaged to Whiteman Air Force Base." A map of Iraq appeared on the big screen on the left. Arrows pointed to 160 targets. "These are the targets we hit last night. Preliminary bomb-damage assessment indicates that a hundred fifteen, or seventy-two percent, were destroyed; twenty-three, or fourteen percent, heavily damaged; and nine, or six percent, were lightly damaged."

"And the other thirteen?" Savane asked.

"We missed," the Marine answered.

"Been there, done that," the senator replied, recalling his missions as a fighter pilot in Vietnam.

"Whiteman is launching twelve sorties tonight," the Marine continued. "All thirteen of those targets will be revisited." The screen on the right scrolled to a new map of Iraq with arrows pointed at the new targets. The screen zoomed in on Baghdad. "Of particular concern tonight is this target. We hit it three nights ago, but it was not totally destroyed."

"Downtown Baghdad," Savane said in a low voice. He was back in time, caught up in his memories. "I was flying over another downtown when I was shot down. Is it worth the risk?"

"We believe it is," Scovill replied, his voice icy calm. His thumb danced on the hand controller in his right hand. "Specifically, this is target I36-8481, an underground command bunker built under the basement of the Al-Rashid Hotel." The screen enlarged to an oblique aerial photo of the hotel.

"My God," Shaw blurted, momentarily losing control. His doctor had warned him about that, and he clamped an iron-hard control on his surging emotions. But an explanation was in order. "That's where the press is staying," he muttered.

Scovill's tight smile was back. "Exactly. On the left screen is the video taken from the attacking B-2's targeting system. The pilot's voice you hear is the mission commander on board the B-2. On the right screen is the simultaneous coverage supplied by a CNC-TV reporter as he reported the attack from the roof of the hotel."

The left screen shimmered with a greenish image of the target as the pilot's voice described the bomb run. "There's the Al-Rashid Hotel." The crosshairs on the screen moved over the hotel. "There's offset one, there's offset two." Again the crosshairs on the screen followed his voice from the hotel to the offsets, each one a distinct target but progressively smaller in size. "Target acquisition now." The crosshairs jumped from the last offset to the middle of a big parking lot. The crosshairs stabilized, and a few seconds later a finger of light flashed at the bottom of the screen. "Bomb gone." A countdown timer in the lower left-hand side of the screen started to unwind to zero.

"The mission commander," the colonel explained, "activated the release system when he went to target acquisition. The computer moved the crosshairs to the no-show target and automatically pickled the bomb when all release parameters were met. When the countdown timer reaches zero, the bomb will impact on the crosshairs. Meanwhile, from the rooftop of the Al-Rashid . . ."

The right screen cycled to the CNC-TV reporter. The skyline of Baghdad was in the background. A series of flashes jumped around the city as tracers lit the sky. "Each flash," the reporter said, "is a precision-guided bomb going off. Radio Baghdad reports three B-2 stealth bombers have been shot down so far."

"As all our aircraft returned," Scovill interjected, "we have reason to believe that this claim is vastly overinflated or that they shot down someone else's B-2s." Savane laughed. "Now," the colonel continued, "direct your attention to the left screen." The crosshairs on the greenish screen disappeared in a little puff of smoke. "Now back to the Al-Rashid."

The reporter on the right screen pointed to the parking lot. "It looks like a bomb hit in the middle of the parking lot but didn't go off. There's been no explosion." A slight pause. "I can see a hole in the pavement now." The camera zoomed in on the hole, a circular black void. "The bomb was a dud." Suddenly a pillar of flame shot out of the hole, followed by billowing smoke. "Oh, my God!" the reporter screamed. "The building is shaking, and I can hear muffled explosions! Oh, no!"—this slightly more composed—"the entire parking lot appears to be caving in." The camera recorded the parking lot collapsing into a big hole.

"The Iraqis," Scovill explained, "had calculated that we would not strike the command post for fear of killing foreign reporters. We want to disabuse them of that thinking. To the best of our knowledge, the only casualties from the first strike were in the command post. Bomb-damage assessment indicates we destroyed the power room to the command bunker and at least two escape tunnels."

"Then why are you 'revisiting' it tonight?" Kennett asked.

"Because," the DCI answered, "we have monitored people still entering and leaving."

"Thanks to TV coverage yesterday," Scovill said, "we were able to identify the main entrance to the command post, which is located here, behind the Al-Rashid." The screen on the left cycled to a photo of what looked like the service entrance to a bakery. "We intend to send a GBU-31 down the main entry—all courtesy of CNC-TV."

Savane tried to look serious, but he was clearly enjoying the briefing. "I do believe that's a gross violation of the freedom of the press."

The Marine couldn't help himself. "I do hope so, Senator. I wanted to send a thank-you note to CNC-TV, but my boss wouldn't let me."

The senator suppressed his laughter. "I can't say I blame him."

"On a more serious note," Scovill said, "the Navy reports contact with three submarines operating in the approaches to the Straits of Hormuz."

Savane caught it immediately. "Hostile signatures?"

"That's affirmative," the colonel replied. "Unfortunately, we can't identify the nationality. One is probably Iranian, the other two may be Chinese."

"But not Russian?" Savane asked.

"Definitely not," General Wilding said. "We're in close communications with our counterparts in Moscow to prevent that from happening."

"That's encouraging," Savane replied. "I assume this has logistical implications."

Wilding stood and walked to the center display screen. He clicked at the handheld controller. A map of the approaches to the Persian Gulf came on the screen. "Yes it does, Senator. We are diverting all our supply ships to Diego Garcia until we can neutralize the threat."

The senator took a deep breath. He fully understood what that would do to the buildup in Saudi Arabia and how it would delay any planned offensive. "Convoy operations?" he asked.

"We are considering it," Wilding replied.

Savane turned to the president. "This is what you wanted me to see, correct?" Turner nodded. The senator's lips compressed so tightly they almost disappeared. "I appreciate your confidence and trust." He thought for a few moments. "During World War Two, General Marshall once said that if you get the objectives right, a lieutenant can write the strategy."

Shaw's anger boiled up. *Another fuckin' strategist!* Just as quickly he squelched it, remembering the warnings. *Damn quack,* he told himself, transferring his anger to his doctor. Then reason took control. *The cancer's not his fault.*

"Mrs. President," Savane said, "I'm not a strategist, but I hope you've considered opening a second front. May I suggest you approach the Germans and try to get them to work independently of NATO and our . . ." He paused, searching for the appropriate, tactful, words. "Shall we say our erstwhile French allies?"

For Shaw it was the equivalent of a revelation. *Savane knows about Leland!* His mental computer shifted into turbo mode as he recalculated the power shift that was taking place. *Maddy might salvage the election yet.*

Savane folded his hands and looked at Turner. "Mrs. President, let me speak bluntly. There is an undercurrent of public opinion against this war, which some of my colleagues want to ride to a victory in November. I totally disagree with that. But at best I can only delay—until you give me something new to work with."

Shaw couldn't believe what he was hearing. Savane wasn't willing to lose a war in exchange for winning an election. *I owe you, Senator.* An image of Senator Leland flashed in his mind. *But not you, you worthless piece of shit.* Secretary of Defense Merritt's image joined Leland's. *Too bad you chose the wrong side,* he thought, thankful that neither man was in the room. That might be enough to send him over the edge. Another thought came to him, and he smiled.

Ankara, Turkey
Thursday, September 30

The ride in from the airport took longer than usual because of the heavy traffic. But Butler didn't mind and napped most of the way. It had not been an easy trip to arrange, but Mazie had told him to make the rendezvous as quickly as possible. Her instructions had been very explicit: "Make them believe." Fortunately, he still had many contacts in the Turkish capital, which was exactly why Mazie had sent him on this mission to begin with.

The cab stopped in front of the Grand Hotel Ankara on Atatürk

Bulvari, across from the Grand National Assembly building. The Grand had lost its former splendor and was no longer the preeminent hotel in Ankara. That honor went to the much newer Hilton or Sheraton. But Butler liked the Grand because of its Turkish flavor. He paid off the cab and walked inside. The woman was waiting for him in the bar.

"My old friend," she said, coming out of her seat, presenting a cheek to be kissed.

"It has been a long time," Butler said as they sat down. He looked around the room to see who was watching them. He was surprised to spot Uri, the old Soviet KGB chief of station who had retired in Ankara after the collapse of the Soviet Union. "I see Uri is still here."

"He works for us now," the woman said. She leaned across the table and held his hand. "It is good to see you." For all appearances, they were two old friends meeting after many years. "And the family?"

"Got 'em all through college," Butler replied. "And yours?"

The woman beamed at him. "Alysha is married. A nice young man." She sighed. "So long ago. We were young then." For a moment the memories were back. Butler had been a young airman fresh out of language school and assigned to a listening post near Trabzon on Turkey's Black Sea coast to eavesdrop on Soviet communications. It was during the height of the Cold War, and Turkish intelligence, not fully trusting its American allies, had sent her to recruit an informer in the American compound. She targeted Butler, and he immediately reported it to his superiors. They in turn told him to develop the contact in order to feed the Turks information. It was a most profitable relationship for all parties, and Butler was established in the intelligence game. But they did the one thing totally forbidden in intelligence—they fell in love. Butler was reassigned and eventually ended up in the Pentagon's basement.

She looked at Uri, who gave her a slight nod. They were clear. "What is of such importance?"

Butler clasped her hand with both of his, palming off a mini-disk. "Your people need to read this."

She laughed, a clear bell carrying over the quiet room. "You know I'm lost when it comes to all this." She spoke in a soft voice, barely audible. "Why is this important?"

"It's hot. Right from Baghdad."

"From the horse's mouth, no doubt."

"We paid enough for it," Butler told her.

"The CIA or the Boys?" she asked.

"The Boys," he replied. Now she was very interested. "The Company gets it tomorrow," he told her. "As soon as I get home."

"After which," she said, "it will disappear into the black hole of Langley, never to be seen again. And you're doing this because we once shared the same bed?"

"Perhaps," Butler replied. He strongly suspected he was Alysha's father. He leaned into her. "It's the UIF's operations order for Kurdish Star. Tell your people to read between the lines." He sensed she was not convinced. "You're next."

"And your masters are desperate," she said, seeing through him. But there was a look of concern in her eyes.

"NATO's not going to get involved, and you're on your own." For a moment he said nothing and only held her hand. Then he stood. "Read it—for Alysha." He walked away.

The woman sat for a few moments, paid the bill, and walked through the main lobby. Uri was standing outside, waiting for a taxi. He gave her a troubled look and a little nod. Now she was very worried.

Central Malaysia
Friday, October 1

A thin trail of smoke drifted over the kampong as the first fire of the morning was lit. A barefoot soldier, his shirt open and pants half undone, walked out onto the veranda of the largest home and stretched, holding a small radio in his left hand. He barked a command, and a teenage girl emerged, a sarong wrapped around her frail body. The man grabbed her breasts as he spoke to her.

Through the binoculars the girl looked very frightened. "One of the pigs," Tel said, passing the binoculars to Kamigami.

Kamigami studied the scene for a moment and then scanned the village. "How many?" he asked.

"Seven," Tel replied.

"Do we know where they all are?"

"Affirmative," Tel answered.

"On my command," Kamigami said, still sweeping the village with the binoculars as Tel spoke into his radio. Below them, twelve men ghosted out of the nearby jungle and moved into the village, their weapons at the ready. A little boy ran out of his house and almost ran into one of the shooters. Kamigami saw it all and tensed. Then he relaxed as the man spoke to the boy, reassuring him. He gave him a little pat on his backside and sent him scurrying for the jungle and safety. The shooter turned in Kamigami's direction and pointed to the boy's house. He held up two fingers and then made a waving motion over the entire kampong. He held up five fingers on his left hand, closed his fist, and held up two more. Two soldiers were in the house and seven in the entire village. Their intelligence was good.

Now the shooters were in position. Kamigami raised the gold whistle to his lips. He refocused his binoculars on the soldier standing on the veranda and gave one long blast that carried over the valley below them. The soldier's head jerked at the sound, and he started to key his radio. But a single gunshot dropped him, the radio falling between the floorboards. At the same time the shooters burst into the houses. Sporadic gunfire echoed through the valley, and it was over in less than ten seconds. The shooters dragged six bodies out of the houses as Tel examined the soldier on the veranda. He looked in Kamigami's direction and signaled that the soldier was still alive but unconscious.

"Keep him that way," Kamigami ordered. Tel spoke into the radio, and bent over the downed soldier, administering a knockout shot. Then he methodically bound up his head wound and stopped the bleeding. Kamigami came to his feet. "Call in the 'copters," he ordered. He walked down to the kampong as Tel made the radio call.

Camp Alpha
Friday, October 1

Colonel Sun paced the ramp as he waited for the helicopters to land. He kept looking nervously to the north, all pretense of calm shattered. "There is one very nervous man," Janice Clark told Pontowski.

"It's not right," Sun told them. "The general should be here, not on operations."

"That's Victor," Pontowski told him. "He leads from the front—always. That's why he needs you, to hold things together." They fell silent as two A-10s took off in formation. They turned out of the pattern, carving a trail against the early-morning sun and cloud-laced sky. "Area familiarization," Pontowski explained. "We need a training range."

Clark made a mental note. "I'll talk to Maggot and arrange something with the MA."

"Good luck," Sun muttered. In the distance they heard the distinctive beat of helicopters. Sun tensed as he waited. "The general insists on radio silence," he explained. Slowly his tension eased as the first two helicopters approached from the north and settled to earth. The lieutenant leading Tiger Red climbed out of the first helicopter and marched over to report while they discharged their precious cargo. He spoke in Chinese, and Sun breathed in deeply, the tension now gone. "Total success," Sun said. "No casualties. The general is on the last helicopter."

Two more Warthogs took off as another two helicopters approached. Three trucks provided by the International Red Cross emerged from under the trees to load the villagers. "We're relocating them to refugee camps near Keluang," Clark explained. Keluang was the nearest town, ten miles west of Camp Alpha. They talked as they waited for the last two helicopters.

"We're settled in here," Pontowski told her. "So I'm heading for Singapore today and checking in with the MAAG. I'm thinking of creating a detachment here to expedite logistics and maintain operational control."

"That'll be a neat trick," Clark said, "if you can bring it off."

"I'd like you to come with me," Pontowski said.

"It might expedite matters," Clark said. She steeled herself as the last helicopter touched down and Kamigami got off. "There he is," she said.

"Let's get this behind us," Pontowski urged. They walked toward the helicopter. Kamigami recognized Pontowski and quickly shrugged off his equipment, shedding over sixty pounds. He handed his weapon and helmet to Tel and jammed a red beret onto his head as he walked toward them. They met in the middle of the ramp. "It's been a while," Pontowski said.

"Not since China," Kamigami replied, telling him the obvious. They shook hands.

"I've got a problem we need to discuss," Pontowski said. Kamigami nodded and waited. "When you cleared the snipers off the base," Pontowski continued, "did you execute either of the two prisoners?"

"No," Kamigami answered. "I let them go."

"But your aide," Clark protested, "said you did. He said it was better that way."

Kamigami shook his head. "Tel doesn't fully understand. He's still learning. He once saw me summarily execute a man who had butchered my family. At the time I set the other prisoners free so they could tell their comrades they met the vampire. I did the same with the two snipers we captured."

"But you did kill a prisoner?" she snapped.

"He wasn't under your jurisdiction," Kamigami replied. His voice was very soft and matter-of-fact. He didn't tell her that it made no difference who held the soldier. But he did owe her an explanation. "They did unspeakable things at my kampong."

"What's this vampire nonsense?" she asked.

"The Chinese tend to be very superstitious. I'm using it against them."

Clark turned to Pontowski. "I'm not sure I want them on my base."

"I don't think we have a choice," Pontowski told her. "For now they stay."

twenty

Atlantic City, Maryland
Friday, October 1

Maddy Turner sat at the head table in the new convention center, and for the first time in twenty-seven days she laughed heartily. The banquet was a major campaign event, with full TV coverage and all the required celebrities in attendance. Below her, the organizers had staged a fashion show satirizing politicians and were gently mimicking not only her but Senator Leland. The actor portraying Leland was a dead ringer for the senator. The only thing wrong was the red tip of the devil's tail that kept sneaking out of his pant cuff with a mind of its own. The audience roared when the woman impersonating the president suddenly sprouted horns, with a pretty bow tied around one. The two actors ended the sketch by joining together to sing "I Got You, Babe" with a very different set of lyrics. Later on, her speech would bring them all back to the serious business of the times. But for now she was thoroughly enjoying herself.

Richard Parrish moved to her side. "Madam President," he said in a low voice, "we have a situation that requires your immediate attention." And for added emphasis: "I'll make the appropriate excuses."

Turner spoke to Maryland's governor and thanked him for the wonderful evening. She rose and quickly followed Parrish out to her waiting limousine. "What's so urgent?" she asked once they were inside.

"The National Reconnaissance Office reports that a satellite monitored six missile launches in Malaysia. Shortly after that we lost contact with our embassy in Kuala Lumpur." Parrish checked his watch. "That was twenty minutes ago. We should have more by now." He spoke into a telephone. "Thank God we've got the first of the FIA satellites up ahead of schedule." The FIA stood for Future Imagery Architecture, the innocuous-sounding name given to the new generation of spy satellites being launched by the NRO. He listened for a moment. "United Press International reports thirteen missile strikes in Kuala Lumpur. That doesn't make sense at all. Our satellites are too damn good." He spoke into the handset as they pulled up to the waiting helicopter for the flight back to the White House. "The ExCom will be waiting when we arrive."

"Please have Serick and Merritt there," she ordered.

Parrish listened on the phone for a moment. "Oh, no," he whispered. "Madam President, CentCom reports the UIF is attacking in Saudi Arabia with tanks and APCs on a wide front."

True to her nature, Turner hated surprises and glared at him. "How did that happen?"

"We'll need to find out," Parrish said.

The White House
Friday, October 1

Shaw was the first to arrive in the Situation Room and found a seat against the back wall. Vice President Kennett was the second, followed by Mazie, the DCI, and Butler. Serick was close behind, and Secretary of Defense Merritt was the last. Only General Wilding was missing. They crowded into the small room and spoke quietly while they waited. The DCI sat at his normal place and nervously thumbed through a stack of reports. He kept shaking his head. Finally the Marine colonel who had briefed them so many times entered and stood by the big monitors opposite Turner's chair. No one said a word. The door opened, and Richard Parrish announced the president. She walked in, still in evening dress, and sat down. She nodded at the colonel.

"General Wilding," Colonel Scovill began, "sends his regrets, but he's fully occupied at the NMCC and will be delayed a few minutes. He'll be here as soon as he can." He pointed at the center display. A large-scale map of the front in Saudi Arabia appeared on the screen. "The UIF has initiated a major attack at these points." The moving symbols on the screen indicated the tanks, APCs, and number of troops the UIF was throwing into the battle.

"How did that happen?" Turner asked, looking directly at the DCI. Everyone in the room knew they were dealing with a major intelligence failure. He didn't answer and only stared at the small computer in front of him.

"We'll get an answer to you as soon as possible," Scovill said. His pointer flicked to the head of a big arrow on the map. "Please note that the spearhead of the attack is directed at the Saudi forces in this area. So far they appear to be holding as CentCom rushes in reinforcements, mostly British." His voice was matter-of-fact as he explained what they were seeing on the screen, all bad. The three screens cycled to Malaysia.

"Simultaneous with this attack," he continued, "six Scuds were launched from this area." A pointer circled the Taman Negara in the center of Malaysia. "Our tracking indicates that at least four were aimed at the Kuala Lumpur area and two launched on a southerly trajectory toward Camp Alpha. So far we have not received strike reports, but the press reports over a dozen explosions in Kuala Lumpur and widespread panic, fires, and looting."

"Four missiles and over a dozen explosions," Turner said. "That doesn't make sense."

"The situation on the ground is confused, Madam President. My guess is that the explosions are being double- or triple-counted. Please remember that Scuds are notoriously inaccurate."

Turner looked around the table. "The situation at our embassy?"

The DCI was still looking at the small laptop computer in front of him. He coughed, but it came out more like a strangling sound. "Madam President," he finally managed, "UPI reports it was hit by numerous explosions."

Turner stood up. "Can we assume those were Chinese Scuds?"

The DCI gulped hard. "No, ma'am, we can't. They don't have Scuds and claim what's going on in Malaysia is strictly local—indigenous farmers out to correct ancient wrongs."

Kennett scoffed. "And how do the Chinese know all this?"

The DCI said, "They have admitted in private conversations that they've given limited support to the rebels, mostly encouragement, but nothing on this level. They also claim that the Libyans are more involved, since the rebels are supposedly Islamic."

Shaw snorted. "It's payback time." As one, every head in the room turned to him. "Yugoslavia, May seventh, 1999," he said. "We bombed the Chinese embassy in Belgrade. Killed three people. Who just happened to be their key intelligence officers. We said it was a mistake and paid four and a half million to compensate the victims. A cheap price to take them off the board." He looked at them as if they were all children. "The Chinese have very long memories."

"Ma'am," Scovill said, pointing to the left monitor, "Camp Alpha reported two explosions approximately ten miles to the north. That correlates with the max range of the Scud, a hundred seventy-four miles."

"So they wasted two Scuds?" Turner replied.

"If those Scuds were from North Korea," Butler answered, "the North Koreans claim a max range of two hundred ten miles."

Shaw snorted. "Sounds like someone got hornswoggled. Sumbitch! Those people can't even play straight with each other."

"They won't make that mistake again," Butler promised.

"Madam President," Scovill said. This time he pointed to the right screen. More reports from Malaysia were flooding in. "We have reports that units of the Malaysian Army guarding Kuala Lumpur are under heavy attack." He stared at the screens for a moment. "Excuse me, ma'am." He quickly cycled through various menus, calling up selected information bases. Then, "Madam President, the situation is unclear, and we need a few hours to sort it all out. The UIF is attacking at what may be the weakest sector. As for Malaysia, it's much worse than we're seeing. I expect Kuala Lumpur to fall within hours."

"Colonel!" Merritt barked, silencing him. Everyone in the room knew that Scovill had made a terrible mistake by giving the president his evaluation, not that of his superiors. "You're not here to speculate." Merritt exercised his authority. "You're relieved, Colonel."

Scovill gave a curt nod. "Thank you, sir. Madam President, with your permission, I'd like to rejoin my old unit."

"Where is it?" Turner asked.

"In Saudi Arabia."

Turner felt a lump in her throat. For a moment she couldn't speak. Then a little nod. "Take care, Colonel. And thank you." She waited until he had left. She looked at the secretary of defense. "Robert, I need a comprehensive evaluation of the situation. Please get one together, and I'll take it to the NMCC. Given the circumstances, we don't need General Wilding and his staff wasting time coming here. Bernie, I want a fresh look at the intelligence picture. Get one together. Sam, track the domestic spin-off and get with the press secretary. Patrick, I'll need a new campaign strategy. Work one out. Mazie, Stephan, give me time to change and meet me in my study in fifteen minutes." She looked around the room. "Go."

The DCI sat staring at the papers in his hands as they filed out of the room, fully aware that the president had totally ignored him.

Mazie and Serick were waiting in the president's private study when she joined them. She was wearing a dark blue pantsuit and low-heeled shoes. Her hair was pulled back into a chignon. She was ready to go to war and got right to business. "We need that second front. Any progress with the Germans and Turks?"

"Everything is in motion," Mazie said. "I'm in contact with von Lubeck, and the Germans are favorable. The problem is with the Turks, and we haven't heard from them. Bernie's working that end."

"Okay, stay on top of it. Stephan, any luck splitting off Iran or Syria?"

"Nothing from Syria, but maybe some progress with Iran. I'm working it, but I have to go through the king of Jordan." He thought for a moment. "I wouldn't place too much hope on it. They're waiting to see if they can break out and threaten Riyadh. That will give them a much stronger bargaining position."

She paced the floor. "Saudi Arabia must remain our number one priority. We don't have a choice. But what can we do about Malaysia?"

Mazie answered. "Not too much at this time, Madam President. We can keep the supply lines open."

Serick nodded in agreement. "SEAC should be able to handle it."

"We need to disengage the Chinese," Turner said. "Tell them we'll respond based on their level of involvement. Everything is on the table:

ending their most-favored-nation trading status, trade sanctions, floating their currency, even breaking off diplomatic relations."

"That should get their attention," Serick said.

"That is the idea," Turner snapped. "Any attempt to stall while they wrap it up in Malaysia to make it a fait accompli will backfire. Make that very clear."

"Perhaps," Serick ventured, "they need to send a special envoy?"

"Only if he has the power to make things happen," Turner said. "And happen quickly." More pacing as she thought. She picked up the phone and buzzed Shaw's office. "Patrick, we need to speak." She hung up and sat down in her rocker. "This was a terrible intelligence failure on all fronts. I need to do something about that." She rocked for a few moments as they discussed that situation. A knock at the door stopped Serick in midsentence. Shaw shambled in. "I have to speak to Patrick in private," she said. Mazie and Serick quickly left. "Patrick, Leland is going to make this a campaign issue, which is the last thing we need at this time. I need to divert his attention."

"That will take some doin'," Shaw allowed.

"Can you do it?"

"I'll work on it," Shaw promised. "It won't be pretty."

"What about the DCI?" she asked.

"Fire his ass," Shaw said.

She buzzed her chief of staff. "Richard, I'm going over to the NMCC. I want to meet with my key policy advisers at seven o'clock tomorrow morning. With any luck we'll know where we are by then. Also, I need a short list for a new DCI." She never mentioned the election.

---

30 Hill Street, Singapore
Saturday, October 2

For the Military Assistance Advisory Group, Saturday morning was just another workday at the U.S. Embassy. As usual, they were very alone in that endeavor, and a Marine guard escorted Pontowski and Janice Clark to their office on the deserted second floor. "Nice duty if you can get it," Clark muttered, marveling at the vacant offices.

The lieutenant colonel and two captains who staffed the MAAG were waiting for them and came to attention when they entered. After the introductions were made, the lieutenant colonel cut to the heart of the matter. "As best I can determine, General, our job is to act as a logistics conduit to Camp Alpha. Unfortunately, we don't have the manpower to manage that type of account."

Clark had a solution. "I can have my resource manager work out of here and keep a satellite office at Camp Alpha."

The lieutenant colonel nodded. "We can do that."

Pontowski listened as they worked out the details and discussed the current logistics situation. While there were problems to solve, there was no doubt it was in good hands. He was about to leave when a civilian burst into the room. "Kuala Lumpur!" he shouted. He collapsed into a chair. "Missiles hit our embassy . . . we're out of contact . . . the city is under attack. I heard on the news."

"Call the DCM," Pontowski told him. He handed the man a telephone to call the deputy chief of mission. He grabbed another phone and dialed the command post at Camp Alpha. The controller answered on the first ring. "This is Pontowski. Turn on the radio and listen to the news. Tell Colonel Stuart he's got the hammer but I'd be generating aircraft. I'll be there as soon as I can." He broke the connection. "I need to get to SEAC headquarters," he said. "We have to work out how to employ our Hogs."

"It's down the road," the lieutenant colonel said. Since SEAC was, at heart, a political alliance, it made sense that it was located close to the major embassies. "I'll take you there." He hesitated. "You're not going to like it."

"Confusion?" Pontowski asked.

"That's a classic understatement," the lieutenant colonel replied. "The younger officers understand what's going on, but the senior generals are . . ." He stopped before he said something he'd regret. "There's a group of younger officers—we call them 'the young Turks.' Very competent, part of the new breed. I'll introduce you. They're the ones you need to work with."

"Let's do it," Pontowski said. "We're running out of time."

The Pentagon
Friday, October 1

Everyone but the DCI was in the battle cab overlooking the NMCC when Turner entered. Wilding escorted her to the center captain's chair overlooking the main floor and sat down next to her. "It's not good," he told her. "They've punched a hole in the center, right through the Saudi position, and are exploiting it in force." He spoke in a calm voice as he detailed the situation on the ground and what they were doing in response. He took care to explain it in terms she understood, devoid of military jargon. "It's going to be touch and go for the next few hours," he cautioned. "But we should be able to contain it."

When Wilding was finished, the vice president said, "Madam President, we've got the situation briefing you asked for ready to go in the conference room." He motioned to the room at the back.

"Where's the DCI?" she asked.

"I imagine he's on his way from Langley," Parrish said as he made a phone call. He spoke to the DCI's assistant and then held his hand over the mouthpiece. "They haven't seen him, and they're checking his office . . ." Parrish's voice trailed off, and his face blanched. "Oh, my God!" he looked at Turner, his eyes wide. "He's dead. He shot himself."

twenty-one

The Pentagon
Friday, October 1

Turner was sitting in the battle cab surrounded by generals when the two FBI agents arrived. Shaw hovered in the background and listened while they introduced themselves and explained how they needed access to the CIA to conduct a full investigation into the DCI's suicide. The president promised them they would get what they needed and no doors would be barred. *The CIA will have something to say about that,* Shaw thought. *No way them boys are gonna open up to you fellas.*

Suddenly it was there, all the pieces on the board. The cancer might have been eating away at his brain, but he was still in the game. He moved a few of the pieces around his mental chessboard as he refined his strategy. *Bait? What's the bait?* He moved a pawn forward and grinned. *Holy shit!* He forced the grin away before someone saw it.

Do I have enough time? He wasn't sure and worked his way to the door. Unnoticed, he slipped into the corridor and forced himself to walk slowly. Fortunately, nothing was wrong with his sense of direction, and he made his way to the main concourse, looking for a bank of public telephones. Luckily, he found one that was tucked away in a corner and deserted. He quickly dialed a number. It was answered on the first ring. He looked around to be sure no one was listening. "I need the URL of a child-pornography site," he said, all traces of his accent gone. There was no acknowledgment or questions, only silence. He waited, counting the seconds. A voice came back with an answer. He jotted it down and broke the connection. "Trace that one," he muttered to himself.

He hurried back to the NMCC, and another piece fell into place when he saw the two FBI agents in a corner comparing notes with two other civilians, obviously Army CID or Air Force OSI agents. He almost laughed aloud as he squeezed into the battle cab that was now overflowing with every general who could think of a reason to be there. He listened for a few moments. "We are now certain," a one-star said, "that the embassy in Kuala Lumpur was hit by mortar rounds and not Scuds. The Scuds served as a cover for special units of the Ninety-second People's Liberation Regiment of the PLA, who are operating in Kuala Lumpur."

About time these boys got their act together, Shaw decided. *It must be Bernie's doin', not the CIA's.* But intelligence wasn't his problem. He inched his way to the conference room at the back and glanced in, finding it still empty. *Luck of the Irish.* He slipped inside and studied the DCI's chair. *Okay, there's got to be something.* There was only a yellow legal notepad and a black pen on the side table. Shaw glanced at the still-open door but saw only the backs of two officers outside. For a moment he hesitated. *Do it!* He used a handkerchief to pick up the pen and quickly copied the URL of the Web site on a corner of the yellow pad in simple block letters. Still using the handkerchief, he carefully ripped the corner off and dropped it into a crack between the chair cushions.

He shuffled back into the battle cab, certain that he had not been seen. *Keep it simple,* he warned himself. He waited patiently until Turner was leaving and followed her out. But he peeled off from the presidential party and headed for the men's room. Again his luck held, and he saw one of the CID officers who had been talking to the FBI agents. He nodded at the man. "Special Agent, ah . . ."

"Carson," the man replied.

Now he was at the tricky part. "CID, right?" Shaw ventured. A slight nod in answer. "You know who I am?" Again the nod. "The SecDef doesn't need any surprises on this one. Keep him in the picture, okay?" Another slight nod. "We never had this conversation, right?"

"What conversation?" Special Agent Carson answered.

"I owe you," Shaw said. He walked into the men's room. *Leland, I'm gonna nail your ass!*

Camp Alpha
Saturday, October 2

The driver dragged the dark green minivan to a stop in front of the concrete barricades blocking the road leading into the base. "Missy Colonel," he said, his eyes full of worry, "this all new. No can go."

The head of a very young security cop popped up from behind the left side of the concrete barricade, then disappeared. For a few moments nothing happened. Then he shouted, "Advance and be recognized."

Before Clark or Pontowski could react, the driver was out of the van, his hands up. "I drive Missy Colonel! She your boss."

Rockne emerged from a sandbagged guard post. "It's okay," he called as he walked up to the van. He was surprised to see that Pontowski was also with them. "General, ma'am, sorry for the confusion. We're real short of people and still getting it all sorted out. We just got the barricades in place." He hesitated for a moment. "I know you're busy, but if you've got a moment, I'd like to do some training. Two minutes max. We're stretched too thin, and I need every opportunity I can get."

"You got it," Clark told him. Rockne placed a small package in a wheel well and walked to the downwind flank of the minivan. He slapped the leash he was holding against his thigh, and Boyca bounded out of the guard post. "Good girl," Rockne said as he snapped the leash on. "Seek," he commanded. He followed Boyca as she moved around the van, searching for the scent of explosives. Once he called "Hup" to get her to search high. Then, to encourage her, "Whatcha got, girl?" When they got to the wheel well, Boyca reacted. She sat with her ears up and looked expectantly at Rockne. He reached into the wheel well and pulled out the package. "You still got it." He pulled out a rubber dog toy and tossed it to her. She jumped up, snagged it, and started to worry it with little growls of contentment. "Good girl." Rockne smiled at Pontowski and Clark. "Thank you." He stepped back and waved them forward. The driver jumped into the van and threaded his way through the barricades.

"The Rock's got 'em jumping," Pontowski said, pointing to two airmen digging a defensive fighting position. Farther down the road another two were doing the same. "Overlapping fields of fire," Pontowski said. "Rockne is good."

"The best," Clark said. They drove past two aircraft bunkers, but the big blast doors were closed and all was quiet. "I can't tell if they're generating," she said.

Pontowski's eyes squinted as he took it in. The goal of an aircraft generation was to get as many of their aircraft fully serviced and uploaded with munitions as quickly as possible for a combat launch. It was a challenge under the best of circumstances but more so since they had just arrived and were still bedding down. "We'll see," he allowed. Their driver had to stop as more barricades blocked the road leading to the command post. But this time there were no guards.

"I guess we walk from here," Clark said. The lone guard at the entrance to the command post cleared them inside. "All things considered," she said, "Rockne is doing a good job with security. But he needs the rest of his people." She made a note on her PalmPilot.

Inside, they found Maggot sitting in the center of a long console in front of a bank of telephones. He was kicked back and sipping at a Coke. He stood up when he saw them. "I take it you're generating," Pontowski said.

Maggot motioned at the big Plexiglas-covered board on the front wall. The AVG's twenty jets were listed by tail number in the far-left column, and by using a grease pencil to fill in the columns, the command post tracked each bird as it was fueled, loaded with ordnance, and assigned a pilot. "We're six hours into it and got nine jets loaded and ready to launch. The jocks are standing by, but without tasking or an ATO, we're pissin' in the wind." An ATO was an air tasking order that sent them into combat.

Pontowski shook his head. "We just came from SEAC headquarters. Total confusion. I asked for an ATO, but no luck. No one seems to know what's going on."

"All they have to do is listen to the radio," Maggot said. "It's even on TV." He waved to a TV set in the corner. Thanks to satellite communications and miniature TV cameras, the deadly chaos sweeping Kuala Lumpur was being documented for the world to see. "Damn! We can help." Doc Ryan walked up to the big boards and made a grease-pencil change to the status of two aircraft. Two more were fully operational and loaded with munitions. "Eleven jets ready to party," Maggot muttered. "And no one to dance with."

"Isn't that Doc Ryan?" Clark asked, wondering why the flight surgeon was in the command post and not the base med station.

"The one and only," Maggot said. "His people are ready, and he wanted something to do. Seems he learned how command posts and aircraft generations worked under Mafia Martini at Okinawa."

"Is he any good?" Pontowski asked.

"You had to be good to survive Martini," Clark answered.

Maggot stared at the ready board. "General, our job is killin' tanks, and based on what I'm hearing on the radio and seeing on the TV, there just might be a few needin' servicing around Kuala Lumpur. Why don't we scramble four jets to go take a look?"

Pontowski shook his head. "What's the threat? What happens if one gets shot down? Besides, without an ATO from SEAC, there's no way I'll let them clear themselves onto a target."

Ryan had been listening, and now he said, "General, I'm in telephone contact with SEAC's command post in Singapore. It's a secure line."

Maggot's eyes narrowed as he hunched over the ONC, or Operational Navigation Chart, in front of him. "Kuala Lumpur's a hundred and twenty-five nautical miles away," he said. "If one of those Hogs was at altitude, he'd be in UHF range and could talk to us. We could coordinate with SEAC and ask for special tasking. Who knows? It might work."

"Sir," Ryan called. He directed his laser pointer at a map of the base tacked up on the far wall and circled two aircraft bunkers. "We might be able to use the First SOS and their helicopters for search and rescue if one of our jets gets shot down. They've got two helicopters on base right now and two out on a mission."

Maggot liked the idea. "Ask 'em." Ryan nodded and reached for the phone.

"It's worth a try," Clark said, urging a decision.

"Better than sittin' here with our finger up our ass," Maggot mumbled.

"Do it," Pontowski said.

Kuala Lumpur
Saturday, October 2

Waldo carved a racetrack pattern in the sky high above the city. Far below, clouds stretched from horizon to horizon. Five thousand feet below his altitude and to the south, he caught a glimpse of the other three Warthogs in his flight as they entered a holding orbit. It was time to call Chicken Coop, the command post at Camp Alpha. He glanced at the Have Quick UHF radio control panel on the left console to make sure he was on channel 20. Even though the frequency-hopping radio supposedly guaranteed that an enemy couldn't monitor their transmissions, he insisted they maintain radio silence as much as possible—just in case they might. He liked to think of it as "sticking to basics." His left thumb nudged the mike switch on the throttle quadrant to transmit. "Ranch flight, radio check." The radio was very clear, with a slight clicking sound in the background.

"Two." As usual, Lurch was abrupt and nasal.

"Three." Bag sounded bored.

A piglike grunt answered for Ranch Four. Waldo made a mental note to mention it during debrief. Probably a comment about the pilot, a slow-talking Native American from New Mexico everyone called Duke, not being able to count to four. "Chicken Coop, Ranch One. How copy?"

"Chicken Coop reads you five by," Doc Ryan replied, his transmission loud and clear.

"Rog," Waldo transmitted. "Solid cloud deck below us at six thou. Can't see a thing on the ground. We've got about thirty minutes of light before sunset. I'd like to send Ranch Three and Four down to take a look."

"Bossman says go for it," Ryan radioed. "Stay above small-arms fire."

Waldo humphed. Pontowski was getting cautious. "Copy all." Now he could get to work. "Bag, you and Duke are cleared in for a look. Shooter-cover." The idea was for Bag to do the looking and Duke to fly cover for Bag and discourage anyone who might think it was a good idea to shoot at him.

"We're in," Bag replied, his voice still bored and matter-of-fact. Waldo watched as the two aircraft broke out of orbit and descended through a small opening in the clouds. Bag was in the lead, with Duke a mile in trail and displaced to the right. Now Waldo had to wait, which he hated.

The radio crackled. "Bag! Break right." It was Duke, now quick and decisive. "Triple A at your deep seven." A short pause. "You're clear."

Waldo ground his teeth as he waited for what seemed an eternity. A Warthog popped out of the clouds. Waldo counted the seconds. A second Hog punched into the open, and Waldo breathed easier as the two joined up and climbed back into orbit with Ranch Two. "Four tanks and troops in the open moving into town along the main road to the south," Bag reported.

"What about the Triple A?" Waldo asked. Because of the A-10's slow speed, antiaircraft artillery was always a big concern.

"Coming from the airport on the south side of the city," Duke radioed. "Some CBU might discourage them." Besides carrying six Mark-82 Airs, five-hundred-pound bombs that were retarded by an inflatable balloon/parachute, Duke was also loaded with six canisters of CBU-58, a cluster-bomb unit that contained 650 baseball-size bomblets.

"Might be friendlies at the airport," Waldo cautioned. Waldo relayed the information to Chicken Coop and got the standard answer given by all command posts.

"Stand by one," Ryan radioed.

"Shee-it," Bag grumbled, dragging the obscenity out into two syllables. They orbited for twenty minutes as the sun set.

"Ranch flight, Chicken Coop."

Waldo keyed his radio. "Go ahead, Chicken Coop."

Ryan's voice was almost jubilant. "You are cleared in against the tanks and the troops on the south side of the city. Simpang Airport is reported to be in friendly hands."

"Then see if you can get them to stop shooting at us," Waldo replied. "Got to hurry. The light's almost gone. Okay, Bag. You got the lead. One pass, haul ass. Me and Lurch are right behind you." Waldo rolled 135 degrees and peeled out of orbit, dropping like a rock to join up on his wingman, Ranch Two, while Bag and Duke disappeared through the clouds.

"I'm in hot on the lead tank," Bag radioed.

"Press," Duke replied. "You're covered. I've got the end tank. Come off to the right and you'll see me at your two o'clock."

Lurch fell in behind Waldo as they dodged through the clouds, descending like falling bricks. At twenty-five hundred feet they broke clear. "Jesus!" Waldo shouted to himself. Off to his far left a bright line of tracers reached out from the airport, cutting the sky behind Duke, who was rolling in on a tank. Waldo punched at his UHF radio and called up Guard, the emergency channel used by aircraft in distress. "Simpang Tower, cease fire! Cease fire! We're friendlies going after the tanks advancing on you." Three seconds later the deadly streak of high-explosive shells cut off. Orphaned, the tracers crossed the sky like a train steaming over a prairie horizon.

Even though the Warthogs were moving across the ground at 560 feet per second, fast by normal human standards, it was way too slow for Waldo's sense of survival. He quickly sorted the targets. Bag was clear of the lead tank, which was now a smoking hulk, and jinking hard. A line of flares popped out behind his A-10 to decoy any surface-to-air missile that might be coming his way. Duke had just launched a Maverick antitank missile at Tail End Charlie and had broken off to the south. That would trap the two middle tanks. "Lurch, take the tank on the right. I've got the one on the left." The end tank disappeared in a satisfying puff of flame as the Maverick did its thing.

Deciding that Duke had the right idea, Waldo called up the Maverick on station nine. His GAU-8 cannon, the seven-barreled, thirty-millimeter Gatling gun, was designed for tank plinking, but he opted for the Maverick on the premise that it was better to launch and leave rather than get up close and personal with an unknown opponent who might have a few nasty surprises of his own. He rechecked the master arm switch, making sure it was in the up position. *No switchology errors today,* he told himself. He mashed the mike switch. "Bag, clear my six when I come off." He dropped down to the deck and firewalled the throttles, his airspeed pushing 340 knots.

When the tank was at two o'clock and three and a half miles away, he popped to a thousand feet and rolled in. What happened next was the product of years of training and fifteen hundred hours' experience flying the Hog. Automatically, his left forefinger played the slew/track-control button on the throttle quadrant and drove the symbol for the Maverick's seeker head in the heads-up display over the tank. His finger mashed the button to lock on, and when the symbol pulsed, his right thumb mashed the pickle button on the stick, sending the Maverick on its way. He hit the transmit switch. "Waldo, rifle." All the while he was jinking hard, making constant, random heading changes to break any tracking solution, and never looked inside the cockpit. Once the Maverick was launched, he turned away and slammed his Warthog down onto the deck. All this took less than eight seconds—which later he would claim was way too long.

"I'm in," Bag radioed.

Clear of the tanks, Waldo looked back and saw Bag's Hog in a low-level pass at six hundred feet. Six canisters of CBU-58s came off cleanly as two lines of tracers reached for the A-10, clearly visible in the fading light. The ground twinkled with flashes as the bomblets exploded. Now Bag was clear, racing for safety on the deck. "RTB," Waldo radioed. "Stick a fork in 'em. They're done."

"Smokin' holes in the ground," Bag replied as the four jets headed for home plate.

Camp Alpha
Sunday, October 3

The voice was bodiless and at a distance, yet it was still close. "General, you're needed in the command post." Slowly Pontowski came awake as sleep yielded to the voice. Doc Ryan was hovering over his bed. "Sorry, sir. But the NMCC is on the secure line."

Pontowski pulled himself to a sitting position and glanced at the clock beside his bed. It was 0130 Sunday morning. "Don't you ever sleep?" he asked Ryan.

"They need help in the command post," Ryan replied, as if that explained everything.

Pontowski pulled on his fatigues and boots. "They better have coffee," he warned.

"Your reputation has preceded you," Ryan replied. He led the way to Clark's minivan, which was waiting outside with her driver, and they rode in silence to the command post. This time there were two guards at the barricade sealing off the bunker. "My medics," Ryan told him. "They hate being security police augmentees, but we haven't got much to do right now. I figure we can help until the rest of Chief Rockne's cops arrive." Pontowski wondered if the doctor was pushing his people too hard. He made a mental note to discuss it with Clark.

Inside the command post, Maggot and Waldo were huddled with Clark in the communications cab. A sergeant he had never seen before stood at the big Plexiglas status board and grease-penciled an ETA on two inbound helicopters. In the notes column he wrote PC: 37.

PC, Pontowski thought. *Precious cargo.* Kamigami and the First SOS had snatched a few more innocent villagers out of harm's way. Then he saw the other number at the bottom of the board: AC: 20. *Twenty aircraft. How many will I lose before this is over?* But for every aircraft lost, there was a human price. *How many pilots?* Because he was half awake and his mental defenses down, the fear buried deep in his subconscious burst free. *How many?* All the numbers were there, beating at him. Maggot and his 30 pilots. The chief of Maintenance with his 309 wrench benders and gun plumbers who kept the aircraft flying and armed. Clark and her support group of 108 personnel who made the base work. Rockne with his 102 cops, most of them too young and inexperienced. Doc Ryan with his 8 medics.

The number 562 beat at him. But it was more than a number. It was 562 faces—each one a living, vibrant individual. *How many will I lose? None today,* he promised himself. Slowly he forced the numbers back into the shadows, promising to deal with them later. But he had forgotten to include himself in the grand total.

"Am I the only person getting any sleep around here?" he asked. The answer was an obvious yes. He sat down at the console.

"General Butler is on the secure line," Clark told him.

Pontowski punched at the monitor button so they could all hear. "Pontowski here. Go ahead, Bernie."

The voice was tinny and crackly, the result of scrambling, a multisatellite relay, and unscrambling. A slight delay was noticeable, but it was not too distracting. "The shit has hit the diplomatic fan," Butler said. "Some human-rights group we've never heard of is claiming you used a secret terror weapon at Kuala Lumpur."

"We launched three Mavericks," Pontowski replied, "expended four hundred fifty-eight rounds of thirty-millimeter ammo, and dropped six canisters of CBU-58." He waited.

"Can you confirm that?"

"We know what we uploaded and what the jets recovered with. The math is pretty simple."

"Did you confirm your BDA?" Butler asked. BDA was bomb-damage assessment, which was always controversial.

"Come on, Bernie. You know how it works with an unknown threat. The jocks were too busy getting the hell out of Dodge. The flight lead, Lieutenant Colonel George Walderman, did a quick visual as he pulled off. He thinks they got four tanks, but didn't hang around to check out the BDA from the CBU."

There was a short break as the system did its magic. "Apparently CBU is now a terror weapon."

"It's the shotgun approach to bombing," Pontowski told him. "It chews up soft targets something fierce, and it's fairly awesome if you're on the receiving end."

Again the pause. "I'll tell Wilding and brief the president."

"We're all loaded out for the morning and waiting on an ATO," Pontowski told him.

A short break. "Don't launch without an ATO. It might be best if you downloaded any CBU."

"What the hell's going on there, Bernie? CBU's damn good area-denial ordnance. It beats the hell out of napalm, which was squirrelly to deliver and only made for good TV coverage. This is no time to start playing politics." He drummed the console with his fingers, waiting for a reply.

Another voice came on the line. "Kennett here. The videos we're seeing are very gruesome. The Chinese have involved the UN, and Senator Leland is calling for a congressional inquiry. You can expect a visit from the GAO." The GAO was the General Accounting Office, the investigative arm of Congress headed by the comptroller general, with over five thousand employees.

Pontowski almost lost it. "What the hell is the matter with you people? You're treating us like some peacekeeping mission. We're not here to stand around wearing a blue beret and watch a massacre."

Maggot made a waving motion to Ryan. "Get him some coffee. Quick. The stronger the better."

It was enough to calm him down. "I apologize, sir. I just don't like hanging my people out to dry."

The pause was longer than normal. “No apology necessary,” Kennett said. “I feel the same way. Coordinate with SEAC and do what you can.”

Butler came back on the line. “The situation in Saudi has gone critical. The UIF has broken out, and it’s touch and go. The president doesn’t need any more distractions right now.”

“Understand all,” Pontowski replied. He broke the connection. He looked at his small staff. “Does anybody have any idea what the hell is going on?”

“You’re getting your ass kicked,” a soft voice said from the doorway. As one, they all turned. Victor Kamigami was standing there with Tel and Colonel Sun.

Clark bristled. “What are you doing here?”

“I called when they landed,” Doc Ryan said, “and asked them to come over. They’ve got good intelligence, and we don’t.”

Pontowski studied the flight surgeon for a moment, not sure whom he was dealing with. An inner voice told him to use the man. “What are you suggesting?”

“We work together,” Ryan said. “We’ve got all this room here, good communications, and not enough people.” He gave a helpless shrug. “Well, it seemed like a good idea at the time.”

Colonel Sun looked around the room, liking what he saw. “We should work together.”

Maggot stood up, shedding his fatigue like a worn coat. “We need forward air controllers on the ground. Can you do that for us?”

“I don’t see why not,” Kamigami replied. He looked at Tel. “Would you like to give it a try?”

“What’s a forward air controller?” Tel answered.

“Ah, shit,” Maggot moaned, sorry that he had brought it up.

Pontowski made a decision. “Let’s do it. Victor, get a liaison officer over here as soon as possible. Doc, you seem to have a clue, so work out the coordination. Maggot, cock the jets for launch at first light. And get some rest. You’re no good to me dead on your feet. Janice, see if you can get the rest of Rockne’s people here ASAP.” He stood up. “We came here to make a difference, folks.”

twenty-two

Washington, D.C.
Saturday, October 2

The sure knowledge that the war had made her a prisoner of the White House grated on Madeline Turner like a rasping hot file, and she saw the election slipping away. But there wasn't a choice, for the demands of handling a two-front war had to take priority. Still, it was a prison she loved, and she certainly had unrestricted visiting privileges. That was another problem, because the growing terrorist threat had forced the Secret Service to sharply curtail the daily tours. Across the street in Lafayette Park, a drummer had taken up a vigil and slowly beat a bass drum in protest over the war. Its dull, rhythmic cadence reached into the residence on the second floor, and when her chief of security suggested that the drummer could be made to disappear, Turner had immediately vetoed it. She would endure.

"It is annoying," she told Parrish as they made their way to the Situation Room for the afternoon briefing. "But that drummer's almost become a tradition." She allowed a tight smile. "And we mustn't disturb tradition." The Marine guard held the door open for her, and Parrish announced her presence. Besides the ExCom, the chief of Naval Operations was waiting for her. She sat down. "Mazie, gentlemen," she said, "before we begin, I would like to announce that General Butler will be the acting DCI until we can identify a replacement. General Butler will be part of the selection process, but he's declined to be the permanent director." To tell from the nodding heads and looks around the table, it was a good decision. "Well, shall we get started?"

The briefing had developed into a set pattern, with a heavy reliance on the monitors and a direct feed from the NMCC. The communications experts in the Pentagon had turned it into a slick and professional presentation geared solely for her consumption and available on demand. The president's face was a frozen mask when the casualty lists flashed on the screen. They were eighteen hours into the renewed fighting, and twenty-six soldiers and airmen had been killed. The numbers beat at her with an intensity beyond anything in her experience, demanding a price. She was not an overtly religious person, but when she stood in front of her Creator, how could she justify so many deaths of the people she was sworn to protect? *And the enemy?* she thought. *Have I no obligation to them?* Yet this war was not of her making and had been thrust upon her by the very people she must kill. She would not shrink from it, but she prayed that there was such a thing as a just war.

The screens with their messages of death and destruction shifted to the closing logos. General Wilding sensed what was troubling his president, and like her, he knew that there was no escape from what he had to do. "We're still in a tactical retreat," he said, "and falling back on prepared positions. It's a tactical strategy that's working well, and the UIF is advancing at a high cost in men and matériel. So far the Saudis have taken the brunt of the fighting and experienced most of the casualties, but we will go on the offensive."

"When?" was all Turner asked.

"As soon as possible," Wilding answered. "But logistics are a problem." He turned to the CNO. "Admiral."

The man that stood up was a throwback to an earlier age, with his weather-beaten face and ruddy complexion. "Madam President, two convoys from Diego Garcia are en route to Saudi Arabia; one to Ad Dammām in the Persian Gulf, the other to the port at Jidda in the Red Sea."

Turner's brow knitted. "I'm worried about those new mines we encountered and any submarines that might be a threat."

"Those mines," the admiral said, "operate on a mass-sensing principle, and we've developed a countermeasure that's almost too simple to believe. But it does appear to be effective. There are still three known submarines operating in the area. However, two Los Angeles–class attack submarines are escorting each of our convoys. If any of those unidentified submarines come within fifty miles of a convoy, those subs will experience a very short but exciting life."

"How soon before they dock?" she asked.

"In six days," came the answer. "On Friday."

She tensed as the prospect of another six days' mounting casualties loomed in front of her. She steeled herself and went on to the next subject. "Malaysia?"

Butler stood up. "The fighting is localized in Kuala Lumpur. Unfortunately, SEAC doesn't seem to know what to do with itself or how to respond."

"Is it a question of supplies?" Turner asked.

Butler shook his head. "No, ma'am. The MAAG reports they can't absorb what we're giving them."

"What about the protests over the AVG?"

Butler humphed in disgust. "All contrived. I talked to General Pontowski less than thirty minutes ago. Four of his A-10s were cleared by SEAC to attack enemy tanks on the outskirts of Kuala Lumpur. They used three Maverick antitank missiles, expended four hundred fifty-eight cannon rounds, and dropped six canisters of CBU-58s on troops they caught in the open. The CBU-58 is a canister-type bomb that spreads grenade-like bomblets over a wide area. That's the terror weapon we're hearing about."

"If you can't win it in combat," Shaw snarled, "win it with the media."

Turner stood. "I'm meeting with Secretary Serick and my foreign-policy advisers in a few minutes. Mazie, Bernie, please join us. General Wilder, I'll take this evening's briefing at the NMCC." She quickly left with Parrish in tow. The briefing had lasted less than twelve minutes.

She would endure.

Camp Alpha
Sunday, October 3

Pontowski was tired. He glanced at the master clock on the front wall of the command post. It was 0630 Sunday morning. *Less than five hours' sleep,* he thought. In one corner the intelligence officer from the First SOS was writing information on a white board with a Magic Marker. He seemed right at home and spoke excellent English. Almost as an afterthought he wrote GULF WAR: DAY 27. Behind the intelligence officer, Kamigami and Sun were speaking quietly to the young-looking major who would man the console. Kamigami looked up, and Pontowski said, "When you've got a moment, Victor." Kamigami nodded and turned back to his two officers.

"Coffee," Pontowski muttered. He wandered out to the small buffet and poured himself a cup. A little TV above the coffeepot was tuned to the BBC channel reporting the chaos in Kuala Lumpur. A reporter was standing in a street lined with burned-out cars and dead bodies. The sound was off, but the camera told the story. "A wonderful thing," Pontowski murmured, thinking of the speed of modern communications and the series of satellites that relayed information around the world in seconds. It was a driving force that set the pace of modern civilization, including war.

Kamigami joined him. He looked fresh and rested even though he had returned from an extraction operation less than six hours ago. "When do you sleep?" Pontowski asked.

"Catnaps," Kamigami replied. "Every chance I get. It's a habit I picked up years ago."

"I've got to learn it," Pontowski said, more to himself than to Kamigami. "Your troops are settling right in."

Kamigami nodded. "This is like their old command post. They like it."

The young intelligence officer rushed up. He skidded to a halt and took a deep breath, composing himself. "Colonel Sun said for me to tell you that Kuala Lumpur has fallen to the enemy."

Pontowski turned up the volume on the TV. "The last of the Malaysian Army units defending the city have surrendered," the reporter said, "and we've been ordered to the airport for immediate evacuation."

"Now it gets interesting," Pontowski said. He turned off the TV.

"Sir," the intel officer said. He showed Pontowski the clipboard he was holding with a small map of Malaysia. "The SA, the Singapore Army, is moving into positions along this line, approximately sixty miles south of Kuala Lumpur." He drew a line from the west coast to the east coast. "The strategy is to anchor this defensive line on Melaka"—he circled a town on the west coast—"and Mersing." He pointed to a town on the east coast. "That will force the PLA to move down the center." He drew a big slashing arrow down the center of the peninsula. "By coming down the middle, it must cross two main rivers and capture the bridges at Bahau and then at Segamat."

Pontowski spanned off the distances, not liking what he saw. The bridges at Segamat were fifty miles to the northwest of Camp Alpha and the last obstacle in the PLA's path. "They're coming right at us. This is going to get up close and personal."

"It would be good to know what's headed our way," Kamigami said. "Maybe a little visual reconnaissance?"

"If we can get below the cloud deck," Pontowski added.

"I'm flying into Segamat this morning," Kamigami said, "to set up forward air control with the SA brigade there. A pilot would be nice to have along. Maybe a little demonstration with a few Hogs?"

"We can do that," Pontowski replied. "Let's talk to Maggot."

Segamat, Malaysia
Sunday, October 3

Waldo hated helicopters and firmly believed they were a flying perversion, a violation of every known law of physics. Only voodoo, or some other occult art, kept them airborne, and something was certain to go wrong at any given moment. It didn't help that he was on a French-built helicopter, but as he had served as a forward air controller at one point in his career, he was the logical choice to go with Kamigami to set up FAC procedures with the Singapore army at Segamat. At first he had wondered about the relationship between Kamigami and his young aide. But he quickly realized it was a combination of uncle-nephew and commander-subordinate. "How can he sleep like that?" he asked Tel.

Tel looked surprised. "General Kamigami? I don't know, but I wish I could."

"Anyone who can sleep on a copter has got a screw loose somewhere," Waldo mumbled. The sound of the rotors beating the air changed pitch as they settled to the ground. He looked out a window on the port side and saw that four officers were waiting for them. Behind them he could see extensive camouflage netting and sandbagging. There was little doubt that this was a brigade that intended to fight.

"Have you ever been a FAC before?" Waldo asked.

Tel shook his head. "I know how to work the radios, and I also speak Malay and Chinese."

"That's a beginning," Waldo said, mostly to himself. The helicopter bumped to the ground, and Kamigami woke up.

Maggot rolled his Hog 135 degrees and headed for the break in the clouds below him. He radioed his wingman. "Duke, I've got a break over here."

"Looks like a sucker hole, white man," Duke replied.

"Looking better all the time," Maggot transmitted. "I can see lots of green below and blue above."

"Don't get them confused," Duke said. He fell in behind his flight lead, and the two A-10s dropped through the clouds. "Segamat at four o'clock, six miles," he radioed.

Maggot rolled to his right and saw the small town surrounded by rice paddies. "Tallyho." He checked the time. "We've got twenty minutes before check-in. Let's look around." He turned northward, toward the Taman Negara. The National Park was over a hundred miles away, but if the intelligence briefing from the First SOS was accurate, that was where the threat would come from. "We could use a Joint STARS," he told Duke. Two clicks on the mike switch answered him, signaling agreement. The Joint STARS was a highly modified Boeing 707 with sophisticated radar that could find, track, and classify any movement on the earth's surface—vehicles, troops, people, or animals. But there was no way they would see a STARS until the Gulf War was over.

Besides a chance to explore his area of operations, it gave Maggot a chance to fly the reengined A-10 they had gotten fresh out of depot maintenance. The jet delighted him and performed with a crispness and acceleration he had never experienced from the old TF34-100 engines. The modification gave the old bird a new lease on life. Duke crossed behind him and zoomed, doing a rolling scissors to fall in behind him. Maggot dodged around a cloud and for a few moments let the twelve-year-old in him out as they worked their way to the north, buzzing villages and the occasional truck or bus. Then reality intruded.

"Traffic's getting heavier," Duke radioed, flying parallel to a main road. "All moving south. Looks like refugees to me." Maggot answered with two clicks on the mike button. Both men had seen it before, when the AVG was in China. "Clouds are starting to move back in," Duke warned.

"Rog," Maggot answered. He had to decide whether to fly lower, turn around, or punch back to altitude while he could still find a hole in the cloud deck above him. The decision was made for him.

"Break left!" Duke shouted over the radio. He had seen the distinctive flash of a shoulder-held, surface-to-air missile as it was launched, and for a few brief seconds he was able to track it before he lost sight. "SAM at your left seven, two miles."

Maggot reacted automatically, slicing down to his left, streaming chaff and flares out behind to defeat any tracking solution. He had to get a visual on the missile coming his way. He didn't see it. But that didn't mean it wasn't there. He loaded his jet with five G's as he dove and turned, seeking sanctuary close to the ground. If it had been the old Soviet-built SA-7 Grail from the 1970s, the combination of flares and maneuvering would have defeated it. But he was being tracked by a much newer version, an SA-14 aptly called "the Needle." Its cooled infrared seeker head easily sorted the flares as it streaked toward the A-10. It closed with an eight-G turn and passed inches over Maggot's left engine exhaust—a near miss. But its graze fusing worked as advertised, and the warhead detonated, sending 4.4 pounds of high-explosive fragmentation into the Warthog.

But the Warthog refused to die and kept on flying. Maggot hauled back on the stick, firewalled his good engine while feathering the left, and zoomed, reaching for every bit of altitude he could find. Duke crossed under him, leaving a string of flares to decoy any missile that might be coming his way. Maggot lost sight of Duke when he punched into the cloud deck, still climbing. Just as he broke out on top, a second missile flew up the right intake and exploded. The entire aft section of the A-10 flared, and only the titanium bathtub surrounding the cockpit saved Maggot from the blast. The stick died in his right hand. He grabbed for the ejection handles at his side and rotated them back with a squeezing motion. The rocket pack sent the Aces II seat up the rails with an eleven-G kick. In less than two seconds Maggot separated from the seat and fell free as his parachute streamed out behind. The canopy snapped open with a satisfying clap, and he was drifting to earth. The Aces II had done its magic. Now he was back in the clouds. He pulled out his survival radio and keyed Guard. "Duke, how copy? I'm in the clouds and okay."

"I'm below you and taking ground fire. Lots of hostiles down here." A short pause. "I'm in."

Maggot descended out of the clouds as the distinctive sound of a GAU-8 cannon roared directly below him. He looked down between his legs and saw Duke pulling off from a strafing attack. He tugged on his right riser line, trying to drift away. His canopy ripped, and he looked up as the distinctive sound of a bullet whistled past. "Taking ground fire!" he radioed. He sawed at the risers, desperate as more bullets ripped into his parachute. He was falling faster as the trees rushed up to meet him. He crossed his ankles and disappeared into the dense foliage.

Maggot's first conscious thought was that he was still alive. He looked down as he swayed back and forth, and calculated he was thirty to forty feet above the ground. He looked up. His parachute was snagged firmly in the branches above him. He heard voices off to his right, on the other side of the massive tree trunk. He managed to catch a branch as the voices grew louder and more distinct. He recognized a few words he had learned in China, and heard the anger. Moving as quietly as possible, he pulled himself onto the top of the thick branch and lay on his stomach. The chest strap of his parachute harness cut into him as he pressed against the branch, willing himself to be invisible. Two soldiers moved into view, and he prayed they wouldn't see his camouflage parachute still hanging in the trees. He held his breath as one looked up, directly at him. Not knowing what to look for, the soldier saw nothing and moved on, chattering aimlessly about something. Slowly Maggot reached for his survival radio and keyed the silent beacon, sending his location and warning Duke that he couldn't talk or receive because he was surrounded.

He released the chest strap of his harness and pressed his cheek against the wood. An insect crawled up his face, but he didn't move.

Washington, D.C.
Saturday, October 2

It was slightly after 9:00 P.M. when Shaw knocked on the door of the residence. Parrish opened the door and let him in. "You wanted to see me, Mizz President?" She patted the couch next to her and glanced at Parrish. Her chief of staff read her look correctly and excused himself. Shaw dropped his bulk down beside her and leaned forward, clasping his hands between his knees.

"Patrick," she began, "is something wrong?"

Whenever he was asked a direct question, Shaw's natural instinct was to lie. He couldn't help it, for he was a natural politician. But he would never lie to his president, the young woman he had befriended when she was a junior state senator in California and marginalized by the "old boys" who ran the state. He had mentored her in the realities of power politics, and she had taken him on the wildest ride of his life, straight into the national arena. "Yes, ma'am. It's the cancer. Six months max."

She held his hand, tears in her eyes. "I'm so sorry, so sorry."

"It's been a damn good run. No complaints, Mrs. President."

"Will it ever be Maddy again?" she asked.

"No, ma'am." How could he explain? She was his guiding star, his reason for living, the daughter he never had, and all that he could never be. He didn't even try to tell her what was in his heart. Instead, "Bobbi Jo is backstopping me on the campaign." Maddy nodded. Bobbi Jo Reynolds was the vice chairman of the reelection committee and Shaw's protégée. She was a heavyset woman with short black hair, thick glasses, and a cherubic look. But underneath lurked the heart of a pit bull and the mind of a Machiavelli. "She can take over if I go lame." He stared at his hands. "Mrs. President, the war is killin' us. End it or we get flushed."

Again the nod. "That's not what I'm worried about."

"I know. It's the casualties. I've seen your face. I know what it's doing to you."

"I'm going to bring the Germans in," she told him. "Please don't ask me how."

"That was the policy meeting this afternoon?"

She nodded. "Mazie's in Germany. Her contact is von Lubeck."

"He is the man over there." Shaw pulled into himself and redrew the power structure of Europe. "I suppose Butler is approaching the Turks?" She looked at him in surprise, stunned that he had divined the strategy. "That's gonna take some fancy dancin' with the facts." He allowed a little chuckle. "Bernie's the man."

"What about Leland?" she asked.

Shaw grunted. "I'm taking care of it. Give me a few days."

twenty-three

Segamat
Sunday, October 3

Kamigami, Tel, and Waldo were with the battalion's headquarters company explaining how a FAC worked when Duke's Mayday came over the UHF radio. Waldo grabbed the mike and acknowledged the call. "Understand Maggot is down. Say coordinates." While he copied the coordinates, Kamigami explained what was happening and Tel translated into Chinese. "Duke, are you in contact with Chicken Coop?" Waldo asked.

"Negative," Duke answered.

"He's too low," Waldo said. "Can we raise 'em on the field telephone?"

"I can try," Tel replied. He spoke to the battalion's communications officer while Waldo plotted the coordinates on a chart. Kamigami hovered like an anxious hawk in the background, eager to escape his tether. "That's it," Waldo finally said, tapping Maggot's position on the chart. "He's down near a ridgeline close to a place called Kemayan, fifty miles to the northwest." He keyed the radio. "Duke, say position of hostiles."

"Hostiles are concentrated along the main LOC south of a village," Duke replied. An LOC was a line of communication, in this case the main north-south road running down the center of the peninsula. "The village is Kemayan, I think. Problems. Lots of refugees on the LOC."

"Can you keep the hostiles away from Maggot?" Waldo said.

"Am I cleared in hot?" Duke asked, sounding much too enthusiastic.

Waldo gritted his teeth. "Stand by one." He hated saying that, but he had to clear it through Pontowski at Camp Alpha. "I've got to coordinate with Chicken Coop," he explained to his listeners. Tel handed him the phone, telling him Alpha was on the line. "Let me speak to Bossman," Waldo said. Pontowski was on the phone in seconds, and Waldo quickly explained the situation.

Pontowski didn't hesitate. "You've got it, Waldo. Duke is the airborne SAR commander for now." SAR was search and rescue. "He's cleared to use whatever he's got but to stay one kilometer away from the LOC. Four Hogs headed your way ASAP." A short pause. "Scrambling now, they should be on station in twenty minutes. Let me speak to General Kamigami." Waldo handed Kamigami the receiver, which seemed to disappear in his huge hand. "Victor," Pontowski said, "can you help us with search and rescue?"

"I thought you'd never ask," Kamigami answered. "Ask Colonel Sun to form up two teams for a ground extraction and send them our way in two helicopters. Bring my gear."

"Copy all," Pontowski replied. Another short pause. "Colonel Sun says they'll be airborne in two hours."

Waldo was listening on an extension and ran the numbers. "Figure another twenty-five minutes' flying time to here, time on the ground, plus another twenty minutes to on station. Three hours." He looked at them. "Too long. The Gomers will have their act together by then."

Kamigami mashed the transmit switch on the phone. "Ask Colonel Sun to be airborne as soon as possible. One hour or less." Although he never raised his voice, the command imperative was loud, clear, and overpowering. There was no doubt that Sun would make the deadline.

Central Malaysia
Sunday, October 3

Below him, the angry voices were growing louder and coming from all sides. *Shit-fuck-hate!* Maggot thought. The soldiers had bracketed his position and were slowly closing in. It was only a matter of minutes before they shook his tree and he fell out. A lone soldier emerged from the brush swinging a machete. He hacked viciously at the trunk of Maggot's tree. He looked around, took another hard swing at the tree, and disappeared into the foliage. *They're not taking prisoners today.* More angry shouts. It was an easy decision. He reached for his survival radio and toggled it to transmit. "Chief," he radioed, speaking as quietly as he could. "They've got me. Strafe my position. I'm in a large tree about forty feet up."

"Can do. Any other options?"

"Not unless the fuckin' Marines are around." This wasn't the way he wanted to die, but he preferred it to what was waiting for him. His voice grew stronger. "Hose the bastards."

"I'm in. Do you have me in sight?"

"Negative. Press." Maggot heard the Warthog, and in his mind's eye he could see it fly a curvilinear approach, 200 to 300 feet off the deck before it popped for the final run in. He pressed his body against the branch, willing himself to become part of the tree. Below, the soldiers heard the approaching jet and shouted warnings as they scrambled for cover. He couldn't help himself and had to look. He raised his head in time to see Duke in the pop, climbing to 800 feet. The Hog rolled 135 degrees as its nose came to the ground and pointed directly at him! He had never been on the receiving end of a GAU-8 cannon. "A bit to the left," Maggot radioed. His voice was amazingly calm. At exactly 2,250 feet slant range, Duke mashed the trigger, and smoke rolled back from the nose of the Hog as the Gatling gun sent a train of death toward him, traveling faster than the speed of sound. The ground below him erupted in a man-made hell as the mix of depleted uranium and high-explosive slugs carved a path in the jungle. Then Maggot heard the growl of the cannon as his tree swayed dangerously back and forth. He held on for dear life as the jet passed over him, its sound wave finally reaching him.

I'll be damned! he thought. *I'm still alive.* He raised his head. Below him, the jungle had been shredded, and shouts blended with cries of anguish echoed back and forth. In the distance he heard the Warthog reposition for a second run. He keyed his radio. "Duke, do it again. This time to fifty meters to the right."

"Sure about the fifty meters?"

"Make it sixty." Again Maggot pressed his body against the thick branch, his arms over his helmet. He didn't look as his world exploded. Four shells hit the tree next to his, and it came apart, sending a shower of splinters into the underside of the branch Maggot was on. "Oh, shit!" he shouted as his perch collapsed from under him. He started to fall, but his parachute was still snagged in the foliage above his head. He swung out, dangling in his harness, still forty feet above the ground. Slowly he raised his helmet's visor. "Whoa," he breathed. The GAU-8 had carved two open alleys in the jungle, leveling everything in its path. But flying splinters had caused the real damage, shredding whatever they hit. A coppery taste flooded his mouth when he saw the body. A long, narrow splinter had pinned the soldier with the machete to a tree. A shower of slivers had turned him into mincemeat.

No wonder they hate us, he thought. The coppery taste was back and he fought the urge to retch. He swung back and forth, clear for anyone to see. *Can't stay here.* He reached for the pocket on the left side of his survival vest and pulled out a lowering device, a long thin strap with a clip and a ratchet. He snapped the ratchet onto the chest strap of his harness and the clip onto one of the parachute risers above his head. He snugged up the strap before pressing the coke clips that released the risers from his harness. He fell about two feet before the strap pulled him up short. He quickly fed the loose end through the ratchet and lowered himself to the ground. He looked around, getting his bearings and listening. But there was only silence.

Segamat
Sunday, October 3

The two team leaders listened as Kamigami explained the drill in his strange mix of English and Chinese. The plan was simple in the extreme. The Warthogs would suppress all ground fire while the lead helicopter, call sign Gold, would ingress to extract the downed pilot. The goal was to spend as little time as possible in the target area and hit with overwhelming force. The second helicopter, call sign Red, would be held in reserve. But the situation was fluid, and they had to be flexible. "I'll be on the lead helicopter with shooters from Dragon Gold," Kamigami said. "Tel, I want you on the second helicopter with the Tiger Red team to coordinate on the radios." He turned to Waldo. "Any changes?"

"The SAR commander's call sign is Air Boss," Waldo replied. "But Duke only has about twenty minutes left on station before he's bingo fuel and has to RTB. Bag will replace him as Air Boss."

"Not good," Kamigami said. "That's about when we'll be arriving."

"Bag's done this before and can hack it," Waldo promised. "We've also got four Hogs holding to the south, play time sixty minutes. Four more will be on station before they RTB for fuel."

"I hope so," Kamigami said. "Okay, any questions?" There were none. "Let's do it." He jogged to the waiting helicopters, holding his helmet in one hand, his MP5 in the other.

Central Malaysia
Sunday, October 3

Kamigami braced himself between the pilots' seats as the big helicopter barely cleared the treetops. The copilot pointed at his watch and held up five fingers, closed his fist, then held up five fingers. They were ten minutes out. Kamigami clutched the mike in his left hand. "Air Boss, how copy Gold on this frequency?"

"Read you five-by," Duke replied. "Maggot is up and talking on Guard. He reports no activity in his area and is unhurt. As you ingress, there's a karst ridgeline running north to south. To the east of the ridgeline you'll see what looks like two cleared paths in the jungle. Maggot is between the paths near the middle. Hostiles have fallen back on the LOC and are using refugees as human shields. Bag's on station and is now Air Boss. I'm bingo minus three and got to go." Duke was three hundred pounds into his recovery fuel and cutting it close.

Bag's voice came on the radio. "I've got it, Duke. Okay, everyone, listen up. The hostiles are fanning out from the LOC in a sweep toward Maggot."

"How far are they from Maggot?" Kamigami asked.

"Less than a kilometer," Bag answered.

Kamigami ran the numbers in his head. They would be arriving in the area about the same time as the hostiles. If they were able to shoot down a Warthog, a helicopter would be twice as easy—unless there was something between them. "Have Maggot move toward that ridgeline to the west. If he can get on the far side, we can use it for terrain masking."

"Copy all," Bag transmitted.

Maggot listened for a moment and then keyed the transmit button on his survival radio. "They're coming my way," he whispered. The radio's earpiece kept falling out of his ear, and he had to hold it in place to hear.

"Beat feet west," Bag told him. "Try to get on the far side of the ridgeline. Help is on the way."

Maggot clicked the transmit button twice in acknowledgment and switched the radio to the silent mode. He checked his compass and pushed into the jungle, fully understanding what he had to do. But it was hard going, and the rain was starting to fall. Branches tore at his flight suit, and he stumbled twice. But the shouting wasn't as loud, and he was pulling away from his pursuers. The foliage thinned out as the terrain started to slope upward. *I might do this,* he told himself. He pushed through a patch of ferns and stopped. "Ah, shit," he moaned, looking directly at a jagged cliff of limestone rising fifty feet above his head. His spirits crashed around his ankles as the shouts grew louder. Again he checked his compass as he heard someone crash through the jungle. He turned south and moved along the base of the cliff. A woman stumbled out of the brush less than five feet in front of him. For a moment they stared at each other. Then she held a finger to her lips and pointed behind her. Then she pointed to the north, in the direction he had come from, and made a waving motion, trying to make him understand. Maggot stood there, not sure what to do. Frustrated, she pushed him, urging him to retrace his steps. He nodded and headed back to the north as the shouts grew louder. The woman watched him go and then turned to the south.

"Maggot's gone silent," Bag radioed. He glanced at the big multifunctional display screen on the right side of his instrument panel and punched at the buttons on the edge, calling up a map display with an SAR function overlay that displayed the location of Maggot's homing beacon. "I'm still picking up his beacon. It looks like he's moving back to the north. I'm going down to take a look." He dropped his Hog to fifty feet above the trees and firewalled the throttles. He crossed the lanes that Duke's cannon had carved in the jungle, jinking hard to avoid any ground fire, and turned toward the ridgeline. He rolled back and forth, finally pulling up to clear the ridgeline.

"Not good," he transmitted. "It looks like the Gomers have reached the base of the ridgeline. But Maggot is still moving."

Another voice came on frequency. "Air Boss, Basher's fifteen minutes before RTB for bingo." Basher was the call sign for the flight of four fully armed Hogs holding in a nearby orbit. "Use it or lose it," the flight lead added.

"Copy all," Bag answered. He knew that another flight of four should be inbound to replace Basher, but he hadn't heard from them. It was time to make things happen. But what?

"Is the crest of the ridgeline clear?" Kamigami asked.

"Affirmative," Bag answered.

"We're in," Kamigami radioed. "Gold's approaching the ridgeline from the west and landing on the backside. Red will stand ready to extract Maggot if he can reach a safe area."

Bag circled to the north and turned south to fly down the western side of the karst formation, keeping the ridgeline between him and the bad guys. Kamigami's helicopter crossed under him and hovered over the edge of the ridgeline, as far back from the eastern side as it could get. Kamigami was the first man out, closely followed by twenty men. The helicopter seemed to fall away and was never exposed to ground fire. Again Bag flew along the ridge. But this time he climbed high enough to see over to the east. He caught a glimpse of the main road, which was still crowded with refugees, but he couldn't see any movement in the jungle or along the base of the ridgeline. A puff of smoke erupted from the edge of the tree line, and Bag slammed his Hog down, putting the ridge between him and the threat. He never saw the Strela missile that passed harmlessly behind him. But he knew it was there.

"Fucking lovely," he muttered under his breath. He checked the display screen. Maggot was still moving to the north. He may have been preoccupied, but the black boxes were still doing their magic.

"We're taking incoming," Kamigami radioed. "Mortars."

Another voice came on the radio. "Air Boss, Loco flight with four, five minutes out, sixty minutes play time."

Now Bag had eight Hogs. He made a decision. "We're running out of time and need to get their heads down. Gold, if you have me in sight, flash your position." He rolled right and watched the ridgeline anxiously. Two flashes blinked at him, followed by two more flashes. "Got you," he radioed. Now he knew Maggot and Kamigami's location. "Gold, can you lay down smoke below you on a bearing of zero-nine-zero?"

For what seemed an eternity, there was no answer. Then a puff of smoke drifted up from the jungle canopy. "Shit hot!" Bag roared over the radio. As best he could tell, Maggot was on one side of the smoke marker and moving north while the hostiles he had seen were on the other side, to the south. It was all he needed. "Gold, keep the smoke coming. Basher Flight, you're cleared in hot. Stay south of the smoke and one kilometer away from the LOC."

"Smoke in sight," Basher lead radioed.

The mortar rounds worked their way along the ridgeline, driving Kamigami and his team to cover. But his mortar team kept at it, lobbing a fresh smoke round into the jungle below and then scooting to a new location. But without a good target, Kamigami wouldn't waste any of their limited ammunition in a vain attempt to discourage the hostile fire. Fortunately, the karst's jagged terrain offered them good cover. But he knew that sooner or later an enemy round would find them. It was just a matter of time. He found the rhythm of the mortars and moved quickly between incoming rounds, using crevices and low points for cover, his radioman right behind him.

Kamigami finally discovered what he was looking for: a long, narrow fissure that cut across the ridge. He dropped into the gap and wiggled to the edge. He scanned the jungle with his binoculars and then reached for the headset his radioman was holding at the ready.

Bag's voice came over the radio. "Maggot, how copy?"

"Read you five-by."

"Rog," Bag replied. "There's a clearing five hundred meters in front of you. Head for it. Break, break. Red, how copy?"

Tel answered. "Read you loud and clear. We're in position and holding." Kamigami allowed a grunt of satisfaction. The boy was doing good.

"Stand by to move in when cleared," Bag ordered.

Kamigami decided it was time to get involved. "Air Boss, this is Dragon Gold. Recommend Red drop his team of shooters here before the pickup."

It all made sense to Bag. Why risk more lives than necessary during the extraction? "Red," he transmitted, "can you do it?"

"Can do," Tel replied.

Kamigami again swept the area with his binoculars. An unusual movement in a tree caught his attention, and he hit the zoom lever on his binoculars. A man was perched high in the branches holding a radio to his mouth—an artillery spotter. Without turning, he said, "I need the L42." The L42 was a sniper rifle carried by one of his shooters, a very proficient marksman. But in this particular case it was something he wanted to do himself. To the south he saw two A-10s in a steep descent as they dropped down to the deck and turned toward him.

"Behind you," his radioman said. He reached back and felt the barrel of the sniper rifle. He pulled the weapon forward and chambered a round. He worked himself into a shooting position and laid the crosshairs in the scope on the spotter's head. He squeezed off a round and watched as the man's head exploded. He didn't fall but slumped forward, still tied to the tree, his radio dangling from a lanyard strapped to his lifeless wrist. A series of mortar rounds walked across the ridge in retaliation, falling wide. "That stirred them up," his radioman said. Kamigami searched for another target but found nothing. Now the lead A-10 was in the pop, climbing to fifteen hundred feet while his wingman stayed low and a mile in trail. Kamigami swung the rifle back to the dead spotter still hanging in the tree. A man had climbed up the tree and was reaching for the spotter's radio. It was a poor shot, but Kamigami took it anyway. The slug hit the man in the right shoulder, knocking him out of the tree just as the A-10 rolled in and released two canisters of CBUs.

Kamigami passed the sniper rifle back, and the radioman handed him a headset so he could monitor the action. Below him, the jungle twinkled with flashes as the CBU bomblets exploded. The second A-10 crossed the flight path of the escaping Hog at thirty degrees, smoke rolling back from its nose. The loud, burring growl of the Hog's cannon echoed over the jungle, punctuated by the bomblets going off.

More mortars walked across the ridge, driving Kamigami's men down. He keyed his radio. "Keep the smoke coming," he ordered. Without the smoke rounds from his team's fifty-one-millimeter mortar marking the jungle, an A-10 might drop a friendly round on Maggot. Over the din he heard Bag radio Red, the second helicopter, and tell it to move farther to the west, using the ridgeline as protective cover.

For the next twelve minutes Kamigami watched the four Hogs of Basher flight work the area over. The aircraft stayed low, circling to the west, using the karst formation for masking. On each run two aircraft would pop out from behind the ridge using shooter-cover tactics. The lead jet would drop ordnance while his wingman flew cover, discouraging anyone who might want to shoot back. It was an effective tactic and suppressed the enemy mortars that were pounding the ridge. Finally the last A-10 was off and heading for home. An eerie silence descended over the carnage below him. It looked as if a giant had stomped across the jungle, crushing the foliage flat with huge boots. Here and there he saw smoke billowing up.

Kamigami crawled out of the crevice and stood up as the big Aerospatiale helicopter carrying Tel and his team of shooters popped up over the western side of the ridge and hovered over a flat, open area. Sixteen men jumped out. The four shooters left on board pushed out equipment bags before the pilot spun the aircraft around and moved away. Kamigami saw Tel giving him a thumbs-up from the doorway just as the helicopter dropped out of sight.

Maggot lay on the ground, his arms wrapped over his head. It took a moment for the silence to register—the bombing had stopped. He rose up on his elbows and shook his head as a raging thirst coursed through his body. But his water bottle was dry. He came to his feet, still unsteady from the pounding his body had taken from the repeated concussions of exploding ordnance. He keyed his survival radio. "Bag, I'm up and moving."

The relief in Bag's voice was obvious. "I'm sending a Jolly Green in now." Jolly Green was a holdover from the past, when SAR helicopters were called Jolly Green Giants.

Maggot was feeling better. "Tell the Hogs they missed. I still got my balls."

"Will do," Bag replied.

Maggot checked his compass and pushed ahead, moving as fast as he could. An insect worked its way up the back of his neck and burrowed under his helmet. "Son of a bitch," he muttered as he ripped off the helmet and brushed the insect away. He tossed his helmet into the brush. He took a few more steps and stumbled into the clearing. For a moment he stood there, breathing deeply and savoring the rain that was starting to fall. He tilted his head back and opened his mouth. Then he mashed the button on his survival radio that keyed the beacon, still looking skyward and drinking in the rain. In the distance he heard the distinctive beat of a helicopter, and he pulled out his pen flare gun. He cocked it and, holding it at arm's length, fired it skyward. The beating of the helicopter grew louder, and he sank to his knees, unbelievably tired.

The screech of an incoming artillery round echoed over the clearing. Automatically, he looked toward the sound. A puff of smoke and flames flashed on top of the ridgeline. Another round echoed over him. "Ah, shit," he moaned to himself. Now he could see the Super Puma as it moved over the clearing and settled to the earth. He ran for it, and two sets of hands pulled him into the open door. He looked up into Tel's smiling face. "We've got to quit meeting like this," he said.

Tel only grinned and strapped him into a jump seat as the pilot lifted off. Tel went forward and stood between the pilots, listening on the radio. He shot Maggot a very worried look as the pilot dropped the helicopter down to treetop level and they raced for safety around the northern end of the karst formation. Through the open door on the other side of the helicopter, Maggot saw two more flashes erupt on top of the ridgeline. Tel pointed out the copilot's quarter panel, shouting something he couldn't understand. Then he saw it—the smoldering wreckage of a helicopter on the edge of the ridgeline.

twenty-four

Camp Alpha
Sunday, October 3

This is a win? Pontowski thought. He was sitting with Colonel Sun at the back of the small room in the hardened aircraft shelter the AVG used for its operations center as Bag went through the postmission debrief. The pilot's flight suit was still damp with sweat and his body racked with fatigue, but he kept at it, covering everything that had gone right on the mission and ferreting out what had gone wrong. *You did good,* Pontowski told himself, giving all the pilots high marks for Maggot's rescue. Unfortunately, the two Singapore helicopter pilots were not used to the way Americans debriefed a mission, and were very reluctant to join in. But Pontowski had to know what had happened. He waited for the right moment. It came when Bag opened a fresh water bottle and took a long swig.

"That was a fine piece of flying," he told the two helicopter pilots. "Very aggressive, with perfect timing. And we honor your fallen comrades." Tel was sitting behind the two and leaned forward, translating in case they missed his meaning. The two pilots nodded in acknowledgment. "But there is one thing I don't understand," Pontowski continued. "Why did General Kamigami insert his team on top of the ridgeline?" The two pilots shook their heads.

"Perhaps," Tel ventured, "he wanted to draw attention away from Colonel Stuart by presenting a new threat."

The helicopter aircraft commander said, "When we were inbound to pick up Colonel Stuart, I heard the general call for Gold to come in for a pickup. But he waved them off when the artillery barrage started."

"So no one was picked up before the helicopter crashed?" Colonel Sun asked.

"I don't think so," the pilot answered. "When we flew past, I didn't see any movement on the ground."

"I can confirm that," Maggot said from the doorway. Everyone turned toward the pilot. He was freshly showered and in a clean flight suit after being checked by Doc Ryan. "I think an artillery round got them." He walked over to the helicopter pilots. "Thank you." He extended his hand in friendship. "You saved my worthless ass." The two men stood, shaking his hand in turn.

"Where did the artillery come from?" Colonel Sun asked.

"I saw three tanks moving down the LOC when I came on station," Bag answered. "PT-76s." The PT-76 was a Soviet-built light amphibious tank. "They sport a seventy-five-millimeter cannon, but I couldn't go after them with all those refugees."

"Old but effective," Pontowski said in a low voice.

"I believe," Tel said, "the PLA is equipped with the Type 63, a much improved version of the PT-76 produced in China. It has an eighty-five-millimeter cannon." He ducked his head, embarrassed for speaking out.

Before Colonel Sun could reprimand him, Pontowski said, "We need to get that information to the pilots. They've got to know what they're going against." *Damn,* he thought. *I screwed that one up.* A hard silence came down in the room, for they all knew it was his order that had placed the LOC off-limits to the A-10s. "They figured that one out fast enough," he said, shouldering the responsibility for the pilots' deaths. "So where are we?"

Bag was relentless as he summarized. "One Hog shot down, one pilot rescued. One Puma downed, two pilots KIA. Thirty-seven men still on the ground."

The burden of command bore down on Pontowski, demanding its price. "Are we out of contact, or have they been captured?" he asked.

"The team has four radios," Sun said. "At least one should be operational."

"So we can assume they've been captured or overrun," Pontowski said.

Tel shot Sun a look, begging to speak. Sun nodded. "I don't think so," Tel said. "He'll contact us when he's ready."

"Why the delay?" Pontowski asked.

"Because vampires are silent," Tel replied.

"That's all I got," Bag said, ending the debrief.

The room quickly emptied, leaving Pontowski and Sun alone to answer the unasked question. "Do we go after them?" Pontowski said, coming to the heart of the matter.

"No," Sun said. "Without radio contact a full-scale rescue mission is premature."

"We can reconnoiter the area," Pontowski replied.

"That might draw unwanted attention," Sun said. "Maybe one flight at first light tomorrow morning. But for now I recommend we wait." He stood up. "Is there anything else, sir?"

Pontowski shook his head. "Thank you, Colonel." Alone, he slumped down in his chair, his chin on his chest. He couldn't avoid the issue. *It was my ROE! Bag would have gone after those tanks in a heartbeat.* He sat there, coming to grips with the deadly cost accounting of combat. But he knew the way the balance sheet worked, and there was more to come before it got better. *Why would a rational person do this?* The answer was obvious—he wasn't a sane man. An image of Maddy Turner demanded his attention. *It's worse for you,* he decided. "Time to go to work," he muttered. He stood up and walked outside.

The rain had stopped, and Clark's driver was waiting for him. "Command post," Pontowski said. "And take it easy." The driver grinned at him, banged the van into gear, and hit the accelerator. They raced down the taxi path and careened around a corner onto the main taxiway. The driver slammed on the brakes and pointed to a moving shadow in the trees, barely fifty meters away. "Good eyeballs," Pontowski whispered. The shadow materialized into a man holding a submachine gun, and the two men bailed out of the van and ran for cover. Pontowski chanced a look back. The man was moving after them, darting from tree to tree. Pontowski put on a burst of speed. Ahead of him he saw the sandbags of a half-completed defensive fire position the security cops had been digging. He dove into it headfirst, with the driver right behind him. Pontowski came up, coughing and spitting dirt. For a moment he pressed his head against the sandbags, still clearing his mouth, as he grabbed his radio. "Chicken Coop," he transmitted, "Bossman. I'm being chased by an unknown and am pinned down." Clark answered, asking for his position. "Halfway down the west taxiway," he replied. But he wasn't sure. His head bobbed up as he chanced a look. "Fifty yards east of"—it took him a moment to remember how the hardened aircraft shelters were numbered—"West One-Two."

"Help's on the way," Clark promised.

Pontowski drew his nine-millimeter Beretta and chambered a round. He held it at the ready, fully expecting an assault. Seconds passed, seeming like hours. He heard a dog bark once in the distance. A security cop leaped over the sandbags from behind and crashed down on him, his helmet banging into Pontowski's face. "Oof," a woman's voice said. She rolled off him and brought her M-16 up to a firing position. She fired off a short burst. "That got his attention," she said.

"Sergeant Maul, I presume," Pontowski said. She nodded. "Lovely day for a stroll." It was all he could think of to say.

"Indeed it is, General." She squeezed off another burst, bobbed up for a look, and dropped down beside him. "The Chief's flanking him."

"Is there only one?"

"I hope so," she said.

They heard a sharp "Get 'em!" off to their left, answered by the distinctive rattle of a Kalashnikov. Silence. Then, "Out!" They waited. "General," Rockne called, "stay where you are while we secure the area."

Jessica breathed easier and sat against the sandbags, holding her rifle upright between her legs. "Are we having fun yet?" she asked. She handed him her canteen. He took a grateful swallow and passed it back.

Boyca limped at Rockne's side as he marched into the command post. He dumped a Kalashnikov-type assault rifle on the table in front of Pontowski and Clark. "It's a knockoff of the AK-47 made in China," he told them. "A Type 56 used by PLA Special Forces."

"Where's the prisoner?" Clark asked.

"I turned him over to the First SOS for interrogation—"

Clark interrupted him. "Is he still alive?"

"Alive and well," Rockne replied. "He can't talk fast enough, and we know he's with the PLA Ninety-second Special Regiment. We'll have all the details before too long. At least we know who we're up against."

"Was he alone?" Pontowski asked.

"He is now," Rockne replied. "We flushed out three others who came across the fence with him. But they wanted to do it the hard way. No survivors."

Clark nodded. "How's Boyca?"

"A bit stiff." He stroked her head, rubbing between her ears. "She's not up to all this activity, but she'll be okay."

"You sent her in against an armed intruder?" Pontowski said.

"Yes, sir. He was preoccupied with you and Sergeant Maul, so he didn't see me. I managed to get within thirty feet, but there was an open space and Boyca was there, sorta like an old fire horse responding to an alarm. I wanted the guy alive, and it seemed like the right thing to do." Rockne allowed a tight smile. "You should have seen his face when he saw her coming at him. He fired wild, but Boyca was on him like shit on . . ." He paused, embarrassed. "He wet his pants."

"What will it take to secure the base?" Clark asked.

"I need the rest of my cops for openers," Rockne told her.

"We've got an aircraft arriving from the States tomorrow morning," she said. "They may be on board." She turned to Pontowski. "Sorry, sir. I hadn't told you but a GAO investigation team is due in."

"Lovely," Pontowski mumbled. "Just what we need." Another thought came to him. "I owe your driver big-time."

Washington, D.C.
Sunday, October 3

Shaw leaned against the doorjamb, watching his dinner companion from Saturday night cook breakfast. She was standing barefoot in his kitchen, wearing only the shirt he had worn the night before. She seemed so young to be a communications analyst at the National Security Agency. But she was old enough to know how to use NSA's sophisticated equipment to monitor domestic phone calls and get away with it. For a moment he couldn't remember what he had done with the first cassette tape she had given him that recorded Senator Leland's conversation with the French ambassador. Then he remembered. He had destroyed the tape after turning down the offer. "You are lovely," he said, telling her the truth.

She tossed her hair and gave him a quick smile. "And you're wonderful," she lied. He wanted to believe her but knew the truth. She might have shared his bed, but his performance had been strictly platonic. He had gotten a good night's sleep, though. She concentrated on the omelet.

"How's things at NSA these days?" he asked, finally coming to the heart of the matter.

Again the toss of the hair. "I thought you'd never ask, not after last time. You seemed so uninterested." She gave him a concerned look. "I was afraid you'd tell the agency about . . . well, you know."

He shoved his hands deep into the pockets of his robe. "Using NSA to monitor domestic phone calls can be hazardous to your health." Without a word she padded out of the kitchen and into the bedroom. She was back in a moment and handed him another cassette before she went back to the omelet. "How much for this one?" he asked, dropping it into a pocket. She shook her head as she studied the omelet in the pan. "Why?" he asked.

She looked at him, tears in her eyes. "Because Leland's a bastard." She flipped the omelet onto a dish and handed it to him.

He took a bite. "This is good." She rushed to him and threw her arms around his neck while he tried to balance the plate in one hand behind her. He felt her tears on his cheek. "Now, what's this, doll?"

"What's wrong, Patrick?"

"Not to worry," he told her. "I'll be okay." She held on to him, and he could feel her heartbeat through the thin shirt.

"Good morning, Mr. Shaw," his secretary said. Shaw grunted his usual answer, not surprised to find her at work so early. The war and impending election had made Sunday just another workday for the White House staff, and the West Wing hummed with quiet but purposeful activity.

"Your desk is ready." He stopped to pour himself a cup of coffee, surprising the woman. "I would have gotten that, Mr. Shaw." He gave her a little nod and carried the mug through to his office. "Well, I never," she murmured to herself. Shaw was not his normal dictatorial, demanding self. She decided he must be sick.

Shaw balanced the mug while he inserted the cassette into the recorder he kept in his desk. He hit the play button and listened. The quality of the tape was outstanding, clearer than anything he had ever heard. "Must be the original clip," he said to himself as he listened to the two very familiar voices of Senator John Leland and Robert Merritt, the secretary of defense.

Merritt: My investigators say the note they found in the DCI's chair was not his handwriting.

Leland: But it was the Web site for a child-pornography ring?

Merritt: That's correct.

Leland: And it was written on paper from his notepad?

Merritt: True.

Leland: Then how in the hell did it get there?

Merritt: We have absolutely no idea. But Security monitored a phone call from a public phone in the Pentagon about that Web site—after the DCI's suicide. This whole thing stinks. I'm telling you, don't use it.

Leland: Damn. A child-pornography ring in Turner's administration, and I've got to sit on it. (A long pause.) That's why he blew his brains out, wasn't it? He was about to be outed. She forced him to it, didn't she?

Merritt: That won't wash, Senator. There's a simpler explanation. We discovered that the DCI was self-medicating for depression and he was under pressure. I'm telling you, don't go there.

The tape ended. Shaw hit the eject button and dropped the cassette back into his pocket. "Go there, Senator," he urged. He settled back into his chair and played with ways to make that happen. The headache that would never completely go away surged back, making him sick to his stomach. He tasted the omelet he had for breakfast as he fought the nausea. He reached for the pills in his desk but stopped short. He knew the side effects. An inner clock told him it was time to step aside. "Not yet," he whispered.

The intercom buzzed. "The election committee is meeting with the president in two minutes," his secretary reminded him.

A shaky hand punched at the intercom. "Tell Bobbi Jo to start without me. I'll be there in a few minutes." He gave Bobbi Jo Reynolds high marks for the way she was managing the minute-by-minute details of the campaign, and there was no doubt she was ready to step in. At least he had done that right. He breathed deeply, forcing the headache and nausea to yield. But each attack was worse than the one before. He came to his feet and headed for the Oval Office, five minutes late.

All the key players on Turner's campaign committee were there when Shaw slipped into the room. The president nodded at him as he sat down, and then turned her attention back to Bobbi Jo. "Leland and his boy are scoring unanswered points," Bobbi Jo said, "and it's costing us in the polls. We're down by five-point-six, well outside the margin of error. The media is picking up on his claim that you're a prisoner of the White House, totally overwhelmed by the war." She consulted her notes. "Leland knows about the diplomatic initiative to split Iran or Syria off. He also knows it didn't work. He's going to hit us with that. It's only a matter of time." She paused. "We need to be preemptive—the sooner the better. I'm thinking maybe we challenge him to an unscheduled debate. Only this time on short notice, here in the White House. Say, tomorrow night, so they won't have time to prepare."

"Why?" Shaw asked.

"That turkey," Bobbi Jo said, refusing to call David Grau by his name, "can't think on his feet. Without his handlers prepping him, he'll step all over his itty-bitty schwanz."

Shaw let out a loud guffaw, now certain Bobbi Jo was ready. He liked the idea, but it needed a little fine-tuning. "First, they'll refuse. When they do, simply point out, very publicly, that if he can't handle a debate on short notice, how in hell can he cope with the crises he'll encounter every day in the White House? Second, they won't do it here, not in the White House. Give in on that point, but make it nearby, maybe at Georgetown University. Third, pass the word to the press corps not to jump on any bandwagons after it's over. When Leland hears that, he'll interpret it as a sign of weakness. That might make him more amenable to hold the debate. Finally, it's all in the timing." He paused, thinking. "Maybe if I can have a word with you afterward, Madam President?"

Turner nodded, and Shaw waited patiently until the meeting was over. At last, he was alone with Turner and Parrish, her chief of staff. "The debate's a good idea," Shaw told them. "Do it twenty-four hours before you open a second front."

"What's the downside?" Parrish asked.

"The media might think we deliberately sandbagged them," Turner answered, looking at Shaw. "That's why the warning to the press about bandwagons. It's a risk I'm willing to take." Her eyes filled with worry. "Are you okay?" she asked.

"Gettin' by, Mizz President. Gettin' by." The headache and nausea were back.

Virginia
Sunday, October 3

The nondescript SUV turned off the Manassas Bypass and crossed the railroad tracks. The onboard navigation and communications system flashed at the driver, telling her that she was cleared to approach the meeting place. She slowed and turned down a country lane, taking her two passengers to a meeting that all would claim until their dying day never took place. Yet, as in the flow of so many events, it was central to everything that would follow, and would elude historians in their quest for the truth. But for the players the judgment of history would have to take a backseat to a more critical need. It wasn't that Bernie Butler believed that the ends justified the means—he knew what that could lead to—but that secrecy was critical to success.

As the acting DCI, Butler now had the resources of the CIA at his beck and call, and the Company was very good at arranging clandestine meetings. Fortunately, the Company also knew who had to be sidestepped at all costs. Even more important, the CIA knew who could be brought in, which explained why the chief of Naval Operations was in the vehicle. But he was not a happy man.

"Look, Bernie," the admiral protested, "this is not the way I work."

Butler groaned inwardly. "Please bear with me, sir. But I think you'll see why we need to keep the SecDef in the dark."

The CNO muttered an obscenity he had learned as a midshipman that related to the sex life of mules. "You can hit Merritt with a spotlight and he'd still be operating in the dark. I'll never understand why Maddy didn't fire him months ago." The driver was cleared in, and she turned into a driveway. She drove directly into an open garage. The two men waited for the door to drop behind them before getting out. "This had better be worth it," the admiral warned as they walked inside. Two men were waiting for them.

"I believe you know Herr von Lubeck," Butler ventured.

"Son of a bitch," the admiral breathed. He was one of the four people in the U.S. government who "officially" knew what Herbert von Lubeck really did.

Von Lubeck was all charm and grace. "Good evening, Admiral. I believe you know my colleague." He looked at the man standing beside him, who was the CNO's counterpart in the German Kriegsmarine. The two admirals shook hands, old colleagues and good friends. A dark-suited aide escorted them into a comfortable library, where Mazie was waiting.

"Okay, Bernie," the CNO said, "what's going down?"

"Why don't we all sit?" Mazie offered. They found comfortable spots, and Mazie came right to the point. "Germany is prepared to open a second front in the northern sector of Iraq. The plan calls for them to strike out of Turkey, drive south to Baghdad, and split the country down the middle. They have a hundred and twenty tanks with supporting units and the necessary logistical buildup in place, and they're ready to move."

The CNO was stunned but quickly recovered. "But what about the Turks?"

Now it was Butler's turn. "We've convinced them they're next if the UIF prevails. They want to get on board and will fall in behind as the second echelon, backing up the German advance and securing the rear."

"Brilliant," the CNO murmured. "Absolutely brilliant. But why is the Navy involved?"

Von Lubeck answered. "We need the offices of you two gentlemen to arrange safe-passage procedures and recognition codes so your Air Force will not attack our tanks once they invade Iraq. Later on we can rely on the conventional channels to coordinate operations."

"The president is concerned about security," Mazie said. "The slightest leak . . . I'm quite sure you understand."

"Merritt," the CNO muttered.

"Let's just say," Butler said, "that he's not totally reliable."

The CNO leaned forward and clasped his hands between his knees. "But I do work for the man."

Mazie tried to explain. "That's why I'm here. I do speak for the president in this matter."

"And General Wilding?" the CNO asked, concerned about the chairman of the Joint Chiefs of Staff.

"General Wilding," Mazie said, "knows you're here. If there's a problem, we can meet with the president and the general."

"But you'd rather not because of the potential for a leak," the CNO said. "Personally, I think there's more of a security problem with the Turks."

"We're aware of that," Butler said. "That's why speed is critical. We figure we've got seventy-two hours at the outside before the UIF gets wind of it."

The CNO stood up. "Then we'd better get working on it. We need to get back to the Pentagon." The German admiral joined him as they headed for the garage. Once they were safely in a car and headed back for Washington, the CNO let his true feelings show. "Playing games with our own people! A hell of a way to run a war."

His old friend understood perfectly. "It happens when politicians believe that what is good for them is best for their country. We have the same problem."

"So where's von Lubeck coming from?" the CNO asked.

"I'm sure you noticed his attraction to Madam Hazelton."

"About as obvious as a bull in rut," the CNO allowed.

twenty-five

Central Malaysia
Monday, October 4

The small group of officers from SEAC headquarters deplaned quickly from the Super Puma and ran for the safety of the sandbagged bunker. They were the "Young Turks," and, to the man, they were neat, trim, well trained, and graduates of Singapore's Armed Forces Training Institute. This was also the closest any of them had been to real combat. Pontowski was the last off the helicopter, and he ducked his head to avoid the rotor blades. He knew he had plenty of clearance, but it was a natural reaction. In the far distance he heard sporadic cannon fire.

Thank God this isn't China, he thought, recalling his days with the American Volunteer Group in the late 1990s. In the grand scheme of things, he was caught up in a low-level conflict, nothing near the intensity of the war in the Persian Gulf. But that didn't make it any less deadly for the participants.

Waldo and Tel were waiting for them in the regiment's version of an ASOC—air-support operations center—which coordinated requests from Army units in contact with the enemy for close air support. Pontowski stood at the back of the small group with Waldo as Tel explained how the ASOC worked. Although Tel gave the briefing in Chinese, all the Young Turks were fluent in English. It was a nice touch the young officers appreciated. "The kid's good," Waldo told Pontowski. "But we need a pilot doing this." Then, "You're not gonna leave me here, are ya?" Like any fighter jock, the last thing Waldo wanted to be was an ALO—an air-liaison officer—directing fighters onto targets out of an ASOC.

"I'm thinking about it," Pontowski replied.

Waldo groaned. "Thanks, Boss." The VHF radio crackled as the flight of two Hogs from Alpha checked in. "Well, this is what they came to see," Waldo said. Tel answered the radio call and jotted down the A-10's time on station, ordnance, and playtime. The radio/telephone operator at a nearby table handed him a clipboard with requests for close air support from units in the field. "Time to go to work," Waldo said. As the ALO, he would select where the A-10s would go.

Suddenly the radio operator was all activity as a new request came in. His fingers darted over the control panel, feeding the incoming call to the loudspeaker above his head. A frantic voice was yelling in Chinese. A stunned silence held the room in a tight grip as Tel ran back to the two Americans. "The PLA has broken through and captured a key railroad and highway bridge over the Sungai Muar."

Waldo rushed to the front and quickly plotted the location on a chart. "Thirty-five miles away," he muttered. "The next major bridge is here."

"The MA should have blown that bridge," one of the Young Turks said.

"But they didn't," Waldo replied. He looked at Pontowski, knowing what they had to do. "It's on the main LOC, packed with refugees. Any change to the ROE?"

"Damn," Pontowski said as the burden of command came back down. It was his rules of engagement that forbade an A-10 to strike within a kilometer of the LOC. "Give me a moment." He had to make a decision and was rapidly running out of time.

The two A-10s cut a lazy racetrack pattern in the sky. Below them, broken clouds stretched to the horizon, with the incredibly green landscape of Malaysia peeking through. Bull Allison, the flight lead, scanned his instrument panel looking for telltale signs of trouble. But his Radar Warning Receiver—RWR for short—was quiet. He keyed his radio and called the ASOC at Segamat. "Hey, Waldo. Make a decision. We haven't got all day."

"Stand by one," Waldo replied.

A bored-sounding voice came over the radio. "Standing by one." It was Bull's wingman, Skid Menke. The tone in his voice asked the main question—why were they turning jet fuel into noise? The Warthogs moved farther west and entered another racetrack pattern.

Waldo came on the radio. "Tulsa Flight, I have tasking."

"Go," Bull answered, his tone hard and quick.

"Visually recce the bridge complex at Bahau and report. Threat unknown."

"Can we shoot back?" Bull asked.

Again the standard answer. "Stand by one." A long pause while the two pilots fumed. "Tulsa Flight, you are cleared to return fire if fired upon."

"How 'bout that," Bull mumbled to himself. "Someone made a decision—finally." He didn't suffer from that problem and keyed his radio. "Skid, ingress from the west, fly up the river at low level, cross the bridge, and get the hell out of Dodge. Shooter-cover." He turned to the north and headed for a break in the clouds as Skid fell in a half mile in trail. Bull rolled 135 degrees as he punched into the clouds and headed for the deck. What looked like a nice break in the clouds turned into a sucker hole, and he was back in the clouds. Immediately Bull was back on instruments as he rolled out and shallowed his dive. Then he broke into the open, fifteen hundred feet above the ground. He kept his rate of descent going and checked his six o'clock for his wingman. Skid dropped out of the clouds inverted, his nose buried, but immediately recovered. "What sort of maneuver was that?" Bull asked.

"An inverted rectalitis whifferdill," Skid answered. "Standard procedure when you follow a blind asshole."

Bull didn't answer as he leveled off seventy-five feet above the river and turned to the east. In his peripheral vision, he caught a glimpse of his wingman in his deep five o'clock, exactly where he should be. He firewalled the throttles. Ahead of him he saw a double span of bridges crossing the river. His RWR gear was quiet as he jinked hard, avoiding any ground fire. He might not have been able to see it, but he knew it was there. He rolled left, then right as he approached the bridge, and overflew it at fifty feet. Both bridges were packed with refugees fleeing southward. He saw the muzzle flash of a ZSU-23-4, an old but still-fearsome antiaircraft artillery weapon, or AAA, at the northern end of the highway bridge. The stick shuddered slightly in his hand as a single round hit his left rudder. Fortunately, the twenty-three-millimeter high-explosive shell did not detonate and only punched a hole through the skin.

"I've got 'em," Skid radioed, rolling in on the offending AAA.

"Refugees!" Bull shouted. "Go through dry!" But it was too late. Skid squeezed off a short burst of cannon fire and pulled off to the south. Bull jinked hard to his right in time to see the ZSU-23 disappear in a flash of flames and smoke. He saw bodies falling off the bridge.

"Looks like a pool party to me," Skid radioed.

"Join up and check my ass," Bull transmitted, wishing Skid had kept his mouth shut. "I took a hit coming off."

Skid slipped into a close formation and scanned his flight lead for damage. "You got a hole in your left rudder; otherwise you scan clean."

"Controllability chcck okay," Bull said. "Ground Hog, Tulsa One."

"Go ahead, Tulsa," Waldo replied.

"The bridge is packed with bodies. Trip A from northern approach. Engaged and destroyed one ZSU-23. I took a hit and we're RTB at this time."

"Say status of the bridge," Waldo replied.

"The bridge is open, and troops are crossing in number with refugees."

Pontowski listened as Waldo copied down Bull's flight rep. "Rog," Waldo replied, "copied all." He gave Pontowski a long look. "They may have gotten some refugees."

One of the Young Turks coughed for attention. "I find no fault here," he said. "We know the PLA uses civilians as shields."

I hope the GAO thinks like you do, Pontowski thought, contemplating the upcoming visit from the Government Accounting Office.

"May I suggest," the same officer said in impeccable English, "that I remain here to train our forward air controllers. I am a pilot and have served as a FAC in the past. That would allow Lieutenant Colonel Walderman to return to his duties with the AVG."

"An excellent suggestion," Pontowski said. It was quickly arranged, and he headed for the helicopter for the return flight to Camp Alpha.

Camp Alpha
Monday, October 4

Clark's driver was waiting for Pontowski's helicopter when it landed at Alpha. "Missy Colonel say you go to command post now," the driver said. In his world Janice Clark's word was law, regardless of Pontowski's rank. He drove at an alarming rate of speed, jamming on the brakes in front of the command post. Pontowski hurried inside, where his small staff was waiting for him. "Okay, folks," Pontowski said. "What's going down?"

As Maggot was the wing commander, he answered. "Tulsa One took a single hit in the left rudder, minor damage, and recovered without incident. Aircraft Battle Repair says they'll have it patched in a couple of hours. Second, Kamigami checked in this morning and has requested resupply."

"What the hell is he doing out there?" Pontowski asked.

"We'll have to ask Colonel Sun," Maggot replied. "Also, we got problems with POL." POL was petroleum, oil, and lubricants—the lifeblood of the AVG.

Janice Clark stood up. "We're not able to tank in enough JP-8 overland to maintain our flying schedule and keep a combat reserve. The roads are jammed with refugees fleeing south, and snipers have attacked three trucks. I'm working with SEAC but haven't come up with a solution." Like a good staff officer, she had a short-term work-around. "The GAO team is coming in on a KC-10. The aircraft has been directed to wait for the team, and we're going to download a hundred fifty thousand pounds of jet fuel while it's on the ground."

Maggot shrugged. "Makes sense. If it can offload in the air, it can offload on the ground."

"Can we get a dedicated tanker until the problem's solved?" Pontowski asked.

"I'll ask again," Clark replied. "But SEAC's having the same problem."

"Any chance my cops on board that KC-10?" Rockne asked.

Clark shook her head. "The MAAG is working on it, but the Gulf has priority." She hesitated for a moment. "General Pontowski, without a full complement of security cops, I cannot guarantee air base defense. In fact, with enemy troops reported less than a hundred miles to the north and our overland supply lines to Singapore coming under attack, we need help." She was a very worried woman.

The sergeant manning the communications cab handed Clark a note. She glanced at it and announced, "The KC-10 is twenty minutes out, VIPs on board." She hesitated for a moment. "I've dealt with the GAO before. I've arranged for quarters while they're here so they can change and discuss whatever they talk about in private." She pursed her lips tightly. "The last thing we need right now is them breathing down our necks."

Pontowski stood up. "A GAO team is power unto itself," he told them. "Tell your people to be polite, answer their questions as simply and truthfully as they can, and do not—I repeat, do not—volunteer any information. It tends to confuse them. Janice, why don't you and I go howdy the folks?" An idea came to him. "Maybe we can assign your driver to them?"

Clark allowed a thin smile. "You're really wicked, General."

The three men and one woman inching their way down the narrow boarding ladder of the KC-10 were not typical government bureaucrats concerned with doing their job and getting on with their private life. They had a mission and the power of Congress to back them up. Consequently, they expected (and usually received) deferential treatment—which they were not getting. The team chief carefully adjusted his safari jacket while he waited for his companions to join him. He studiously ignored Pontowski and Clark. After conferring briefly with his team, he turned to Pontowski.

"Jason P. Willard," the team chief said, presenting Pontowski his identification. He didn't wait for a reply. "Please have our driver take us to our quarters, where we can shower and change. Later we will need to tour the base and interview certain individuals." He handed Pontowski a list of names. "Please have them available."

"Certainly, Mr. Willard," Pontowski replied. "May I present Lieutenant Colonel Janice Clark, the base commander?"

Willard looked at Clark the way someone would examine roadkill. "As Colonel Clark is on the list to be interviewed, any contact at this time is inappropriate." He turned to Clark's waiting minivan and driver. "Our transportation, I presume."

"Of course," Pontowski said. He escorted the team to the minivan and waited while they climbed in. "May I escort you?" Pontowski offered.

"Does the driver know his way around the base?" Willard asked.

"Of course," Pontowski replied. "But under the circumstances—"

Willard interrupted him. "General Pontowski, apparently you don't appreciate why we are here. We must operate independently in order to learn the truth of the matter. Any unwarranted contact at this time would be prejudicial to our investigation."

Pontowski stepped back and saluted as Clark's driver jammed the minivan into gear and stomped on the accelerator. "Welcome to Camp Alpha," he muttered as the van careened around a corner and disappeared.

"Charming people," Clark said. Together they walked back to the command post.

The Scud hit two hours later.

The first reports flooding into the command post indicated that the missile had hit on the extreme southwest corner of the base, missing the main complex by a thousand meters. Pontowski leaned over the center console as he listened to the damage reports. When the runway was reported as clear and undamaged, he ordered the KC-10 to launch and hold south of the base. "Any casualties?" he asked.

A sergeant answered. "The Rock says two security cops were in a defensive fire position near the point of impact. Doc Ryan is there now."

"Stay on top of it," Pontowski ordered. "Colonel Clark, any word on the GAO team?"

"The last I heard they were still at operations interviewing pilots." She punched at her communications panel and called the hardened shelter. She spoke briefly to Maggot and broke the connection. "They say the GAO's left and are coming our way," she told him. "They should be here any moment. Apparently they're not happy campers."

The GAO team that ran into the command post had definitely lost some of its self-composure but none of its arrogance. "General Pontowski," Willard barked, "what exactly do you think you're doing?"

Pontowski was confused. "What am I doing?"

"First this missile attack and now our airplane taking off without us."

Pontowski handed him a phone. "You really need to speak to the PLA about the missile. As for the KC-10, I ordered it airborne for safety. We can recall it when you're ready to leave."

Willard was shouting. "Recall it immediately!"

"Certainly," Pontowski said. "I take it your investigation is complete."

"No, it is not!"

"Can I be of any help before you leave?"

Willard took a deep breath and wiped the sweat from his face. "Did you order the use of CBU-58s at Kuala Lumpur?"

"Directly order? The answer is no. But I am responsible, as I cleared my pilots to engage. Further, I allow them to use the best tactics to ensure their survival and the weapons best suited for the target. I don't second-guess them, Mr. Willard."

"Then you're also responsible for the attack on the innocent civilians on the bridge at Bahau this morning?"

"If you're referring to the attack on the ZSU-23 that shot at and hit one of my aircraft, the answer is yes."

"Have your rules of engagement been approved and published?"

"Approved by whom?"

Willard was not used to being questioned, and he turned a light shade of purple. "The national command authority. Who else would I be talking about?"

"Do you mean by President Turner?"

Willard's face turned a deeper purple at Pontowski's intransigence. "I mean by the legal controlling authority of our government!"

"At the risk of forever confusing you, sir, the American Volunteer Group is under the operational command of Southeast Asia Command. Further, I seriously doubt if the 'legal controlling authority of our government' has a clue when it comes to the ROE in this theater."

Janice Clark interrupted him. "General." She cast a glance at the doorway, where a haggard-looking Doc Ryan was standing with Rockne.

"I couldn't save them," Ryan said. He turned and left.

"Your two cops?" Pontowski asked Rockne.

Rockne's face matched his nickname. "It was a direct hit." He pulled himself erect, almost at attention. "Sir, when the KC-10 lands, can we hold it long enough to load the body bags? Sergeant Maul can escort them."

"Absolutely not!" Willard shouted.

Pontowski turned and fixed him with a hard stare. "Mr. Willard, that KC-10 is not taking off without them."

"We'll see about that!"

"Please do."

For a moment the two men stared at each other, locked in a contest of wills. Willard broke and scurried out. "You haven't heard the last of this!" he shouted, determined to have the last word.

Clark shook her head and muttered an obscenity under her breath. "Why," she wondered, "do I get the feeling we're being hung out to dry?"

The White House
Monday, October 4

The muffled beat of the drum coming from Lafayette Park was barely audible in the president's bedroom. But it was there, pounding at her subconscious with its unrelenting message. Maddy's eyes snapped open, and she sat up, her heart racing. *What was I dreaming about?* The luminous hands on the clock announced it was just after four in the morning. She breathed deeply, and soon her heart slowed. She hesitated before turning on the light. She knew that simple signal would send out waves like a huge rock splashing into a placid lake, until the White House was awash in activity, fully alert and tuned to her needs.

She reached out and turned on the bedside lamp. Within seconds there was a discreet knock at the door. It was her maid, ready to be of service. "Coffee, please," Maddy called, starting the day. She padded into the bathroom and turned on the shower. For a few minutes she let the hot water course over her body, savoring the moment. Her maid was there with a warm robe when she stepped out. She ripped off her shower cap and shook her hair. "I'll wear the dark blue jumpsuit with the presidential logo for now," she said. The older woman looked at her in a state of mild shock, and Maddy smiled. "Well, if Winston Churchill could wear his 'siren suit,' I can, too." Another thought came to her. "We start at the normal time today," she said.

"It's too late, Madam President," the woman replied.

Exactly eight minutes later Turner walked into the Situation Room. The three officers on duty had been warned she was headed their way and were ready. She sat in a chair next to the big monitors instead of her normal chair across the table. "A quick update," she said, picking up a hand controller. DAY 29 flashed on the center screen, and within seconds she was scrolling through the Spot Update, the current synopsis of the war the NMCC updated every thirty minutes. The UIF was still driving hard to the south, but the air-interdiction campaign was slowing them down.

"The Saudis are fighting like demons," a duty officer said. It was true. They were in the thick of it, throwing every unit they had into the front line and taking heavy casualties. "By the way, we know how the UIF is moving supplies south." He called up a map display tracing the UIF's supply net into Saudi Arabia. "They took their lessons from the North Vietnamese and the Ho Chi Minh Trail," he explained. "But lacking a jungle for cover, they adapted to the desert. First they dug a series of tunnels under the border." His pointer circled eight dashed lines that started in Iraq and reached south, across the border, aiming toward King Khalid Military City. "They range from five to twelve miles long. Our analysts estimate it probably took them three years to construct them. Once clear of the border, they leapfrogged ahead and built aboveground tunnels to serve as drive-through storage bunkers." Another chart showed a spiderweb of truck trails reaching into the desert. "They made no attempt to hide the truck tracks, and we've destroyed over two thousand trucks moving south."

"Where did we think all these trucks were coming from?"

"Because of the tunnels," the officer answered, "we couldn't detect them crossing the border. So we assumed they were ours, captured when King Khalid City fell. Then they made sure we saw exactly what we wanted to see. The entire road net is littered with burned-out hulks. What we didn't see were these aboveground bunkers."

A high-resolution image showed a truck track in the desert paralleling a ridgeline. "This is fairly typical. All they did was extend the side of the ridge, much like a snow shelter on a railroad track in the mountains. If you look close, you can see how a truck can dart in here from the main track, drive down the tunnel, and come out here, rejoining the main track. We estimate as many as a hundred trucks can hide in this tunnel until any threat has gone away. Then they dash for the next tunnel."

"Why haven't we bombed these tunnels?" she asked.

"This is new, very new. The CIA and DIA just put it together. The big lesson here is that low tech still works, if you're willing to pay the price. The analysts are calling it 'Saddam's Spider.'"

"So this desert pipeline—Saddam's Spider, if you will—is in full flow?"

"Packed with men and supplies," came the answer. "That's how they were able to mount and sustain the current offensive."

Turner's fingers drummed a tight tattoo on the table as an idea began to form in the back of her mind. She hit the advance button on her hand controller to cycle the screens. The casualty status report was next. The total number of Americans killed in action had reached 2,011. She hit the pause button when the names of the current casualties appeared. "Yes, ma'am," the duty officer said, "we saw it, too." The name of Colonel Robert Scovill was at the top of the list.

"What happened?" she asked.

"As best we know, he had just arrived at his battalion headquarters when the enemy broke through. It was a rout. But he formed up a unit of stragglers and led them in a counterattack. They held on long enough for reinforcements to arrive and turn it around. It was afterward . . . a dudded mortar round exploded."

She fought for her breath. Then, "Please, give me a moment." The three men quickly left. *I last saw him when? Friday night.* Tears formed in her eyes. *How long ago was that?* Her relentless mind drove her on, offering no refuge. *Fifty-six hours ago. Not even three days. Oh, my God! How much can I ask of them?* Her body shuddered with a wrenching sob. His name flashed at her. *I will remember,* she promised. Then the tears flowed, not just for Robert Neil Scovill but also for all of them. Slowly she regained her composure, as an icy calm descended over her soul. *I will not forget!* She dabbed at her eyes with a tissue and hit the intercom button. "Please have my staff join me here."

"They're in the hall, Mrs. President."

Richard Parrish was the first through the door, closely followed by Nancy, her personal assistant. Turner stood while the rest filed in and found seats around the table. Mazie was the last to enter, and she stopped, not sure what she was seeing. "We're going to end this war," the president said. She looked around the room. "Not as soon as I would like, but soon enough. And we will not lose the peace. Richard, get with Stephan at State and Mazie and develop an end-game strategy. Also, I will be making an announcement in thirty minutes in the Press Room."

"Ma'am," Parrish said, "it's only five o'clock. No one will be there."

"Then I'll be talking to an empty room." She fixed them with a steady gaze. "And by the way, we're going to win this election. Please excuse me. I have to call Colonel Scovill's family." Her staff quickly left, not sure what to make of what they had just experienced.

The small Press Room was packed when the president walked in. She stood at the podium and looked around the room, bending each one to her will. "Earlier this morning I learned that Colonel Robert Neil Scovill, USMC, was killed in action within hours after joining his unit in Saudi Arabia. I believe many of you knew Colonel Scovill from the briefings he gave at the Pentagon. He also briefed me numerous times, the last being Friday evening. I had come to rely on Colonel Scovill and trusted his judgment. But he was never happy here and wanted to be with his men. Colonel Scovill was first and last a Marine, and he gave his life fighting for the freedom of others. I can only honor his sacrifice." She paused and looked at her hands.

"Second, my worthy opponent in this election has repeatedly charged that I am a prisoner of the White House, unable to meet the challenges of this conflict and afraid to make a decision. He is right about one thing: I have given my full attention to this war and as a consequence have been held close to the White House. Personally, I would like to see how he responds to the demands of the moment. Therefore, I'm offering to meet him in a debate to last no longer than ninety minutes, within the next thirty-six hours at a place of his choosing—as long as it's not too far from here." A wave of laughter worked its way around the room. "No moderator, no set format, no prearranged questions. He gets to make the first statement, and we go from there. The offer is on the table."

She turned and left the stage.

Wilding arrived at the Situation Room at exactly seven o'clock to meet with the ExCom and the president. His eyes burned, and he felt a weariness that was dragging him down. "General Wilding," Turner said, "thank you for coming." She stood and paced the floor. "Mazie, when can we expect the Germans to launch their offensive?"

"H-hour is 0100 hours local, Thursday morning," Mazie said. "That's five P.M. Wednesday evening here. The vanguard starts to deploy and move to the border tonight."

"General Wilding," Turner said, "I just learned about Saddam's Spider. I assume you will be targeting it in the very near future."

"Starting today," Wilding said.

"Focus initially on the southern end of the Spider," she said. "I want—"

Wilding stood up. "Madam President, we've been through this before."

She nodded. "Indeed. But hear me out. The moment the Germans launch their offensive, seal off the northern end of the Spider. I do not want any supplies returning north."

Wilding's head came up as his fatigue disappeared. "Brilliant. We hit the southern end hard, they push more supplies into the Spider to make up for the losses and keep their offensive going, the Germans attack, and we seal off their logistical effort in the Spider." His face grew hard as he looked at her, the pieces falling into place. "They've dug their own graves."

"Exactly," Turner said, returning his gaze.

The lights were on in the Oval Office when Bobbi Jo Reynolds and the election committee sat down to meet with the president. "Thanks for staying so late," Turner said.

"Thanks for the dinner," Bobbi Jo replied. The small group went to work, bringing the president up to date on the campaign. "There is bad news, Mrs. President. We're running out of money. Campaign contributions have slowed to a trickle, and our supporters appear to be in a wait-and-see mode." A serious matter, but they were all pros and knew how to work around the problem of diminishing finances. They were about finished when the door opened and Patrick Shaw slipped into the room.

He gave them all a big grin. "I just got off the phone. Leland and his boy have agreed to a debate. Tomorrow evening, six P.M., at Georgetown University." His news was greeted with approval all around, and the committee rapidly finished its work. Finally they were gone, and her day was over. "Well, Mizz President," Shaw said, "you gotta render that son of a bitch tomorrow."

"Any suggestions on how to do that?" she asked.

"If we're lucky, he'll bang the drum on three issues: leadership, failed intelligence, and diplomacy." Shaw could hardly contain himself. "You know the answers—but give them the last word every time."

twenty-six

New Mexico Military Institute
Monday, October 4

Zack and Brian arrived ten minutes early for the afternoon briefing in Dow Hall. Neither teenager's strong suit was punctuality, and ten minutes early set a new record for them. But it was a wasted effort, as every seat in the room was taken and they had to stand at the back. Just as the Army captain giving the update on the war stepped up to the podium, two football players came through the door and edged in front of them. "What happened to practice?" Brian muttered.

The bigger of the two players, a defensive lineman, stepped on his foot. "Hey, this is where the action is."

The captain looked around the room. "We're going to have to find a larger place," he said. Zack and Brian agreed with him as the two football players squashed them against the back wall. The computer-driven projector clicked on, and the captain quickly summarized the fighting in the Gulf and in Malaysia. "The UIF's rate of advance toward Riyadh appears to be slowing, but there is still some hard fighting ahead for the coalition forces before it is stopped. The arrival this Friday of two major convoys will certainly improve the logistics situation. However, the situation on the Malay Peninsula is much bleaker. At the rate the PLA is advancing, it appears Singapore will fall within two to three weeks."

"Hey, Pontowski," the lineman said, "it looks like your old man is gonna get his ass kicked."

"Asshole," Brian muttered.

The captain called up another image on the screen. "Today I'd like to look at the win-hold-win strategy being pursued by the United States. I think it's fair to say, given the circumstances, it is the only viable option." He outlined the details of the strategy, focusing on the lack of strategic airlift necessary to make it work. He finished, "Unfortunately, the timing is all wrong, and I seriously doubt that we can win the war in Saudi Arabia in time to redeploy to Malaysia and save the hold. It looks like SEAC and the American Volunteer Group are being hung out to dry."

The briefing was over, and the room rapidly emptied, but before Zack could escape, the football player stopped him. "Hey, man. I didn't mean it the way it sounded. I mean, well, shit, I mean, I wish I was there . . . with your dad." His big hand pounded Zack's left shoulder. "I'd follow your old man anywhere." Embarrassed by his show of emotion, he spun around and hurried out the door.

"Can you believe that?" Brian said. Zack shook his head, and they walked in silence back to the barracks. "Your dad is something else again," Brian finally said.

Zack looked at his best friend, his eyes filled with worry. "Do you think that asshole might be right?"

"About your dad getting his ass kicked if Singapore falls?" Zack gave a little nod. "No way my mom would let that happen," Brian assured him.

Central Malaysia
Tuesday, October 5

The Super Puma flew through the early-morning dark, relying on GPS navigation to keep it on course and clear of high terrain or any obstacles. The bright moonlight also helped the crew navigate, but they were drenched in sweat as they neared their destination. The terrain flattened out, and instinctively the pilot dropped lower to the ground. He had never flown so long at night, much less over enemy territory. Two minutes out he asked his copilot to recheck the coordinates for the landing zone he had punched into the GPS. The copilot did as ordered and confirmed they were the same as those in Kamigami's message requesting resupply. When the display read two-tenths of a kilometer to go, the pilot reached for the throttles overhead and inched them back, slowing the big helicopter.

On cue, a small clearing appeared in the moonlight and a light flashed, clearing them to land. The big helicopter settled to earth as the gunner slid open both doors in the cargo compartment. Men ran from the surrounding trees and, in less than two minutes, offloaded a ton of ammunition and supplies. Two wounded men were helped on board as a tall, lanky figure jumped off the Puma.

Tel turned and watched as the helicopter lifted off and disappeared over the treetops, heading back to Camp Alpha. He shouldered his heavy bergen and followed the men into the tree line, where Kamigami was waiting. "Good morning, sir," Tel said. Kamigami gave him a studied look but said nothing. "Colonel Sun suggested I join you."

"Suggested?" Kamigami said.

"Well, he did want me to outline a possible operation. There is some urgency."

"We have to move out," Kamigami said. In his world of special operations, movement was life, and he assumed, rightfully so, that the helicopter had been detected. Someone would be investigating at first light, and they had to be miles away by then. However, he planned to leave a few interesting "surprises" behind to discourage anyone who might want to follow them into the jungle. Kamigami quickly packed his portion of the supplies that had been offloaded, and then checked on the two claymore mines that had been rigged as booby traps. He personally set the timers that would detonate them in thirty-six hours if some hapless soldier didn't trigger them first. He lifted his bergen and picked up an ammunition box. "Go," he said, his voice barely audible. Two corporals took the point and led the way down a trail. Tel adjusted his night-vision goggles and fell in behind Kamigami.

For the next hour the thirty-six men ghosted through the jungle, moving fast and spread out over a quarter of a mile. No one had to urge them to maintain a killing pace. Finally Kamigami called a halt. He removed his night-vision goggles and rubbed his forehead. "What possible operation?" he asked Tel.

Tel took a long drink from his canteen. "SEAC wants you to take out the bridges at Bahau."

"Where the tanks are," Kamigami said. It wasn't meant to be a question.

"The tanks are still on the northern side," Tel replied. "They'd like to keep them there."

"The AVG can drop those spans in a heartbeat."

"Unfortunately," Tel told him, "the PLA's using refugees as human shields to protect the bridges from bombing."

Kamigami scoffed. "The ROE won't allow Pontowski to bomb civilians on an LOC, and the PLA figured it out days ago." He stared at the ground. "The Americans never learn." He thought for a moment. "For us to go after the bridges is a suicide mission." A distant explosion echoed over them, and Kamigami checked his watch. "They got there sooner than I expected." They heard a second explosion. "They're aggressive—they'll be after us in a few minutes."

"Do they have dogs?" Tel asked.

"Not for long. We also booby-trapped the trail."

"Won't the dogs sniff out the detonators or trip wires?"

Kamigami shook his head. "Hope not. We used motion-detection detonators." He passed the word to move out, and the men set a blistering pace, fully aware they were being chased. Ninety minutes later Kamigami motioned for a halt and quickly checked their position with a GPS. "I've got an idea about the bridges. But it will take some coordination." He called for his lieutenant and two sergeants. The three men joined him, and he outlined his plan. "How long will it take you to move two mortar teams into position?" he asked the lieutenant.

The lieutenant thought out loud. "The max range of the L9 is seven hundred fifty meters." The L9A1 was a fifty-one-millimeter-caliber mortar, light and accurate, but with limited range. "We'll have to infiltrate to get in range." He considered his options. "We go in tonight, hide during the day, attack at sunset so we can E-and-E out at night." E and E was escape and evasion.

"That will give us plenty of time to coordinate with the AVG," Tel said.

"Let's do it," Kamigami said. He gave them map coordinates for a rendezvous and told the lieutenant to select two other men and a radio operator.

"Can I go?" Tel asked.

The lieutenant gave him a long look. "How many mortar rounds can you carry?"

In the distance they heard the muffled explosion of the last booby trap. "Aggressive bastards," Kamigami said, paying their pursuers a compliment.

Camp Alpha
Tuesday, October 5

Pontowski's small staff gathered around him while he read SEAC's latest air-task order that sent his A-10s into combat. He snorted as he reread it and he paced the command post like a caged animal. He waved the offending message in front of them. "Two missions?" he asked angrily. "Four jets in twenty-four hours?"

"That's all, boss," Maggot replied. "I told SEAC we could launch sixteen Hogs on the first go, twelve on a second go, and eight on a third."

Pontowski let his disgust show. "Why are we even here?"

Colonel Sun coughed politely for attention. "We received a message from General Kamigami earlier this morning. You might find it of interest." He handed Pontowski and Maggot copies to read.

"This is more like it," Maggot said.

"Timing is critical," Sun told them. He passed out target folders his intelligence officer had put together. "The plan calls for two mortar teams to shell the northern approaches to the bridges at 1750 hours, approximately ten minutes before sunset, tomorrow evening. The teams will walk the barrage toward the bridges and seal off the approach. If it goes as planned, the people and soldiers on the highway bridge will run for cover to the south, leaving the bridge clear. However, given the short range of the mortars, the teams will come under immediate attack and have to withdraw. But there should be a narrow window of opportunity for your Warthogs to attack."

"And we coordinate the attack," Maggot said, "so the mortar teams can withdraw under the cover of darkness."

"Exactly," Sun replied.

"I'll get Weapons and Tactics on it," Maggot said. Weapons and Tactics was the planning section made up of pilots who were experts in weapons employment and tactics. "Four Hogs should do the trick. Two on each span."

"We can have a Puma in the area if search and rescue is required," Sun added.

"Will we need SEAC's blessing?" Maggot asked.

A frown crossed Sun's face. "Perhaps," he hedged, "it would be best if only Mr. Deng knew."

An image of the tall, elderly man in charge of Singapore's Security and Intelligence division flashed in Pontowski's mind. "Why Gus?" Pontowski asked. "What's going on?"

"Shall we say," Sun said in a low voice, "that there are problems with security within SEAC."

"Lovely," Maggot muttered. "Can't tell the players without a program. Hell of a way to fight a war."

"Does that explain the lack of tasking on the ATO?" Pontowski wondered. From the look on Sun's face, he knew he had touched the truth of the matter. "I'm going to Singapore to sort out the ATO. I can talk to Gus then about the bridges."

"Please," Sun said, "keep this very close-hold."

"I understand," Pontowski said. He looked at the others. "Anything else while I'm down there shaking the bushes?"

Clark studied her notes. "Can you check with SEAC about a dedicated shuttle for fuel?"

"I'll put the pressure on," Pontowski promised.

Rockne stood. "I know I'm sounding like a broken record, but we do need the rest of our cops."

"I'll check with the MAAG," Pontowski said. "But I doubt if I'll have much luck."

"Well," Rockne replied, "I could use a truckload of mines and a dozen or so M-60s." The M-60 was a light machine gun firing a 7.62-millimeter slug. Combined with land mines, it was an excellent weapon for denying terrain.

"Doc, do you need anything?" Pontowski asked.

"Arrangements for air evac would be nice," Ryan replied.

Pontowski stepped up to the big situation chart on the sidewall. "I don't like what I'm seeing. They're driving straight for Singapore, and we're directly in their path." He measured the distance from Camp Alpha to the edge of the battle area. "Seventy-five miles away." He sat down and leaned back in his chair, his chin on his chest. "Start thinking evacuation, folks."

Rockne closed his eyes and took a deep breath. If that happened, he knew who wouldn't be leaving. "I really need those mines and M-60s," he said. "A few antitank weapons would be nice. I suppose tactical nukes are out of the question."

Nobody thought it was funny.

Singapore
Tuesday, October 5

Pontowski sat in the backseat of the dark blue staff car as it turned out of the embassy's garage and eased into the late-afternoon traffic. "Have you ever met Mr. Deng?" the driver asked.

"I met Gus in Washington," Pontowski replied. He decided to get right to it. "Mr. Stans, I take it you're not an administrative services officer."

"Call me Tom, sir. Whatever else would I be?"

"CIA? Chief of station?"

Stans gave a little laugh. "Is it that obvious?"

"And you're hoping to be part of this meeting," Pontowski replied.

"One does hope. But we would appreciate a back brief. Don't be taken in by Gus's grandfatherly image. This is his territory, and he'll cut your throat in a nanosecond if he thinks you're a problem."

Pontowski shook his head. "I guess I don't want to be a problem."

"That's encouraging," Stans said. The traffic was very heavy, and they were late when they turned into the large estate. Two extremely fit young men wearing flak vests and carrying Uzi submachine guns were waiting for them. "I'm glad they know you," Stans mumbled under his breath.

A third man opened the car door. "Mr. Stans, you're more than welcome to join Mr. Deng and General Pontowski." Stans couldn't believe his good luck and followed Pontowski inside.

Gus was waiting for them on the veranda. "Ah," he said, standing to greet them. "Mr. Stans, I presume. Your reputation precedes you." He turned to the two beautiful young women with him. "May I introduce LeeAnn and Cari?" The introductions made, the girls left. Gus came right to the point. "How may I help you?"

"First," Pontowski said, "the AVG is not getting tasking, and we're sitting on our thumbs at Alpha while the PLA's coming straight at us. Use us or we're going home."

Gus nodded in acknowledgment. "Ah, yes. The air-task order. That is a problem. Shall we say there are certain factions here who are reluctant to use the AVG for fear of making the situation worse."

"How can we make it worse?"

"These same factions," Gus explained, "are hoping for a negotiated settlement."

"The PLA will negotiate," Stans said, "when you surrender."

"Quite so," Gus said. "I hope to convince these gentlemen that they are misguided."

"Also," Pontowski continued, "Kamigami and Sun have a plan to attack the bridges at Bahau."

"I've seen Victor's message," Gus said. He smiled at their surprise. "Nothing of significance happens in Singapore without my knowing. I believe a mortar attack will clear the bridges, and it does solve your problem with your ROE. But it also puts the mortar teams at some risk." He hesitated. "I assume your aircraft can destroy the bridges."

"In a heartbeat," Pontowski promised. "But we need clearance from SEAC to launch."

"The word of your plan will reach the proper ears." Gus's face was impassive. "I assume you haven't solved your problem with fuel supplies at Alpha and that you want to increase your air base defense posture."

"That's correct," Pontowski said, wondering where he got his information. The answer was obvious. "Can I assume that Kamigami and Sun are operating under your personal direction?"

"You may assume that. Perhaps we can discuss your problems over a light supper?" Without waiting for an answer, Gus smiled at the two girls, who were waiting to escort them inside. "Tell me about this man you call 'the Rock.'"

It was dark when Stans drove Pontowski back to the embassy. "Nieces, my ass," the CIA agent said under his breath.

"They are beautiful," Pontowski said.

"Damn good thing you didn't take him up on the offer to spend the night. One of them would have been waiting for you in bed. That would have put you in his pocket."

"I figured that one out on my own," Pontowski said.

A siren started to wail, and Stans pulled over to the side of the road. Two flashes lit the sky, and two dull booms rolled over them in quick succession. Then another flash was followed by another boom. A streak of light reached up from the ground and headed into the sky, only to end in a bright flash and falling debris. "A Patriot missile got that one," Pontowski said. A much louder explosion rolled over them, shaking the car. "That was way too big for a missile."

"More like a truck bomb," Stans muttered. He got out of the car and studied the sky. "Damn. Nothin's gonna move here for a while. We better walk." Pontowski got out and followed him down a side street. But it was obvious that Stans was not headed for the embassy. They came to another main road, and Stans pointed to a raging inferno two blocks away. "That was SEAC headquarters." He snorted. "Gus just blew away the pro-PLA faction in SEAC. That leaves the Young Turks in charge."

"I've met some of them," Pontowski said. "They want to fight, but will the politicians let them?"

Stans gave him a long look. "That's always a question."

twenty-seven

Central Malaysia
Wednesday, October 6

Tel wanted to warn the lieutenant that they were moving too fast and they had plenty of time. He checked his GPS and confirmed what he already knew. They were in mortar range of the bridge and needed to use the remaining hours of darkness before sunrise to site the mortars and find an LUP, a lying-up point. But the lieutenant pushed ahead, leading the five men past a dark kampong. Tel paused and listened. He had grown up in a very similar kampong and recognized all the signs. It was deserted. He stepped behind a low fence used to corral pigs and relieved himself. A single shot rang out, and loud shouts split the night air. He fell to the ground, and the six mortar shells he was carrying dug into his back.

He slipped out of the shoulder straps, shedding his heavy load, and listened. Sharp commands in Chinese drifted back to him. A shadow moved toward him, and he drew his knife. Then he recognized the corporal whom he was following. "Over here," he said in a low voice.

The corporal fell down beside him. "The lieutenant walked right into them," he said.

"How many?" Tel asked. The man held up three fingers. A guard post. Tel made a mental wager that they did not have a radio or telephone. So was the single shot a warning? In the distance he heard the sharp crack of another rifle shot. Or were they dealing with trigger-happy guards afraid of the night? It was time to find out. He checked his MP5, ensuring that the silencer was tightly screwed on. He motioned the corporal to stay where he was, and slipped into the night, moving exactly as Kamigami had taught him. He circled the guard post and listened to the three soldiers decide what to do with their bag.

He inched closer until he could see. The lieutenant was lying on the ground in a pool of blood, and the other three were sitting on the ground, their hands tied behind their backs. One of the soldiers rummaged through their bergens and passed out various items. From the way the two other men grabbed the food bars, it was obvious they hadn't eaten in some time. The oldest soldier started to argue with the youngest, a teenager, telling him to report back to their sergeant and ask what to do with their three prisoners and the dead lieutenant. The teenager refused to leave until he had finished eating. A kick finally sent him on his way.

Tel followed him, astounded at how easy it was. He slipped up behind the teenager and slit his throat. He held his face down in the soft earth, muffling any gurgling sounds as his life drained away. Tel moved quickly, returning to the guard post. The two soldiers were standing over their prisoners, sharing a pack of cigarettes. Tel shook his head in disgust at their disregard of basic security. He lifted his MP5 and thumbed the select lever to single-shot, then squeezed off two quick rounds. The incredibly smooth bolt action made a light clattering sound, not much louder than the two pops from the silencer. The soldiers fell to the ground. One rolled over on his side, and Tel was on him in a flash, jabbing his knife in an upward motion under the sternum. The man shuddered once and lay still.

Tel moved fast and cut the men free. One of the sergeants started to say something, but Tel cut him off, issuing orders and taking command. Within minutes they had hidden the three bodies and repacked their equipment. Tel scoured the ground until he found the two spent shells and all other traces of their presence were erased. Then he led the team back to the abandoned kampong to join up with the corporal he had left behind. One of the sergeants wanted to abort the mission and leave immediately while they could still move under cover of darkness. "Do you need a lieutenant to fire a mortar?" Tel asked, ending the debate. "We've got work to do."

Again he issued orders, sighting the two mortar tubes and camouflaging their position. Then he selected a tree and climbed into its branches with a radio. It was a good choice. He could see the river and both spans of the bridge. He settled in to wait as the first glow of light split the eastern horizon. He checked his watch—exactly twelve hours to go. He fell asleep.

Washington, D.C.
Tuesday, October 5

Shaw was waiting in the wings with Bobbi Jo when the president arrived at the auditorium of Georgetown University. She was exactly five minutes early for the debate, which was scheduled to start at 9:00 P.M. He studied Turner, looking for any telltale signs that she wasn't ready. He relaxed and smiled at Bobbi Jo Reynolds, absolutely certain that she also was ready. Turner walked toward him. "Any last words?" she asked.

"Knock 'em dead, Madam President." He stepped back as she moved past. A searing pain shot through his head, making him sick to his stomach. *Not yet!* he commanded, willing the cancer to obey. Slowly it yielded a notch. He looked across the stage and saw Leland with his man, the honorable David Grau, former boy wonder of the House of Representatives, governor of Leland's home state, and now candidate for the presidency of the United States. Grau's stage makeup was perfect, and his salt-and-pepper hair immaculately coiffed to create an older image. But to Shaw he resembled a slicked-down seal.

Leland leaned into the boy wonder, his hands moving, as he gave him last-minute instructions. An image of a football coach sending in his quarterback for the critical play in the closing moments of the last quarter flickered in Shaw's mind. A well-known political commentator took his place at a podium downstage left and made a brief introduction. "As agreed," he said, "Governor Grau will make the opening statement, and the debate will run for ninety minutes. There are no other rules or conditions." On cue, Turner and Grau walked onstage from opposite sides, shook hands, and stood behind their respective podiums. With that the battle was joined.

Grau fixed the audience with a somber look. "This is the thirtieth day of a terrible war," he began. "A war that has been characterized by poor leadership, missed opportunity, massive intelligence failures, and a total breakdown in diplomacy."

Shaw felt like cheering. *"Missed opportunities." I left out that one. But three for four in this business ain't bad.* He watched Turner's face as she listened to Grau's charges. *Give him all the rope he needs.*

Finally it was her turn. "The governor is correct," she began, "when he speaks of intelligence shortfalls. We're working hard to correct the neglect of the intelligence community of the last ten years. I would like to remind the governor that when he served in the House of Representatives, he voted against every attempt to increase our intelligence posture—"

"Which is a total misrepresentation of the facts," Grau said.

Turner was condescending. "Please, I didn't interrupt you while you were speaking."

Easy, easy, Shaw thought. The pain was back, and he sat down. But it was different this time. "Water," he said, half aloud. Bobbi Jo rushed for the water fountain while he fished the small bottle of pills out of his coat pocket. His hands fumbled with the childproof cap. Somehow he managed to get two pills to his mouth. Bobbi Jo was back with a cup of water. He gulped it down, fully realizing what the pills would do to him. He breathed deeply while the pills worked their magic. The pain faded into the fog. He reached into his pocket and felt the cassette. Shaking, he handed it to Bobbi Jo. He fought for the right words, but all he could manage was "Listen alone." The pain came roaring back, consuming him in agony. "Hospital," he whispered.

Bobbi Jo punched at her cell phone while Grau went on the attack. "Failures on the diplomatic front have led to disaster on the Malaysian peninsula. Your win-hold-win strategy will not work, and the American Volunteer Group is little more than a blood offering, sacrificed on the altar of a failed strategy." An audible gasp escaped from the audience at the blunt severity of his accusation.

Shaw raged to himself. *I didn't see that one coming!* He struggled with the words, but nothing came out.

"It's okay," Bobbi Jo said. "The ambulance is on the way."

Shaw turned his head to the stage. He could see Maddy talking, but he didn't hear her words as the fog and pain claimed him.

The doors to the waiting room at Bethesda Naval Hospital swung open as four Secret Service agents led the way for the presidential party. The two doctors standing by the counter had been warned and were nervously waiting as the president rushed in. "How is he?" she asked.

"Stable," the lead doctor said. "He's heavily sedated."

"How bad is it?"

The doctor shook his head. "We took a CAT scan. I don't know how he hung on this long."

"How long?"

"Days, maybe a week."

"Can I see him?"

"Certainly. But I doubt if he'll recognize you." He held the door for her and led the way to Shaw's room. "Other than make him comfortable, there's not much we can do."

"I know," she said. She stood by the bed and gazed at him, her eyes moist. "Please," she said, wanting to be alone. The doctor nodded and closed the door. For a moment she didn't move. Then she held his hand. "Oh, Patrick. I didn't want it to end like this." An eyelid moved as if it were trying to blink. "We've come a long way. I couldn't have done this without you." She felt a little squeeze, and her spirits soared. He was still with her! Of all the people she knew, Patrick Flannery Shaw was the least sentimental and given to self-pity. He was first, last, and always a political animal. That's all he was. She started to talk, telling him what he wanted to hear.

"You should have been there for the end. I gave him the last word, and he walked right into it. Would you believe I've lost the war and there's nothing but defeat left?" Again she felt a little pressure in her hand. Or was it a nervous reaction? "Oh, Patrick. You're trying to tell me something. What is it?"

But there was no reaction, and he lay there, barely breathing.

Central Malaysia
Wednesday, October 6

The readout on his watch flicked to 1750. Tel held the radio to his lips. "Radio check." A quick "One" and "Two" answered. "One, fire." The dull *whomp* of a mortar shell reached him high in the tree as he trained his binoculars on the two bridges in the distance. He saw a flash and puff of smoke. "Long," he radioed. "Decrease thirty." A second *whomp* echoed over him. This time it hit the road.

"Two, fire." He watched as the third round hit the road, less than ten meters from the second. Now he could see people scattering, running away from the bridges. "One and Two, fire for effect. Right traverse." The air filled with thunder as the two mortar teams walked round after round down the road, toward the northern approaches to the two bridges. He focused on a truck as it accelerated onto the bridge and rammed its way into the people trying to make their way across. More rounds slammed onto the approaches. "One, left traverse," he ordered. Now half the rounds worked their way back to the north while the other half pounded at the bridge. In the distance he heard the A-10s.

The refugees on the bridge flowed off the southern end, leaving it clear. "Cease fire!" Tel commanded as a counterbattery round screamed overhead. "GO!" It was shoot and scoot, and they had to run for their lives. He dropped the line he had tied to the tree and rappelled down, hitting the ground running. Another round passed overhead and hit nearby. They were getting the range. He ran for the abandoned kampong. An A-10 passed overhead on its attack run, barely clearing the treetops.

A second A-10 crossed behind the first, only to disappear in a blinding flash of light. Tel never slowed as he ran.

Camp Alpha
Wednesday, October 6

Maggot was waiting when Bag taxied to a halt outside the shelter. The ground crew swarmed over the jet, inserting safety pins and hooking up a tow bar. In less than two minutes the A-10 was backed into the shelter and the big doors were cranking shut. A boarding ladder was placed against the right side of the cockpit, and the pilot climbed down. Halfway down the ladder he paused and looked at Maggot. He shook his head and dropped to the ground. A crew chief handed him his helmet. "She okay, sir?" he asked, wondering about the status of his jet. Bag gave a little nod in answer and headed toward Maggot. Together they walked into one of the rooms built into the shelter's sidewall.

"What happened to Lurch?" Maggot asked.

"I don't know. We turned inbound, he was a mile in trail. I could see the bridge. It was clear. I saw a flash at my deep six, and Skid called me off. I broke right and saw where he went in. Smoking hole in the ground. No chute. All things considered, it seemed like a good idea to abort the mission."

They fell silent, waiting for the two pilots from the second flight, Skid and Waldo, to join them. Skid was the first to arrive. "I never saw what hit him," he said.

Maggot tried to focus on what Bag and Skid said while a sergeant from Intelligence debriefed them on the mission. But he couldn't get past two burning facts—he had lost a pilot and two aircraft under his command. He wanted to rationalize it, telling himself that it went with the territory, which all combat commanders had to deal with. But there was no escape. Finally the sergeant was finished. "Where's Waldo?" he asked.

"Right here," Waldo answered. He had walked over from the shelter where his Hog was parked, and his flight suit was streaked with sweat. "A SAM" was all he said, telling them that a surface-to-air missile had destroyed the Warthog and killed the pilot.

"Jesus H. Christ!" Bag shouted. "Lurch was in the weeds. What kinda SAM can do that?"

"I saw a rocket plume," Waldo told him.

"Maybe one of the newer SA series," Maggot said. The latest generation of Russian-built SAMs was reported to be good down to thirty feet. "If Russia sold the Chinese any." He steeled himself for the coming messages. "We need to get an Op Rep out." An Op Rep was an operations report detailing the results of a mission.

"Are we going back after the bridge?" Waldo asked.

Maggot hesitated. Then he shook his head.

twenty-eight

Singapore
Wednesday, October 6

The airliners formed an unbroken procession in the night as they took off from Changi Airport and headed straight ahead for Pulau Tekong, the large island four and a half miles away. The pilots were careful to maintain runway heading and not climb above two thousand feet until they were abeam of the island's reservoir. Then it was a hard-right climbing turn to the south and, for the relieved passengers on board, the promise of safety. But in SEAC's makeshift command center in Singapore's basic military training camp, which was located on the island, it was a constant roar that made face-to-face conversations difficult and turned telephone conversations into screaming matches.

The Air Force major who escorted Pontowski and Gus into the command center was typical of SEAC's Young Turks: educated, well trained, and smart. He shouted his apologies above the din. "The operations planning staff is with the general," he said. "They should be free in a few moments to meet with you about the ATO." He hurried off to make it happen.

Gus played with his right earplug in a futile attempt to make it fit. A plane rumbled overhead, lower than usual. "They need to move," he shouted.

Pontowski looked around, and wasn't sure. The truck bomb that had leveled SEAC's headquarters in the city had also flushed the old leadership, leaving the Young Turks in command. Everywhere he looked, there was a crispness and focus that announced SEAC was a military organization and not a collection of generals playing at politics. "Or have Changi change their departure procedures," he replied. Gus sat down to wait while Pontowski studied a wall map. After a few minutes he wandered outside for a breath of fresh air. A string of aircraft anticollision lights winked in the night as the airliners turned almost directly over his head.

Gus joined him, massaging new wax earplugs. "Changi should be taking off to the south," Pontowski told him. "If they've got to take off our way, then the pilots should make an immediate climbing turn as soon as they get the gear up." Gus agreed with him, and they stood there watching the string of departing aircraft. "Oh, no," Pontowski said, pointing to the sky. A short plume of flame reached up from the narrow Johore Strait that separated Singapore from the Malaysian mainland and headed for the string of anticollision lights. Then it went out. Pontowski had time to say "Rocket motor burnout" before a bright flash consumed an anticollision light.

Gus's voice was icy calm. "What type of surface-to-air missile was that?"

"Probably a Grail," Pontowski answered, his eyes padlocked on the stricken airliner. "Or some similar type of shoulder-held missile." Now they could see flames trailing from the right side of the airliner. "He's turning back for Changi." The big Airbus flew directly overhead, its one good engine bellowing at full power.

"Will he make it?"

Years of flying experience could not be denied. "No. He's turning into the dead engine. He'd be better off ditching straight ahead." But the Airbus pilot kept the turn coming. "Ah, shit," Pontowski moaned as the aircraft approached a stall. The Airbus seemed to shudder as it fell off on its right wing and tumbled into the water, less than a half mile from them. Almost immediately the water turned into a sheet of flame. There would be no rescue attempts.

"I'll relay your suggestion about the departure pattern," Gus promised. A siren started to wail in the main camp. "That's an air-raid warning," he said. "Perhaps we should go inside."

Pontowski followed Gus into the relative safety of the sandbagged walls of the command center. He sat down, chin on his chest, while Gus worked the phones. Now he had to wait. *Will Changi change the departure pattern?* he thought. *Do they even have a choice?* It was the age-old dilemma of all commanders—making decisions when there were no good alternatives. It helped not knowing who went down on the Airbus. They were just faceless numbers, just so many casualties. Outside, he heard the siren sound an all-clear. The major escorting them came back. "Any damage reports?" Pontowski asked.

The major checked the clipboard he was carrying. "One missile hit the causeway." The causeway spanned the Johore Strait, linking Singapore with Malaysia.

"That's one lucky hit for a Scud," Pontowski said, thinking of the missile's notorious inaccuracy.

"We don't think it was a Scud," the major replied. He stepped up to the wall map and pointed to the Taman Negara in Malaysia. "Our early-warning radar tracked it from here. Given the range and accuracy, perhaps it was a CSS-7?" The CSS-7 was a Chinese-built tactical missile with a range of 530 kilometers. "Unfortunately, the aqueduct under the causeway was cut."

"How serious is that?"

Gus overheard the conversation and joined them. "Very," he said. "Because of our small size and dense population, water is always a problem. We treat over one million cubic feet a day and have many reservoirs, but without the aqueduct . . ." He shook his head, not able to estimate how long before the reservoirs ran dry.

A sergeant hurried over to the major and handed him a message. He read it as he added it to the pile on his clipboard. Then he stopped and handed it to Pontowski. "It's an Op Rep from Alpha, sir. The attack on the bridge."

Pontowski read the operations report without a word and handed it to Gus. The bridge was still standing, and the AVG had lost an aircraft and, more important, the pilot. The number three beat at Pontowski—he had lost three people under his command. But this time there was no body to send home. *You've lost people before,* he told himself. He tried to rationalize. *It's a risk that goes with the business.* But nothing helped, for each number had a face. "A SAM got him. It had to be more sophisticated than a Grail. Maybe one of the new Strelas." He thought for a moment. "I hope it's not a Gadfly." The Gadfly was a Russian-built missile guided by monopulse radar that could engage high-performance aircraft down to fifty feet off the deck.

"Is that a problem?" Gus said.

"I went against those puppies in the Middle East. I was flying a Strike Eagle and almost didn't make it. A Hog's a sitting duck."

The major coughed for their attention. "We have four F-16s that are configured for air-defense suppression. So far we haven't used them."

"It's getting tough out there," Pontowski said. "We're going to need them." As if to punctuate his statement, the siren started to wail again. "I'd guess that's another missile."

Gus stood at the wall map, his eyes fixed on the Taman Negara. "We need to do something about that."

Central Malaysia
Thursday, October 7

The night air steamed around the five men as they pushed their way up a small stream. They rounded a bend, and a cloud of gnats descended on them, burrowing under the straps of their night-vision goggles. Tel kept moving, and soon they were in the open and free of the irritating insects. He checked his watch. They had been evading through the jungle for eight hours, and he planned to make good use of the hours remaining before sunrise. Aware that his night-vision goggles were growing dim, he called for a break to replace the batteries. He motioned his men to cover on one bank and told a corporal to retrace their steps to stand lookout. He quickly replaced the batteries, but before donning the goggles, he checked their position with his GPS. They were making good time and should make the rendezvous with Kamigami that afternoon. He decided to take a break.

The corporal was back, his hand flashing a warning—soldiers were coming. Tel could hardly credit that their pursuers had kept up, and that irritated him more than the gnats. He decided to end it. He slipped out of his bergen and sent his men into a quick-reaction drill. But this time it was not for practice. Satisfied that they were ready, he and the corporal moved back downstream. They didn't have to wait long.

Two men waded upstream, their weapons at the ready. They passed by, and four more soldiers came into view. Tel let them also go by. A sixth man brought up the rear, his eyes darting from side to side. He angled over to the bank directly below the corporal and sat down, his back to them. At first Tel couldn't determine what he was doing. Then the distinctive smell of urine wafted back to him. The soldier was relieving himself as he sat on the sloping bank. Tel pointed to the soldier and made a chopping motion with his hand. The corporal nodded and silently moved out of cover. He took two quick steps and rabbit-punched the side of the soldier's neck. But it didn't work. The man screamed twice before the corporal could pound him into silence.

Tel unlimbered his MP5 as loud shouts echoed from upstream. A grenade exploded, followed by five quick bursts of submachine-gun fire. A soldier stumbled back downstream, and Tel fired twice, putting two bullets in his head. He waded out to make sure the soldier was dead as another body came floating down. He dragged both bodies to the bank and quickly searched them.

"What do I do with this one?" the corporal asked, standing over the unconscious body.

"Drain it," Tel said.

Washington, D.C.
Wednesday, October 6

Bobbi Jo Reynolds's voice was flat and unemotional as she tallied the fallout from the previous evening's debate. "Most of the media are repeating verbatim what that asshole said." Like Shaw, she refused to call David Grau by his name. But for the other five people gathered with the president in the Oval Office for the afternoon recap, her words were the death rattle of Turner's election campaign. "What's amazing," Reynolds said, "is who has *not* jumped on the bandwagon. The *Washington Times,* of all things, and CNC-TV have adopted a wait-and-see attitude."

"The polls aren't quite as bad," Parrish said. "But the trending is down. Grau and group are hitting us with too many unanswered charges. The GAO has issued a report highly critical of the AVG, and Congress is getting on board. The Senate is going ahead with the investigation into the fall of King Khalid Military City, and Leland is pushing for the hearings to begin before the election."

Turner rocked back in her chair, feeling the gloom in the air. "That's nice of him." Her instincts told her it was time for the half-time locker-room pep talk. But how much could she tell them without compromising the impending operations in the Gulf? "Please trust me on this. We have to hunker down for the next few hours and take the hits. But we come out swinging tomorrow. Until then no comment to the press or anyone else." From the look on Bobbi Jo's face, Turner knew she wasn't reaching her.

The door opened and Nancy entered. "Madam President, it's time for the afternoon briefing in the Situation Room."

Turner stood up, a decision made. "Bobbi Jo, please join us. I think you'll find it very interesting." She led the way down to the basement, discussing the next day's schedule with Parrish. Bobbi Jo followed, not sure why she was there.

Wilding was waiting with the ExCom, eager to start the briefing. He glanced at Bobbi Jo and arched an eyebrow. "Bobbi Jo is taking Patrick's place," Turner said. She patted the chair where Shaw normally sat. Suddenly Bobbi Jo understood. Patrick Flannery Shaw was gone, and she was now walking in his shoes.

"Madam President, ladies and gentlemen," Wilding said, "Operation Saracen will commence in two minutes." The big center monitor came to life with a map of northern Iraq on the screen. It zoomed onto the area where the Tigris River flowed south across the Turkey-Iraq border. "Two German panzer regiments with one hundred thirty-four Leopard tanks and lighter armored vehicles are in position to sweep down the eastern bank of the Tigris. The first objective is Mosul, eighty miles away."

"When do they expect to reach Mosul?" Turner asked.

"If everything goes as planned," Wilding answered, "within twenty-four hours." The left screen came on with a report that the Iraqi air-defense net was reporting massive air strikes against its northern radar net and missile sites. "Luftwaffe Tornados launching out of the airbase at Diyarbakir in Turkey are tasked with kicking the door open," Wilding said. He watched the screen as Iraqi radar and missile sites disappeared from the map one by one. "It appears the door is open." He called up the latest information being downlinked from an orbiting Joint Stars aircraft. A remarkably detailed radar picture of vehicular movement along the northern Turkey-Iraq border appeared on the right screen. He used a laser pointer to indicate a bright line. "This is as near real-time as we can get. This radar return is an armored column." More information appeared on the screen, identifying and classifying the vehicles. "Definitely German," he said, his lips a grim line.

"So they're off to a good start," Vice President Kennett said.

"They've started as planned," Wilding replied.

Butler looked worried. "A plan never survives the first thirty seconds of combat," he intoned.

For the first time in four weeks, Wilding smiled. "I think this one will. And for good reason. The first convoy arrived eighteen hours early and is docking as we speak. We will have the troops and equipment in place and ready to commence Operation Anvil Monday. The Air Force has destroyed the tunnels at the northern end of Saddam's Spider, and nothing is moving on the southern end." He looked at his president with deep respect. "Madam President, your strategy to trap the bulk of the UIF in the Spider was brilliant."

Bobbi Jo couldn't contain herself. "When can we go public with this?"

"For now," Turner replied, "we're not. We're simply going to let the facts speak for themselves." She looked around the table. "I've got an election to win. Is there anything else?"

"Yes, ma'am," Butler said. "But given the sensitivity, perhaps it would be best if Miss Reynolds . . ."

"Bobbi Jo," Turner said, "would you be kind enough to meet with me later?"

Butler waited until Reynolds had left. "Madam President, I'm very worried about Malaysia. If I may." He punched at a hand controller, and the center screen changed to a map of central Malaysia. "The PLA is pushing hard down the center of the peninsula. SEAC's main forces have taken up a defensive line anchored on the town of Segamat and are reported in contact with advanced elements of the PLA. The analysts at DIA don't think SEAC can hold Segamat and will have to fall back to here." He pointed to Camp Alpha. "Alpha is not defensible, and my analysts expect it to fall within days. There is nothing between Alpha and Singapore to stop them."

Turner stood up. "How soon before we can redeploy to Malaysia?"

"We have some hard fighting ahead of us in the Gulf," Wilding said. "Without Operation Anvil, the Germans are at risk."

"I'm not asking for you to be a miracle worker," Turner told him.

Wilding thought for a moment. "Two weeks at the earliest."

Bobbi Jo floated back to her office on the second floor of the West Wing. *Grau,* she thought, calling up an image of a barbecued seal, *you're dead meat.* She sat down at her desk and kicked back as it all fell into place. "Lordy, Lord, Lord," she sang. "Patrick, you should have been there." She cocked her head, thinking. She rummaged in her gigantic handbag for the tape cassette he had given her at the debate. The clarity of the tape surprised her when she played it, and she instantly recognized Leland's voice. *Is that the secretary of defense?* she wondered. *Where did Shaw get this?* She replayed it, and all the pieces fell into place. "Oh, my God!"

Shaw had trained her well.

twenty-nine

Malaysia
Thursday, October 7

It was still dark when the pilots gathered at the back of the hardened shelter for the mass briefing. Pontowski and Maggot stood at the back while Waldo went down the lineup, detailing each pilot to an aircraft and going over the ATO Pontowski had delivered just after midnight. In principle it was simple enough. SEAC wanted them to keep two A-10s for close air support on station throughout daylight hours, with two more on five-minute alert. When the first two had expended their ordnance or had to return to base to refuel, the two alert birds would launch. Then two more Hogs would come on status, ready to launch in five minutes. But as Waldo pointed out, the simple things are always hard. Then he turned it over to an Intelligence officer to update the situation.

It was the young lieutenant's first briefing, and his face was somber and his voice matter-of-fact as he reviewed what they were up against. "The PLA is in contact with SEAC here, sixty miles to the northwest." He pointed to the town of Segamat. "If the PLA can capture the bridge across the river at Segamat, there'll only be three minor river crossings, all fordable, between them and us."

"Can we go home now?" a pilot called.

"I'm working on it," the lieutenant replied, never missing a beat.

The weapons and tactics officer was next. He quickly outlined how the Singapore Air Force would have two F-16s on station for SEAD, or suppression of enemy air defenses. SEAD was a three-dimensional chess game in which the goal was to kill surface-to-air missiles and cheating was required. Then it was Maggot's turn. "This is the big Kahuna," he told them, "the reason we're here. Let's do it right."

The pilot called Neck, short for Red Neck, taxied his heavily loaded Hog into position on Waldo's left side. He gave Waldo the high sign that he was ready to go. Waldo ran his engines up and released his brakes. Neck punched at the clock on his instrument panel, starting the elapsed-time hand. Fifteen seconds later he ran his engines up and, when the second hand touched twenty, released his brakes. The Hog rolled down the runway, slowly at first, then gaining speed. He eased the stick back, and the nose gear came unstuck. He caught a glimpse of Pontowski standing beside his car at the first taxiway intersection. Just as he lifted off, Pontowski threw him a salute.

Waldo turned out to the left, giving Neck cutoff room to join up. Neck slid into an easy route formation on the left. "Fence check," Waldo ordered. Neck's hands flew over the switches, making sure his Hog was ready for combat. He double-checked everything, leaving only the master arm switch in the off position. Four minutes later Waldo radioed the ALO, the air-liaison officer, at Segamat. The ALO cleared them into the area and told them to contact the FAC, the forward air controller, on the ground. High above, two F-16s cut a graceful arc, trolling for action. Almost immediately Neck's radar warning gear was screaming at him. He glanced at the scope. A monopulse radar was active, signifying a SAM launch. Above him, the two F-16s jinked hard, splitting apart. One rolled in on a target, buried its nose, and then pulled up. A missile streaked by, not able to turn with the F-16. The F-16 did a violent Split-S as a second missile flashed by. Then the second F-16 was in. An antiradiation missile leaped from under its left wing. It was Neck's first combat mission, and he would not have believed the speed of the antiradiation missile if he hadn't seen it. His warning gear continued to scream at him, and he turned the volume down. He saw a flash on the ground, and his RWR gear went quiet. The antiradiation missile had done its job.

Waldo contacted the FAC, who asked if he had the green smoke on the northern edge of town in sight. "Affirmative," Waldo answered, his voice calm. The FAC cleared them to engage any target north or northwest of the green smoke. "Understand cleared in hot," Waldo transmitted. "Take spacing," he ordered, dropping to the deck. As they had briefed before taking off, Neck peeled off to the left and leveled off at a hundred feet above the ground to run in at a cross angle behind Waldo. He double-checked his armament-control panel: bombs ripple, stations three and nine, high drag, nose fusing, gun high rate of fire. He was ready. He breathed faster. Ahead of him, Waldo was pulling off, and he saw the silver ballutes, inflatable balloon/parachutes, deploy behind each bomb, slowing them so Waldo could scamper to safety and avoid the bombs' blast.

"Your six is clear," Neck radioed. "I'm in." He headed for the road running north out of the town. Four trucks and what looked like two armored vehicles were at his ten o'clock position. People were scattering in all directions, running for cover. He pulled back on the stick and popped to fifteen hundred feet. He rolled the Hog and apexed at eighteen hundred feet, too high, as he brought the nose around, placing the lead vehicle at the top of his HUD, or head-up display. The target moved down the projected bomb-impact line and into the bomb reticle. Looking good. He depressed the pickle button so the system would automatically release the bombs when all delivery parameters were met. For a fraction of a second the pipper was on the target, centered in the bomb reticle. Six bombs should have rippled off the ejection racks, but nothing happened.

"Go through dry and check your switches," Waldo radioed.

Neck's eyes darted over the armament-control panel. The master arm switch was still off, and he suppressed a groan. He had made a switchology error. Furious with himself, he ruddered the Hog around, now determined to kill the trucks and armored vehicles. He moved the master arm switch to the down position. A mental Klaxon sounded, warning him not to pop to altitude. He firewalled the throttles and stayed low as he ran in. The black boxes in the A-10's weapon-release systems did their magic, and this time six bombs separated cleanly, walking across the trucks.

He pulled off to the left. "Flares!" Waldo shouted over the radio. Neck hit the flare switch on the right throttle. Eight flares popped out behind him just as a Grail homed in. The shoulder-fired missile exploded, sending high-explosive fragmentation into the tail of Neck's Warthog. The aircraft shuddered as he fought for control. He rolled the wings level as four high-explosive twenty-three-millimeter rounds passed overhead. A fifth round hit the left side of the fuselage, just below the canopy rail, while eight more rounds passed underneath.

Pontowski sat back in his chair, his feet up, chin on his chest, as Waldo debriefed the mission. The words came at him in packets of bad news, telling a tale he had heard many times. "Switchology error . . . reattacked . . . my fault, should have been one pass, haul ass . . . a Grail and ZSU-23 working together . . . bad juju." Waldo stood there. "So do we keep at it?"

It was a fair question that demanded an answer. Pontowski looked at Maggot, not willing to take the decision away from him. The monkey was on Maggot's back, and he knew it. "It's the first goddamned ten days of combat," Maggot said. "If we can get a jock through it, his chances of survival go sky high." He paced the floor. "Neck made three basic mistakes. A switchology error, he hung around to reattack when he should have gotten the hell out of Dodge, and he was late hitting the flare switch."

He stared over their heads and thought out loud. "A Grail alone can't do it. It messes up the control surfaces something fierce, but the Hog can handle that. And the tub normally works." The tub was the titanium armor plating that surrounded the A-10's cockpit like a bathtub. "We know the F-16s can get their heads down." He made the decision. "As long as we got F-16s for SEAD, we keep flying. Brief the pilots that from now on it's one pass, haul ass, stay in the weeds, keep the flares coming, and jink like a son of a bitch."

"Too bad it cost us a Hog to relearn what we already knew," Waldo said.

Maggot reached for the phone, punched the button for the med clinic, and asked to speak to Ryan. "Hey, Doc, how's Neck?" He listened for a moment. "Good enough. Give him back when you're done."

Central Malaysia
Thursday, October 7

It was late afternoon when Tel and his team reached the rendezvous point. It was just a spot in the jungle, totally devoid of distinctive features, and Tel checked his GPS. Certain they were at the correct coordinates, he sent his men into defensive fire positions. "Very good," a voice said from the shadows.

Tel shook his head. "We never saw you."

"You weren't supposed to," Kamigami replied. "How'd it go?"

"Lost the lieutenant when we stumbled into a guard post. But we cleared the bridge as planned. The A-10s were on time, but one was shot down before it could release its bombs. We were taking counterbattery fire and had to withdraw."

Kamigami appreciated his understatement. "And the bridge?" Kamigami asked.

"The last I saw, it was still standing. I don't know if the AVG went back after it or not. We had other problems. I got to admit, those bastards chasing us were good. Luckily, it was night, or we would've never made it."

Kamigami asked him more questions and reconstructed the mission, approving of the way he had ambushed his pursuers. Without doubt, Tel had proven himself. "We've got marching orders," he told the young man. "We're going after the Scuds in the Taman Negara. We rendezvous with three helicopters tomorrow morning and switch out the men before insertion."

"I want to stay," Tel said.

Kamigami shook his head. "I need you back at Alpha for a formal debrief." It was a weak excuse, and both men knew it. "Get some rest. We move out in an hour." Tel turned to leave and find a tree to rig his hammock. "One thing," Kamigami said, stopping him. "What happened to the midnight pisser the corporal took out?" One of the hard facts of special operations was that you couldn't take prisoners in the field.

Tel hesitated. Did he want to admit that he had stripped the unconscious man, strung him up by his heels over the stream, and punched two holes in his neck? "He's still there, hanging around." He couldn't help himself. "Someone will find him."

Washington, D.C.
Thursday, October 7

The ExCom gathered in the Situation Room for the ten o'clock meeting and quietly found their places. Vice President Kennett looked across the table and nodded at Mazie and Butler. "Well done," he said.

"The waiting was the hardest part," Mazie said. "I wasn't sure if von Lubeck could deliver."

"It is a new role for the Germans," Butler said. "Personally, I was more worried about the Turks." He fell silent when the door opened, and came to his feet when the president entered. Everyone in the room joined him.

For a moment she stood there, her eyes bright and clear. Then she smiled. "The drummer's gone."

Butler hoped his face did not give him away. As acting DCI, he had a few options not available to the average human being, not to mention politician, and had simply exercised one. Madeline Turner smiled at him, and the color drained from his face. There was no doubt that she knew. "Please be seated," she said, letting him off the hook.

"The protesters hate success, Madam President," General Wilding said. "May I offer my congratulations for Operation Saracen?" He searched for the right words, not wanting to sound like a brown-nosing apple polisher. "Convincing our allies to open a second front was brilliant."

"The credit belongs to Mazie and Bernie," she said.

Wilding allowed a tight smile—he knew how it worked. "If I may," he said, starting the briefing. For the first time in weeks the news was good, and all the tension and worry that had borne down on him with a relentless and crushing weight was finally lifting. "Operation Saracen is going well, and the Germans reached Mosul two hours ago, nine hours ahead of schedule. The Iraqis have fallen back into the city and are showing unexpected resistance. The Germans plan to leave a covering force in place, bypass the city, and drive for Baghdad. In the south, Operation Anvil is hammering hard at Saddam's Spider." He warmed to the subject, venting his pent-up frustration while reveling in the change of events. "We plan to open a major offensive in seventy-two hours. We're going to hold them by the nose while kicking them in the butt." But then reality intruded, and he clamped a tight control on his emotions. "We still have some hard fighting in front of us, Madam President. But we have the logistics and personnel in place to do the job now."

Turner tapped her fingers together. "Malaysia?" she asked.

The screens on the TV cycled, and Wilding took a deep breath. "The situation is unclear, Madam President." He pointed to SEAC's defensive line centered on Segamat. "It appears that SEAC is holding. Unfortunately, the AVG lost another aircraft earlier today, but the pilot was unhurt and has returned to duty."

"Stay on top of it," Turner ordered, "and do what you can." Her voice turned to steel. "I hope you've started planning for redeployment to Malaysia."

"Indeed we have, Madam President," Wilding replied. "But the lack of airlift is the limiting factor."

The briefing was over, and Turner came to her feet. The ExCom stood with her. "We'll fix that problem when this is all over," she promised. She paused for a moment. "I can't thank you enough." Her voice cracked with emotion, and she quickly left. Outside, in the corridor, shouting and cheering coming from the main floor echoed down the stairs. Nancy reached for her personal communicator to warn the staff that the president was returning to the Oval Office, but Turner stopped her. "Let them enjoy the moment," she said. "They've earned it."

Rather than return directly to her office, she strolled through the West Wing, keeping in the background. Everyone was clustered in front of TVs and bouncing with excitement as reporters and political pundits searched for the right words to describe the turn of events. Even the most hostile commentators were comparing Operation Saracen to General Douglas MacArthur's Inchon landing in the Korean War.

"A brilliant maneuver . . ."

"Governor Grau strangely silent . . ."

"Syria's ambassador to the United Nations has petitioned for an in-place cease-fire."

A loud "No way!" chorused from her staff.

"I'd like to speak to the press," Turner said to Parrish.

"Yes, ma'am," he sang. He punched at his communicator, warning the press secretary as he followed her down the hall. Ahead of them, they could see reporters running for the Press Room. "Give them a few moments," he said. They spoke quietly, going over what she should say.

"Ignore Grau and Leland," Parrish counseled. "Keep it brief and make them focus on what's ahead."

Madeline Turner closed her eyes for a moment. Then she nodded and led the way into the Briefing Room. As one, the reporters stood and applauded.

thirty

Central Malaysia
Friday, October 8

Kamigami maintained a relentless pace, pressing his men to make the rendezvous with the three helicopters. They had been in the field almost five days, and in the world of special operations that was an eternity. By now it was a certainty that someone was out there looking for them. The answer was movement and speed. Thanks to night-vision goggles, superb charts, and a GPS, they could move through the jungle at night and make good time. But it wasn't easy.

They reached the landing zone just after midnight, seventeen minutes before the Pumas were scheduled to arrive. The men collapsed to the ground, breathing deeply and gulping water. Half of them knew they were going home and started to relax. But Kamigami was merciless. He posted lookouts and briefed his four team leaders. "The two teams returning to Alpha board the last helicopter, the rest get on the second Puma. I'll board the first aircraft with the replacement teams. Helicopters get attention, so minimum time on the ground. I want us out of here in less than a minute. Count your men; no one gets left behind. We all lift off together and egress the area together. Once clear of the area, we split. One and Two head north, Three returns to Alpha." The muffled sound of the helicopters brought them to their feet. "Move," Kamigami ordered. He pulled Tel aside. "It's easy going in; it's the getting out that's hard. Remember that."

"Good hunting," Tel said. They shook hands as the first Puma settled to the ground. Kamigami ran for it without looking back and climbed in the side door. The eighteen men returning to Camp Alpha clambered on board the last helicopter. For a moment Tel hesitated. Then he ran for the second aircraft.

The helicopters lifted off in quick succession and flew low over the jungle canopy, heading to the southeast. Sixteen minutes later they flew up a river valley and entered the Gunong Besar mountain range. The river glowed like a silver ribbon in the moonlight, and the helicopters dropped even lower. When the river split, the first two Pumas turned north, toward the Taman Negara, and the third continued to the south, heading for Camp Alpha, fifty miles away. For the forty-two men on board the two northbound helicopters, it was a bumpy ride, as the pilots used terrain masking to escape detection. Exactly thirty-six minutes later the two Pumas hovered over a jungle clearing and the men jumped out. Tel was the last off and made his way through the tall grass, trying to look inconspicuous.

Kamigami was crouched beside a tree, giving his team leaders last-minute instructions. "You've got three hours before daylight," he told them. "Use it." He gave them the rendezvous coordinates and sent them on their way. Without looking up, he said, "Tel, get your ass over here." He waited. "The next time I give you an order, do it."

"Yes, sir," Tel answered, not the least bit intimidated.

Camp Alpha
Friday, October 8

Clark's driver accelerated across the runway at the midfield intersection, leaving the main base behind them. Once clear of the runway he drove down the road that led to the weapons-storage area. Clark pointed to a muddy dirt track, and the driver made a hard turn off the asphalt, sending a wave of water over a recently dug defensive fire position. He jerked the minivan to a halt when he saw Rockne and Boyca standing beside a bigger, heavily reinforced bunker. He jumped out and ran around to open the sliding door, grinning at Clark. "We here, Missy Colonel." She climbed out, followed by Pontowski and Doc Ryan.

Rockne threw them a crisp salute and led the way down into the bunker. "This is the operations bunker for Whiskey Sector," he explained. They gathered around a wall chart as Rockne detailed the base's defense plan. "I've divided the base into three sectors: Whiskey, Yankee, and Zulu." He traced the boundaries of the sectors on the chart, which reminded Pontowski of a big T. Two long sectors lay side by side, parallel to the runway, and formed the stem while an oblong sector crossed the T, like a big cap. Rockne circled Zulu, the northern sector that formed the cap. "Any attack will most likely come from the north. That's why the Malaysian Army laid a big minefield in this area before we arrived. Unfortunately, they didn't make a plan of the minefield. The really bad news is that they laid it inside the tactical boundary."

"So why did they plant the mines there?" Clark asked.

"Because it's outside the base perimeter fence line," Rockne explained. "They never considered the tactical boundary. At least there's nothing in this sector, so I've turned it into a kill zone." Four jets took off, forcing him to wait for the noise to subside.

Pontowski checked his watch. "The first go of the morning," he told them. He tapped the chart, pointing to the sector on the western side of the T's stem. "It looks like everything important is in Yankee sector—the runway, command post, aircraft bunkers."

Doc Ryan said, "It looks like the base medical station and the command post are at the hub."

Clark studied the map. "It all makes sense," she said. "If we come under heavy attack, we can give ground and fall back in concentric rings to the hub. One thing I don't understand. Only the fuel dump and the weapons-storage area are on this side of the runway. Wouldn't it be better to place Whiskey Sector ops bunker on the other side of the runway where you can better defend it?"

"We thought about it," Rockne said. "We rigged the fuel dump and the weapons igloos with demolition charges in case we have to withdraw. But there was no way we could get the firing wires across the runway. We have to detonate them from here."

Pontowski saw it first. "Neat, Chief, very neat." His eyes narrowed. "If we come under attack and have to give up Whiskey, we can blow the fuel and ammo dumps."

"Exactly," Rockne said. "Whoever gets caught in Whiskey is going to have a very bad day." He showed them the panel that activated the charges.

"Let's hope," Ryan said, "it won't come to that and we'll all be long gone."

"In an evacuation," Clark told him, "the security police are the last to go." Worry filled her eyes. "If they go."

"Oh, no," Ryan said, at last understanding.

"It goes with the territory," Rockne said, trying to be philosophical about it.

Clark checked the time. "We've got an inbound C-130 with more personnel. It might be some cops. Why don't we go meet it?"

"Sounds like a plan," Pontowski said.

Rockne led the way in his pickup with Boyca. Doc Ryan trailed along with Clark and Pontowski in her van and sat in silence, calculating how to evacuate wounded if they abandoned the base. A dull explosion brought him back to the moment. "It came from the north," he said.

Clark keyed her handheld radio and called the controller in the main command post. But before the controller could determine the source of the explosion, Rockne's pickup was racing for Zulu, the northern sector. The controller in the command post was back on the radio. "Two civilians are in the minefield. One is down, the other is waving for help."

Clark's driver floored the accelerator, trying to pass Rockne. "Slow down!" Clark shouted in Malay. He did and followed Rockne to the edge of the minefield. Behind them, two fully loaded A-10s lifted off.

Pontowski watched them as their landing gear came up and they turned out of the pattern. "Those were the alert birds," he told them. "I've got to get back to the command post." Clark told him to use her van and that she'd stay with Rockne.

"I'll stay here," Ryan said.

Rockne grabbed a pair of binoculars out of his pickup and swept the minefield. "They're kids," he said. He pressed the zoom lever. "One's down, the other is standing there, not moving."

"How are we going to get them out?" Ryan asked.

"It's for damn sure I'm not sending anyone in there without a map," Clark told him. "How long will it take to sweep a path?"

"A couple of hours," Rockne replied, still studying the two boys. "The one kid is indicating his buddy is hurtin' bad. I don't think we got the time."

Ryan shook his head. "So we're going to let him die?"

"Maybe not," Rockne answered. "Come," he called. Boyca jumped out of the pickup and trotted to him. He knelt down beside her and pointed to the boy standing in the minefield. Then he patted the ground. "Seek," he commanded. Boyca sniffed the ground and started to range. She stopped. She had found a mine. "Good girl," he said. "Seek." Again the dog sniffed the ground and stopped. "Good girl." He pointed toward the boy. "Seek." Boyca did as commanded and worked her way toward the boy, stopping whenever she found a mine.

"I didn't know she could do that," Clark said.

"Neither did I," Rockne replied, his voice full of pride. "Oh, no," he moaned. "Doc, what the hell do you think you're doing?"

Ryan was walking slowly into the minefield, a first-aid kit slung over his shoulder. "Following her path," he called. "Muddy footprints."

"Doctor!" Clark shouted. "That's dumber than dirt!" But he kept on walking. She sucked in her breath and waited. "Losing a dog is one thing," she grumbled. She exhaled in relief when he reached the two boys.

"Boyca," Rockne called. "Stay." The dog sat on her haunches and waited while Ryan worked on the boy. Then he stood and gave a thumbs-up. He handed his bag to the uninjured boy before picking the other one up in a fireman's carry. "Boyca," Rockne called. "Seek." He slapped her leash against his thigh, hoping she would seek and come at the same time. She did.

Two more A-10s took off, heading north as two entered the pattern for landing while Ryan walked out of the minefield. Clark was beside herself with anger. "Doctor, that was dumb."

Ryan ignored her. "We need to get him to the med station."

"For his sake," Rockne said with a straight face, "I hope you know what you're doing this time." He looked up as a C-130 entered the pattern. "Let's go," he told the two officers. They loaded the boys into the back of his pickup, and he deposited the doctor and the boys at the medical station before dropping Clark off at the command post. Then he hurried back to the parking apron where the C-130 was unloading. He parked and clipped the leash to Boyca's collar. Together they walked across the ramp, where a familiar figure was waiting with a group of thirty-three security cops. "Welcome back, Sergeant Maul."

"It's good to be back, Chief," Jessica said, meaning it. She knelt down and stroked Boyca's head. "You been a good girl?"

"The best," Rockne replied. He looked at the waiting cops and stifled a snort when he saw Tech Sergeant Paul Travis and Staff Sergeant Jake Osburn. "I thought you two were minding the squadron at Lackland."

"We were," Travis replied. "But we got backfilled from the reserve."

Jake nodded in agreement. "We thought you might need some help."

"We'll find something to do with your worthless bodies," Rockne allowed.

Clark stood at the back of the command post and waited. Maggot was at the center console talking to Maintenance Control while Pontowski was in the communications cab on the secure phone to SEAC headquarters. Pontowski waved her into the glassed-in booth when he saw her. "We're surging," he told her. He held up a hand and listened for a moment. "We'll do what we can," he promised. He broke the connection. "The PLA's broken through at Segamat. Singapore's two regiments gave a good account of themselves before withdrawing. It's bad."

Maggot stuck his head through the doorway. "Two Scuds just hit Changi Airport and Pulau Tekong. SEAC headquarters got shook up, but they're okay."

"Those weren't Scuds," Pontowski said. "SEAC better move before they find the range."

Taman Negara
Friday, October 8

It was near sunset when Kamigami stepped out onto the jungle trail, looked both ways, and sniffed the air. Someone was bivouacked nearby and cooking. He ordered his team into a quick-reaction drill, and within seconds they had shed their heavy bergens and were ready to engage. "We've been on this trail before," Tel told him. "We're twenty kilometers from the PLA's base camp." He quickly checked his GPS and plotted their position on a chart. "Sorry," Tel muttered, "we're twenty-one kilometers away."

"Close enough," Kamigami allowed. He motioned Tel to silence when he heard movement on the trail. Almost immediately a man trudged into sight, bent under a heavy load. Kamigami's eyes narrowed as he took the man's measure. This was a soldier, not a porter. Then another came into view, and Kamigami started to count. Every six to eight seconds a heavy-laden soldier passed in silence, totally unaware of the men hiding less than six meters away. Two hours later a bevy of officers brought up the rear, totally unencumbered and talking loudly. Finally the trail was deserted. "How many?" Kamigami asked.

"Nine hundred and eighty," Tel answered.

"Close enough," Kamigami said. He had counted 983. "I make it a battalion."

"That's a big battalion," Tel replied, comparing it to what he had been taught.

"God favors big battalions," Kamigami told him. They heard movement and fell silent as another man came down the trail. Again they counted as a long line of men tramped past. As before, the officers brought up the rear. But this time there was no break before a third battalion plodded past. When the last group of officers passed, an eerie silence descended over the jungle. "Make that big regiments," Kamigami said. "They're traveling at night and bivouacking during the day." He thought for a moment. "Think you can play FAC?"

"I can try."

"Good. Take a radioman and follow them. I'm guessing they'll make camp before morning. I'll radio SEAC, and with a little luck we can have a few Hogs on station first thing in the morning. Your job is to get them on target."

"Is this what I get for not obeying orders?"

Kamigami ignored his question. "Your call sign is Gopher Hole."

Central Malaysia
Saturday, October 9

Tel wiggled onto the rock outcropping near the crest of the ridgeline and scanned the top of the jungle canopy with his binoculars. As Kamigami had predicted, the regiment had marched all night and made camp while it was still dark. Below him, the smell of campfires being lit drifted up. He tried to find the smoke, but since he was looking directly into the sun as it broke the eastern horizon, he couldn't see a thing. His radio crackled to life. "Gopher Hole, this is Mudfighter with two. How copy this frequency?"

Tel took a deep breath and squeezed the transmit button. "Gopher Hole copies you five-by. Your target is troops bivouacked under trees." He quickly read off the coordinates.

"Gopher Hole," Mudfighter replied, "I see smoke coming through the canopy in maybe fifty different places."

"Those are cooking fires," Tel answered. "Hit the smoke."

"Rog," Mudfighter replied. "Do you have safe area coordinates?"

This was new for Tel. "Sorry, I don't understand."

"Where do I punch out if I have to eject?" the pilot replied.

Tel gave him the coordinates where he had left Kamigami. "You're cleared in hot," he said.

"One's in," Mudfighter radioed. "Jaws, go tactical. Ninety cross, separate to the south, one pass, no reattack." The flight lead was using verbal shorthand to set up the attack.

"Copy all," Jaws replied. "Your six is clear."

Tel scanned the area with his binoculars but couldn't find the Warthogs. Where were they? For a moment he was certain they were bombing some other place and that he had screwed up. Suddenly a loud noise beat at him, and he looked up, directly into the cockpit of a Warthog less than fifty feet above him. The pilot had used the ridge Tel was hiding on for terrain masking and had run in from the backside. He popped to eight hundred feet to clear the crest, rolled 135 degrees, and pulled the Hog's nose down to the valley. Tel watched as six canisters rippled from under the Hog's wings, walking along the line of campfires. The canisters opened like clamshells and sent their lethal load of bomblets into the trees. The pilot honked back on the stick and pulled off to the right as flares streamed out the back to defeat any surface-to-air missile.

"I'm in," Jaws radioed. Again Tel could hear but not see the aircraft. Below him, he saw flashes in the trees as the bomblets cut a swath through the jungle. The second Warthog arced around the southern end of Tel's ridge, barely a hundred feet off the deck. Suddenly it was climbing and rolling as it gained altitude. Its nose came down like a bow in a deadly minuet as it crossed ninety degrees to the first aircraft's heading. Six Mark-82 Airs rippled off. "Off to the south," Jaws radioed calmly. Six explosions erupted, blowing huge gaps in the jungle canopy. Now Tel could see the ground below the trees.

"You're clear," Mudfighter radioed. "Join up on my left. We go home."

Tel's ears were still ringing, and he didn't know what to say. Belatedly he keyed his radio. "Thanks for the help."

"Anytime," Mudfighter replied.

Tel waited for over an hour as bomblets with delayed-action fusing exploded. He constantly scanned the area, looking for movement or signs of life. But there wasn't any. Finally he motioned to his radioman, and they worked their way down the ridge and onto the valley floor. He wished he hadn't, and knew he had crossed the border into hell when he heard cries for help mingled with groans of pain. He took a few more steps and found himself on the edge of the blast effects of the five-hundred-pound pounds. But even two hundred meters from the point of impact, the carnage was horrendous. Wounded men were everywhere, parts of bodies were blown into the trees and scattered over the ground, and a sweet, sickly smell assaulted his nostrils. The buzz of insects homing on the blood grew louder as he moved toward the epicenter of the attack. He stopped when his radioman started to retch. *All this in less than four minutes,* Tel thought as nausea and guilt swept over him. Then he remembered his village.

A soldier stumbled toward him, dazed but unhurt. For a moment they stared at each other. The man begged for mercy in Cantonese. "This is the vampire's land," Tel replied in the same language. He turned and headed for the rendezvous with Kamigami.

Washington, D.C.
Friday, October 8

The hostess was beside herself when she saw Secretary of Defense Robert Merritt standing in the vestibule of her lavish Georgetown home. There was no doubt the party would now be an outstanding success. "Mr. Secretary," she gushed, taking his arm. "I'm so pleased you could come." She escorted him into the big lounge, ensuring that everyone was aware of her triumph. "I know it must be so hectic," she soothed, "but the news is so wonderful. Such a change in the landscape." They both knew she meant the political landscape. "The president must be pleased." A scattered round of spontaneous applause broke out.

"It was a gamble," Merritt said, loud enough for everyone to hear. "It's far from over, but we are confident of success." Knowing heads nodded in agreement, for this was the power elite of Washington, the inner circle of men and women who could, and did, make things happen. They were all experts at reading political tea leaves and sensed that the totally unexpected turnaround of the Gulf War had changed the political landscape. What had been a millstone dragging Maddy Turner to defeat in the election was now the springboard for victory. And common sense, not to mention political survival, demanded they shift positions accordingly.

The hostess led Merritt into the library. "Senator Leland is hoping to speak to you," she confided. She glanced up the stairs.

"I can't imagine why," Merritt said dryly as he turned to shake more hands and bask in the praise the media were heaping on the administration. A short, very dapper man came up. "Well, Robert, are you going to accept Syria's offer of an in-place cease-fire?"

Merritt smiled. "CENTCOM is of the opinion they should surrender first."

The man was aghast. "Do you always listen to your generals?"

"Only when we want to win a war." Merritt moved on, enjoying the moment. Finally he climbed the stairs to the elegant study on the second floor, where he suspected Senator John Leland was waiting. He wasn't disappointed.

Leland didn't waste time and came directly to the reason for the meeting. "Have you seen the polls?"

Merritt shrugged. "That happens when you get caught on the wrong side of a war. Your boy's looking like an unpatriotic idiot."

"We were set up. Fuckin' Shaw. He was behind this, wasn't he?"

"I don't think so. Maddy did this one all on her own. Brilliant, wouldn't you say?"

Leland was as close to losing control as he had ever come in his political career. He paced the floor, then spun around to face Merritt and jammed a rigid forefinger into his chest. "That child-pornography ring, the one the DCI was involved in."

"Like I said before, there's nothing there. One slip of paper with the address of a Web site does not—"

Leland interrupted him. "Then how did it get in his chair in the first place? Tell me that!" More pacing. "I'll tell you how. It fell out of his pocket or briefcase, that's how."

"Don't go there," Merritt pleaded. "My investigators have totally discounted it. There's that phone call I told you about and—"

"I want it," Leland said, his voice firm. Merritt gave in to the inevitable and recited it from memory. "Damn it. Are you hard of hearing or just stupid? I want the actual note. The gloves are off, and I'm going to render that bitch."

"You'll have it first thing tomorrow morning," Merritt promised. Leland shot him a look of triumph as he turned and left. Merritt walked to the sideboy and poured himself a drink. It was ginger ale, for no sane politician drank at a time like this. He considered his options and, like everyone at the party, knew it was time to shift positions. But how? He sank into a deep leather chair and wished that Shaw were not in the hospital. He made a mental note to call Parrish the moment he got home. But he didn't like that option. Then the image of Bobbi Jo Reynolds flashed in front of him, and he changed his mind.

thirty-one

Camp Alpha
Sunday, October 10

The first explosion shattered the two windows on the end wall. Luckily, the heavy duct tape that crisscrossed the windowpanes held, and most of the glass shards were embedded in the blackout curtains. Instinctively, Pontowski rolled out of his bunk, hit the floor, and rolled under the bed. For a moment he breathed hard, getting his bearings. "Son of a bitch," he mumbled. He checked the time. It was 0528, a half hour before sunrise. The second explosion rocked the building off its foundations and cracked the ceiling, sending a cloud of dust and debris onto the bed. He coughed twice and waited. Nothing. He heard running feet in the hall, followed by a banging on his door. "General! Are you okay?" It was Janice Clark.

"Yeah," he answered.

"We're on fire. Get out!"

Pontowski rolled out from under the bed and pulled on his boots. He didn't stop to tie them and grabbed a flight suit as he bolted out the door. Clark was ahead of him, running down the hall, banging on doors to make sure the building was clear. Smoke chased them both out of the building. They ran for the bomb shelter and crashed through the narrow entrance. In the half-light of early morning, he could see about a dozen people crowded inside. He leaned against the sandbags and pulled off his boots so he could don his flight suit. "Ah, Colonel," he began, "I think you need to . . ."

The base commander was only wearing a T-shirt that showed a generous amount of leg. "Tough shit!" she barked. She paused as a heavy silence came down. "Sorry, sir. That wasn't called for." Someone handed her a radio, and she called the command post for a status report. They all heard the on-duty controller detail what looked like two missile strikes. Outside, they could hear a siren wail the all-clear. "Better late than never," she grumbled. "Sir, can I meet you in the command post in a few minutes?" Without waiting for an answer, she darted out the door.

Pontowski had to stifle a grin when he heard her driver's voice. "Missy Colonel! Where you clothes?" Little snickers and guffaws moved around the bunker as the tension shredded.

"What does that guy do?" someone asked. "Sleep in his van?"

"As a matter of fact," Pontowski replied, "he does." He finished tying his boots. "Okay, let's go. We got work to do." The bunker rapidly emptied. The officers' quarters were half consumed in flames and sending billows of smoke over the base. In the distance he heard two Warthogs lift off for the first go of the morning. He ran for the command post.

Maggot looked up from his console in the command post when he saw Pontowski. The wing commander had been up most of the night, and his eyes were bloodshot, his face drawn. "It was definitely two missiles. One hit the fuel dump, the other here." He pointed to the main dormitory where half of the AVG was billeted. "Thank God almost everyone was at work. Doc Ryan is there now with the rescue crews."

Janice Clark joined them, now dressed in a fresh set of fatigues. She didn't bother to explain how her driver had rushed inside the burning officers' quarters and found her clothes and a brush and comb. She studied the base map. "They went after the two biggest high-value targets that weren't revetted," she told them. "Damn good intelligence, if you ask me."

"With that accuracy," Maggot said, "it means they weren't Scuds."

"Colonel Clark," the controller called from the communications cab. "All land lines are down, but we're still in radio contact with SEAC."

"Get with the Malaysian Army," Clark told him, "and see what they can do. This is their base."

"The MA's not answering the phone or radio," the controller said.

"General Pontowski," the liaison officer from the First SOS called, "Colonel Sun will be here in a few moments. He says it's urgent."

"Any reports from the fuel dump?" Clark asked.

"Negative," the controller told her. "The crash wagon and fire truck are at the dorm. The security police report the fuel dump is burning like hell . . . hold on." He called Maintenance Control and asked for the fuel status. He listened for a moment. "Maintenance says the only fuel they got is in the lines and the holding tanks. Maybe enough for twenty-four hours. That's all."

Colonel Sun walked in just ahead of Rockne. "Two missiles hit Singapore this morning," Sun announced. "One hit the main petroleum terminal, the other destroyed the largest refinery on the main island. Many fires. Many riots, and the people want peace."

"First they cut the city's water supply," Pontowski said. "Now they're going after POL. Sounds like a blockade strategy."

"Mr. Deng," Sun continued, "has ordered an all-out search for the missile launch sites. He wants them destroyed." He paused, searching for the right words in English to convey the urgency of the situation. "This is most critical."

"We got other problems," Rockne said. "The MA is gone."

Clark was on her feet, almost shouting. "What do you mean 'gone'?"

Nothing betrayed Rockne's anger, and he could have been discussing a training exercise. "The Malaysian Army battalion assigned to defend the base has deserted en masse. We're uncovered."

"We're not going to be hung out to dry," Pontowski promised. "Colonel Sun, can one of your helicopters fly me to Singapore? ASAP." The wiry colonel jerked his head yes and reached for a phone to alert a crew. Pontowski came to his feet in one easy motion and paced the floor. He jabbed a finger at the situation chart tracking the fighting fifty miles to the north of them. "We've got to slow the bastards down, so fly as much close air support as you can. I'm going to beat the bushes and get the airlift we need to get the hell out of Dodge. Meanwhile, keep launching sorties."

"The helicopter will be ready when you arrive," Colonel Sun told him.

"I'm on my way," Pontowski replied. "Colonel Clark, Chief, ride with me so we can talk." He turned to Maggot. "Dwight, you've got the stick here. My gut tells me all hell is about to break loose."

"I can't imagine why," Maggot said straight-faced. For a moment they stood there, looking at each other. "Hell, General, you never promised me a rose garden." They shook hands. "You'll have to excuse me, sir. I've got a war to fight here." He turned around and picked up the phone to Operations. "Waldo, brief the jocks for a surge."

Pontowski nodded in agreement and walked out with Clark and Rockne in close trail. He used the short ride to the First SOS and the waiting helicopter to go over the details of base defense. "Sir," Clark said, "regardless of what happens, we're going to need jet fuel to keep on flying." Her driver halted the van by the helicopter. This time Clark was out before he could run around to open her door. She walked with Pontowski to the helicopter, still going over last-minute details. The four-bladed rotor started to turn as the turboshaft engines wound up. She stepped back and threw a crisp salute. Pontowski wanted to hug her, but that was out of the question. He returned her salute and climbed on the helicopter while she ran for the minivan.

Her driver was holding the door. "You go home now, Missy Colonel. Please. Before too late."

The Puma lifted off as Pontowski strapped in next to the right-door window and donned a headset. He pressed the mike switch. "Any chance of checking out the roads?" he ventured. The pilot was agreeable, and they headed south, paralleling the main road. As Pontowski suspected, the road was clogged with refugees and nothing was moving north. They had been airborne less than six minutes when a loud bang and sharp jolt buffeted the helicopter. It tilted wildly to the left as Pontowski held on. Over his headset he heard the pilots yelling at each other in Chinese as they feathered the two engines. Smoke poured into the cabin, and he searched for an oxygen mask. But he couldn't find one. Desperate, he reached for the door handle to roll the sliding door back. He cracked it an inch before it jammed. He stuck his face against the crack and took a deep breath. Then he hit the quick release to his lap belt and grabbed on to the seat frame. He half swung and half fell across the cabin, only to bounce off the crew chief and slam against the left door. The door handle jammed into his back. He fumbled in the heavy smoke until he felt the top seat tube. Holding on, he released the door handle and slid the door back.

He almost fell out before the pilots righted the helicopter. The smoke cleared, and he could see holes punctured in the floor near the aft bulkhead. Now the nose of the helicopter came up as it autogiroed to earth.

He had mere seconds before they hit the ground, and he tried to strap back in. But he could find only the left strap of a seatbelt. The Puma hit the ground and bounced, twisting and pitching forward as he held on with a death grip. It hit again and corkscrewed back into the air, this time throwing Pontowski out the door.

Clark stood in front of the four body bags lying on the ground. Behind her, the dormitory was a smoking hulk. Slowly she clenched her fist and relaxed. Without a word, she climbed into the van and ordered her driver to take her to the medical station. She had to talk to Doc Ryan. She was there in two minutes and hurried down the concrete ramp that led inside. She was immediately assaulted with the heavy antiseptic odor that announced she was in the presence of medical wizardry. Ryan was bent over the casualty, talking quietly as he stitched up the man's inside thigh. "You are one lucky dude. It missed your balls and got the fleshy part of your thigh."

"Doc, how many wounded?" Clark asked.

Ryan looked up from his task. "Six. Two critical. We need to air-evac them out. Soonest."

"I ain't goin' without my buddies," the man lying on the exam table announced.

Ryan grunted. "Your call."

Clark's radio squawked at her. It was the controller in the command post asking her to return ASAP. "I'll get back to you," Clark promised, running from the bunker. This time it was quicker to run to the command post than drive and she was there in less than a minute.

Maggot told her the bad news. "The control tower monitored a Mayday from Pontowski's helicopter. They took ground fire and augered in about ten miles south. I've scrambled Waldo and Buns to take a look."

Clark clamped an iron control over her emotions and was all business. "We're hurtin' for POL. You might want them to recover at Tengah for refueling." Tengah was a Singapore Air Force base.

"That's doable," Maggot said. "But we'd have to bring 'em here for rearming."

Waldo checked in on the radio. "Rocker One and Two rolling now."

In her mind's eye Clark could see the two Warthogs roaring down the runway and lifting into the clear air, and like Maggot, she had to wait. But that wasn't in her temperament. She strode into the communications cab. "I need to speak to the MAAG in the Singapore embassy. And I mean now."

Southern Malaysia
Sunday, October 10

The pain was a tiger, ripping and tearing at him when he tried to move. But he had fought the tiger before and willed himself to move. Inch by inch he pulled himself across the rice paddy, barely keeping his head above water. He tried to move his left arm, but his shoulder roared with pain, making him dizzy. He stopped and used his right hand to position his left forearm across his chest. That helped, and he lay on his right side, pulling himself toward the low dike that bounded the rice paddy. Every time he tried to take a deep breath, more pain coursed through his body. He was certain he had broken a rib and had pierced a lung. Finally he reached the low mound of dirt and pulled himself into a half-sitting position, careful not to move his left arm. The pain in his chest subsided, but he knew the tiger was still there, ready to leap out of the fog that bound him tight. He tried to take a deep breath, but that only unleashed the tiger. Slowly the fog eased, and he could think.

Breathing, bleeding, and bones, he thought, reverting to the basics of first aid. He already knew about the breathing, so he checked for bleeding. Nothing. He forced himself to hack up some phlegm. Again the tiger roared, but what he spit out was clear. *Okay, bones.* He ran his good hand over his body. Other than a bruise on his left temple and the big hump protruding on top of his left shoulder, he was okay. He touched the hump and flinched with pain. "Broken collarbone," he muttered.

The wind veered and sent a puff of black smoke over him. He pulled himself up the dike until he could see over the top. The smoking Puma was upside down two or three rice paddies away. He studied it, looking for fire. But there wasn't any. *Did they make it?* he thought. His question was answered when he looked toward the nearby kampong. A group of soldiers was clustered around two inert bodies lying on the ground. He saw the flash of a machete blade as the men yelled and screamed obscenities. He stopped counting the hacks when he reached twenty. But he couldn't take his eyes off the grisly scene.

Two A-10s roared overhead, driving the soldiers to cover. The lead Hog pulled up and ruddered over to swoop down on the grim tableau like an avenging bird of prey. *Waldo,* he thought, recognizing the style. The A-10 pulled off and circled the kampong at two hundred feet, baiting the defenders to shoot at him. They did. The A-10 jinked hard, pulling away as the second A-10 rolled in, its cannon firing. Reddish brown smoke rolled back from under the nose as the rounds walked up to the kampong. "Buns," he muttered. "You always did bunt." Waldo was in a sharp climb, popping to fifteen hundred feet for a low-angle bomb run. The maneuver was a study in perfection as he rolled and brought the Hog's nose to the target. Two bombs separated cleanly, and their ballutes deployed, slowing the bombs while Waldo escaped, crossing at ninety degrees to Buns's strafing attack.

Pontowski slipped down the dike for protection from the blast as the kampong disappeared in a series of deafening explosions. The two A-10s orbited the area on opposite sides of the circle. He was certain they were looking for him, and he crawled onto the dike to be seen. But two teenage boys were running toward him, crouched low, anxious to escape the wrath of the two raptors circling overhead. They saw him and shouted. But his ears were still ringing, and he couldn't hear a word. He glanced up as the two Hogs joined together and climbed into the sky.

One of the boys raised the M-16 rifle he was carrying. His right hand moved as he charged a round.

Camp Alpha
Sunday, October 10

Waldo sat in the command post and took a long pull at a water bottle. "All I saw were two bodies lying on the ground outside the kampong."

"Were they wearing uniforms?" Maggot asked.

"Flight suits, maybe," Waldo muttered. "They were pretty well hacked up."

"The general was wearing a flight suit," Clark whispered.

Waldo looked at them in agony. "It could have been him."

"We were taking ground fire from the kampong," Buns added.

Waldo gave them a hard look. "So we morted the muthafuckers."

Taman Negara
Sunday, October 10

The sun had set when the big diesel fired to life in the underground warren deep in the ridgeline. Smoke belched from the center tunnel as the transporter/erector/launcher moved out of hiding, its huge twelve wheels slowly turning. The missile it carried was heavily camouflaged and resembled a long, bushy caterpillar moving slowly down the rough trail. The sergeant hiding on the ridgeline noted the time and motioned for his runner. The lance corporal listened to his instructions and pulled back from the observation post, little more than a shadow moving silently in the night. Once clear of the ridge, he moved fast and reached Kamigami in less than twenty minutes.

"That's two," Kamigami told Lieutenant Lee, his team leader.

"Do we take them out?" Lee asked.

Tel knew the answer before Kamigami replied. The Taman Negara was essentially a staging area for the PLA, and all around them supplies were dispersed in the jungle waiting for transport south. However, side by side were large numbers of soldiers being fed into the maw of combat, and for Kamigami that was the real threat. It was only a matter of time before one of his four teams was discovered. Tel calculated they had two or three more days at best before they had to withdraw.

"For now our mission is to observe and report," Kamigami told the lieutenant. "Get a message out." But even that was not easy. Although their PRC319 radio was capable of sending an encrypted, short-burst transmission that defied decoding, simple triangulation would warn the PLA that intruders were in the Taman Negara. A runner would have to take the message miles away for transmission. However, nothing could be written down in case the runner was captured, so the message had to be committed to memory.

"Sir," Tel said, "should we include the coordinates of the tunnel?" Kamigami didn't answer. "I mean the exact GPS coordinates of the entrance," Tel explained.

"How do you propose we get those?"

Tel never hesitated. "We send someone down there with a GPS. All he has to do is press the fix button."

"And if he gets caught?"

"We shoot him," Tel replied.

"I'll do it," the lance corporal volunteered. "Those missiles are targeted at my family in Singapore."

Kamigami agreed and huddled with the team, telling them exactly what he wanted. The lance corporal changed into a worker's dungarees and pocketed a small GPS before he moved out. After he had left, Kamigami handed Tel an M-16 with a night-vision sight. "This was your idea," he said.

Tel's face blanched. "What if I miss?"

"Don't," Kamigami warned.

Tel lay beside the sergeant in the observation post overlooking the tunnels and sighted the scope. The greenish image was unbelievably clear as he zeroed in on the entrance. It was all familiar from the time when he and Kamigami had first discovered the base camp. But now it was swarming with people. He estimated the range at five hundred meters and dialed it in. "Five-fifty," the sergeant said. Tel changed the setting. The sergeant pointed to the shadows to the left of the tunnel entrance, and Tel glued his right eye to the eyepiece.

A figure shambled out of the shadows and crossed in front of the center tunnel. It was the lance corporal. In the direct center he stopped and fished a pack of cigarettes from his pocket. A guard stepped out of the tunnel and challenged him. The corporal said something, and the guard laughed. The corporal tapped two cigarettes from the pack and offered one to the guard. He shouldered his submachine gun and took one of the cigarettes. The corporal struck a match and lit the cigarettes. Even at that distance it was a flare, washing out a small part of the scope. Tel moved the crosshairs slightly to the side so he could see. The corporal shoved the pack of cigarettes into his pocket and hesitated for a moment as he keyed his GPS. Then he withdrew his hand and walked on across as the guard stepped back into the shadows.

Tel exhaled in relief.

Washington, D.C.
Sunday, October 10

The ExCom was waiting in the president's private study off the Oval Office early Sunday morning. They talked quietly until she arrived. Kennett automatically did a quick appraisal of his president, deeply worried that she wasn't getting enough rest. "Good morning," she said, her voice calm and not showing the fatigue that was drawing her down. "First, the UN is going to consider a cease-fire resolution this afternoon."

"H-hour for Operation Anvil is 0100 hours Gulf time tomorrow morning," General Wilding said. "Our forces are in place, and the UIF knows it's coming. This is nothing but an attempt to stop it."

"That's not going to happen," Turner assured him. "I'll have our ambassador delay any vote in the UN as long as possible. But if it comes too early, I fully intend to ignore it until the UIF surrenders. Period."

Wilding carefully considered his next words. "Madam President, this is going to be a max effort. That means heavy casualties."

"I understand," Turner said. "What else?"

"I talked to Herbert last night," Mazie said. "The EU is demanding that the Germans halt their drive on Baghdad. The French are really putting the pressure on, and Herbert isn't sure how long they can ignore it."

Turner caught Mazie's use of von Lubeck's first name and arched an eyebrow. "Tell von Lubeck to delay as long as possible. What else?"

It was Butler's turn. "The situation in Malaysia is critical. The PLA has broken out and is driving hard toward Singapore."

"We may be able to do something on the political front," Turner told them. "The Chinese special envoy, Zou Rong, arrived yesterday. Stephan is meeting with him at noon and thinks he may have an offer."

Butler frowned. "I wouldn't count on that, Mrs. President."

Turner glanced at the TV. "I think there's something you'd like to see." She hit the remote control, and the logo for *Meet the Press* appeared.

"Madam President," Kennett said, "why do you torture yourself this way?" The commentator's face, which reminded the vice president of the "muffin boy," filled the screen as he introduced his guest, Senator John Leland. Kennett's missing left arm started to itch, which was always a bad sign. "This is bad. He likes Leland."

"Because the good senator feeds him inside information," Butler observed.

"Leland's desperate," Mazie said worriedly. "There's a rumor he's got an 'October Surprise' in store for us."

"I'm *not* surprised," Turner said. "Not with a little over three weeks before the election." They fell silent as the interview began. Leland's face was a mask while the commentator summarized the latest poll results that linked what was happening in the Gulf to Turner's sudden surge in popularity. There was no doubt that if the election were held tomorrow, Turner would sweep David Grau under the political carpet. But Leland didn't take the bait and started to talk in his rolling tones, pontificating on the state of Turner's administration. "Here it comes," the president warned.

On cue, Leland turned to the camera, his face solemn. "This has gone far beyond politics. Increasingly, we're dealing with a state of moral degeneration in this administration that transcends anything we've ever seen."

Nancy Bender knocked on the door and entered. Without a word, she handed a note to the vice president, glanced at the TV, and left. Kennett read the note, and his face paled. "That's a very serious charge," the TV commentator said, playing the straight man.

"And I don't make it lightly," Leland said with pain in his voice. "During the investigation into the suicide of the late DCI, it was discovered that he was involved in a child-pornography ring on the Internet. But this line of inquiry was dropped."

The commentator was outraged. "Are you suggesting it was covered up?"

"It appears so." Leland folded his hands in front of him, the stern judge. "It's entirely possible that the DCI was about to be outed and was driven to suicide by forces within the Turner administration."

Turner laughed, and everyone looked at her in shock. "First Grau shoots his foot off," she said, owing them an explanation, "and now Leland." She was obviously enjoying the moment. "For the time being, we have no comment. Talk to Bobbi Jo. She knows what to do."

It was a rare moment, and Kennett hated that he had to spoil it. He handed her the note. "Madam President." He waited.

"Oh, no," she whispered. She came to her feet, wadding up the note in her hand. "It's Matt," she said. "The helicopter he was on was shot down. About twelve hours ago." She fought back the tears, refusing to give in. She turned to Wilding, an unspoken plea on her face.

"I need to return to the NMCC," the general said. "Unfortunately, we're fully engaged in Operation Anvil. We don't have much in the area. Maybe Okinawa."

"I know that," she admitted.

thirty-two

Camp Alpha
Monday, October 11

Smoke from the still-smoldering fire in the fuel dump drifted over Alpha, holding the base in an eerie silence. To the north the constant rumble of artillery was a grim reminder that the fighting was coming their way. Occasionally a train of weapons trailers emerged out of the smoke and crossed the runway to deliver its deadly load. The big blast doors at a shelter would crank open far enough to move one or two trailers inside. Then the tug would move on to the next shelter. Inside, Maintenance worked hard to ready the Warthogs for combat while the pilots tried to catch some rest in one of the rooms at the back.

A lone pickup drove around the perimeter road as Rockne checked on each fire team he had posted in a defensive fire position. Although he could not see their faces in the dark, he could sense their worry. One young airman summed it up best. "Damn, Chief. I'd feel a hell of a lot better if the general was here or we were outa here." Rockne agreed with him and moved on to the next position.

A C-130 Hercules with Singapore roundels on the fuselage touched down at 0108 hours and taxied into parking. The pilots kept the engines running as the ramp came down at the rear of the big cargo plane. Six big fuel bladders that resembled black sausages rolled out the back while an ambulance waited with the two litter patients and three walking wounded from the missile attack. The Air Force lieutenant colonel from the MAAG hurried down the ramp and ran over to the van where Janice Clark was waiting. "I've got the plane for at least one more shuttle," he told her. "We can start evacuating nonessential personnel."

"What the hell is going on?" she yelled over the roar of the engines.

He gestured to the north. "The front is collapsing. Singapore is a mess. I'm screaming for help, but no one seems to be listening. I was lucky to pry the Hercules loose." He glanced at the C-130, where two litters were being carried on and Doc Ryan was giving instructions to the crew chiefs. "I should be back in an hour or two."

Clark watched as the lieutenant colonel ran for the Hercules. He climbed on board, and it fast-taxied for the runway. Satisfied that the fuel bladders were taken care of, she told her driver to take her to the command post. He drove in silence, obviously worried. He dropped her at the entry control point and said, "Missy Colonel, I need to see family." She told him to go, fully aware that she would never see him again.

Inside the command post she radioed for the chief of Maintenance, Doc Ryan, and Rockne to join her. While she waited, she went down the AVG's personnel roster: 30 pilots including Maggot, 304 maintenance troops, 134 cops including Rockne, 108 support personnel, and 9 medics including Doc Ryan. *Five hundred and eighty-five,* she thought. *Can I get them out?* The simple question beat at her like a sledgehammer. She answered her own question out loud: "Every damn one." Again she scanned the list, checking off those who would go first. But reality could not be denied—the cops would be the last to go. If they went. Once again she scanned the list, forgetting three names: Clark, Pontowski, and Boyca.

Rockne was the first to arrive. "Your driver is outside," he told her. "He wants to speak to you." Clark quickly explained how they were going to start an evacuation before she walked outside to see what her driver wanted. She found him squatting on his haunches outside the entry control point. Much to her surprise, she was glad to see him.

"I know where general is," he told her.

Washington, D.C.
Sunday, October 10

The hostess swept through the downstairs of her elegant Georgetown home, ensuring that all was ready for the arrival of her last guest. A quick glance at the clock in the vestibule: two minutes before noon. She took a deep breath. It had been a wonderful weekend, first with the party on Friday night and the meeting between Secretary of Defense Merritt and Senator Leland, and now this. Her star was certainly rising, and she could see a future. The clock struck twelve, and she opened the door. On cue, a black sedan drove under the portico and stopped. An aide emerged from the front passenger seat, looked around to confirm they were not observed, and opened the rear door.

She smiled graciously as Zou Rong emerged and hurried up the steps. Nothing betrayed her inner anxiety when Jin Chu stepped out of the car and followed Zou inside. The hostess was neither slow nor stupid and recognized her immediately. But she was not prepared for the sheer beauty and natural grace of the woman. For a moment she considered asking to have her fortune told, but she quickly discarded the notion. But why was Jin Chu there? The hostess's contact at the State Department who had arranged the clandestine meeting had not mentioned it.

"Mr. Ambassador," the hostess said, escorting Zou upstairs, "this is indeed an honor." Zou ignored her. She opened the door to the study where Merritt and Leland had met. This time, the secretary of state was waiting inside. She closed the door and descended the stairs. Should she offer Jin Chu tea?

The two men exchanged the formal courtesies dictated by the circumstances. As he represented the host country, Serick was the first to broach the reason for the meeting. But it was done in the time-honored way of his profession, carefully nonconfrontational and with tact, leaving room to maneuver without committing his side to a course of action or policy. "My government is worried about the situation in Malaysia."

What he got in return was a full artillery barrage. "Your government is worried about Singapore," Zou corrected. "Fortunately for the peace-loving peoples of Asia, it is beyond your control."

Serick was stunned. Belligerents talked this way to the press and on TV, and then it was for home consumption. He pulled off one diplomatic glove. "Mr. Ambassador, you have traveled too far to recite propaganda. I was hoping for a more productive conversation."

"Please tell your president that we will have many things of mutual interest to discuss in a few days. That is why I'm here."

Serick pulled off the other glove. "You're wagering you can capture Singapore before we can respond."

Zou was a gambler at heart and liked the analogy. "Our friends in the Middle East have given us the race." He smiled contentedly.

"When you back the wrong horse," Serick replied, "don't blame the horse."

"It won't even be a photo finish," Zou told him. "As your president will shortly learn."

Serick tried a different tack, determined to at least send a message. He did it in terms even an adolescent could understand. "There will be a price to be paid."

"There is a new economic order emerging. I suggest you seek ways to make an accommodation before it is too late." Zou stood, bringing the meeting to an end. "Please tell your president there is always a price to be paid for being in the wrong place. Which we are explaining to her General Pontowski." He gave a little bow and left.

Serick was in a state of shock and didn't move. His eyes narrowed as he considered what he should do next. But all his options were gone. There was nothing left except fighting, death, and destruction. "Well, so be it," he murmured, accepting failure. He reached for his cane and stood up. Suddenly he felt very old. His hostess was waiting for him at the bottom of the stairs. She keyed off Zou's abrupt departure and looked very concerned. "Thank you so much," he told her.

"It was my pleasure, Mr. Secretary. I'll always remember meeting Miss Jin. What an adorable lady. And her English is exquisite."

"Jin Chu was here? The fortune-teller?"

"Why, yes. I thought you knew."

"What did she say?"

"We talked about the weather, of course." She thought for a moment. "The conversation took a most unusual turn. She mentioned the Chinese love of gambling." Serick's shaggy eyebrows shot up, an unspoken command to repeat exactly what was said. The hostess caught it. "She said, 'Not even the gods wager on horse races.'"

Serick kissed her hand, still the gracious Old World courtier. "Madam, you have done your country a rare service." He hobbled down the steps, surprising her with his speed.

Turner tapped her fingers together as a heavy silence ruled the Oval Office. "That was a diplomatic slap in the face," she finally said.

"Actually," Serick allowed, "it was a bludgeoning."

She made no effort to hide her anger. "If he thinks he's here to dictate surrender terms, he's going to die an old man waiting." She stood up and looked out the windows, her back to her advisers. "They're deluding themselves if they think they can blackmail me into an agreement."

Mazie and Butler exchanged glances, both certain she was talking about Matt Pontowski. "Madam President," Butler said, "regardless of what Zou said, we can't be sure they have captured the general. I keep asking myself why he brought the woman with him. Very bizarre, to say the least."

"Madam President," Mazie said, "we're on a Chinese roundabout. I think we're getting two messages here."

Turner turned and faced them, deadly calm. "Then it's time to send them a message they'll have no trouble understanding. General Wilding, how long before we can reinforce SEAC?"

Wilding thought out loud. "The problem is airlift. Everything we've got has been dedicated to the Gulf and the buildup for Operation Anvil—which commences in five hours. With sealift finally open, I can start redirecting aircraft on return flights out of the Gulf."

"Redirect," the president ordered.

"I'm hesitant to commit forces piecemeal, Madam President. I want to go in with at least a division. I'm thinking the Third Marine Division in Okinawa. We can deploy it at less than full strength and have it in place in . . ." He hesitated, not sure of the numbers. It was a complicated calculation dependent on so many factors. He committed. "We can have a vanguard regiment in place, ready to fight, in seventy-two hours." Every instinct warned him to hedge for time, but the look on Turner's face was ample warning not to do it.

"Seventy-two hours," Turner repeated. She crossed her arms in defiance, her eyes hard. "I will not allow Singapore to fall. Tell SEAC to hold. Help is on the way."

Camp Alpha
Monday, October 11

Jessica felt like a dwarf as she stood behind Paul Travis and Jake Osburn in the Base Defense Operations Center. She shouldered her way through and moved to the front of the chart table. She wasn't about to be left out because of Travis and Jake. "It's 0215 in five seconds," Rockne said. "Three, two, one, hack." The nine security cops set their watches. Rockne studied his team, taking their measure. Satisfied that he had the right people, he circled a railroad junction eleven miles south of Alpha. "Our source claims that General Pontowski is being held in this area by no more than three or four soldiers. We know the PLA has long-range patrols operating in the area. If they are PLA, and if the general is wounded, they're probably waiting for a pickup. Our mission is to rescue him before that happens, while we've still got surprise on our side. The bad news is that the roads are flooded with refugees and we can't move by vehicle."

"What about the First SOS?" Jessica asked. "They've got helicopters."

Rockne's face matched his name. "We called, but all their choppers are on other missions and only the command element is here. So we're going in by foot. The good news is that we've got a guide who knows a back way."

"How reliable is this guy?" Paul Travis asked.

"He's Colonel Clark's driver and seems pretty loyal to her," Rockne replied. "I want to be in and out before sunrise. That means an eleven-mile slog in three hours. I'm betting there's so much confusion out there that no one will want to mess with us and we can blow right by them. With a little luck, we can do it. Regardless of what happens, we got to try. Any questions?"

"This is not a hell of a lot to go on," Jake Osburn said. "Where do we rendezvous if this turns to shit?" Rockne pointed out their rendezvous, and they punched the coordinates into their GPSs.

"Chief," Jessica said, "Boyca's real good at picking up a scent."

"That's why she's coming," Rockne replied. "Okay, let's do it."

Southern Malaysia
Monday, October 11

Jake Osburn set the pace for the team as they moved silently along the path that led between two kampongs. Clark's driver was carrying only two canteens and had no trouble keeping up, but the others were struggling under their combat loads. Rockne checked his watch. They were making good time, and he called a break. "Five minutes," he told them. Jessica collapsed to the ground and pulled out a canteen. She sloshed some water into a small plastic pan for Boyca before drinking any herself. Then they were up and moving as Jake lived up to his reputation as an animal.

Their pace slowed as they neared the railroad junction and ran into refugees. Rather than take a chance, they went to cover while the driver went ahead to clear their way. Then they were moving again, reaching the railroad junction while it was still dark. Clark's driver pointed to the compound. "There" was all he said.

Rockne swept the area with his night-vision goggles. He could make out two railroad-maintenance sheds, at least five shacks, and two more substantial cement-block buildings. "Which one?" he muttered. The driver gave an expressive shrug. "Fuckin' lovely."

"Okay," he told his team, "me and Boyca will lead the way in and try to pick up the general's scent. If we can identify the building, Jess, you take a four-man team inside." Paul and Jake stiffened but said nothing. "Go in on my command," Rockne said, "and do it by the book." He pulled Pontowski's flight cap out of his rucksack and held it for Boyca to sniff. He unsnapped her leash. "Seek."

Boyca ranged back and forth as she moved into the compound. Behind her, Rockne moved from shadow to shadow, staying out of sight. He was about to give up and return to the team when Boyca started to move back and forth as if moving toward the apex of a cone. She had picked up the scent, and Rockne followed her, moving in the deep shadow of one of the maintenance sheds.

A man stepped out of a doorway and called to Boyca, the Malay equivalent of "Come here, doggie." He squatted on the ground and called again, beckoning to her. But Boyca refused to move and stood still. The man pulled out a knife and inched toward her. Boyca sensed the danger and darted away, directly toward Rockne. Rockne laid his M-16 on the ground and carefully removed his goggles. Boyca came up to him, panting. Without a word, he stroked her ears and drew his knife. The man was almost to the shadows, totally unaware of what was there. Again he spoke in Malay, cajoling Boyca to come to him. His right hand dangled at his side, still holding the knife.

Rockne went into a linesman's stance, as if he were playing football. The man took another step toward him, paused, raised his knife, and then took another step. Rockne exploded out of the shadows, his left hand sweeping the man's knife aside as his own knife flashed in an upward motion. He drove it into the man's sternum, lifting him off the ground. The man hacked up a cough, but it died with him. Rockne pulled him back into the shadows and rolled the body under the shed. He quickly donned his gear, but Boyca was already moving. She stopped and lay on her stomach, paws outstretched, her head up, looking directly at the door of a cinder-block building.

thirty-three

Southern Malaysia
Monday, October 11

Paul, a young airman called Spike, and Jake lined up behind Jessica in the shadows as they waited for the command to move on the building. But Boyca was still lying in front of the door, an obstacle in their way. The first half-light of the approaching sunrise cut at the shadows, and Jessica's night-vision goggles began to wash out. She ripped them off and jammed her helmet back on. The men did the same as her eyes adjusted to the ambient light. Now she could see Rockne's dark mass against the wall of the shack, gesturing at Boyca, trying to get her to move out of the way. Finally he gave a low whistle, and Boyca scampered to him, clearing the path.

"Go," Jessica said in a low voice. As one, her team moved out, trying to stay in the rapidly dissipating shadows. They made it to the door as the upper limb of the sun cracked the horizon. Automatically, they stacked against the wall, boots touching. Jake, the last man, squeezed Spike's arm, signaling that he was ready. Spike relayed the signal to Paul, who passed it to Jessica. She reached for the doorknob and tested it. The door swung open, and she moved quickly, bursting through the "fatal funnel." She buttonhooked to the right and into the corner, never stopping as she moved down the sidewall. Paul was right behind her, moving to the left wall, clearing his side of the room.

Before Spike could move through the door, a burst of gunfire raked the doorway, knocking him backward. Jessica fired a short burst into the muzzle flash and was rewarded with a scream of pain. A weapon clattered to the ground as Jake came through the door.

"Don't shoot!" Pontowski shouted. A flashlight snapped on and swept the room. Pontowski was on the floor, a dead body lying across him. "One more in the next room," he said.

Paul never stopped moving and went through the next door as Jake fell in behind him. They were a team and moved as one with blinding speed. Another short burst of gunfire. Silence. "All clear," Paul said.

Jessica stepped around him and took a deep breath. A man was down on the floor, crunched over his weapon, an M-16. "What the hell?" Jessica muttered to herself. She examined the body. It was a teenage boy wearing a Malaysian Army uniform. She kicked the M-16 aside and picked it up. "Jammed," she said. "You are one lucky dude," she told Paul. She hurried back into the first room to check on Pontowski. He was still under the body.

"Mind untying me?" Pontowski muttered. "Damn, that was fast."

"That's the idea, sir," Jessica said, relief in her voice. "Who else is in the building?" she asked.

"That's it." He rolled clear of the body. "They were deserters. Malaysian Army. Kids scared silly."

"Check on Spike," she told Paul and Jake.

"He's dead," Rockne said from the doorway. He knelt beside Pontowski. "You okay, sir?"

"Just my shoulder. Broken collarbone, I think."

"Can you travel?"

"Yeah, I think so."

Rockne stood and walked to the doorway. He spoke into his whisper mike, asking for a status report from the men posted outside. "We've got lots of movement out here," a staff sergeant told him. "The gunfire must've stirred 'em up. It's hard to tell in this light, but I think they're all civilians."

"Find a wheelbarrow or a cart and get ready to move out."

"That's not necessary," Pontowski told him. "I can walk."

"It's for Spike, sir. No way am I gonna leave him here."

Camp Alpha
Monday, October 11

The three men clustered around the chart table in the back of Alpha's command post. "SEAC is pressing us hard to take this one," Maggot said. "Singapore can't take many more missile strikes and think this will stop it. But if this is what they say it is, it's got to be heavily defended."

Waldo carefully plotted the GPS coordinates in the tasking message and spanned off the distance. "One hundred and sixty nautical miles. Thirty minutes' flying time." He visualized the terrain and different attack headings. "All we need are a couple of F-16s to discourage any SAMs."

"I already asked," Maggot told him. "None available."

"This is very important," Colonel Sun said. He searched for the words to make the two Americans understand. "In Singapore the people are so packed in, a single missile kills many. They are so helpless."

Maggot shook his head. "If we had something cosmic like an AGM-154, that would give us enough standoff distance and we could send one right down the entrance." An AGM-154 was a fifteen-hundred-pound standoff glide bomb with an inertial or GPS guidance system that under the right delivery conditions could fly up to forty miles.

Waldo thought for a few moments. "We got some AGM-65Gs." He looked at Colonel Sun. "That's a Maverick with a double IR seeker head and a three-hundred-pound blast-fragmentation warhead. It's good for taking out tanks and hardened targets. Pretty accurate with the right jock."

Maggot shook his head. "The Maverick has a standoff distance of fourteen miles max. But you're going to have to get a lot closer than that."

"Innocent people are dying," Sun murmured. "My family is there."

Waldo heard the pain behind his words and committed. "We don't know for sure what they got for defenses. We may be able to get close enough to acquire the entrance and get a lock-on."

"We know they got Gadflies," Maggot reminded him. "Max range twenty-one miles, and it can come down into the weeds and get you."

Waldo looked hopeful. "So if a monopulse radar comes up talking, we get the hell out of Dodge. It sure wouldn't hurt to send two Hogs up to take a look."

Maggot relented. "You and Neck got it. Launch ASAP." His palms were flat on the chart, and he leaned forward. "But I want my jets back." He was really saying he wanted Waldo and Neck back.

Waldo grinned. "No problemo, boss." It was the first time anyone had called Maggot "boss."

Taman Negara
Monday, October 11

"Target on the nose at thirty," Waldo radioed. Neck answered with two clicks of the transmit button. Waldo glanced at his radar warning display. No threats were showing, and only an early-warning search radar at their deep six was active. He decided it was probably friendly and disregarded it. A loud chirping noise blasted his ears. He turned the volume down. "Neck," he radioed, "I got a Firecan in search mode." A Firecan was an old AAA radar. If the radar shifted to a higher frequency and focused its beam on one aircraft, then it was locked on and in a guidance mode and tracking.

"Got it," Neck replied. "Maybe a fifty-seven. Looks like it's coming from the target." Both men were confident they were up against either an old thirty-seven- or fifty-seven-millimeter antiaircraft artillery battery with a max effective range of two and a half miles. And they knew how to kill one of those.

Waldo made a decision and mashed the transmit button. "Trick-fuck," he said, calling for the tactic they would use. "I'm the fuck."

"I'm the trick," Neck replied, confirming his part so there would be no confusion. The pilots had given a crude name to a tactic that worked very well against a single defender. The plan called for one aircraft, the trick, to act as a diversion while the other aircraft hit where the defender wasn't looking. Waldo broke out of formation and dropped his Hog down to the deck, below radar detection. He set up a tight orbit and throttled back while Neck flew a wide arc around the target. When he was well away from Waldo, Neck climbed until the radar found him, getting the gunner's attention. Then he dropped behind a ridgeline for a little more cat and mouse. He popped up long enough to allow a radar lock-on and then back down behind the ridge, baiting the gunner. When he was on the opposite side of the circle from Waldo, he radioed, "The trick's ready."

"Go," Waldo replied.

"Trick's in," Neck transmitted. He turned into the target, firewalled the throttles, and jinked hard. His warning gear came alive as the radar found him and locked on. "Lock-on," he radioed. He had the gunner's undivided attention and was still out of range.

"Fuck's in," Waldo radioed. He pressed from the opposite side of the circle, betting that the gunner was fully focused on Neck. If at any time the radar found Waldo, the attack was off and he would turn away. Neck darted behind a ridge and broke the lock. But the radar was waiting for him the moment he cleared the protective terrain. He reversed course, heading away, until the radar locked on. Immediately he turned behind a ridge, broke the lock, and popped up so the radar could find him again. It locked on as he streaked along the top of the ridge, away from the target. This time he made no effort to break the lock. "Six miles out," Waldo radioed. He was rapidly closing on the target.

Now the timing was critical. Neck pulled up and reversed again, turning toward the radar. He headed for the target and dropped down to the deck, breaking the lock-on. When he was four miles out, he pulled up to fifteen hundred feet, allowing the radar to lock on. His warning gear blasted at him as he came into range. "The trick is good," Neck radioed.

"I'm in the pop," Waldo replied. He pulled back on the stick and climbed, going for a visual. He wasn't disappointed. Eight rapid puffs emerged from thc trcc canopy as the gunner fired a short burst at Neck. "Break left!" Waldo transmitted, just in case Neck hadn't seen the smoke. He had and was already in the break, finding safety next to the ground. Although neither pilot saw them, the eight rounds passed overhead and wide. Waldo's left hand flew over the armament-control panel as he selected BOMBS RIPPLE. Why waste a Maverick when a pair of Mark-82 AIRs would do the trick? The five-hundred-pound bombs may have been "dumb," but the weapons delivery system in the Warthog, the low-altitude safety and targeting enhancement system, or LASTE for short, was anything but. The target marched down the projected bomb-impact line in Waldo's HUD. When all the delivery parameters were met, the bombs pickled automatically.

Neck pulled up to get a visual on Waldo. He saw the other Warthog as the two bombs flashed. A fraction of a second later a third explosion ripped the top of the jungle canopy. Waldo had gotten a secondary, a big bonus in the world of tactical fighters. Almost simultaneously he saw the tunnel entrances. "Target in sight," Neck radioed. He rolled in and called up a Maverick. He glanced at the TV monitor on the right side of his instrument panel and drove the crosshairs over the middle entrance.

Waldo passed underneath as he ran for safety, away from the gun he had just killed. His RWR gear came alive with a new warning—a monopulse radar. "Break it off!" he shouted over the radio. But it was too late. Two missiles were streaking at the doomed A-10. "Eject!" Waldo yelled as the jet disappeared in a blinding flash. What he didn't see was a Maverick missile homing in on the tunnel. A deadly calm settled over him as he ruddered his Hog around and dropped below fifty feet, flying below two ridgelines and heading directly for the area where the two missiles came from. He saw what looked like a pile of brush moving down a dirt road. Again he kicked the rudders and brought his Hog's nose around as he mashed the trigger. A long burst of cannon fire walked through the jungle and up to the camouflaged vehicle.

It disappeared in a fiery cloud.

Tel's ears were still ringing when he reported back to Kamigami. "I saw it," he said. "A missile flew right into the middle tunnel entrance and exploded."

Kamigami listened without comment as Tel filled in the details and other reports came in. "So," he finally said, doing the grim cost accounting, "one missile on target, one Triple A battery bombed, and one Gecko surface-to-air battery destroyed for the price of a Warthog."

"No parachute was seen," Lieutenant Lee told them.

Another report came in from the team watching the tunnels. Four camouflaged transporter/erectors, each loaded with a missile, had exited and were moving south. "They must have a blast shield inside," Kamigami said. His chin slumped to his chest. "Not a good exchange." He looked up. "Send a message."

Camp Alpha
Monday, October 11

Waldo's flight suit was still wet with sweat as he recapped the mission. There was no attempt to gloss over the simple fact that he had lost his wingman. "I called for a trick-fuck."

"It may have worked in the Gulf or South Africa," Maggot said, "but the PLA is a different cat. My guess is they build their defenses in layers, with one weapon system covering for another. What got Neck?"

"I got a radar warning for a monopulse radar. That's when I called to get the hell out of Dodge." Waldo thought for a moment, trying to recall every detail. "Wait a minute. The symbol . . . it was different . . . it may have flashed at me." He looked at Maggot, now clearly distraught. "Oh, shit. A Land Roll." The Land Roll radar was matched to the SAM system NATO called the Gecko, a self-contained, highly mobile system with six missiles on a six-wheeled vehicle. "When did they get those?"

Maggot shook his head. "Who knows? But it looks like the Russians are their supplier of choice. What else do they have?"

Janice Clark joined them. "You need to see this," she said, handing Maggot a message.

Maggot scanned it and then carefully reread every word. "It's from Kamigami. Neck got a Maverick off. Flew right into a tunnel. A shack." He crumpled the message into a wad. "It didn't do any good. Twenty minutes later four tactical missiles moved out." He stood up and took a deep breath. "No parachute was observed." He slumped into his chair, thinking. Finally he stood up. "Any word from Rockne?" Clark shook her head. "Okay, folks," Maggot announced. "We're evacuating. When's the next C-130 due in?"

"No word yet," Clark told him. "They said they'd be back but weren't sure when." She was deeply worried. "They might not make it."

"We'll be ready if they do," Maggot said. "Have a group standing by ready to board the moment it lands. We can pack ninety to a hundred bodies on board at a time." He paced the floor. "We'll shanghai that fucker if we have to."

Clark parked her minivan under the camouflage netting behind the aircraft shelter and then walked to the rear entrance. Even though it was a short walk, she was sweating and wished her driver were back. By being available, literally at her beck and call, he had increased her efficiency, and she needed him. She banged on the small blast door until someone answered. Inside, a group of men were waiting for her. She checked her clipboard and ticked off the names. "Okay, listen up," she called. "We've got a C-130 due to land in a few minutes. When I give you the high sign, I want you out of here and running for the parking ramp, which is about a hundred yards through the trees. Everyone know where that is?" Nods all around. "Great." She paused, searching for the right words. "We tried to make a difference here. But it wasn't in the cards. Now it's time to go home." One man headed for the rear door. "What's the problem?" she called.

The man stopped and turned around. "No offense, Colonel Clark. But I was with the AVG and the general in China. We got chased out of there and, damn it, as long as we got Hogs flying, I ain't gettin' chased out of here." He released the two locking levers and pushed the door open. Two men followed him out.

Clark erased the ticks by their names and looked up. "I promise you this," she told the men, "I will get them out." She walked over to the phone on the wall and called the command post for the status on the C-130. "Okay, it's on short final. GO!" A crew chief hit the switch for the main blast doors, and they started to roll back. The men streamed out, running for the trees. She followed them as the doors cranked closed. She was still in the trees when the Hercules touched down and reversed its props. By the time she reached the parking ramp, it had cleared the runway and was rolling fuel bladders out the back. Then she saw it. The pilots had no intention of stopping for passengers.

She dropped her clipboard and ran for the exit leading to the runway. It was a race between her and the big plane, which was now turning toward the runway, free of its cargo. She won and stood in the middle of the exit, blocking the C-130. But the big bird kept coming, its props howling. She drew her Beretta and used a two-handed shooter's stance as she aimed directly at the pilot sitting in the left seat.

He got the message and stopped. The crew entrance door flopped open, and the lieutenant colonel from the MAAG stood in the doorway. She could barely hear him over the roar of the engines. "NO PROBLEM . . . DIDN'T UNDERSTAND."

"Yeah, right," she grumbled as the rear cargo door raised and the ramp lowered. The waiting men rushed aboard, and she stepped aside, holstering her weapon.

"WE'LL BE BACK," he shouted, pulling the entrance door up.

Clark threw the pilot a salute as the Hercules taxied past, and much to her surprise, he returned it. She walked across the ramp and picked up her clipboard. She pulled out her pen and changed the numbers: 104 gone, 481 to go. Then she walked briskly back to her minivan.

"Missy Colonel," a familiar voice said. "Where you want to go?"

"You're back!" She almost hugged him in relief. "About time." He opened the door and she climbed in. "Command post" was all she said.

"General at doctor, not at command post."

"Is he hurt?"

"Broken bone. But he walk back." The driver pulled a long face. "Rockne . . . he very mean man. Kill a man who want to eat Boyca."

Clark shook her head, wondering what the story was behind that. "I imagine he would."

The driver stopped beside the med station and ran around to open her door. But Clark was already out and running down the ramp. "I go get general some clothes," he called to her back. Inside, she found Pontowski sitting on an examination table as Doc Ryan taped his left shoulder. His boots were off, and the upper half of his flight suit was cut away and hanging around his waist. He was filthy, encrusted with dried grunge from the rice paddy, and he had a distinct aroma about him.

For a moment she said nothing as relief flooded over her. "Damn, General. You do need a shower."

Pontowski cocked an eyebrow. Then the grin was back. "The Hilton was having a few problems with their staff."

"You are one lucky man," Ryan said. "Not many walk away from a crash. Other than your shoulder and a few cracked ribs, you seem okay. But God only knows what was in that rice paddy you landed in." He prepared a syringe. "Antibiotics. Just in case." He glanced at Clark, who turned away. "Drop your trousers and bend over, sir. This will feel a little warm." He finished and pointed to the back. "Take a shower while we find you some clothes."

"My driver is bringing them," she said. She stood outside while Pontowski showered, and talked through the doorway, bringing him up to date. He was toweling off when a dull thud rocked the bunker. A little dust rained down from the ceiling. "What the hell?" she wondered aloud. Two more thuds, this time more distant, shook the walls. She ran for the entrance, where her driver was standing holding Pontowski's fatigues and a clean pair of boots.

His eyes were wide. "Mortars. Missy Colonel, you go home now?"

"Not yet," she told him, taking the clothes from him. The wail of warning Klaxons echoed over the bunker as another mortar round slammed into the base. She closed the blast door and dogged it down.

Washington, D.C.
Monday, October 11

Mazie leaned back in her chair and closed her eyes. She knew she should go home and get some rest, but an inner need held her close to the White House. A gentle snore drifted across from the couch where Bernie Butler was stretched out. Like her, he couldn't leave. She glanced at the clock—two in the morning. Again she closed her eyes, but her restless mind drove her on. Upstairs, in the residence, the president was sleeping—why couldn't she? "Damn," she muttered, sitting upright. It was Operation Anvil. The Gulf offensive was in its ninth hour, and she needed an update. Maybe then she could go home. She stood and walked out, careful not to disturb the sleeping Butler.

The duty officer in the Situation Room stood when she entered. He knew why she was there, and called up the current status reports coming from the NMCC. "It's going well," he told her. Slowly the tension that held her tight gave way. "Casualties are much lighter than expected." His fingers danced on the keyboard, and the three monitors changed displays. "In the north the Germans are driving hard for Baghdad."

The door opened, and Bernie Butler entered. He glanced at the monitors and sat down. "I couldn't sleep," he said. He focused on the center screen. "Lord love a duck. They're collapsing." It had taken the United States thirty-six days to halt the UIF's incursion, build up its forces, and go on the offensive. Now, with the Germans advancing from the north, the UIF was being hammered on the anvil of combat and surrendering en masse. He couldn't believe what he was seeing. "It's all over but the shouting." Gradually a huge smile spread across his face. "Thirty-six days! Fan . . . *tas* . . . tic!" He drew the word out in exultation, savoring the moment. "Should we wake the president?" he asked.

Mazie shook her head. "She needs the rest." The right screen scrolled, and the news got better. Pontowski was safe at Camp Alpha with only minor injuries. Mazie relaxed in her chair and dozed while Butler considered what he had to do. As the acting DCI he could start the process of reform the CIA needed so desperately. Deep in thought, he missed the message on the left screen that Changi Airport in Singapore had been struck by a tactical missile. He made notes on a legal yellow pad as he outlined the changes he had in store for the agency. He would drag the CIA kicking and screaming into the twenty-first century and break the deadly combination of Cold War and bureaucratic mentality that had led to so many failures. Another thought hit him with the force of a train wreck—he was the man to do the job.

The display on the center screen was overridden with a flash message and a loud gong for emphasis. Mazie's eyes snapped open as Butler's head came up. The missile that had hit Changi was armed with a nerve-gas agent. Another gong echoed in the room: two more airfields in Singapore had been hit with tactical missiles. They waited as the tension surged. A fourth message came in: Camp Alpha was under mortar attack. The hot line from the NMCC rang, and the duty officer picked it up. He listened for a moment, and his face paled. "Every airfield in Singapore," he announced, gesturing at the three screens, "has been hit with tactical missiles carrying nerve-gas agents."

Mazie stood up, her knees weak. "We better wake the president."

thirty-four

Washington, D.C.
Monday, October 11

The Army staff car bringing General Mike Wilding and Secretary of Defense Merritt from the Pentagon made record time and turned into the gate leading to the West Wing at exactly 0403 hours. The men waited impatiently while two guards and a dog inspected the car. Not willing to wait, Wilding jumped out and let a guard run a wand over him. Merritt was right behind him, and they ran for the side entrance. Again they had to endure a search before bolting down the stairs to the Situation Room. The Marine guard recognized them and held the door open.

The president was waiting with Mazie, Butler, Parrish, and the vice president. "Thank you for coming so promptly," Turner said, fully aware that they were held captive in the NMCC, catching a few hours of sleep when they could. "How bad is it?"

Wilding checked the monitors to see if there had been a change since he had left the Pentagon. Nothing significant was on the screens, and he visibly relaxed. "We have a problem, Madam President. Seven short-range tactical missiles have hit our arrival airfields in Singapore and southern Malaysia and effectively closed them, denying us entry. The Third Marine Division on Okinawa is mobilized and ready to go. As of thirty minutes ago nine C-17s and three C-5s were on the ground at Kadena Air Base and loading. Another hundred and seventy-eight aircraft inbound for Okinawa are being diverted until we can open the pipeline."

"They did that with seven missiles?"

"All were armed with nerve gas, Madam President. Apparently it's a new agent that disperses over a wide area and is very persistent. It may be days before we can get started landing aircraft. Given enough time, we can do it."

"Time is the one commodity not available," Turner snapped. Only the low hum of a computer filled the silence.

Butler spoke in a low voice, confident and with authority. "My analysts"—he really meant informants and spies—"tell me the PLA has no more than six CSS-7 missiles left in country. Further, the PLA is stretched to the breaking point."

"How can you be so sure?" Kennett asked.

"It's the missiles," Butler replied. "It's all or nothing—go for broke."

Mazie was on the same wavelength. "As long as it's quick. The world has a very short memory. They know there's a political price, but they're willing to pay it."

"If the geopolitical payoff is right," Butler added.

"Which it will be if they capture Singapore and the Strait of Malacca," Turner said. She looked at them. "My God! What are we dealing with here?"

Mazie answered. "Power politics redefined for the twenty-first century, with asymmetric warfare the final determinant."

"Not on my watch," Turner said. It was a simple statement of fact with little emotion. "General Wilding, we need a breakthrough force. Make it happen."

"Yes, ma'am. There is another matter. We're in direct contact with the command elements of the UIF. They're begging for a cease-fire."

"Not without an unconditional surrender," Turner said, her voice deadly calm.

"They're aware of that," Wilding replied. "However, they said it was an unacceptable demand."

Turner's face was a perfect reflection of her resolve. "Apparently they do not have a full appreciation of the situation, which needs to be made clear to them. There will be no premature cease-fire."

"Ma'am," Wilding said, "if there's nothing else, I do need to return to the NMCC."

"Fifty-seven hours," Turner said, a firm reminder of the promise he had made fifteen hours earlier to reinforce SEAC within seventy-two hours. Merritt rose to leave with him. "Robert, I'm meeting with my election committee at eight this morning. Can you be there?"

Everyone in the room knew it was not a request. "Certainly, Mrs. President."

The president stopped her general before he could leave. "General Wilding, thirty-six days. Well done."

"Thank you, Madam President."

Camp Alpha
Monday, October 11

Pontowski sat on the floor of the base med station and leaned against the wall. He studied his watch and did a mental countdown. At the count of "two," a dull *whump* echoed through the thick walls. "Two seconds early," he announced. The constant mortar bombardment was taking its toll, and he could sense the fear and anxiety that filled the bunker like a fog, at times wispy and ephemeral, then dense and oppressive. It was time to do something about it. "Six rounds an hour," he announced. "Just enough to keep our heads down while conserving ammo."

"It's working," Clark groused. "We're buttoned down, and no one is moving."

"Five rounds spaced twelve to thirteen minutes apart," he said, "followed by a sixth round one minute later. Then the sequence repeats." He checked the wall clock. "The next round is due in thirty seconds." On cue, a mortar round exploded. But this time it was farther away. "Next round due at 1706," he declared. "Spread the word." He forced a casual, laid-back nonchalance he didn't feel. He waited while the tension ratcheted up. Every eye was on the clock as the minute hand touched the six. Nothing. Pontowski grinned, maintaining the image. "Wait for it. The sons of bitches may not be able to tell time." A dull thud echoed in the distance. He stood up. "Next round at 1717. I'm going to the command post." He walked to the blast door and threw it open. "Coming?" he said to Clark.

She was right behind him. Outside, Pontowski made himself walk, making light conversation over the distant thunder of artillery. "Sounds like it's getting closer," he told her. Ahead of them, a security policeman peeked at them from his defensive fire position outside the command post. "Next mortar round at 1717," Pontowski told him. He ambled by as the airman spoke into his radio, spreading the word and adding to the Pontowski legend. "How 'bout that?" Pontowski said to himself as Rockne emerged from the heavily sandbagged Base Defense Operations Center.

"Got your message, sir," Rockne said.

"What message?" Pontowski asked.

"About the mortars. Time to do something about it."

They walked inside, where Maggot was waiting. He quickly recapped the situation. "We've got four Hogs on the ground at Tengah Air Base. They're safe enough in shelters but can't move because of nerve gas. Here we got twelve Hogs, nine good to go and three down for maintenance. Maintenance should have two fixed and ready to go in the morning."

"And the last jet?" Pontowski asked.

Maggot shook his head. "Waldo's old bird. The one he crunched at Kelly Field and barely got here. Needs an engine change. Which we ain't got. Gonna cannibalize it for parts."

"Fuel?"

"Right now," Maggot replied, "we have enough in the lines and holding tanks for twenty-nine more sorties." He thought for a moment. "Tengah's got lots of fuel but no munitions."

"And lots of nerve gas," Clark added.

"True," Maggot replied. "But if Tengah opens up, we get our birds back. If that happens, we can launch out of here, fly a mission, recover and refuel at Tengah, and then fly here to upload. We can top the tanks off or just fly a shorter mission."

"If the artillery I heard outside is any indication," Pontowski said, "the action's coming to us and we're not going to be flying long sorties."

"Those fuckin' mortars aren't doing much damage," Maggot grumbled. "Just bounce off the shelters, but they're keeping us from moving."

Now it was Rockne's turn. "We pinpointed their firebase." He unfolded the 1:50,000-scale chart he was carrying. "Two of my cops found a counterbattery radar the MA left behind. Maintenance got it working and installed it on top of the control tower." He circled an area to the east of the base, on the far side of the weapons storage area. "As best we can tell, they got two tubes in this area and they ain't movin'."

"Movement is life," Pontowski intoned.

"Exactly," Rockne said.

"Time to return the favor," Maggot said.

Waldo sat at the mission director's console and waited. Like everyone's in the command post, his eyes were fixed on the master clock. At exactly 1732 hours they heard a dull thump as a mortar round hit on an aircraft shelter. The radios came alive as Maintenance reported no damage. Now they had to wait for the security police. The phone from the BDOC buzzed, and Rockne picked it up. "The counterbattery radar reports no change on the mortars' location," he told them.

Waldo's fingers flew over the communications board. "Thresher One and Two, scramble." He kicked back from the console and, like the rest, waited.

Like clockwork, the big doors on two shelters rolled back as the pilots, Bull Allison and Goat Gross, brought their A-10s to life. The engines had barely come on line when the crew chiefs pulled the wheel chocks and motioned them forward. Bull's crew chief stepped back and came to attention, throwing him a salute as he cleared the shelter. Goat fell in behind Bull as they fast-taxied for the runway. There was no end-of-runway check, where crew chiefs gave each bird a final inspection and pulled the safety pins from the munitions hanging under the wings. All that had been done before engine start. Instead they turned onto the runway, paused briefly to run up, and rolled down the runway in a formation takeoff.

Immediately the pilots snatched the gear up and at fifty feet did a tactical split, each turning away twenty degrees for five seconds before returning to the runway heading. A mortar round flashed in the open area where they would have been had they not split, ample proof the base was closely watched. "Missed," Bull radioed. "Arm 'em up." He reached out and hit the master arm switch. They turned into the setting sun, never climbing above two hundred feet, and headed to the west. Below them, the main road was packed with refugees, still fleeing south. A convoy of military trucks heading north was stalled, unable to push through the desperate people. Farther to the west, people were flooding down the railway tracks.

Well clear of the base, the two Hogs cut a big arc to the north, turning back to the east. The sun was almost to the horizon, and they had only a few minutes of light left. "Split now," Bull ordered. Goat peeled off to the right and took spacing as Bull headed back for the base. He checked his GPS and followed the bearing pointer to the spot in the jungle east of the base, a no-show target pinpointed by the counterbattery radar. He double-checked his switches and centered up on the target-designation box in his HUD. One last glance at the master arm to ensure that it was in the up position. He jinked and mashed the flare button on the throttle quadrant, sending a stream of flares out behind him. Then he mashed the pickle button on the stick, giving his consent to release when all delivery parameters were met. He climbed to four hundred feet, stabilized for a fraction of a second, and felt the six canisters of CBU-58s ripple off. Again he jinked hard as he dropped down to the deck.

"Your six is clear," Goat radioed. "I'm in."

"Reversing to the north," Bull radioed.

"Got you in sight," Goat replied. "I'm at your nine o'clock."

Bull's eyes darted to the left, and he saw Goat inbound to the target, crossing at a ninety-degree angle to his bomb run. Like Bull, he laid a string of flares out to decoy any SAM that might be coming his way. Under the jungle canopy, bright flashcs popped like flashbulbs as the last of Bull's bomblets exploded. Goat's deadly load separated cleanly, and he pulled off to the north, falling in behind Bull. A dazzling light bloomed behind them—a big secondary. "What the hell was that?" Bull radioed.

"Beats the shit out of me," Goat replied. "I didn't see a thing." The CBU-58 dispersed its bomblets over a wide area and was very effective against soft targets like unarmored vehicles—and people. But they didn't make for good secondaries. "Must've been big."

"Shooter-cover," Bull said. "I'm gonna take a look." He turned back to the target as Goat moved out to the left to cross behind him. Numerous fires and a column of smoke belched skyward, a beacon in the rapidly darkening sky. But there was enough light to see by. "Nothing but dog meat down there," Bull pronounced, pulling off.

"Roger on the puppy chow," Goat said.

Janice Clark studied the big situation chart, trying to make sense of it. She tuned out the voices behind her as Maggot and Waldo used the landlines connecting them to the shelters to debrief Bull and Goat. Since the mortar shelling had stopped, there was no doubt as to the effectiveness of the mission. But the dull thunder reaching into the command post spoke for itself. The fighting was coming closer. "Frustrating," she murmured to herself.

"Indeed it is," Pontowski said from behind her. "Supposedly we have the best communications system in the world, and here we sit, thirty miles from the front, without a clue what's happening."

She corrected him. "We know it's coming our way. Damn. I feel like we're stranded on a rock in the middle of a raging stream that's rushing past us." She turned to face him. "We could sure use a lifeline to get us off it."

"We'll get out of here," he assured her. "The shelling's stopped, runway's open, and we're ready to launch sorties at first light."

"General Pontowski, Colonel Clark," the controller called from the communications cab. "The tower reports a C-130 is inbound."

"How many you got ready to go?" Pontowski asked.

"Ninety-eight," she replied. "That leaves three hundred eighty-three."

"Let's go see them off," he said. They hurried out the door to where her driver was waiting. A light rain was falling as they sped toward the parking ramp. "I'm not going to miss this place at all," he told her.

"Did we make a difference?"

"We slowed them down a bit." They rode in silence, each deep in thought. The van skidded to a halt. "Let's do it," he said. Together they walked toward the C-130 that was taxiing in. A group of men emerged from the trees, running toward them as fuel bladders rolled out the back of the Hercules. It stopped, and the men charged up the cargo ramp. The lieutenant colonel hopped off the ramp and hurried over.

"I need empty bladders," he told them.

"What's going on?" Pontowski asked.

"I wish I knew," he told them. Even in the dark they could see he was fatigued to the point of collapse. "As best I can tell, SEAC is in a tactical retreat and giving ground slowly. Tactical missiles carrying nerve gas have hit every airfield and closed 'em down. We're landing on highways." He fished a message out of his pocket and handed it to them. "I received this about two hours ago." He snorted. "I don't think it's gonna happen." He looked at the C-130. "Got to go. I'll be back." He ran for the aircraft, which was starting to move. He jumped on the ramp and disappeared inside.

Pontowski watched the big cargo plane taxi out of the parking ramp. His head snapped up as the shrill shriek of an incoming artillery round split the air. "Incoming!" he shouted, dropping to the ground and dragging Clark with him. The C-130 disappeared in a blinding explosion. Pontowski rose up on all fours, shaken but unhurt. The Hercules was nothing but a mound of fire and smoke on the taxiway.

Clark staggered to her feet, raging in the night. "Goddamn you to hell!"

The command post was silent as a tomb, every eye on Pontowski as he sat, his chin on his chest. Finally he stood up. "Don't forget them," he said. His back straightened, and he studied the aircraft boards. "We got enough fuel now to fly thirty-five, maybe thirty-eight sorties. When we run out of gas, we can suit the pilots out in APE and recover at Tengah." APE was aircrew protective equipment that protected the wearer from chemical and nerve-gas agents.

"Got it," Maggot said, determined to make it happen.

How much more can I ask of them? Pontowski thought. He collapsed into a chair and ran through his options. *None good.* He pulled out the message Maggot had given him, and reread it for the third time. He knew what he had to do. "Colonel Clark," he said, "we need to talk. In private." She followed him into a back office and he handed her the message without a word.

She read it twice. "So the vanguard from the Third Marine Division is due to arrive no later than midnight Wednesday." She returned the message. "Remember what the lieutenant colonel said? He didn't think it was going to happen." She stared at him. "Because that requires airlift, and there's no place to land."

"Yes there is," Pontowski told her. "Here. I don't know why we haven't been hit with chemical or nerve gas, but I suspect it's because they haven't got the resources to do it, or they want to capture the base intact so they can use it."

She saw it immediately. "Which explains why they haven't cratered the runway. Or maybe they've got too many of their own people in the area."

"It doesn't matter," he said. "We're going to hold as long as we can." He hesitated, hating what he had to say. "Janice, it could get very ugly here. For you . . . all the women . . . personally. I want you out at the first opportunity."

She stood up to leave. "General, there's two other women on base besides myself. I'll make them the same offer, and they can decide for themselves. But as for me, I'll leave when you leave." She changed the subject. "By the way, Rockne wants to talk to us."

They found him sitting on the floor in the hall sound asleep. Boyca was curled up beside him, her head on his lap. She came alert when Pontowski and Clark approached. It was enough to wake Rockne, and he stood up. "I think we got an intruder on base," he told them. "A good one who is acting like a spotter for artillery. Think about it. For most of the time the mortar fire was purely harassment. Twice, when it really mattered, it got accurate as all hell. Once when the Hogs launched. If they hadn't've done a tactical split like they did, that mortar round would have nailed them. They were waiting for us to take off."

Clark's eyes narrowed. "And the second time was the C-130."

"Exactly," Rockne said. "I'm gonna find the little bastard."

Pontowski checked his watch. "You've got nine hours. I want to launch at first light."

"Got it." He spun around and left.

How much more can I ask? Pontowski wondered.

Washington, D.C.
Monday, October 11

Stephan Serick stumped down the hall, his usual grumpy self. But not even he could put a damper on the euphoria pervading the West Wing. The news from the Gulf was simply too good, too positive to let the secretary of state ruin the best Monday morning they had experienced in over a month. The president's secretary was waiting and immediately ushered him into the Oval Office for the 8:00 A.M. meeting. He was ninety seconds late. Turner was sitting in her rocker, surrounded by her key policy advisers. She patted the arm of the couch next to her, where she wanted him to sit. He dropped his bulk onto the couch, his cane upright between his knees. "My apologies, Madam President, but I was on the phone to the Chinese embassy."

Turner made a mental note. Serick had mentioned the phone call only because it warranted her attention. They would discuss it later. "First," Turner began, "I fully expect the honorable senator to continue with his October Surprise today." They all knew she was talking about Leland and his allegations about the late DCI. She looked directly at the secretary of defense, Robert Merritt. "That would be a mistake on his part, and I urge him not to go there."

"Madam President," Merritt replied, "I'll be glad to relay the message." It was the reason she had told him to be there. Bobbi Jo Reynolds, the head of the reelection campaign, smiled at him, reminding him of a shark—or Patrick Shaw.

"Well, Stephan," Turner said, turning back to the secretary of state, "do the Chinese have a message for us?"

Serick's hands had a death grip on his cane as he tried to strangle it. "Not a message, Madam President, a demand. The ambassador told me to be at their embassy at ten o'clock this morning to meet with Zou Rong."

The shock that went around the room was palpable, intense, and immediate. The Chinese demand was shattering, totally beyond the carefully scripted world of diplomacy. An ambassador simply did not give orders to high-ranking officials in the government he was accredited to. The president came to her feet and crossed her arms. She stood in front of them. "Oh, my. Did the ambassador indicate what the meeting was about?" Her voice was soft and reasonable.

"No, ma'am, he did not. But I suspect it involves Singapore and Malaysia."

"I see," she murmured, a concerned look on her face. "Well, I suppose we must respond."

"We can return the ambassador's letter," Serick ventured. The return of his formal letter of accreditation from the Chinese government was tantamount to declaring him persona non grata and breaking off relations with China.

"No, not yet. I want to appear reasonable—for now." She thought for a moment. "Is there a word in Chinese for 'piss off'?"

Taman Negara
Monday, October 11

A gentle rain misted down from the trees as the two men ghosted out of the dark. For a moment the incessant buzz of insects halted while they paused to make sure the way was clear. One spoke into the whisper mike pinned to his shoulder, and they moved on, bent under the weight of their heavy bergens. A voice spoke in the night. "Sergeant Hu, over here." The two men halted and spun around, weary and fatigued. A dark shadow materialized into human form as Tel moved away from a tree. Like them, he was wearing night-vision goggles and resembled some strange nocturnal creature.

Again the sergeant spoke into his whisper mike. A few moments later Colonel Sun led the rest of the team into the rendezvous. He gave an order, and the fifty-four men disappeared into the dark. "You made good time," Tel said. "I just arrived." He appreciated the distance they had traveled from their insertion point, the closest helicopters could get without drawing attention.

Sun slowly lowered his bergen. He was tired to the point of collapse, and his face was streaked with sweat. He pulled off his goggles. "How much farther?"

"Thirty miles" came the answer.

"How soon can we get there?" He swayed with exhaustion.

Tel worked the problem, balancing the distance with the threat. "Tomorrow night, if we're lucky. Probably sometime early Wednesday morning. We have to do the last ten miles at night to avoid patrols."

Sun cursed under his breath. "Not in time. F-16s are going to bomb the tunnels tomorrow, and we're supposed to mop up."

"I hope they've got something better than the A-10s," Tel said. "They put a missile into the entrance. Twenty minutes later missiles moved out."

"Then we'll do it alone," Sun said. "Those missiles have to be destroyed." There was steel in his voice. "As soon as possible."

Even in the dark Sun saw the surprise on Tel's face as the pieces came together—the heavy combat loads they were carrying, the urgency. "A daylight attack is suicide."

The colonel didn't answer.

thirty-five

Camp Alpha
Tuesday, October 12

The six team leaders who trooped down the ramp and into the BDOC at two o'clock in the morning were soaking wet. Jessica watched from the back wall as they removed their helmets and gathered around Rockne to report in. Rockne listened impassively as each leader confirmed that his team had not found a single intruder, much less one with a radio, GPS, and laser range finder. "Did you check every tree?" he asked.

The answer was unanimous. If they couldn't visually scan the branches, they sent someone up.

"Okay," Rockne said. "Good work. We had to check it out." He studied the map of the base as they left. "He's here. I can feel it in my bones."

Jessica joined him. "He's in the northern end of Whiskey Sector," she said. "Probably outside the fuel dump. That's where the trees are the heaviest and he can see the northern end of the runway, where the mortar shell landed and they got the C-130."

He agreed. "It makes sense. But you heard. It was a good sweep."

"Let me and Cindy take Boyca and have a look." Rockne didn't answer. "Wouldn't hurt anything," she cajoled.

"Do it. But I want my dog back."

The pickup crossed the runway at midfield and stopped at the intersection of the roads leading to the fuel dump to the north and the weapons storage area to the south. Jessica and Cindy hopped out of the back and adjusted their fighting loads. Cindy moved the ammunition cases so she could lie comfortably in the prone position if she had to, while Jessica got Boyca out of the passenger seat. They buckled their helmets and adjusted their night-vision goggles as Boyca strained at her leash, sensing action. Without a word, they moved into the night, Boyca ranging ahead of them.

It was slow going as they crossed back and forth through the trees, always careful to report their position so the teams manning the defensive fire positions wouldn't fire at them. At one DFP they found the two men asleep. "Do you have any idea what the Rock would do to you?" Jessica asked.

Cindy answered the question. "He'd rip your balls off and feed them to you for breakfast." One of the cops snorted in disbelief. "Believe it," Cindy warned. They continued the search, constantly moving northward, toward the minefield that formed a giant cap on the base. Finally they reached the edge of the minefield and sat down to rest. Cindy squatted against a tree, her M-16 lying across her lap. "Nothing," she said, resignation in her voice.

"It's the rain," Jessica said. "It washed away the scent." She radioed the BDOC and reported in. They sat in silence, totally defeated. Above them, the clouds scudded across the sky, breaking up in a gentle breeze and allowing moonlight to shine through. To the east the first glow of sunrise marked the horizon. Jessica removed her helmet and pulled off her heavy goggles. She wiped the sweat from her forehead. "I hate these damn things." Boyca came alert and growled, straining at her leash. Jessica looked in the same direction. "She's onto something."

A short burst of gunfire shattered the dark. "Oh, shit," Jessica said, jamming her helmet back on. She came to her feet and pressed her back against a tree, shielded from the gunfire. Another burst raked their position. Silence. Jessica counted to ten. Nothing. She counted to ten again. She keyed her radio to call the BDOC. "Rat Hole, this is Lima One." Her voice squeaked as adrenaline pumped through her. She forced herself to calm down and tried again. "Rat Hole, this is Lima One. We're taking fire."

Rockne answered. "Roger, Lima One. Are you in the same place?"

"That's affirmative," Jessica replied.

"Lima One," Rockne radioed, "help's on the way. If possible, proceed to the empty defensive fire position a hundred yards to the west, next to the runway, and occupy."

"Copy all," Jessica replied. She broke the connection as more gunfire erupted. Then it was quiet. "Go," Jessica ordered. They bolted for the DFP, but Boyca was moving in the opposite direction.

"Follow her," Cindy said.

"Oh, shit," Jessica whispered. She fell in behind Cindy as the dog moved through the trees. Boyca lay down on her stomach, her head up as she looked directly at a tree. A shot rang out, and the dirt kicked up inches in front of her nose. Jessica reacted automatically. She brought her M-16 up as she stepped from behind a tree and fired in the direction of the muzzle flash.

"You muthafucker!" Cindy yelled. "Leave the dog alone!" She fired Rambo style as she darted from tree to tree, closing on the shooter.

"Cindy! No! Take cover!"

The airman skidded behind a tree and stopped firing, her breath coming in ragged gasps. Cindy hit the eject button on her rifle and slapped in a fresh magazine. "He's running!" she shouted.

Jessica's head darted out from behind her tree and back, chancing a look. She caught a glimpse of a shadow moving in the rapidly improving light. "Got him!" She fired blindly. A short burst of gunfire in reply chewed at her tree. A coppery taste flooded Jessica's mouth as fear coursed through her. Cindy fired from a different spot, and Jessica realized that Cindy had moved, using her fire for cover. Now it was Jessica's turn to advance as Cindy fired. She darted to the next tree. Safe, she fired a short burst.

Boyca moved off to the left. "Stay!" Jessica commanded. The dog stopped, frozen in motion, a stationary target. A mistake. "Come!" Jessica shouted. The dog came to her as three slugs ripped into the ground where she had been a second before. Cindy fired a short burst from yet another position. A woman screamed in a language they didn't understand. Silence. Another shout, the same words. "Hands up!" Jessica shouted. A shadow moved, and the woman stood in the open, hands in the air. "Cover me," Jessica said. She moved toward the woman. Up close, she was staring into the face of a frightened young girl, no more than eighteen or nineteen years of age. She was wearing black tennis shoes and pants with a military green tunic. A web belt hung around her waist with a canteen, a radio, and an empty ammunition pouch. A small GPS hung on a lanyard around her neck. Jessica spun her around, frisked her, and pushed her to a spread-eagle position. "It's okay," she told Cindy.

With Cindy guarding the girl, Jessica searched until she found her weapon. "She was out of ammo." She keyed her radio. "Rat Hole, we've got the spotter." Before Rockne could answer, a single shot rang out. Jessica froze, stunned by the scene in front of her. Cindy had shot the girl in the head.

"Say status of prisoner," Rockne radioed.

Jessica paused, the coppery taste back. "Prisoner is dead."

"Search the body and proceed to the DFP as assigned," Rockne ordered. "We'll pick up the body later."

The two women stared at each other in silence as the sun cracked the horizon. The sound of a jet engine cranking to life rolled across the runway as another burst of gunfire from the eastern perimeter split the air. "Why?" Jessica whispered.

"I had buddies on the C-130."

Washington, D.C.
Monday, October 11

Marine One lifted off from the south lawn at exactly 6:18 P.M. for the forty-two-minute flight to Norfolk, Virginia. Turner settled into her chair and for a moment gazed out the window. Floodlights bathed the base of the Washington Monument, but the tip was caught in the fading evening twilight. *It's Tuesday morning in Malaysia,* she thought. The lights of Alexandria winked at her as they headed south. Across the narrow aisle Bobbi Jo ran through the campaign speech one last time before handing it to her.

"Patrick always called Norfolk 'Leland Loony Land,'" Bobbi Jo said, having second thoughts about the wisdom of delivering a critical campaign speech in the heart of the Confederacy.

"A lot of nice people live there," Turner said.

"I wonder how many of those 'nice people' are listening to him right now?" Bobbi Jo said. "He's on the local TV." Turner punched a button on the arm of her chair, and the small TV screen in front of her came to life with Leland's face. They listened for a moment, and Bobbi Jo snorted. "This is a preemptive strike if I ever heard one."

It was true. Leland was hitting hard, determined to undermine any positive effect the president's speech might have. ". . . involved the country in an unwise war, sacrificing our boys and girls on the altar of big oil."

Turner scanned her speech, committing key phrases to memory. *The defense of freedom is not optional.*

Leland continued to rant in the background. ". . . a morally degenerate administration unable to cleanse itself."

Another line from the speech burned with emotion. *So many have answered the call for service, and they should be honored for their sacrifices.*

Leland built to a climax. "This note in my hand"—the camera zoomed in to read the printing—"was deliberately buried by the administration to cover up the suicide of the director of Central Intelligence!" The camera panned to Leland's face and caught the iron set of his jaw.

The two women exchanged glances, and Bobbi Jo let out a war whoop that filled the passenger compartment. "There is a God!"

Turner handed the speech back to her and looked out the window as the Sikorsky S-61V settled to earth on the helipad near the convention center while a high school band struck up "Hail to the Chief." The entrance door lowered, and two Marine guards came to attention. As if to prove the impossible, their salutes were sharper than usual as the president descended the steps. She nodded, her way of acknowledging the salute. "Thank you, Madam President," one said, breaking all protocols. But there would be no reprimand. She stepped onto the red carpet, and the two Marines turned to face her back, ready to be of instant service—and to protect her at all costs.

A reporter yelled, "What about Malaysia?"

A second joined in. "Can you answer Leland's charges?"

But the crowd chanting "Maddy, Maddy!" drowned him out. "MADDY!" It grew to a roar as she entered the building.

Bobbi Jo joined the press pool and stood by Liz Gordon, CNC-TV's star political reporter. Neither could speak over the commotion. Finally the noise died away. "Who would've believed a reception like this?" Gordon said. "Right in the heart of Leland land. But I don't think it's going to last. Enjoy it while you can." Bobbi Jo didn't respond. "Leland is going to be on the front page tomorrow," Gordon said, egging her on. Still no answer. "You can't ignore him."

Bobbi Jo handed her a tape cassette. "You need to listen to this, in private. And I assure you, it is authentic." She turned to follow the president inside.

Camp Alpha
Tuesday, October 12

The sergeant popped out of the command post's communications cab. "General, a C-130 is inbound, due to land in twenty minutes."

Pontowski glanced at the master clock on the wall: 0809 hours. He looked around for Clark but couldn't see her. "Relay that inbound to Colonel Clark," he said, heading for the entrance. Outside, the thunder of artillery rolled over him. "Damn," he muttered. It was too close for comfort and getting louder. He jumped into his pickup and raced for the hardened aircraft shelter where Clark was marshaling the evacuation. He drove around to the backside and stopped. A guard saw him and banged on the small entrance door to let him in. "How's it going?" Pontowski asked.

The young security cop tried to make a show of it but failed miserably. "Sir, I'm scared as all hell." He made a vague motion in the direction of the thunder.

"It's okay to be scared," Pontowski told him. "Just don't freeze." The sound of two Hogs taking off demanded their attention. In his mind's eye Pontowski saw their gear come up as they turned out of the pattern. They'd be back on the ground about the time the C-130 landed.

The door swung open. "Sir," the cop said, "there's a rumor going around that we've been hung out to dry and ain't getting out of here."

"We're getting out of here," Pontowski promised. He stepped inside the shelter, where Clark was waiting.

"I got the message, sir. I've almost got everybody here. My driver's out collecting a few more."

Pontowski nodded. That explained why he didn't see her van and driver. "How many you got going out?"

She checked her clipboard. "So far, a hundred and nine." She handed him the clipboard as the entrance door opened and six pilots walked in. "Make that one-fifteen," Clark said, correcting the total.

He studied the numbers, worried about who was left: 184 maintenance troops, 55 support personnel, 9 medics, 133 cops, and 22 pilots. He changed the total remaining to 403 and returned the clipboard. The number beat at him—403. Could he get them all out? For the first time he wasn't sure.

Taman Negara
Tuesday, October 12

Kamigami lay motionless as insects buzzed around him. One landed on his forehead and crawled along his brow, finally moving onto the binoculars jammed against his eyes as he swept the area below him, watching for movement in the tunnel entrances. Nothing. In the distance he heard the sound of jets, and he checked his watch. The F-16s were late. The sharp double-barreled crack of two SAMs launching drifted down the shallow valley. He made a mental note that they were employed in pairs. Then he heard a distant, very faint explosion. He scanned the sky and saw a tumbling fireball. At the same time a shadow flashed across his line of sight as a rapid-fire antiaircraft artillery battery opened up.

He dropped the binoculars in time to see a dark object streaking toward the tunnel entrances. Experience told him it was a smart bomb, either laser or infrared guided. It flew right into the center entrance and exploded as the antiaircraft battery continued to sweep the sky. Now he could hear a single jet receding into the distance. Again he swept the skies, looking for a parachute. There wasn't one. He made another mental note—one aircraft and one pilot exchanged for one tunnel.

The antiaircraft battery ceased firing, and he waited. The cough of a diesel engine starting echoed out of a tunnel. Soon he heard the unmistakable sound of clanking treads as a bulldozer went to work. The sound of the laboring diesel grew louder, and a mound of dirt and debris was pushed out of the central tunnel. Dark smoke from the exhaust mushroomed out as the bulldozer emerged. The driver, wearing a respirator, continued to clear the entrance. Finally he was finished and pulled off the mask. Behind him, a transporter/erector with a missile emerged into the morning sunlight.

Kamigami made another mental note: there had been no exchange. The missile disappeared into the jungle, reminding him of a giant slug he'd once stepped on by accident. He decided to do it again, this time intentionally.

thirty-six

Camp Alpha
Tuesday, October 12

Janice Clark felt her heart pound as the C-130 taxied for the runway. The image of the last one burning on the runway was seared into her mind, and fear held her tight. But she couldn't look away. "Come on, come on," she whispered. The big bird turned onto the active runway, pointing to the south. The pilot paused and ran the engines up, a heavy drone against the erratic beat of artillery fire. "GO!" she shouted, unable to contain her worry. The pilot released the brakes, and the cargo plane moved forward, accelerating quickly to takeoff speed. The pilot honked back on the yoke and lifted off. Immediately the gear came up as he leveled off thirty feet above the runway and accelerated. Barely able to breathe, Clark watched as the Hercules pulled up and turned sharply to the west, its right wingtip a few feet above the treetops. Then it was out of sight.

She ran for her van. But her driver was already coming her way, and he slammed the vehicle to a halt, pausing only long enough for her to pile in. He raced for the command post. Her radio came alive as the tower announced that an A-10 was inbound with battle damage and a wounded pilot. They passed a crash truck headed for the runway. The ambulance was right behind it. "Follow them," she commanded. Her driver spun the van around and hit the throttle.

Doc Ryan was standing beside the ambulance when the van pulled up at the midfield intersection. Clark got out and joined him. "There," he said, pointing to the west. She saw the Hog and held her breath. It seemed to hang in the sky as smoke and flames trailed out behind. A pickup truck drove up, and Waldo got out. "Why doesn't he eject?" Ryan asked.

"It's Goat," Waldo answered. "He's wounded pretty bad. Probably can't survive an ejection. The jet's in manual reversion, but he's gonna try to land it."

"Where's he wounded?" Ryan asked.

"A round shattered the canopy," Waldo replied. "Tore up his right shoulder, split his helmet. He's flying with his left hand." They stood there, all hoping or praying in their own way. Waldo's left hand moved, trying to control the throttles. "Push it up!" he shouted as the Warthog turned final. But he knew what was coming, and his hand fell helplessly to his side. "Oh, no," he moaned. The jet never rolled out of the turn. Instead it fell away to the left, arcing toward the ground. The canopy flew off, and the rocket pack kicked the Aces II ejection seat out of the doomed bird with an eleven-G kick. The seat cleared the bird, and the drogue chute streamed out behind. The Hog crashed into the trees and fireballed as the pilot separated from the seat and the main chute deployed. Waldo looked away.

"He made it," Clark said. Waldo didn't answer and only stared at the ground.

"Oh, Lord," Ryan moaned as the fireball sucked in the descending parachute.

The thunder was growing closer when Clark reached the command post. For a moment she stood and looked at the column of smoke rising out of the trees where Goat had died. A loud explosion rolled over her, and she felt the ground shudder. A cannon round had hit the base. One of the cops in the DFP outside the command post waved her on, and she ran for the entrance, holding her holster to keep it from bouncing. She skidded through the door, and it banged closed behind her. She hurried into the main room and sat down at her console. An orchid was lying on her desk. She looked at Maggot and Pontowski. "Where did that come from?" There was a catch in her voice.

"Your driver," Pontowski answered. He handed her a bottle of water. "We're talking to Chief Rockne on line one." She punched at the button and listened.

"There's only one battery in range doing the shelling," Rockne explained.

"Do you know the location?" Maggot asked.

"According to the counterbattery radar, they're shooting and scooting. We should get another round or two in twenty or thirty minutes."

Pontowski studied the grim story on the aircraft status board. The AVG had arrived with twenty A-10s but was now down to fifteen. Four Hogs were still trapped on the ground at Tengah Air Base, and they had eleven on base. However, only ten were good to go, and one was a hangar queen. But the real problem was fuel. "How many sorties we got left?"

"Twenty-eight," Maggot replied. "Unless more fuel came in on that C-130."

Clark shook her head in answer. "No fuel. We got a hundred and nine out." She subtracted Goat's name from her count. "Two hundred ninety-three to go."

Pontowski's eyes narrowed. "If it's only one battery, we can kill it."

The two artillery rounds came in quick succession, falling well short of the DFP on the northern side of the base, where Jessica and Cindy had taken refuge with Boyca. Cindy checked in with the BDOC, confirming that the rounds had fallen outside the base. Across the runway the big doors of a shelter cranked back, and a Hog fast-taxied for the runway. The pilot, a young captain called Stormy, never slowed as he took the active runway at midfield. A green light blinked at him from the control tower hidden in the trees. On top of the tower the small antenna of the recently installed counterbattery radar spun at a high rate, searching for more incoming artillery fire. Stormy firewalled the throttles, taking off to the south. The Hog came unglued with two thousand feet of runway remaining, and Stormy snatched the gear up. Immediately he turned hard to the left before turning back to the south. He disappeared over the treetops with a single radio transmission: "Stormy's clear."

The command post monitored the radio call, and a sergeant marked the boards. "I hope this works," Clark said.

Pontowski's voice was flat, without emotion. "They may be able to shoot, but they can't scoot fast enough." Now they had to wait for the next salvo. It came twenty-one minutes later. The controller in the tower instantly transmitted a set of coordinates. "The radar got him," Pontowski said.

Stormy did not acknowledge the radio transmission from the tower as his fingers punched the coordinates into his GPS. The number one bearing pointer and range indicator in his horizontal-situation indicator cycled to the target along with the display in his HUD. He turned toward the target-designation box in the HUD. When the box was on his nose, he flicked the radio button on the throttle quadrant. "Stormy's in." He flew across the base at fifty feet. Below him, Jessica and Cindy covered their ears, rocked by the noise that pounded at them. Cindy poked her head up in time to see the Hog clear the minefield as it headed to the north. Stormy jinked hard, never holding the same heading for more than two seconds. He was vaguely aware of a rocket plume flashing behind him, a Grail launched way too late. His left forefinger pushed the flare-dispensing button on the throttle quadrant, and six flares popped out behind in time to decoy a second missile that he never saw.

The range indicator on his horizontal-situation display indicated seven miles to go. The target box started to move down his HUD. He climbed a few feet, trying for a visual sighting. Nothing. He climbed a few feet more and saw a muzzle flash at his ten o'clock position. He jinked hard and descended. Without consciously thinking about it, he marked the location. He might have a chance to settle that score later.

"Tallyho the fox!" he radioed. The target was at his two o'clock at two miles, exactly where it was supposed to be. Figures were scrambling furiously around an artillery tube, hooking it up for transport while others threw equipment into the back of a truck. He popped to twelve hundred feet and rolled in as he hit the flare button again, sending more flares out in his wake. He hit the pickle button and waited. Six Mark-82 Airs rippled off, walking across the gun emplacement below him. The truck was racing for safety, shedding its camouflage as it accelerated.

He pulled back on the stick and kept his Hog low to the ground as he escaped to the north. Once clear of the blast, he ruddered the jet back around and looked for the truck. It was still racing down the dirt road, its back end on fire and streaming smoke. He arced in on a perfect strafing run and mashed the trigger. The big cannon gave off a burring sound as he fired forty-eight rounds, literally cutting the truck in half. He pulled off and came around, selecting CBUs. He walked them across the area, ensuring that the message was received.

"Scratch one artillery tube," he radioed.

"Rog," Maggot answered. "RTB. Save the gas."

Disappointed that he couldn't go after the muzzle flash, Stormy turned south. He landed four minutes later and taxied into his shelter with over half his fuel remaining.

"General Pontowski," the controller in the communications cab called. "A U.S. communications advance team has arrived in Singapore, and we're back in contact." He handed Pontowski a stack of four messages. "More's coming."

Pontowski settled down to read them, only to jump to his feet. "The dumb—" He cut off the obscenity that was on the tip of his tongue. "They want us to increase our sortie rate and hold at all costs." He stormed back and forth.

"Who ordered the hold?" Maggot asked.

Pontowski checked the message. "The national command authority."

"Does that mean the president?"

"What it means is that someone in Washington hasn't got a fuckin' clue. Screw that noise. We're getting out of here."

"General," Clark said from her console, "the BDOC is reporting heavy small-arms fire on the eastern perimeter." She stepped to the base map on the wall and circled in red the DFPs that were taking fire on the far side of the base. "Any chance we might get a Hog to return the favor?" she asked, thinking of the artillery battery they had silenced.

The sergeant waved another message at Pontowski. "Sir, Tengah was just hit by another missile with nerve gas. And we got a request for immediate close air support." His eyes widened when he realized where the request came from. He handed the message over and retreated into the communications cab.

Pontowski read it and passed it on to Maggot. "We got to do it."

Maggot never hesitated. He punched at his console. "Basher One, scramble. Basher Two, scramble. After takeoff contact FAC, call sign

Bravo Zero One, on one-two-four-point-oh. If unable to recover at home plate, your alternate is Hang Nadim Air Base, heading one forty-five degrees at seventy."

"Basher One scrambling now," Waldo replied, his voice sounding bored and matter-of-fact.

"Stalwart fellow," Maggot said sotto voce. But no one laughed.

Four minutes later Waldo radioed, "Basher One and Two rolling."

Maggot dialed in the forward air controller's radio frequency to listen. "I'd rather be up there than here," he muttered to himself.

"Roger that," Pontowski said, totally agreeing with him.

They listened as Waldo checked in with the FAC. Both men came to their feet when they heard Bravo Zero One say, "Tanks have broken through south of Paloh."

"Son of a bitch," Maggot said. "That's fifteen miles from here."

"Jammer," Waldo radioed to his wingman, "ingress line abreast. You work west of the railroad tracks, I'll take the east side. One pass, egress to the west. I'll fall in behind and cover your six."

"Copy all," Jammer replied.

Pontowski recognized the tactics Waldo was employing. "They're going in with Mavericks," he said to no one.

"Beats getting up close and personal with the gun," Maggot told him.

"Waldo, rifle," Waldo transmitted as he launched his first Maverick. His voice was higher-pitched, and the words were coming fast. "Waldo, rifle." His second Maverick was on the way.

"Jammer, rifle," Jammer radioed as he launched a Maverick.

"Shack!" Waldo called as his first missile hit home.

Jammer was back. "Jammer, rifle." His second Maverick was on the way.

"Jammer! Break left! Trip A at your six!"

Jammer's voice was labored as he pulled four G's to avoid the stream of high-explosive shells. "Coming from the flatbed on the tracks." Then, "I'm clear."

Pontowski and Maggot visibly relaxed. "I got the fucker in sight," Waldo said. "I'm in."

The tension was back, and in his mind's eye Pontowski could see Waldo's Hog as it rolled in on an antiaircraft battery firing at Jammer's escaping A-10. The wait seemed to take forever. "Scratch one Trip A,"

Waldo said. "Winchester Mavericks." He had expended all his antitank missiles.

"Same-oh," Jammer replied.

"RTB home plate," Waldo ordered.

Four minutes later the two jets taxied clear of the active and raced for their shelters. The mission had taken less than twelve minutes, they had expended four Mavericks and two Mark-82 Airs, killed four tanks, obliterated an antiaircraft artillery battery, and cut the railroad tracks in the process. Pontowski and Maggot exchanged glances in relief, a visual high-five. But Clark was on the phone to the BDOC and brought them back to reality. "The cops are bringing in two casualties from across the runway." She listened for a moment. "Whiskey Sector's perimeter is heating up. It looks like they're coming from the east."

The Pentagon
Monday, October 11

Marine One approached from the south as it returned from Richmond, and touched down on the helipad outside the River Entrance. General Wilding was waiting and saluted when the president climbed down. "Thank you for coming, Mrs. President." She nodded, and he dropped the salute. "I understand the folks in Richmond gave you a warm welcome."

She smiled graciously. "Southern hospitality at its best." It was classic understatement, for the campaign speech had been an unqualified success. "But they did seem receptive."

Wilding couldn't contain himself. "I'm quite sure you'll find an equally receptive audience here." They walked in silence to the NMCC, each deep in thought. Inside, she stepped into the battle cab overlooking the main floor. Below her, the floor was crowded with people, all looking up and awaiting her arrival. Applause swept the room and rattled the glass in front of her, drowning out any conversation. Finally she had to lean over and speak into the boom mike in front of her.

"Thank you," she said. Her voice echoed from the loudspeakers. She waited for the clamor to subside. "I hope this applause is for yourselves and your comrades. You deserve it, not me." She stood as the big room thundered an ovation. The UIF had unconditionally surrendered, and the fighting had stopped.

Turner sat down and closed her eyes. The war in the Gulf had stopped three hours short of the thirty-eighth day, at the cost of 3,114 lives. She corrected herself—3,114 American lives. For a moment a raging doubt assailed her. Was it worth it? She put the question aside for the historians to debate from their safe and secure towers with all the benefits of hindsight and time. Now she had to win the war in Asia. Her eyes opened. "Singapore and Malaysia?" she murmured.

Wilding spoke into his telephone, and the map on the big screen at the front of the room cycled to the Far East. It zoomed in on southern Malaysia and changed again to a computer-generated cartographic display. The map came alive with strings of lights snaking down the peninsula, crawling toward the island city. An illuminated arrow highlighted the map as Wilding spoke. "We now have a Joint Rivet aircraft in place and monitoring the ground situation. This is a real-time downlink. As you can see, the PLA has broken out here"—the pointer circled the village of Paloh—"and is advancing on the American contingent at Camp Alpha." The pointer paused over the base. "The AVG is still launching sorties flying close air support for the Singapore Army and have been instrumental in slowing their advance. However, four aircraft have been diverted to Tengah." The pointer moved onto Singapore. "Advanced communications and command teams have arrived at SEAC and are assessing the situation. We have parachuted decontamination teams and equipment into these air bases." The pointer circled Changi and Tengah. "We should have them open within twenty-four hours."

"But until that happens," the president said, "we have no place to land." She paused. "Have you considered paratroops?"

"Yes, ma'am, we have. We have elements of the First Airborne en route from the Gulf. Indonesia has given us permission to land and stage out of Djakarta"—the pointer circled the airport—"some five hundred nautical miles away. But I'm hesitant to commit them piecemeal."

Turner stood and studied the flashing lights on the main map as they moved slowly southward. "How long can the AVG hold?" she asked.

"I can't answer with certainty," Wilding replied. "We are getting reports of small-unit action around the base." Silence. "Madam President, we may have waited too long. I should have recommended a withdrawal when we had time." She looked at him, an unbelievable sadness in her eyes, and shook her head. He stared at her, at last understanding.

"You said seventy-two hours," she reminded her general.

"Yes, ma'am," he replied.

Georgetown
Tuesday, October 12

It was after midnight when Mazie arrived at the opulent town house. As expected, her hostess was waiting at the side door. "What wonderful news from the Gulf," she gushed. Mazie smiled in return but said nothing as they walked up the stairs. Instead of turning to the right and into the library, her hostess led the way to the guest suite. She knocked twice and opened the door. "Please ask if you need anything," she cooed. Then she closed the door behind the national security adviser and sighed. "La," she murmured to herself.

Herbert von Lubeck was sitting in an easy chair and reading. He rose to his feet in a graceful motion when he saw Mazie, and came to her. He was wearing an open-necked shirt, slacks much too casual for public wear, and hand-sewn Italian loafers. He took her hand and held it. "It was a very close thing," he told her. "My government was under enormous pressure to halt the advance." He didn't release her hand.

"Please relay President Turner's thanks," she said. "Your armored units were magnificent."

"I do hope you are as successful in the Far East. Unfortunately, there is little we can do to help you there." She nodded at his concern. "Perhaps we can broker a prisoner exchange," he added. "So unfortunate that President Turner did not withdraw your AVG in time."

"She had no intention of withdrawing them," Mazie told him.

Von Lubeck dropped her hand and sat down, stunned by the revelation. *"Du lieber Gott,"* he whispered. "They're a hostage force." The pieces all fell into place. "She will sacrifice them."

"If she has to," Mazie said.

His respect for Turner went over the moon. She was, without doubt, a superb politician and strategist, able to enter the world of power politics and force her will on vain and vicious tyrants. He elevated her to his pantheon of statesmen, above FDR and nudging Bismarck for first place. "It could mean a wider war."

"I doubt it. Sooner or later the Chinese will realize what's happened."

"So simple," von Lubeck said. "American casualties guarantee American involvement when the political situation would otherwise prevent it." He looked at her with admiration. "You were part of this?" A little nod in answer. "Was it your idea to involve my country?" Another nod of her head. His face lit up. "There is always a quid pro quo."

"Really?" she answered, arching an eyebrow and playing the game. "Which is?"

"You." He was deadly serious and not playing games. "We will have beautiful children."

Mazie was shocked. "I'm married."

"Divorce him. We will create a dynasty for the new century."

For a moment they stood frozen in time. Then she stepped out of her shoes and led him into the bedroom.

thirty-seven

Camp Alpha
Tuesday, October 12

We got wounded coming across the runway," Clark said. She paused, listening to the radio traffic on the security police net. "One litter case and two walking."

"Got it," Pontowski said. He glanced at the status board. They had ten A-10s good to go, but fuel was still the limiting factor. "Maggot, how many sorties we got left?"

"Twenty-six, sorta." They both understood the "sorta" to mean that three birds were down to half fuel.

"Top 'em up," Pontowski ordered.

Clark came to her feet. "We're taking mortar rounds on the taxiway in Yankee Sector." She fought the panic that ripped at her. The heart of her base—the aircraft shelters, the medical station, command post, and the BDOC—were all in Yankee Sector.

"Are the shelters buttoned down?" Pontowski asked, equally worried.

"That's affirmative," she answered.

"We ain't gonna be scrambling jets if we're taking mortar rounds," Maggot said, telling him the obvious.

Pontowski thought for a moment. "We got four jets at Tengah. They got fuel but no munitions. How they doing on the gun?" Each Hog carried 1,170 rounds of thirty-millimeter ammunition when fully loaded. "We might get a sortie or two out of them."

"I'll find out," Maggot replied. He punched up the line to the communications cab and went to work.

Clark stood up. "The BDOC reports two DFPs are falling back." She hurried to the base map and drew slashing red *X*'s through two defensive fighting positions on the eastern perimeter. She pressed her headset to her head, trying to understand the chatter coming in. Then she lost it and screamed, "A tank's in Whiskey and firing!" A dull thud rocked the command post, and debris laced with dust cascaded from the ceiling.

"What was that?" someone yelled.

"We're gonna die!"

Pontowski stood up and took command. "I hope not. I haven't shaved today." The remark was so totally unexpected that everyone looked at him in surprise. Then Maggot snickered. "Calm down, folks," Pontowski said. "My guess is that we took a direct hit that dudded. So we got lucky. Now let's kill the bastard before he does it again. Janice, call Rockne and get a fire team on that tank. Maggot, get a Hog airborne outa Tengah that's got some thirty mike-mike left and hose the shit outa him." He stood there, defiant. "Come on, folks. Make it happen."

The two sergeants stared at each other. "The Rock wants us to do what?" Paul Travis asked.

"Take out that damn tank," Jake Osburn answered, looking at his radio in disbelief. "I didn't join up to be a fuckin' hero." They looked toward the clanking sound coming from the trees. "I think it's going away," Jake said.

Paul picked up the LAW, a light antitank weapon, leaning against the side of their dugout. "Then a HEAT round up his ass will get his attention." He was out of their DFP and running for cover, the LAW in one hand, his M-16 in the other.

"Shit," Jake muttered. He grabbed his M249, better known as a SAW, or squad automatic weapon, and followed his buddy. They were a team, honed by years of training and playing weekend football, and they instinctively moved together. Paul skidded to cover behind a tree and chanced a peek. His hands flashed, motioning Jake to his far left. He waited and looked again. Now he could see the tank. It was not what he expected, but smaller, with a forward-mounted turret. The barrel was raised and firing randomly across the runway. He counted six men moving with it. He motioned to Jake and darted through the trees, trying to get closer. He needed to get within two hundred yards to get in range. But half that distance would significantly increase the probability of a kill. And he understood probability and range. On a football field a hundred yards is a far distance. In combat it qualifies as up close and personal. But thanks to countless football games, he knew exactly what a hundred yards looked like. He crouched and checked the LAW. It was ready. Jake crawled into position and set the bipod for his SAW. He signaled he was ready.

Paul lay on the ground and sighted the weapon. He depressed the trigger on top, and the sixty-six-millimeter round fired. At the same time Jake opened fire, spraying the area and cutting into the six soldiers. He emptied the magazine and pulled back while Paul rolled behind a tree. He grabbed his M-16 while Jake slapped a fresh magazine into his SAW. Again Jake signaled he was ready. Paul shoved his weapon around the trunk and squeezed off a short burst, firing blindly. A fraction of a second later Jake was moving, firing Rambo style. Paul ran for the next tree and crouched, his breath coming in ragged pants. He chanced a look. Smoke poured from the engine compartment at the rear of the tank, ample indication that the LAW had worked as advertised. A submachine gun clattered, driving him back behind the tree as splinters cut into his face and shattered his goggles. He ripped them off and could see again.

Jake fired again. Now all was silent except for a whirring sound. Paul looked and froze. The sound was coming from the tank's turret as it traversed toward Jake. "Run!" Paul yelled. Jake started to run, but it was too late. The whirring sound stopped as Jake dove for cover. The cannon fired, and the round passed inches above Jake's head. A burst of submachine gun fire cut into the tree where Paul was, pinning him down. The turret whirred again, slewing toward him, and Paul knew he was dead.

But Jake had other ideas. He was up and firing. The submachine gun fell silent as the turret turned. Paul broke from the tree and ran for all he was worth, but the turret kept coming. "Buttonhook!" Jake yelled. Paul jerked to his left as the cannon fired. It missed.

The tank exploded.

The sharp crack of projectiles traveling faster than the speed of sound reached them. Then they heard the GAU-8 cannon firing, a loud buzzing sound. The last to arrive was the Warthog itself. It flew over, rocking its wings. Paul gasped for air. "Fuckin' silent death," he muttered. There was no other way to describe what it meant to be on the receiving end of a Warthog's cannon.

Jake walked through the carnage, poking at the bodies and checking the tank. He kept mumbling "Son of a bitch" over and over. He stopped and threw Paul a triumphant look. "Where's the cheerleaders when you need them?"

Maggot pressed the transmit button to acknowledge the radio call from the Warthog. "Chief, this is Gopher Hole. Good work on the tank." He gave Pontowski a thumbs-up as he spoke. "Understand you're Winchester ammo. Recover at Hang Nadim." Maggot relaxed for a moment and then was back at it. "That leaves three Hogs at Tengah."

"We're still taking sporadic gunfire on the eastern perimeter," Clark reported. "But it's quiet everywhere else. Hold on." She listened to the voice in her headset. "We have problems at the med station. Too many wounded. Doc Ryan needs to make room."

"How many's he got?" Pontowski asked.

"Twelve," Clark answered. "Maybe we can bring some here."

"Do it," Pontowski said.

Clark hit the phone button, but the line linking her to the medical station was dead. "Line's down," she said. "I better go see what's happening."

"Be careful," Pontowski said.

Jessica stroked Boyca's head while she fed her the last of the Nibbles in her butt bag. "Sorry, girl," she said. "That's it." She stood up and scanned the minefield with her binoculars. "I got movement on the far side." Cindy stood beside her and squinted. She was looking almost directly into the afternoon sun and shaded her eyes. She reached for her M-16. "What are you doing?" Jessica asked.

"Gonna waste the bastard." She laid the barrel across a sandbag.

"He's too far. Maybe a quarter of a mile." The M-16's effective range for a point target was half that distance. "Why draw attention?"

Cindy sighted the weapon and waited. "It won't matter if he's dead."

"Give it up," Jessica said. She set back down and stroked the dog's head. But Cindy didn't move. Jessica fell asleep.

Her eyes snapped open at the sharp crack of a single shot. "What the hell?"

"Got him," Cindy said, sinking down beside her. Jessica stood and scanned the minefield. A body lay crumpled on the far side. Sporadic gunfire echoed from the east, well over a mile away. The distinctive shriek of artillery passing overhead split the air.

Taman Negara
Tuesday, October 12

Kamigami pushed through the heavy brush in the river valley, following the grinding sounds coming from the missile transporter. Bravo Team's sergeant was right behind him and spoke in English. "It sounds like the transmission's going out." Kamigami agreed and checked the time—1607 hours. They had been tracking the missile for five hours, keeping back from the road and hiding in the jungle. Although the big transporter/erector/launcher was going only at two miles an hour as it moved down the rough track, it had been a constant slog to keep up. The sound stopped.

Kamigami called for a much-needed break while he checked his GPS. He shook his head. "It's not the best location," he told the sergeant. "But they could launch from here."

"Maybe they don't have a choice," the sergeant said, thinking about the grinding sound. Then a different sound echoed through the brush. "Maybe we should take a look."

"Go," Kamigami said. "Rendezvous here." The sergeant motioned for a corporal to follow him, and the two men disappeared into the brush. Kamigami studied his chart and spanned off distances. He thought for a moment and pointed to the team's sniper. "What's your max range?"

The corporal answered with the maximum effective range of his rifle. "A thousand meters."

"To hit a moving target?" Kamigami asked.

"Seven hundred meters," the corporal replied. Just under half a mile.

"Think you can do twelve hundred?" Kamigami asked, setting the challenge. The corporal's eyes were wide, for his buddies had heard. "*I* can't do it," Kamigami said, letting him off the hook. He shrugged in resignation. "Just a thought. It's an impossible shot."

The corporal stiffened. "I can make it."

It was exactly what Kamigami wanted to hear. He pointed to his chart and circled the valley's ridgeline. "Take a backup and go here ASAP. If they launch, try for a single shot to the aft end of the missile. The rocket motor will cover the sound. Rendezvous back here. Go." The corporal heard the urgency in his voice and quickly moved out with another corporal. Kamigami sat down to wait, honestly doubting if the sniper could make the ridgeline in time, much less make the shot. But they had to try. He went to sleep.

"Sir," a soft voice said, waking him. It was the sergeant, back from reconnoitering the missile. "They've erected the missile and are preparing to launch. The crew is wearing heavy protective equipment and gas masks. They are being very careful, and it's slowing them down. I think it's a chemical warhead."

"Most likely nerve gas," Kamigami said. He reached for his radio to call the sniper who was still climbing the ridge. Then he thought better of it. The corporal would make the shot if he could. He went back to sleep.

Free of the heavy vegetation that tore at his clothes, the corporal scampered up the last fifty feet to the crest of the ridge. A loud roar echoed up from the valley as he pulled his rifle out of its protective case. He snapped on the telescopic sight, ignoring the smoke belching from the valley floor. He slapped a ten-shot magazine into the British-made weapon and charged a single round as the missile lifted out of the smoke. He rolled into a prone shooting position and pressed his cheek against the stock as he sighted. Through the scope he saw the missile as it slowly rose and accelerated. He squeezed the trigger.

Camp Alpha
Tuesday, October 12

The security cop manning the counterbattery radar in the control tower saw the missile on the radarscope the moment it came into range. He hit the warning siren and stepped on the button to transmit over the security net as a loud wail carried over the base. "Incoming missile!" He fell to the floor, his arms over his helmet.

The CSS-7 missile arcing down had been built in 1999 and originally deployed opposite Taiwan as part of the buildup to intimidate the feisty islanders. But it had not been properly sheltered, and the sea air had caused small spots of corrosion in the aft section, near the motor mounts. Sloppy annual inspections had not caught the corrosion, as it was mostly on the small clips that held the wiring harness in place. The sniper's single bullet had passed through the missile, causing little damage, but it did cut one of the wiring clips. Combined with the heavy vibration experienced during launch, two more of the corroded clips broke free and allowed the wire bundle to flop free. The gimbaling motor pushed the wire bundle to one side, causing a slight imbalance.

It was a very minor thing—but enough to cause an imperceptible wobble. As the missile accelerated on its downward trajectory, the wobble turned into a major vibration, overloading the guidance gyros. The missile tumbled and corkscrewed through the sky.

The security cop lifted his head and looked at the radarscope. The missile had hit harmlessly to the east. He pressed the all-clear button.

Inside the command post, Maggot had to make a decision. They had enough fuel for sixteen more sorties and four urgent requests for close air support. Since A-10s always fought in pairs, that meant launching eight aircraft, which left two on base with enough fuel for eight more sorties. But if they did it right and the Hogs recovered with fuel still on board, they might be able to squeeze out ten or twelve sorties and still have enough to fly to safety. It was worth a chance. "Boss," he said to Pontowski, "we can scramble eight and recover here. But it's gonna be tight."

"Do it," Pontowski replied. Maggot scrambled the first two jets as Clark ran into the room.

"We got two Pumas inbound," she announced. "We can evacuate the wounded."

Pontowski hated what he had to do. "Walking wounded only." She stared at him, demanding an explanation. "Litters take up too much room," he said. "We'd be lucky to get eight stretcher cases loaded. But we can get forty walk-ons out."

"Then I'll prop 'em up," she shot back.

"That works," he said. "Talk to Doc Ryan and make it happen." She hurried out. "Be careful," he called. He checked the time—less than an hour to sunset. Could he evacuate the AVG during the night? He could always fly the Hogs out at the last minute, and the helicopters proved that SEAC had not abandoned them. But SEAC simply couldn't supply enough airlift to get everyone out. Could they escape and evade over land? He had to talk to Rockne. But equally important, he had to get out and be seen, talk to the troops and sense their morale. "Maggot, I'm going to take a short tour. I'll start at the BDOC and go from there. You got the stick."

"Got it," Maggot replied, scrambling two more A-10s.

Pontowski walked outside and spoke to the two security cops manning the DFP. No problems there, but one cop did wonder why it had gone so quiet. That's when it hit Pontowski—all he heard was the sound of two Hogs taxiing out. He hurried over to the BDOC, where he found Rockne bent over the base defense chart. "The command post said you were on the way," Rockne told him. "Bad news. SEAC is reporting nerve gas a mile to the east." He pointed to an area beyond the base's tactical perimeter. "As long as the wind holds from the west, we'll be okay."

"Make sure everyone is suited out," Pontowski said.

"I got patrols out right now checking on everyone." He paused. "You know what I think, sir? That missile that missed was carrying nerve gas and hit right in the middle of their main force. They assholed their own troops."

"Gas cuts both ways," Pontowski said. "We learned that lesson ninety years ago in World War Once."

"According to what SEAC is saying," Rockne continued, "it takes about eight to twelve hours for the shit to dissipate. That might explain why it's so damn quiet right now."

Pontowski nodded slowly. "That's part of it. But we know they regroup at night, and we're forty minutes from sunset." The two men fell silent for a moment. "Chief, level with me. Can we evacuate out of here over land?"

"There's a lot of small units floating around out there. We might be able to get some of our people through. How many, I don't know." He considered the odds. "Sir, if we go, we got to go as soon as it's dark. It's going to get very interesting in a few hours."

"When the nerve gas dissipates," Pontowski added.

Rockne didn't answer. The last two jets took off.

The White House
Tuesday, October 12

Maddy stared into the cold fireplace as the elegant grandmother clock in the corner of the family room chimed six o'clock. She cupped the mug in her hands and took another sip. Maura came through the door and joined her. "Did you get any sleep?" There was no reproach in Maura's voice, only a deep concern for her daughter.

"A few hours." She took another sip. She picked up the remote control to the TV. "This should be interesting."

The screen filled with the words CNC-TV SPECIAL REPORT, the words then displaced by the channel's star reporter, Liz Gordon. "A bombshell exploded in the nation's capital last night with the latest revelation growing out of the investigation into the suicide of the director of Central Intelligence."

"I'm sick of this," Maura murmured.

"Wait," Maddy said.

The commentator's face turned even more serious. "A tape monitoring a telephone conversation between Senator John Leland and Secretary of Defense Robert Merritt revealed that Leland knew beforehand there was no connection between the existence of an alleged child-pornography ring and the late DCI."

The screen faded to an interview with Leland. "This is a blatant attempt by the Turner administration to discredit my investigation," Leland blustered.

A voice off camera said, "Secretary Merritt has confirmed the authenticity of the phone call."

"Merritt is a lying turncoat," Leland fumed. "That is not my voice on the tape."

The voice was relentless. "Three experts have analyzed the tape and compared it with your speeches. They all say it is you."

Leland drew himself up, filling the screen with righteousness. "Let me make this perfectly clear: the person who recorded this tape committed a crime that will not go unpunished. It is a violation of federal law."

Again the voice was there. "An unidentified source claims that Patrick Flannery Shaw was the source of the tape."

Leland was shouting. "Do you know who Shaw is?"

"Was, Mr. Senator. Patrick Shaw died early this morning."

Maddy clicked off the TV. "Oh," Maura said. "I didn't know."

"He passed away two hours ago."

"You were there?" Maura asked. A gentle nod answered her. "I'm so sorry."

"It wasn't unexpected," Maddy said. She rose and walked to the mantel over the fireplace. She reached out and touched the small hand bell resting in the place of honor. "Do you remember when he gave it to me?" She held the bell as tears coursed down her cheeks.

thirty-eight

Taman Negara
Tuesday, October 12

Twilight in the tropics is very brief, and it was dark when Colonel Sun and the rest of the First SOS made the rendezvous shortly after 1900 hours, a good eight hours ahead of schedule. The men dropped their heavy loads and sank to the ground, too weary to appreciate what they had done. "How many?" Kamigami asked.

"Fifty-four," Sun replied. With Kamigami's forty-two men, they had ninety-six shooters.

"Where's Tel?" Kamigami asked.

"Tel was on the point when we ran into a patrol," Sun explained. "He saw them first, but before we could retrograde, they saw two men. Tel took a four-man team to lead them away. With luck, they may think they're chasing a long-range patrol."

Kamigami's eyes narrowed as he fought the urge to reprimand the colonel. He should have waited and covered the last ten miles at night. But Sun was no fool and understood how critical the element of surprise was to special operations. "Why the hurry?"

"Singapore is under incredible pressure from missile attacks. We've been ordered to take them out as soon as possible—before morning."

Kamigami had experienced it before where the priorities of a higher headquarters overrode tactical considerations, often at the risk of the mission itself. It was also a measure of SEAC's desperation. "I understand," Kamigami conceded. Sun swayed from fatigue, and Kamigami gave in to the inevitable. "Get some rest." He checked his watch. "I'll lay out the attack at 2300 hours, and we'll go in before first light." Four hours of rest was all they were going to get.

Rest was the one luxury Tel did not have. He kept his small team moving, urging them on with hand signals, barely ahead of the men in hot pursuit. It was a calculated gamble to lead the patrol they had inadvertently stumbled across away from the Taman Negara. So far it had worked. But he wasn't certain for how much longer. He kept thinking "ambush," but he needed time to set it up. He also needed to know how many men were chasing them. Given the way the PLA did business and judging by the noise they were making, he suspected it was a rather large number.

Finally it was dark enough to do something. He ordered his team to drop their heavy bergens and strip down to fighting loads. Then they were up and moving, now much faster. Eventually he found an open area where the trees thinned out but the underbrush was still thin and undeveloped. He sent his four men into hiding, all within ten meters of the trail. He quickly checked to make sure they were not visible to night-vision goggles before spreading ground pepper on the trail where it entered the clearing. He took cover.

He didn't have to wait long. Two men came into sight, moving cautiously down the trail. He evaluated their movements with a practiced eye and decided they weren't very good. Then he saw the dog. He forced his breathing to slow as the dog sniffed at the trail. The dog sneezed four times, and the two men halted. They took their time studying the clearing. The dog sneezed again, and one spoke into his radio, ample proof they were in contact with a larger group. They stood beside the trail and smoked cigarettes while they waited for the main body to come up. Tel didn't move as the dog started to range, only to start sneezing again.

The patrol came up the trail, and the two men kept smoking, waving them through the clearing. Tel counted fifty-three soldiers as they passed. An officer brought up the rear with a radio operator. He paused while he spoke into his handset, reporting his platoon's location and what they had seen. Tel caught enough of the report to worry him. The officer moved on, and a second platoon came down the trail. This time Tel counted fifty-eight men. He was dealing with a company-strength patrol. Finally the two men were alone, and they fell in behind, now the rear guard.

Tel waited until they were out of earshot and spoke into his whisper mike. "Take them out," he ordered. He waited.

A voice spoke in his earpiece. "We got them."

Tel stepped onto the trail and moved forward. The two soldiers were lying beside the trail, their throats cut. "Where's the dog?" he asked. But no one had seen it. Tel made a decision. "Pick them up and head for the rendezvous. We'll dispose of them when we can." Two of his team shouldered the bodies in a fireman's carry and headed back in the direction they had come from. Tel scoured the area, removing any traces of the fight or their presence. He took one last look around and followed.

Camp Alpha
Tuesday, October 12

Clark counted the twenty men piling onto the first helicopter while Doc Ryan and two medics pulled the last stretcher patient out of the crash wagon. Willing hands helped pull the wounded man onto the laps of the six men crammed onto the rear bench of the second Puma. Clark took one last count—four litter patients and fifteen men—and gave the pilots a thumbs-up. The two helicopters lifted off and disappeared over the treetops. She ran for the crash wagon and jumped into the back with the doctor. They raced for the med station as an artillery shell exploded on a nearby empty aircraft shelter. "How many left?" she asked.

"Two," Ryan answered.

"I wanted to get them all out," she said.

The doctor shook his head. "Better this way. They're not in pain." It was triage in the raw. The two men not evacuated were going to die no matter what miracles modern medicine might perform. Their places on the helicopter had been given to patients who could be treated—and to men who could still fight. The crash wagon's radio crackled. Two more wounded were coming across the runway, both the enemy.

The truck parked in the hardened shelter nearest the med station, and Clark ran for the command post. Pontowski was waiting for her. "How many left?"

She ran the numbers from memory. "We got two hundred thirty-seven to go. Twelve pilots, seventy-eight maintenance, a hundred and twenty-two cops, nine medics, and seventeen support—that includes the two controllers in the tower, two in the command post, and two in intelligence. The rest are augmenting the cops."

"We got ten Hogs good to go for one more sortie, so that leaves two extra pilots."

"When are you going to launch them?" she asked.

"At first light." Pontowski glanced at the master clock. It was 2206 hours. "In about eight hours, if SEAC has still got any kind of defensive line left."

Clark pulled on her headset to listen to the security police net. "All quadrants except the north are taking sporadic small-arms fire," she reported. "Rockne is reinforcing the perimeter." She moved to the base defense map and circled each defensive fighting position as it reported in. "The minefield is keeping the north clear, and he's only manning two DFPs on the northern side." She circled the two defensive fire positions, one on each side of the runway. When the last team checked in, she counted each position and wrote a big "56" on the board.

"Jess," Cindy whispered. "Someone's out there."

Jessica stood up and looked through the night-vision sight fitted to Cindy's M-16. "I don't see anything." She turned the objective-focus ring, sharpening up the image. Still nothing. Then she turned off the reticule brightness. The sight was good out to four hundred meters, and still nothing appeared. She sensed movement at the extreme edge of the sight's amplification. "I got it," she said. The image became more distinct. "Someone's moving along the ground." She watched for a moment. "He's clearing mines."

"Can we get a flare?" Cindy asked.

Jessica handed the M-16 back and called the BDOC. Rockne answered. "You still got my dog?" he asked, fully aware everyone on the net was listening.

"That's affirmative," Jessica replied.

"Good. Feed her Cindy if she gets hungry."

Jessica snorted, but it did help break the building tension. "Very funny. Any chance of getting a flare over the minefield?"

Paul answered. "We got a tube. A sixty-millimeter, courtesy of the long-departed MA." An enterprising security cop with a touch of larceny had found sixteen mortars abandoned by the Malaysian Army and had distributed them over the base.

"I hope you clowns know how to use it," Rockne said.

"On the way," Paul said. A dull *whomp* echoed out of the trees, and a single round arced over the base. It popped over the minefield, and a bright flare drifted down.

"Look at that," Cindy whispered. At least twenty men were on the far side of the minefield working their way across. She squeezed off a shot. "Keep the flares coming," she said. Jessica asked for another flare as Cindy fired again. "I got one." She fired again. Jessica stood up and fired with her. Across the minefield a soldier stood up and ran for cover.

"Let him go," Jessica ordered. They watched as the rest of the men followed his example and bolted for safety. A cloud of dirt and smoke mushroomed up, catching the red glow of the flares. The dull report of a mine exploding rumbled across their DFP. "Well," Jessica said, her voice shaking, "that's one way to clear a minefield."

The radio net came alive. "Tanks!"

Taman Negara
Tuesday, October 12

It was drizzling when the team leaders joined Kamigami and Sun under the camouflaged shelter. Four hours of rest had performed a minor miracle for most, but Sun was still showing the effects of the forced march. As always, Kamigami carefully evaluated each man, looking for any telltale sign that could turn into a major problem once the action started. After talking to Sun for a few moments, he was certain the colonel could hack it. He turned over a chart to reveal a sketch of the area. "We're here," he said, pointing to their position. He ticked the base camp four miles away.

"Approximately two to three hundred enemy are between us and our objective." He circled the three tunnel entrances near the base camp. "We know the PLA has dug a major complex under the ridgeline. Exactly how big, we don't know. How many missiles are left, we don't know." He looked around the small group. "So what does all this tell you?"

"We don't know very much about our objective," Lieutenant Lee answered, "which is a recipe for disaster."

"Exactly," Kamigami said. "So we're not going to destroy the tunnels." Stunned looks answered him. "We're going to close them up and turn them into tombs."

"What about the troops in the base camp?" Sun asked.

"First we have to convince them they want to be in the tunnels," Kamigami answered. He fingered the gold whistle around his neck. "Once that happens, we blow the entrances." His face hardened. "Once we've secured the area, we'll find the ventilation shafts and seal them."

Camp Alpha
Tuesday, October 12

Rockne keyed his radio and tried for the third time to raise Whiskey Sector's command post on the opposite side of the runway. "Whiskey Ops, this is BDOC. How copy?" Again there was no answer. "Damn," he muttered. More reports streamed in as he tried to make sense out of what was happening. Since each team manning a defensive fire position had a unique call sign based on its sector and number in line, a definite pattern started to emerge. At least three tanks supported by troops were maneuvering on the eastern perimeter. But where were they going? "Whiskey Zero-Five," he radioed, "do you have tanks in sight?"

Paul answered. "Whiskey Zero-Five has three tanks with troops at four hundred meters."

"Are they moving?" Rockne asked.

"Negative," Paul replied.

Rockne radioed the next DFP in line. "Whiskey Zero-Six, do you have tanks in sight?"

"That's affirm," a shaky voice answered. "No movement."

Back to the problem of Whiskey's command post. "Whiskey Ops, how copy?" No answer. Rockne thought for a moment. Who could check it out the quickest with the least risk? He hit the transmit button. "Zulu Zero-Two, proceed to Whiskey Ops bunker and find out what the hell is going on."

Jessica answered. "Zulu Zero-Two is on the way."

Paul was back on the radio, his voice urgent. "Those fuckers are coming straight at us!" Rockne heard the rattle of a SAW over the open frequency.

"Paul!" Rockne shouted, ignoring all radio discipline. "Get the hell outa there!" But there was no answer. "Whiskey Zero-Six," Rockne said, radioing the DFP next to Paul and Jake. "Are you engaged?" Again there was no answer. More reports flooded in as the entire eastern perimeter was taking fire. He made a decision. "Whiskey Sector," he radioed, "DFPs Whiskey Zero-One through Whiskey One-Five fall back to secondary positions. Acknowledge." He checked off the DFPs as they checked in. All but Zero-Five and Zero-Six were accounted for. If he read the situation right, the enemy was coming through a very narrow funnel directly into the weapons storage area. A very bad mistake. He called the command post. "Colonel Clark, we got a major attack forming on the eastern perimeter. Three tanks with troops. We're falling back."

"I'm coming to you," Clark answered.

The two women hugged the tree line that paralleled the runway as they ran. Boyca loped along beside Jessica, apparently enjoying the exercise after the long confinement in the DFP. Off to their left the rattle of a heavy machine gun momentarily drove them to cover. Then they were up and running again. The sharp retort of cannon fire split the air, followed by a loud bang. The cannon stopped firing. Encouraged, they ran faster. When they reached the runway intersection at midfield, they slowed and turned down the dirt road that led toward the weapons storage area. Ahead of them, they saw the outline of the bunker. As expected, it was dark. "What do you think?" Cindy asked.

"Where's the sentry?" Jessica replied. She motioned for Cindy to spread out, and they slowly approached. Boyca sank to the ground, her head up, ears back. She let out a low growl.

Clark leaned over the chart and frowned. "They punched through here," Rockne explained, touching two DFPs. "Whiskey Zero-Five and Zero-Six." The radio net blared at them as the fire teams on the secondary line came under attack.

"BDOC, Whiskey Zero-Five," Paul radioed, his voice barely audible. Rockne's head came up. "Troops coming through the fence at my location. Battalion strength."

Rockne looked at the chart, his mouth a grim line. "Aren't you going to acknowledge?" Clark asked.

"No. He's ratholed and already off the air. He doesn't need a radio squawking at him." He paused for a moment and then keyed his radio. "All mortar teams commence firing on Whiskey Zero-Five and Whiskey Zero-Six." He dropped the mike and stared at the floor. "Shit-fuck-hate," he muttered.

"There wasn't a choice," Clark said. "But it will slow them down."

"Not for long," Rockne answered. He pulled himself up. "We're gonna have to withdraw to the runway and blow the fuel dump and weapons-storage area."

"From Whiskey Ops," Clark said. He nodded. "Blow it on my command. Not before."

He nodded and hit the transmit button on his mike. "Zulu Zero-Two. Say position."

"Zulu Zero-Two is outside Whiskey Ops," Cindy answered.

"What's wrong with the inside?"

"It's occupied, and we don't think they're friendly."

Clark went rigid. "You better get over there. We can handle it here." The other two security cops manning the BDOC nodded in agreement, neither anxious to leave the security of the bunker.

"Tell Zulu Zero-Two I'm heading their way." He slapped his flak vest closed, and grabbed his helmet and M-16 as he hurried out. Then he stopped and pointed to one of the sergeants. "You're with me."

The two men ran outside and jumped into Rockne's pickup. The steady *whomp* of mortars from across the runway reached out and demanded their attention. "Chief, do we have to do this?" the sergeant complained.

"You bet your sweet ass." Rockne gunned the engine and raced for the other side of the base. The speedometer touched sixty miles an hour when they crossed the runway. He slowed to make the turn onto the dirt road leading to the bunker. A long burst from a submachine gun cut into the right side of the pickup's windshield. Glass sprayed over the two men, and a single 7.62-millimeter round hit the sergeant in the neck, killing him instantly. The impact threw his body against Rockne, which probably saved Rockne's life. Two more slugs slammed into the sergeant's vest. The last round hit Rockne's helmet and ricocheted off. But the force of a round fired at short range is enormous, and it rocked Rockne's head back and twisted his neck, momentarily knocking him out. The truck careened out of control and rolled onto its side as it skidded to a halt. Another burst of gunfire cut into the underside and punctured the gas tank.

Rockne climbed out and staggered away from the truck, keeping it between him and the gunfire. But that was all he had. He sank to his knees, too dazed to move, as another burst of gunfire ripped into the truck. He tried to stand but sank back to the ground and vomited. Jessica saw him as he collapsed. "Cindy, it's the Rock! Go!" The two women ran toward him as the truck exploded. A soldier stepped around the burning truck and saw Rockne kneeling on the ground. He never saw the women coming his way as he walked over and held the muzzle of his submachine gun inches from Rockne's head. Jessica skidded to a stop in the shadows, still fifty meters short. She raised her M-16, but she couldn't take the shot. Boyca was in the way.

Boyca was a blur as she barreled toward the soldier. She let out a single bark and kept coming. The soldier looked up, not believing what he saw. He swung the muzzle of his submachine gun around just as Boyca's powerful hind legs dug in. She leaped at him, fifty-six pounds of concentrated fury. The soldier fired a short burst. The first two rounds missed, but the third struck Boyca in the chest. She crashed into him, and her jaws clamped down on the soldier's left arm. He screamed in pain when the small bone in his forearm shattered. He fell to the ground as Boyca jerked her head back and forth, refusing to let go. Then she released him. The soldier rolled free of Boyca's lifeless body and reached for his weapon, only to look directly into the muzzle of Jessica's M-16. She shoved it into his mouth and pulled the trigger.

Cindy was there. "Jesus, Jess," she breathed. Together they helped Rockne to his feet and dragged him into the tree line.

"Call BDOC," he groaned, still too dizzy to stand unassisted.

Cindy keyed her radio. "BDOC, this is Zulu Zero-Two. We've got the Chief, but he's injured."

Clark answered. "Zulu Zero-Two, tell the Chief to blow the weapons storage area and fuel dump ASAP."

"How do we do that?" Jessica wondered.

"Get me into the Whiskey Ops bunker," Rockne rasped.

The two women looked at each other, not sure what to do. Suddenly Jessica ripped off her helmet and dropped her webbed harness, shedding over thirty pounds of fighting load. She grabbed a grenade and pulled the pin. "Cover me," she said. She ran for the bunker, darting from shadow to shadow and keeping in the trees. A burst of gunfire flashed from a firing port, but she kept running. Cindy snapped off four rounds, chipping at the sandbags around the firing port. Another burst of gunfire and Jessica went down. Just as quickly she was up and running again, now less than thirty feet away. A long burst of gunfire swept the area, and two rounds cut into her. She pitched forward and threw the grenade. "You muthafuckas!" she screamed. The grenade arced true and sure into the firing port. They heard it detonate, and the gunfire stopped.

Rockne was on his feet, a little more stable. "Go!" Cindy propped him up, and they hobbled toward the bunker.

Each second was an eternity as Clark waited. She never took her eyes off the base defense chart as each firing team checked in when they reached the DFPs near the runway. A loud explosion shook the beams overhead, and she looked up. But it didn't die away and continued to build as it rippled through the weapons storage area. Another boom, this time from the fuel dump, punctuated the rolling thunder. But there was little fire, as the tanks were dry and contained only vapor. It was enough, however, to set the trees on fire. Wave after wave of intense heat belched out of the fuel dump as the tanks exploded, adding to the conflagration. A compulsion she would never understand drove her outside. She had to see. The entire eastern horizon was on fire, explosion after explosion sending sparks and smoke into the night sky.

Rockne steadied himself against the wall of the bunker and took a shallow breath. His neck ached beyond belief, and he was certain someone had driven a spike into his skull. He connected the last two firing wires to the firing device and twisted the small handle. He braced himself as another detonation shook the bunker. "We got to go," he told Cindy.

But she only rocked back and forth, bent over Jessica's body, as tears streamed down her face. She looked up at him. "She was my buddy."

"I know," he said. "That's why we're here."

Slowly Cindy reached under the body and pulled Boyca's leash out of Jessica's rear pocket. She stood and wiped at her tear-stained face. Then she handed the leash to Rockne.

thirty-nine

Taman Negara
Wednesday, October 13

The teams moving into position were little more than shadows in the night. Twice they had to take out sentries who posed a threat, but for the most part they bypassed the guard posts. Lieutenant Lee's team was the last to reach its assigned position, less than three hundred meters from the tunnels. He radioed two words when his team was ready: "Tiger Red."

Colonel Sun's radio operator copied the transmission and relayed it to Kamigami. "Get ready," Kamigami told his team. He raised the gold whistle to his lips. Again he checked on his men. They were alert and waiting. He blew on the whistle, faintly at first and then crescendoing to a long, hard blast. The sound carried down the low valley, echoing between the karst formations. The moment he stopped, the team broke cover and ran. Kamigami fell in behind, hard-pressed to keep up. Six minutes later they halted, and again Kamigami gave a long blast on the whistle. He let it dangle around his neck as they listened. They could hear shouts and movement from the main camp less than a hundred meters away.

"They got the message, sir," a sergeant said. It was true. The legend of the vampire inhabiting the area was too strong, too vivid for many of the superstitious soldiers to ignore, and panic swept the camp. At first there was general confusion, while officers and senior NCOs tried to restore order. But the second whistle had sent a few racing for sanctuary in the tunnels. Kamigami helped it along by a third blast, and what had been a trickle turned into a torrent flowing into the tunnels.

A few officers managed to reach the entrances and were beginning to regain control when Kamigami blew the whistle for the fourth time. Then he dropped the whistle and sent his team into the camp. Fear had started the soldiers moving, and now survival drove them on, as Kamigami's team annihilated what little opposition remained on the perimeter.

From the far side of the camp another team opened fire, catching many of the soldiers in a deadly crossfire. Now it was a general rout, as the survivors made for the tunnels. But an officer gathered three NCOs and started to regroup, blocking the fleeing soldiers. Lieutenant Lee signaled for his sniper to take the officer out. Compared to the missile, it was an easy shot.

But the three NCOs were made of stern stuff and didn't give up. Slowly the flow into the tunnels stopped. Lee radioed for support. Farther back, Sun gave the order, and the two fire teams on the ridge saturated the area with mortar rounds. Gradually they drove the defenders away from the tunnels and back into the camp. A squad of seven soldiers emerged from the left tunnel, commanded by a gutsy NCO, and headed directly for Lee's position. Again the sniper fired, and the NCO fell to the ground. Lee redirected the mortar fire, and the squad took a direct hit. Three survivors crawled back into the tunnel, leaving their wounded behind.

Ropes dropped from above the tunnels, and three men rappelled down the face of the ridge. The center man stopped at a big outcrop and shoved two satchel charges into the deepest cracks. He climbed back up, trailing the firing wires behind him. The man on the left had to descend almost to the entrance as gunfire splattered around him. The sniper fired at the muzzle flashes, and the gunfire tapered off as the man swung back and forth, slapping limpet charges on the brow of the tunnel. He swung farther to the left and caught a handhold, then pulled himself into a chimney and worked his way back to the top, safe from hostile fire. A burst of submachine-gun fire cut into the third man, leaving him swinging back and forth over the right entrance.

With two men safe, the team leader above the tunnels blew the charges. The big outcrop above the center entrance caved in on itself, and most of the ridge collapsed into the center. The charges on the left were less effective but still collapsed the roof of the entrance, partially sealing the tunnel. The right tunnel remained open.

A sixth sense told Kamigami that resistance in the main camp was stiffening and it was time to withdraw. He spoke into his radio, giving the order, and started to fall back. The gunfire slowly died away, as dust and smoke rolled down the valley and into the jungle. A lone mortar round crashed into the camp, followed by the sharp crack of a sniper rifle. Kamigami counted his men as an eerie silence came down.

Camp Alpha
Wednesday, October 13

Doc Ryan took one look at Rockne and went back to work on the Chinese soldier lying on the operating table. "Have a medic check you out."

"And take two aspirin?" Rockne said. He was much better and feeling foolish for even coming to the base medical station. But Clark had been most insistent.

"In your case, four."

Rockne grunted and did as he was told. Outside, he paused, surprised by how quiet it was. But "quiet" was all relative. Dull explosions still reverberated from across the runway and mixed with distant cannon fire. He hurried to the BDOC, steadier on his feet and thankful that his headache had subsided to manageable stabs of pain. Clark met him on her way out. "Bossman wants us in the command post. We got a white flag near the gate."

Clark held a white flag out the window as her driver slowly maneuvered through the concrete barricades at what once was the main gate. Rockne sat behind him and guided him through the minefield. A small group of men were waiting on the far side, also holding a white flag. The driver stopped and got out, holding the white flag above his head.

"Okay," Pontowski said, "play it cool and just stand behind me. Don't say a word." Rockne and Clark nodded in agreement. Rockne got out and carefully adjusted his black beret, convinced that appearances still mattered. Clark was right beside him, looking neat and trim as always. They fell in behind Pontowski and marched toward the group waiting for them. Halfway there, they stopped. For a moment nothing happened. "I guess they don't want to talk," Pontowski said. He turned to leave.

"They're coming," Clark said. Pontowski turned back around and stood at parade rest.

The three men coming toward them were tall and wore neat and well-tailored uniforms. Pontowski recognized the rank of the middle officer, a major general. As he was junior in grade, Pontowski saluted first. The general waved a salute back. "General Pontowski, I presume?" His English was impeccable and carried the trace of an English accent.

"How may I help you?" Pontowski said, dropping his salute.

"By surrendering, of course."

"That might be a problem," Pontowski replied. "We don't have the facilities for processing and feeding all your men."

The two-star general allowed a little smile. "Please, do not play games."

"I assure you, sir, I am not playing games."

"And neither am I. I am in direct contact with our embassy in Washington, and our special ambassador informs me that your president refuses to discuss your situation, which, to say the least, is untenable. Apparently you are expendable."

"Ah," Pontowski replied, taking a wild chance. "Mr. Zou no doubt. How wrong can he be?" The general caught the pun on Zou Rong's name and frowned. A mistake. Pontowski leaned forward and lowered his voice. "How many of your men died in your last attack?" He motioned to Whiskey Sector across the runway. "Must this go on?"

The general went rigid and snapped his fingers. Behind him, there was a flurry of activity, and two soldiers dragged a tall security policeman out of a truck. They shoved him forward. "Paul Travis," Rockne said in a low voice. In the half-light of the van's headlights they saw he was dirty, battered, and bruised. But there was something in his stance. His right eyelid started to blink as Rockne stared at him.

"Do you wish to see this man executed as a war criminal?" the general said, his voice calm.

"He's not a war criminal," Pontowski said.

"I take it," the general said, "that we have nothing else to discuss."

"Apparently not," Pontowski replied. The three men spun around and marched back. "General," Pontowski called to their backs, "take good care of Sergeant Travis. I want him back."

Clark's driver brought up the van, and they climbed in. "Okay, Chief," Pontowski said, "what was the message?"

Clark didn't understand. "What message?"

"Did you see Paul's right eye blink?" Rockne replied. "Morse code."

"What did he say?" she asked.

"'Jake dead. Resist. All bluff.'" Rockne let it sink in.

Artillery rumbled in the distance, but it was getting closer. "That doesn't sound like 'all bluff' to me," Clark said. Her driver floored the accelerator and sped toward the command post.

"It may be a last gasp," Pontowski said. "Why else the white flag?"

The driver slammed the van to a halt. "Missy Colonel, you go home now?"

An artillery round shrieked across the night sky. "Incoming!" Rockne shouted.

Taman Negara
Wednesday, October 13

The dull *whomp* of a mortar round echoed out of the base camp and over the valley. A few seconds later the round hit in the jungle eighty meters behind the ridge where Kamigami and Sun were hiding. "They're wasting ammunition," Sun said.

"They're ranging," Kamigami said. "Spread the word to take cover." He focused his night-vision scope on the tunnel entrances. There was movement inside the right tunnel, ample indication that it was open. The entrance to the middle tunnel was totally collapsed and permanently sealed. He zoomed in on the left tunnel. The entrance was half filled with rubble and big boulders, but there had been no cave-in and the roof was still standing. The sound of a diesel engine resonated from the right tunnel. "Something's coming out." He panned to the right entrance as the engine raced and dark exhaust billowed out. Then the base camp erupted. The defenders launched a mortar barrage, sending a wave of projectiles into the surrounding ridgelines. At the same time a light tank emerged from the tunnel, its cannon firing. It laid a trail of heavy smoke as it raced for the far end of the valley where the road disappeared into the jungle. Another diesel engine labored in the smoke, totally obscured from view. Kamigami caught a glimpse of a transporter/erector carrying a missile before the smoke rolled back over it. The mortar barrage grew heavier as men poured out of the tunnel, running for the base camp. Machine-gun fire from the surrounding ridges raked the smoke. The mortar barrage from the camp stopped, and the smoke slowly dissipated. Thirty or forty bodies littered the ground, but it had been a successful breakout.

"They're getting organized," Kamigami told Sun. "There's more to come."

"What about the missile?" Sun asked.

"Send a team to track it down and kill it."

Sun spoke into his radio to make it happen. He listened for a few moments. "Tel's coming in."

"Time to withdraw," Kamigami said. "Call in the team leaders." They had violated two of the basic rules of special operations—never hold ground, and hit and run. So far they had hit. Now it was time to run and remember the first rule.

The small group of men who gathered a few minutes later understood what had to be done, but they were reluctant to disengage. True to their culture, no one openly raised the issue as Kamigami detailed the sequence for withdrawal. Finally Tel broke the silence. "Sir, they want to try once more to close the tunnel."

"An attack during daylight is suicide," Kamigami said.

"Those missiles are killing their families," Tel replied. The simple statement pounded at Kamigami as he remembered his own family. Tel pressed the argument. "We've got another hour before sunrise."

Lieutenant Lee stepped forward. "I can take a team from Tiger Red in."

"You'll have to blow the entrance from inside," Kamigami said. "Who knows how to clear a tunnel?" There was no reply to his question. It was just as well, for the First SOS had to withdraw while it was still dark. But the faces of his family kept coming back.

Tel crawled into position with the sniper and gave three quick clicks on the transmission button of his radio, initiating the attack. Mortars slammed into the base camp, driving the defenders to cover. More mortars laid down a smoke screen in the open area. Ropes tumbled from the ridgeline above the left tunnel, and four men rappelled down. The first man, Lieutenant Lee, landed on the rubble piled in the entrance and released his rope while the other three men hovered above. A big shadow rappelled down Lee's rope as the lieutenant raised his head and looked inside, his night-vision goggles making him look like a giant insect perched on a rock. He pumped his fist up and down, and the three men hanging above swung in just as the last man reached the entrance. He swung in after them. Lee scampered over the rocks and disappeared inside. Tel clicked his radio twice, ending the barrage. Kamigami and four shooters were inside.

Kamigami motioned Lee and two men to the far side of the tunnel as he got his bearings. He inched along the wall, looking for a cross gallery connecting the three main tunnels. Voices echoed out of the dark, coming from deep inside. The tunnel curved, and he motioned Lee on. The lieutenant dropped to all fours and crept forward. Then he pulled back and motioned Kamigami forward. Kamigami chanced a look. A dim light was coming from a side tunnel. Kamigami's internal clock was running, and it told him they had only seconds before being discovered. He lifted his night-vision goggles and darted toward the light. He looked around the corner. They had found a cross gallery, and forty meters away he could see the center tunnel that intersected the gallery at a right angle. He motioned Lee up, and the men stacked against the wall behind him. They lifted their goggles, and he gave them a few seconds for their eyes to adjust. The last man tapped the elbow of the man in front, signaling he was ready. The signal was passed up to Kamigami. He burst around the corner, and the men moved as one. Automatically, Lee took the far side of the gallery, following at an oblique angle to Kamigami.

They reached the intersection with the center tunnel, still undiscovered. Loud voices and the sound of movement echoed around the corner. Kamigami never hesitated. He pulled off his helmet and goggles and tucked them under his arm. "Walk across," he said. He pointed to Lee to lead the way. The lieutenant ambled across the tunnel to the other side of the cross gallery. Kamigami was next. He looked down the tunnel as he crossed. A large group of soldiers was sitting on the ground around two transporter/erectors parked in line. He stepped into the shadows next to Lee. The lieutenant pointed down the gallery to their objective. The last tunnel was forty meters away, but a group of soldiers was standing in the intersection. The next shooter made it halfway across before a sergeant saw him. He yelled at him in Cantonese, and the shooter shouted back. But it was the wrong answer. He bolted across, joining Kamigami and Lee.

All that counted now was overwhelming violence. The two shooters left behind knew they were the rear guard. One fell to the ground and held his M-16 around the corner and fired blindly down the center tunnel. The other shooter stood over him and jammed his M-79 grenade launcher around the corner. He squeezed off four shots, sending forty-millimeter grenades into the densely packed men. He pulled back and waited. His partner was up and retreated down the cross gallery to the left tunnel, slapping a fresh magazine into his M-16.

At the same time Kamigami and Lee ran for the next intersection, with the shooter right behind them. Kamigami fired as he ran, cutting into the men standing there. Most of them died in the first hail of gunfire, but one crawled free. Kamigami skidded to a halt and slammed his body against the wall. He motioned the shooter forward and made a tossing motion.

Four quick concussions rocked the center tunnel as the grenades went off. The shooter held his M-79 around the corner and fired again. His partner had almost made it back to the left tunnel when a grenade rolled around the corner, coming directly at him. He kicked at it wildly. The grenade rolled off the shooter's boot, and he kicked again, half scooping it around the corner with his boot. The grenade detonated with a sharp crack, taking the shooter's foot with it. He fell to the ground, still alive, his body protected from the full blast by the corner.

The shooter with Kamigami tossed a grenade down their tunnel as Lee fired blindly in the other direction, out the open entrance.

The lone shooter at the center tunnel fired, sending three more grenades into the hell he was creating. The last round ricocheted off the tunnel wall and hit the side of the missile loaded on the first transporter/erector. It exploded, cutting into the missile's solid-fuel propellant.

The shooter with Kamigami threw another grenade down the tunnel as the first one detonated. The blast blew the second grenade back, directly at Lee. Lee fell on the hand grenade at his feet and took the blast in his stomach, saving the shooter and Kamigami.

The missile in the center tunnel started to cook off as the shooter emptied his magazine and pulled back to reload. He glanced down the gallery toward the left tunnel and saw his partner crawling toward him, leaving a trail of blood.

Kamigami fell to the ground and crawled to Lee, not to help him—it was too late for that—but to use his body as a shield. The shooter with him was out of grenades and was firing down the tunnel with his M-16.

In the center tunnel the rocket motor partially ignited, sending a plume of fire back over the missile behind it.

Two soldiers ran around the corner of the intersection at the left tunnel and fired down the cross gallery. The shooter at the center tunnel crumpled to the ground. His wounded partner stopped crawling and rolled a grenade at the two soldiers, yelling and cursing like a madman as the grenade exploded.

Kamigami reached Lee and grabbed the satchel charge he was carrying. "Cover me!" he yelled at his shooter. He crawled for the entrance, dragging Lee's satchel charge with his own.

In the center tunnel the uneven thrust of the rocket motor pushed the transporter/erector forward, carrying the missile with it. The wheels rolled over the men trapped there as it headed out the tunnel. But the entrance was solidly blocked by the cave-in.

Kamigami crawled along the ground, almost to the open entrance, as bullets ricocheted off the walls. In the half-light coming from inside, he saw a large fissure that split the wall. He jammed the two satchel charges into the crack and pulled the tabs, igniting the fuses. He had sixty seconds. Kamigami looked back and motioned his shooter out. The shooter started to run, but a hail of gunfire from deep in the tunnel cut him down. He screamed in pain, and Kamigami crawled back to get him.

The transporter/erector accelerated as it rolled past the cross gallery.

Kamigami saw it and put on a burst of speed, finally reaching the downed shooter. But he was dead.

The transporter/erector crashed into the blocked entrance. But the high-explosive warhead did not detonate. Instead it combined with the burning propellant and the transporter's diesel fuel to send a wall of fire back down the tunnel and out the cross gallery. The fire engulfed the second transporter and its missile, starting the process all over. Kamigami saw the wall of fire coming at him down the cross gallery and got to his feet, running for the entrance. The fiery blast washed over him, knocking him down. He rolled on the ground, desperate to extinguish his burning clothes. He shed his web harness as he rolled, taking patches of burning cloth and skin with it. He tried to come to his feet but couldn't. He tried a second time and staggered forward, racing the burning fuses. He was almost to the entrance when a gunshot echoed from outside. The bullet ripped into his abdomen. He clutched the wound with both hands and lurched out the entrance. He fell to the ground and crawled around the corner as the satchel charges blew, mangling his legs.

The sniper squeezed off a shot, dropping the soldier who had gunned down Kamigami. Tel was up and running for all he was worth, as more gunfire kicked up the dirt around him. Before Colonel Sun could give the order, every man in the First SOS was firing. The earth rumbled as the ridge above the tunnels collapsed.

Camp Alpha

Wednesday, October 13

The concussion reverberated through the command post. "Damn," Maggot muttered. "That fucker was close." He drew a diagonal line through the four marks he had made counting the cannon rounds. "Five." Every head was raised, looking at the heavy beams in the ceiling, wondering if a direct hit could penetrate. Frustrated, Maggot punched up the line to the control tower. "Has the counterbattery radar got a fix yet?"

"He's constantly moving," the controller answered. "Range twelve miles."

"And he's big," Maggot added. Tension boiled beneath the surface as they waited for the next round.

"They only got one," Pontowski told them. From the looks on their faces, he had to tell them more. "My guess is that they're stretched to the limit and it's go-for-broke time. They know that come morning, when we can fly close air support, we're going to hurt them. Bad. So we got to hang on till then."

"All we got is fuel for ten sorties," Maggot said. "The jets won't be recovering here."

"It may be enough," Pontowski said. A loud boom shook the bunker, and dust drifted down from the ceiling. A second explosion rocked them, this time much harder. "That was a secondary," he told them.

Clark monitored both the radios and the phone bank as reports trickled in. It seemed to take forever. "A shelter took a direct hit," she finally announced.

"Did they get a Hog?" Pontowski asked.

She shook her head. "Two casualties." She listened. "Oh, no. It was the shelter next to the med station, and the fuel holding tank ruptured. Fuel is flooding the med station, and Ryan is evacuating." Another round slammed into the base, this time farther away. Then, "Mortars on the southern perimeter." A slight pause. "Heavy small-arms fire at the gate." Her eyes were wide with fear, but there was no panic in her voice. "APCs on the western perimeter with troops." APCs were armored personnel carriers.

In his mind's eye Pontowski could see the chaos outside. Could he sort it out in time to get his Hogs airborne? He made a decision. "Maggot, you got it here. I'm going to the BDOC." He slapped a fresh battery pack into his radio and dropped a second one into a pocket. He reached for his helmet and ran for the entrance. Much to his surprise, Clark's driver was right beside him.

"I drive for you," he said. They jumped into the van and made the short dash to the BDOC.

Rockne was waiting for him and reported his arrival to Clark. "What about those APCs?" Pontowski asked.

"I can kill fuckin' APCs," Rockne snarled. "But I need more fire teams. And I just ain't got them." Another artillery round hit the base, this time in Whiskey Sector. "And I'm gonna kill that bastard." Like the infantry, Rockne was growing to hate artillery.

Pontowski studied the base defense chart as a sergeant marked which DFPs were engaged. They were holding, but he wasn't sure for how much longer. "We gotta hold." He was running again, talking on the radio to the command post. "On the way to Maintenance. Tell them I'm coming." He piled into the van. "Maintenance Control. Go!" An artillery round landed in the trees a hundred yards to their right. Fortunately, a hardened shelter deflected most of the blast away from them. The driver clutched the wheel and gritted his teeth as they raced down the taxiway. The big blast doors of the shelter cranked back when they approached, and the van drove straight in. The doors were closing before they halted.

The chief of Maintenance, a reservist colonel who had served Pontowski so well, was waiting. "Thank God you made it," he said.

"You got seventy-eight troops left, is that right?" He didn't wait for an answer. "How many do you need to launch the Hogs?"

"Two per jet," came the answer. "Twenty."

"That leaves fifty-eight. Tell them to grab their helmets and whatever weapons they got and report to the BDOC. We need them for fire teams."

"Rockne trained some of them for guard duty when we first got here," the colonel said. "Give me a few minutes to switch around, and I'll send them." He pointed to seven men sitting against the back wall. "They can go now."

"Load 'em in the van," Pontowski ordered. "Where are the two pilots not assigned to a Hog?" The colonel pointed to the room at the back of the shelter. "Hey, I need some jocks out here," Pontowski shouted. Waldo and Bag ran out and joined him. "You two think you can organize some type of close-in defense so crew chiefs from one shelter can give covering fire to another shelter when it launches a jet?"

"Can do, Boss," Waldo answered. He snorted. "Why do we always do this the hard way?"

Pontowski ignored him and ran for the van. It started to move the moment he piled in. The shelter's blast doors cranked open. "BDOC," he ordered. Outside, heavy smoke rolled across the taxiway, dropping visibility to thirty feet. But the driver knew his way and had them at the BDOC in less than four minutes. "Follow me," Pontowski told the seven mechanics. He led the way into the bunker. "Chief," he told Rockne, "match these guys with a cop." He had just given Rockne seven more fire teams. "You got about fifty more coming."

He radioed the command post as he ran out. "Tell the doc I'm on my way." The med station was less than a hundred meters from the BDOC, but still he drove, not wanting to lose track of the van. The smoke grew heavier as they approached, and he rolled up the windows. Then he saw the source. The med station was engulfed in flames, black smoke rolling out in waves. He couldn't believe it when two medics ran out of the bunker, their arms full of supplies. "Where's Ryan?" he yelled. The man pointed to a nearby aircraft shelter. He dumped his load on the ground and ran back inside. Clark's driver jumped out and followed them inside. Pontowski ran for the shelter.

Doc Ryan was in the middle of the floor, bent over a wounded man in a litter. He stood up when he saw Pontowski, and shook his head. "How many?" Pontowski asked.

"Twenty-six all told," he answered, gesturing around the shelter. "Eleven EP." Enemy prisoners. Pontowski walked the floor, talking to his men. Most were going to make it. He stepped across the imaginary line that separated the two groups. A soldier looked up at him, certain that Pontowski was going to execute him. "We'll take care of you," he promised. The soldier did not speak English, but he heard the meaning. He said the only two words of English he knew: "Thank you."

The blast doors moved back, and the van drove in. The two medics jumped out and offloaded the medical supplies they had retrieved from the burning med station. The driver reeked of smoke. "We got two wounded at the gate," Ryan called. "But we can't get them here."

"I go," the driver said. Pontowski sent him on his way and checked in with the command post.

"We have intruders on base," Clark told him. "We're buttoning up, so stay where you are. The chief is sending two fire teams to your position."

"Copy all," Pontowski replied. He took off his helmet and rubbed his forehead. He looked at his watch. It was one hour to sunrise.

forty

Camp Alpha
Wednesday, October 13

Waldo nervously paced the floor of Maintenance's deserted shelter, frustration itching at him. A shell whistled overhead and hit the southern edge of the base. "Give me a Hog and I'll mort that fucker," he promised, his frustration turning to anger.

"Just give me a Hog," Bag lamented. Like Waldo, he wanted to do something. "Who did we piss off?" he asked, wondering why neither of them had been assigned a jet.

"We were out of the rotation," Waldo answered. "And you know Maggot. And then Clark couldn't get us on a helicopter to beat feet out of here." Another round whistled overhead, and he grunted an indecipherable obscenity. "At least the bastard hasn't got the range."

"Without an observer it's just harassment fire," Bag said.

"Well, it's working," Waldo muttered. More pacing. He came alert. "I think it's stopped." Both men listened, and the minutes dragged, each one longer than the previous. Waldo hurried to the small door at the rear of the shelter and cracked it open. "Yeah, it's definitely stopped." Smoke drifted in and stung their eyes. Waldo closed the door and dogged it down. "Not good."

"What do you mean, not good?" Bag asked.

"What comes next is definitely not good," Waldo replied. On cue, his radio came alive. "Shit! Tanks have busted through on the southern perimeter and are heading this way."

Bag ran to the big blast door and listened. "I can hear gunfire."

Waldo held up a hand, still listening to the radio traffic. "Three tanks with troops have broken through."

"Son of a bitch," Bag moaned. "Caught like fish in a barrel. I didn't want to buy it this way."

Waldo snorted. "I ain't no fuckin' fish." His head jerked up as an image flashed in front of him. It was the hangar queen, the A-10 that couldn't be repaired and was being salvaged for parts. He looked at the big doors in front of him, imagining them as they rolled back. "Bag, think you can play crew chief?" He didn't wait for an answer. "Come on." He led the way out the small entrance at the rear and ran for the next shelter. The rear entrance was unbolted, and he ran inside. A Warthog was parked inside, the right engine missing, the canopy gone, the left rudder partially disassembled, and numerous panels removed where parts had been cannibalized.

"No way this hangar queen can fly," Bag said.

Waldo scampered up the bordering ladder and lowered himself into the cockpit. "Who said anything about flying? Check the gun and pull the pins." His hands flew over the panels, running the before-engine-start checklist. He hit the battery switch. Nothing. "I need power." Bag hurried to the APU and started it. The sound was deafening in the enclosed shelter. Fortunately, the exhaust was vented outside. Bag plugged in the electrical cord on the right side of the fuselage just aft of the cockpit. The electrical busses came alive, sending power to the instruments. The rounds counter indicated that there were 734 rounds in the cannon's ammo drum. "Shit hot!" Waldo roared. "Open the doors!" Bag ran to the control box and hit the switch. Slowly the big blast doors cranked back. Waldo started the Hog's internal APU and lifted the left throttle over the hump. The engine spun up, and at 20 percent, fuel automatically started to flow. The igniter worked, and the motor kicked off. Waldo gave Bag the thumbs-out signal to remove the wheel chocks. Bag disconnected the power cord and jerked the blocks free. Waldo fed power into the one engine, and the Hog taxied out of its nest.

Bag motioned Waldo forward and snapped the traditional salute a crew chief gives his departing jet. He held it while Waldo taxied past. Waldo turned onto the main taxiway and disappeared in the smoke. Bag ran for the controls to close the doors. "What the fuck for?" he wondered aloud. He stood there for a moment, not knowing what to do. Then he ran for a shelter with a good Warthog. At least he would have company.

Waldo turned on the aircraft's radio. Nothing. He turned up the volume on his personal radio and screwed the earpiece into his ear, holding the radio to his lips. "Chicken Coop, Waldo. I'm in the hangar queen and taxiing south."

"Say intentions," Maggot radioed.

"I got a gun on this puppy and figure I can taxi around and use it to kill a few tanks."

Maggot answered with the traditional reply of all command posts when faced with something new. "Stand by one."

"Stand by too fuckin' long," Waldo shouted, his adrenaline in full flow, "and you'll get a tank up your ass!"

Maggot ignored him as he coordinated with Rockne. "Roger, Waldo, say position."

Waldo calmed down. "On the west taxiway, headed south"—he peered into the smoke—"passing shelter West-Three."

"Gotcha," Maggot answered. "You've got a tank with troops approximately a thousand meters at your twelve o'clock heading toward you. Hold at shelter West-Two until we can get fire teams to support you."

"Now, that's a plan," Waldo said. He slowed as he approached the next shelter. Three fire teams emerged out of the smoke, two men on his left and four on his right. He pushed up the throttle. "How do I make this happen?" he said to himself. He hit the ground override switch on the back of the left console and moved the master arm switch to the up position. But the lights on the weapons-armament panel were out. He turned on the HUD to get a gun-sight display. Nothing. "Doesn't anything work!" he shouted. "Oh, shit," he breathed. A tank emerged out of the smoke and darkness, barely a hundred meters in front of him. He pressed the trigger, half expecting the cannon not to fire. The GAU-8 roared, and reddish brown smoke poured out the vent. The aircraft shook, pounding at his kidneys, and shot backward. The recoil of the cannon was so great that it had stopped the Hog's forward motion and backed it up. Waldo released the trigger. The cannon on the A-10 has a slight downward tilt, and the rounds had hit the ground seventy feet in front. Not only had he missed, but the rounds had cut a trench in the concrete as he backed up. He had to get the nose up, but how?

The tank fired. Like Waldo, it missed, and the round whistled overhead. The muzzle lowered slightly as it reloaded. "Fuck me in the heart!" Waldo shouted as he firewalled the throttle. The Hog leaped forward. He was vaguely aware of his fire teams laying down a barrage. He pumped the brakes. The Hog's nose rocked up and down as he held the engine at max throttle. Waldo mashed the trigger and held it. Again the cannon gave off its deafening roar, sending rounds into the sky and then down into the concrete, kicking up dirt and debris and blinding the tank's gunner. Eight rounds ripped into the tank's carapace a fraction of a second before its cannon fired. The thirty-millimeter depleted-uranium slug was designed to kill a heavily armored tank at a distance of over two thousand feet. At less than three hundred feet, the lightly armored Type 63 simply came apart. The turret blew back as the cannon fired, sending the eighty-five-millimeter round arcing high over the base. Fire belched from the hole left by the turret as an explosion literally blew the engine out the back.

Waldo coughed, gagging on the smoke from his own cannon. He retarded the throttle as he taxied past the wreckage. "Shit oh dear," he muttered, stunned by the carnage. Until that moment he had no idea of what the GAU-8 did to the enemy. He held his radio to his mouth. "Chicken Coop, Waldo. Scratch one tank. Say position of next target."

"Roger Waldo," Maggot replied. "Stand by one."

"Absolutely fuckin' lovely," Waldo grumbled, his fangs now fully out.

Pontowski moved across the shelter, talking to the wounded men lying on the floor. He knelt beside the one man Doc Ryan held little hope for. The security cop opened his eyes and managed a half smile. "I'm gonna make it, sir," he promised. Pontowski held his hand until he died. Then he slowly came to his feet and walked to the next man. A series of sharp clanging rings filled the shelter, and he dropped to the floor. He looked up and saw Ryan pointing to the blast doors. It was small-arms fire ricocheting off the outside.

Another fusillade raked the doors, and Pontowski ran for the telephone on the sidewall, his ears ringing. He punched at the button for the command post, and Clark answered immediately. "We're under attack," he told her.

"Help's on the way," she promised.

"Your driver is bringing in wounded," he said.

"I'll try to raise him on the radio and warn him off." She broke the connection.

Waldo taxied south on the west taxiway. Eventually he would loop around the south end of the base, pass the exit to the main gate, and turn back north on the east taxiway, toward the command post and the base med station. He stopped when two more fire teams joined up and talked to the three teams already with him. The smoke seemed less dense, and he squinted, looking to the east. The first glow of dawn marked the horizon. A sergeant gave him the thumbs-up when the teams were in place, and he nudged the throttle forward. The Warthog moved down the taxiway with the fire teams spread out in a V behind him.

"Waldo," Maggot radioed. "Say position."

"Passing shelter West-One heading for the exit to the main gate."

"A tank is reported in that area," Maggot told him.

"Copy all," Waldo said. He pushed the throttle up, forcing the fire teams to run to keep pace. The rattle of a heavy machine gun carried over the sound of his engine as he made the loop to the south. He was surprised when Clark's van cut across in front of him and disappeared through the trees, heading north. "What in hell is she doing out here?" he wondered aloud to himself. The point man on his left waved furiously at him, then gestured down the side taxi path leading to the first hardened aircraft shelter on the east side, East-One. He saw the rear end of a tank stopped on the taxi path and firing point-blank into the empty shelter. "Okay by me if you want to waste your ammo," he muttered.

He turned down the narrow taxi path as his fire teams engaged the soldiers with the tank. He lined up at the tank's six o'clock. "It's the guy you never see who kills you," he said to no one, repeating one of the truisms fighter pilots live and die by. The tank's turret started to traverse to the rear, but it was too late. Waldo pumped the brakes and squeezed off a short burst, now getting into the rhythm of it. The tank disappeared in a flash of flames and smoke. "Always check six," he muttered. The gunfire died away as the soldiers ran for safety. He looked around and groaned. The destroyed tank was blocking his way, and the taxi path was too narrow for the Hog to turn around and return to the main taxiway. He yelled at his fire teams and pointed to his rear. "Hey, I need a push!"

The phone on the sidewall buzzed, and Pontowski picked it up. "I can't contact my driver," Clark said, "but he did pick up two wounded and was last reported heading toward your shelter."

"We're still taking small-arms fire here," Pontowski replied.

"Rockne says he's got two fire teams on the way."

"We'll get the van inside," Pontowski promised. He hung up and ran to the doors. "Doc!" he yelled. "The van is coming in with wounded." Ryan ran for the peephole and unbolted the shutter to look out. Pontowski heard a horn honking furiously.

"Open the doors!" Ryan shouted. Pontowski hit the switch, and the doors moved back. The gunfire grew louder. "Oh, shit!" Ryan yelled. He ran outside. Pontowski hit the switch and stopped the doors. Another burst from a submachine gun echoed outside, and he saw the nose of the van emerge between the open doors. Ryan was pushing the bullet-riddled van into the shelter. Pontowski ran to help and pushed against the side of the van, getting it over the door tracks. He ran for the switch to close the doors. Another burst of submachine-gun fire clanged against the doors as they slowly winched closed. Ryan was leaning against the back of the van, panting hard, when a grenade rolled in. He scooped it up and threw it back out. It cleared the doors and exploded. But fragments cut into Ryan, knocking him back. The doors jarred to a halt, jammed open.

"Medic!" Pontowski shouted, but a medic was already running for Ryan. He skidded to a halt and went to work while two more medics ripped open the side door of the van.

"Wounded!" one of the medics shouted, calling for help.

Pontowski saw the driver slumped over the wheel and ran to his side of the van. He jerked the door open and pulled him out. Somehow, in spite of his massive wounds, the man was still alive. Pontowski gently laid him down. "You tell Missy Colonel go home now," he whispered. He exhaled and lay still.

"I didn't even know your name," Pontowski said, his head bowed. But he knew, without doubt, that this man had been worth fighting for. His head snapped up when he heard the distinctive clank of tank tracks.

"Waldo!" Maggot shouted over the radio. "A tank's at the med station!"

"On the way," Waldo transmitted. He looked over his shoulder as he slowly backed up. Just a few more feet to go. "Go! GO!" he shouted. The men responded, and the Hog rolled onto the main taxiway. He firewalled the throttle, fast-taxiing to the north and leaving his fire teams behind. The big jet touched forty miles an hour as it rumbled down the taxiway. He passed the BDOC, and two men ran after him. Ahead he saw the burned-out hulk of the med station. He never slowed as he headed for the nearby shelter. Now he could see the tank. Its muzzle flashed, sending a round into the partially open blast doors.

A heavy machine gun raked the side of the Hog as it lumbered past. But the titanium tub that shielded the pilot easily deflected the slugs. One of the cops following the Hog fired his SAW, taking out the machine gun. The tank commander saw the Hog coming at him, and the turret traversed, coming to bear on the charging A-10. Waldo firewalled the throttle and mashed the trigger, holding it down, pumping furiously on the brakes. The tank fired at the same instant. The A-10 disappeared in a thundering fireball as the tank came apart. Then it exploded, sending a column of smoke and flames skyward that joined with the rising fireball of Waldo's Hog.

The rattle of a SAW cut into the soldiers running for cover. The gunfire stopped.

"Oh, my God," Pontowski breathed. "How's the doc?" he shouted.

"He's pretty bad," the medic tending Ryan said.

Pontowski chanced a look out the door. Rockne was striding down the taxiway, a SAW at the ready. The big man stopped and looked skyward. Pontowski followed his gaze and heard it—the distinctive sound of a C-130. He ran outside in time to see a Hercules fly down the runway at five hundred feet. Paratroops poured out the jump doors, their chutes snapping open in quick succession, catching the first light of the rising sun. He sank to one knee.

Another sound came to him. Shelter doors were cranking open, and the shrill whine of starting engines filled the air. A Hog taxied out as another C-130 flew past. More parachutes lined the sky, and in the distance he heard the sound of a third Hercules. Pontowski came to his feet and walked back into the shelter to check on Ryan. He was a bloody mess, but alive and conscious. "That was a pretty gutsy thing, Doc." Ryan tried to muster a smile, but it wasn't there. "You made a difference when it counted," Pontowski told him.

Pontowski slowly walked toward the burning hulk of the A-10. A tower of black smoke rose skyward, a beacon marking Waldo's funeral pyre. Tears streaked Pontowski's cheeks. Was it the smoke? He didn't care. "Damn, Waldo. You did good." He blinked away the tears, then turned and headed for the command post.

Taman Negara
Wednesday, October 13

The rain misted down through the jungle canopy, filtering the early-morning light into a gentle haze over the makeshift canvas shelter. Tel stood with Colonel Sun beside the shelter as water dripped from their helmets. Under the canvas a medic worked on Kamigami. He tightened the tourniquets on what was left of his legs and tried to bandage the gaping wound in his abdomen. But there was nothing he could do for the burns. Finally he administered a shot of morphine and stepped back. He had done all he could. "He's in terrible pain," he said.

"Can you make him comfortable?" Tel asked.

The medic shook his head. "That was the last of the morphine. Nothing else I've got will work."

Kamigami's lips moved, forming one word. "Tel."

Tel ducked under the shelter and knelt beside him. "I'm here."

Kamigami tried to focus his eyes but gave up. His right hand came up and touched the whistle around his neck. The effort exhausted him, and his hand fell to the ground. "Take it," he whispered, every word an effort. His body shook with pain as Tel gently lifted the chain over his head.

"End it. Now."

Tel shook his head. "Hold on, you'll make it."

"It's over."

"I don't understand. What's over?"

A long silence. "They killed my family. I killed them." At last Tel fully understood. Kamigami had not sought this fight, it had come to him, and he had responded in the only way he knew. He was a warrior, a samurai bound by his own code of conduct. Kamigami's words from an earlier time came back, now clear and full of meaning: "This is what I am."

Kamigami gathered his strength and fumbled for the sidearm still at his side. He managed to half extract the Beretta before his hand fell away. Tel pulled the weapon free. The grips were worn with use, and he wondered how many men it had killed. "It's okay," Kamigami whispered, his words racked with pain.

Tel looked at Sun, not knowing what to do. "There's no helicopter," the colonel said. Tel touched the slide on the Beretta, mustering his courage. He chambered a round.

A single shot rang out, carrying through the jungle, only to fade away in the mist.

Washington, D.C.
Tuesday, October 12

General Wilding's staff car arrived at the entrance to the West Wing at exactly 7:00 P.M. He jumped out of the backseat and returned the Marine's salute as he hurried down the steps to the basement. Mazie and Parrish were waiting for him in the corridor outside the Situation Room. "How long has she been waiting?" Wilding asked, concerned that he should have arrived much sooner.

"She's been here all day," Parrish said.

"Why didn't someone tell me? I'd have come . . ."

Mazie's gentle look stopped him in midsentence. "There was nothing you could have told her. She was just waiting."

Wilding took a deep breath and pushed inside. "Madam President," he began. He stopped. She was alone, sitting in her chair, and sound asleep. For a moment he didn't know what to say. He turned to leave.

"General Wilding," Maddy said, her eyes still closed. "You promised seventy-two hours. You did it in fifty-one."

"Yes, ma'am. It was a very near thing."

"Thank you," she murmured.

epilogue

Travis Air Force Base, California
Tuesday, October 19

Air Force One was parked at the western end of the huge ramp, next to a brace of war-weary C-5s. On board, Madeline Turner was in her office, working at her desk as she waited for the arrival of the C-17 Globemaster carrying the last of the AVG. Richard Parrish handed her a schedule of events. "As you requested," he said, "the base is keeping it low-key. They'll get off the plane and go through a short reception line. Their families will be right there to meet them. Then you'll say a few words and, if you want, informally greet them."

"I want," Maddy said.

He frowned. Unable to contain himself, he blurted, "Madam President, it's a missed opportunity. It's a slow news day, the media can't get enough."

She held up a hand, stopping him in midflow. "This is their day, not mine." She looked up at the knock at the door. Mazie entered, a strange look on her face. She handed Maddy a hard copy of a message received only moments before. "It's from Bernie," she said in a low voice. "Zou Rong. He's been murdered."

Maddy read the message. "Bizarre." She handed it to Parrish. "Are they sure the woman did it?" she asked.

Mazie nodded. "She was his mistress. Apparently it happened

moments after Jin Chu learned my father had been killed. She cut Zou's throat and then hanged herself with a silken cord."

Nancy Bender entered. "It's time, Mrs. President." Maddy stood and walked into the lounge, where Maura, Brian, and Sarah were waiting. The president led her family to the front of the aircraft and stood in the entrance. In the distance a huge crowd roared "Maddy! Maddy!" when they saw her, their shouts of approval growing and crescendoing as she waved at them.

"We tried," Parrish explained. "But they kept coming. There's a traffic jam outside the main gate three miles back."

Overhead, a dark gray C-17 entered the pattern and turned final, landing to the east, as the presidential party descended the boarding steps. The general commanding the base saluted and, as he had been briefed, received a nod in acknowledgment. He escorted the party to a line of waiting electric carts, and they drove to the reviewing stand. Maddy climbed the four steps to the platform and turned to watch the C-17 taxi in. A gentle Delta breeze ruffled her hair and her skirt, creating a most charming effect not lost on the TV cameras.

The big cargo plane slowly rolled by an honor guard of fourteen battle-scarred A-10s, each pilot standing by the nose of his aircraft. Maggot stood in front and called his pilots to attention. One by one, they saluted as the C-17 moved past. A crew chief marshaled it to a stop, and the engines spun down. Pontowski was the first off the aircraft, and he worked his way down the reception line, taking salutes and shaking hands. He stood to one side as the AVG deplaned. He smiled when Janice Clark picked up her two children. He hadn't realized they were so young.

"Dad!" Zack said, running to meet him. He skidded to a halt, not sure what to say. Then he motioned to the crowd where Bloomy and half the staff from the library were waving. "They wanted to be here," Zack said.

Pontowski waved back. "Bloomy!" he called. She looked at him, startled. "Whatever turned up about Gramps's missing year?"

His question surprised her. "You mean 1944 to 1945?"

"Right. That one. Maybe we should find out?" She gave a little nod. "See you at work."

Rockne was the last off the plane. For a moment he stood in the doorway, holding Boyca's leather leash in his left hand, scanning the crowd that milled around below him. His eyes crinkled when he saw Paul Travis engulfed by his wife and four children. The sergeant had returned with honor. Rockne descended and made his way down the reception line. Free of that duty, he stood alone. Cindy Cloggins was standing thirty feet away, also alone, shifting her weight from one foot to the other. "Chief," she called. "This sucks. Cops don't report in this way."

He agreed with her and pointed to a spot on the ramp. "Cloggins, you're the guide-on." She took five quick steps to the spot and stood at parade rest. He slapped the leash against his thigh. The sound cracked with authority. "GROUP!" he bellowed, drawing the word out. "FALL IN! On Cloggins." An electric shock went through the milling airmen, and suddenly they were security cops again. They swiftly formed up in ranks of eight. Not to be left out, the chief of Maintenance called for his men to fall in. An expectant hush fell over the crowd as the AVG formed. "GROUP," Rockne called, his voice echoing down the ramp. "A-ten-HUT!" As one, they came to attention. Rockne did a left face, toward Pontowski, and snapped a salute. "Sir, the Group is formed."

Pontowski understood. He returned the salute and took his place beside Rockne. "GROUP," Pontowski called. "For-ward HARCH!" The AVG moved forward, their ranks ragged at first but slowly straightening. Rockne called the cadence as they marched across the ramp, directly toward the reviewing stand. "Hup, two, three, four." Then, "Hup, two, three," and a sharp crack echoed over the AVG as he slapped Boyca's leash against his thigh on the count of four. Again, "Hup, two, three," crack. Rockne looked straight ahead as they marched. And Boyca was with him.

"Well," Maura said to her daughter, never taking her eyes off the marching men.

"Well, what?" Maddy asked.

"Do what you have to do."

For a moment Maddy hesitated. Then she stepped down from the reviewing stand. The TV cameras recorded her long strides and the wind whipping at her hair as she walked toward the men.

"GROUP," Pontowski called. "HALT!" He stopped four feet away from his president and saluted. "American Volunteer Group reporting for duty, ma'am."

He stood there holding his salute. Then she nodded as a little smile played at the corners of her mouth. "What took you so long?" she asked.

South China Sea
Thursday, October 21

The graceful bow of the prahu knifed through the clear emerald green water while Tel stood at the tiller. His eyes squinted against the sea spray, searching for familiar landmarks along the shore. When he saw the grove of casuarina trees backed by the tall palms, he turned toward land. He bumped the boat up onto the sand, half expecting his family to run down to meet him. But he was alone. He jumped out and set the anchor in the sand before retrieving a shoulder bag from the boat. He crossed the beach and walked into the trees, toward his kampong. But he stopped short when he saw it, now overgrown with low vegetation that hid the charred ruins. He sniffed the air, relieved that the odor of death and decay was gone. The jungle did work fast. He skirted his old home, no longer a part of it.

He pushed through the heavy brush that blocked the path leading to the casuarina trees farther down the beach. How many times did he walk this path as a child? He saw the shrine and stopped. Now he could smell the water and hear the gentle waves lapping at the shore. He gazed out to sea and for a moment didn't see it. Then he realized that the three offshore oil platforms were gone. Were they also a casualty of war? He hoped so.

Tel knelt in the sand in front of the small shrine he and Kamigami had built to hold the ashes of their families. He closed his eyes and tried to remember their faces. But they were fading from memory and growing indistinct. He reached into his shoulder bag and brought out a small tin box. Gently he placed it in the shrine, next to the nine already there. A little smile played across his mouth. True to life, the box holding Kamigami's ashes was bigger than the others. He settled back on his knees, his hands resting on his thighs as he watched the light fade from the sky.

The moon was already up and cast a willowy light across the water.

Tel fingered the gold whistle hanging from the chain around his neck. He lifted it over his head and started to lay it in the shrine. But an inner voice that sounded like Kamigami told him, "No, not yet." He raised it to his lips and gave a long whistle that echoed pure and sure down the beach and across the water, chasing the moonlight.

Slowly he rose to his feet and came to attention. He saluted. Then he turned and walked away, the whistle still in his hand.